...and applies Kant with lethal resul... in this dazzling philosophical adventure ... this is really walking the literary high wire, and Roberts not only keeps his balance, he makes the spectacle compelling'

Guardian

'Using lit-fic techniques and by not playing by the genre rules, [Roberts] rises to the challenge that Mitchell sets down' *SFX*

'*The Thing Itself* is evidence of Adam Roberts' inimitable brilliance' Tor.com

'I do appreciate a novel that makes me think while also entertaining me. *The Thing Itself* marries the two to perfection. There is so much packed within these pages and, without doubt, it's one of those memorable novels that will stand to repeated readings over the passing of time. A book of the year for me, for sure' For Winter's Nights

'Personally, I found it deeply fascinating ... The closest reference point for me was Philip K. Dick's VALIS trilogy which fits in the same general literary area but *The Thing Itself* is definitely much more fun' Upcoming 4 Me

Also by Adam Roberts from Gollancz:

Salt
Stone
On
The Snow
Polystom
Gradisil
Land of the Headless
Swiftly
Yellow Blue Tibia
New Model Army
By Light Alone
Jack Glass
Twenty Trillion Leagues Under the Sea
Bête

THE THING ITSELF

ADAM ROBERTS

First published in Great Britain in 2015 by Gollancz
an imprint of The Orion Publishing Group Ltd
Carmelite House, 50 Victoria Embankment
London EC4Y 0DZ

An Hachette UK Company

1 3 5 7 9 10 8 6 4 2

A CIP catalogue record for this book is
available from the British Library.

ISBN 978 0 575 12773 9

Typeset at The Spartan Press Ltd,
Lymington, Hants

Printed and bound by CPI Group (UK) Ltd,
Croydon, CR0 4YY

MIX
Paper from
responsible sources
FSC® C104740

www.adamroberts.com
www.orionbooks.co.uk
www.gollancz.co.uk

This tale of the world turned upside down is dedicated to Rachel.

Syncretism refers to that characteristic of child thought which tends to juxtapose logically unrelated pieces of information when the child is asked for causal explanations. A simple example would be: 'Why does the sun not fall down?' 'Because it is hot. The sun stops there.' 'How?' 'Because it is yellow.'

G. H. Bantock

CONTENTS

Thing and Sick

Unity

The beginning was the letter.

Roy would probably say the whole thing began when he solved the Fermi Paradox, when he achieved (his word) *clarity*. Not clarity, I think: but sick. Sick in the head. He probably wouldn't disagree. Not any more. Not with so much professional psychiatric opinion having been brought to bear on the matter. He concedes as much to me, in the many communications he has addressed to me from his asylum. He sends various manifestos and communications to the papers too, I understand. In all of them he claims to have finally solved the Fermi Paradox. If he has, then I don't expect my nightmares to diminish any time soon.

I do have bad dreams, yes. Visceral nightmares. I wake sweating and weeping. If Roy is wrong, then perhaps they'll diminish with time.

But really it began with the letter.

I was in Antarctica with Roy Curtius, the two of us hundreds of miles inland, far away from the nearest civilisation. It was 1986, and one (weeks-long) evening and one (months-long) south polar night. Our job was to process the raw astronomical data coming in from Proxima and Alpha Centauri. Which is to say: our job was to look for alien life. There had been certain peculiarities in the radioastronomical flow from that portion of the sky, and we were looking into it. Whilst we were out there we were given some other scientific tasks to be keeping ourselves busy, but it was the SETI task that was the main event. We maintained the equipment, and sifted the data, passing most of it on for more detailed analysis back in the UK. Since in what follows I am going to say a number of disobliging things about him, I'll concede right here that Roy was some kind of programming genius – this, remember, back in the late 80s, when 'computing' was quite the new thing.

The base was situated as far as possible from light pollution and radio pollution. There was nowhere on the planet further away than where we were.

We did the best we could, with 1980s-grade data processing and a kit-built radio dish flown out to the location in a packing crate, and assembled as best two men could assemble anything when it was too cold for us to take off our gloves.

'The simplest solution to the Fermi thing,' I said once, 'would be simply to pick up alien chatter on our clever machines. Where are the aliens? *Here* they are.'

'Don't hold your breath,' he said.

We spent some hours every day on the project. The rest of the time we ate, drank, lay about and killed time. We had a VHS player, and copies of *Beverly Hills Cop*, *Ghostbusters*, *The NeverEnding Story* and *The Karate Kid*. We played cards. We read books. I was working my way through Frank Herbert's *Dune* trilogy. Roy was reading Immanuel Kant. That fact, right there, tells you all you need to know about the two of us. 'I figured eight months' isolation was the perfect time really to get to grips with the *Kritik der reinen Vernunft*,' he would say. 'Of course,' he would add, with a little self-deprecating snigger, 'I'm not reading it in the original German. My German is good – but not *that* good.' He used to leave the book lying around: Kant's *Critique of Pure Reason*, transl. Meiklejohn. It had a red cover. Pretentious fool.

'We put too much trust in modern technology,' he said one day. 'The solution to the Fermi Paradox? It's all in here.' And he would stroke the cover of the *Critique*, as if it were his white cat and he Ernst Stavro Blofeld.

'Whatever, dude,' I told him.

Once a week a plane dropped off our supplies. Sometimes the pilot, Diamondo, would land his crate on the ice-runway, maybe even get out to stretch his legs and chat to us. I've no idea why he was called 'Diamondo', or what his real name was. He was Peruvian, I believe. More often, if the weather was bad, or if D. was in a hurry, he would swoop low and drop our supplies, leaving us to fight through the burly snowstorm and drag the package in. The contents would include necessaries, scientific equipment, copies of relevant journals – paper copies, it was back then, of course – and so on. The drops also contained correspondence. For me that meant: letters from family, friends and above all from my girlfriend Lezlie.

Two weeks before all this started I had written to Lezlie, asking her for a paperback copy of *Children of Dune*. I told her, in what I hope was a witty manner, that I had been disappointed by the slimness of *Dune Messiah*. I need the big books, I had said, to fill up the time, the long aching time, the (I think I used the phrase) terrible absence-of-Lezlie-thighs-and-tits time that characterised life in the Antarctic. I mention this because, in the weeks that followed, I found myself going back over my letter to her – my memory of it, I mean; I didn't keep a copy – trying to work out if I had perhaps offended her with a careless choice of words. If she might, for whatever reason, have decided not to write to me this week in protest at my vulgarity, or sexism. Or

3

to register her disapproval by not paying postage to send a fat paperback edition of *Dune III* to the bottom of the world. Or maybe she *had* written.

You'll see what I mean in a moment.

Roy never got letters. I always got some: some weeks as many as half a dozen. He: none. 'Don't you have a girlfriend?' I asked him, once. 'Or any friends?'

'Philosophy is my friend,' he replied, looking smugly over the top of his copy of the *Critique of Pure Reason.* 'The solution to the Fermi Paradox is the friend I have yet to meet. Between them, they are all the company I desire.'

'If you say so, mate,' I replied, thinking inwardly *weirdo!* and *loser* and *billy-no-mates* and other such things. I didn't say any of that aloud, of course. And each week it would go on: we'd unpack the delivery parcel, and from amongst all the other necessaries and equipment I'd pull out a rubberband-clenched stash of letters, all of which would be for me and none of which were ever for Roy. And he would smile his smarmy smile and look aloof; or sometimes he would peer in a half-hope, as if thinking that maybe this week would be different. Once or twice I saw him *writing* a letter, with his authentic Waverley fountain pen, shielding his page with his arm when he thought I wanted to nosy into his private affairs – as if I had the slightest interest in fan mail to Professor Huffington Puffington of the University of Kant Studies.

He used to do a number of bonkers things, Roy: like drawing piano keys on to his left arm, spending ages shading the black ones, and then practising – or, for all I know, only pretending to practise – the right-hand part of Beethoven sonatas on it. 'I requested an actual piano,' he told me. 'They said no.' He used to do vocal exercises in the shower, really loud. He kept samples of his snot, testing (he said) whether his nasal mucus was affected by the south polar conditions. Once he inserted a

4

radiognomon relay spike (not unlike a knitting needle) into the corner of his eye, and squeezed the ball to see what effects it had in his vision 'because Newton did it'. He learned a new line of the *Aeneid* every evening – in Latin, mark you – by reciting it over and over. Amazingly annoying, this last weird hobby, because it was so particularly and obviously pointless. I daresay that's why he did it.

I tended to read all the regular things: SF novels, magazines, even four-day-old newspapers (if the drop parcel happened to contain any), checking the football scores and doing the crosswords. And weekly I would pull out my fistful of letters, and settle down on the common room sofa to read them and write my replies, whilst Roy furrowed his brow and worked laboriously through another paragraph of his Kant.

One week he said, 'I'd like a letter.'

'Get yourself a pen pal,' I suggested.

We had just been outside, where the swarming snow was as thick as a continuous shower of wood chips and the wind bit through the three layers I wore. We were both back inside now, pulling off icicle-bearded gloves and scarves and stamping our boots. The drop package was on the floor between us, dripping. We had yet to open it.

'Can I have one of yours?' he asked.

'Tell you what,' I said. I was in a good mood, for some reason. 'I'll sell you one. Sell you one of my letters.'

'How much?' he asked.

'Tenner,' I said. Ten pounds was (I hate to sound like an old codger, but it's the truth) a lot of money back then.

'Deal,' he said, without hesitation. He untied his boots, hopped out of them like Puck and sprinted away. When he came back he was holding a genuine ten-pound note. 'I choose, though,' he said, snatching the thing away as I reached for it.

'Whatever, man.' I laughed. 'Be my guest.'

He gave me the money. Then, he dragged the parcel, now dripping melted snow, through to the common room and opened it. He rummaged around and brought out the rubberbanded letters: four of them.

'Are you sure none of them aren't addressed to you?' I said, settling myself on the sofa and examining my banknote with pride. 'Maybe you don't need to buy one of my letters – maybe you got one of your own?'

He shook his head, looked quickly through the four envelopes on offer, selected one and handed me the remainder of the parcel. 'No.'

'Pleasure doing business with you,' I told him. Off he went to his bedroom to read the letter he had bought.

I thought nothing more about it. The three letters were from: my mum, a guy in Leicester with whom I was playing a tediously drawn-out game of postal chess, and the manager of my local branch of Lloyd's Bank in Reading, writing to inform me that my account was in credit. Since Antarctica was hardly thronged with opportunities for me to spend money, and since my researcher's stipend was still going in monthly, this was unnecessary. I'm guessing it was by way of a publicity exercise. It's not that I was famous, of course; even famous-for-Reading. But it doubtless looked good on some report somewhere: *we look after our customers, even when they're at the bottom of the world*! I made myself a coffee. Then I spent an hour at a computer terminal, checking data. When Roy came back through he looked smug, but I didn't begrudge him that. After all, I had made ten pounds – and ten pounds is ten pounds.

For the rest of the day we worked, and then I fixed up some pasta and Bolognese sauce in the little kitchen. As we ate I asked him: 'So who was the letter from?'

'What do you mean?' Suspicious voice.

'The letter you bought from me. Who was it from? Was it Lezlie?'

A self-satisfied grin. 'No comment,' he smirked.

'Say what?'

'It's my letter. I bought it. And I'm entitled to privacy.'

'Suit yourself,' I said. 'I was only asking.' He was right, I suppose; he bought it, it was his. Still, his manner rubbed me up the wrong way. We ate in silence for a bit, but I'm afraid I couldn't let it go. 'I was only asking: who was it from? Is it Lezlie? I won't pry into what she actually wrote.' Even as I said this, I thought to myself: *Pry? How could I pry – the words were written to be read by me!* 'You know,' I added, thinking to add pressure. 'I *could* just write to her, ask her what she wrote. I could find out that way.'

'No comment,' he repeated, pulling his shoulders round as he sat. I took my bowl to the sink and washed it up, properly annoyed, but there was no point in saying anything else. Instead I went through and put *Romancing the Stone* on the telly, because I knew it was the VHS Roy hated the most. He smiled, and retreated to his room with his philosophy book.

The next morning I discovered to my chagrin that the business with the letter was still preying on my mind. I told myself: get over it. It was done. But some part of me refused to get over it. At breakfast Roy read another page of his Kant, and I saw that he was using the letter as a bookmark. At one point he put the book down and stood up to go to the loo, but then a sly expression crept over his usually ingenuous face, and he picked the book up and took it with him.

It had been a blizzardy few days and the dish needed checking over. Roy tried to wriggle out of this chore: 'You're more the hardware guy,' he said, in a wheedling tone. 'I'm more conceptual – the ideas and the phil-horse-o-phay.'

'Don't give me that crap. We're both hands-on. Folk in Adelaide, and back in Britain, they're the *actual* ideas people.'

I was cross. 'Philosophy my arse.' At any rate, he suited up, rolled his scarf around his lower face and snapped on his goggles, zipped up his overcoat. We both pulled out brooms and stumped through light snowfall to the dish. It took us half an hour to clear the structure of snow, and check its motors hadn't frozen solid, and ensure its bearings were ice free. Our shadows flickered across the landscape like pennants in the wind.

The sun loitered near the horizon. A cricket ball frozen in flight.

That afternoon I did a stint testing the terminals. With the sun still up, it was a noisy picture; although it was possible to pick up this and that. At first I thought there was something, but when I looked at it I discovered it was radio chatter from a Spanish expedition on its way to the Vinson Massif. I found my mind wandering. Who was the letter from?

The following day I eased my irritation by writing to Lezlie. *Hey, you know Roy? He's a sad bastard, a ringer for one of the actors in* Revenge of the Nerds. *Anyway he asked for a letter and I sold him one. Now he won't tell me whose letter it is. Did you write to me last week? What did you say? Just give me the gist, lover-girl.* But as soon as I'd written this I scrunched it up and threw it in the bin. Lez would surely not respond well to such a message. In effect I was saying: 'Hey you know that love letter you poured your heart and soul into? I sold it to a nerd without even reading it! *That's* how much I value your emotions!'

Chewed the soft blue plastic insert at the end of my Bic for a while.

I tried again: *Hi lover! Did you write last week? There was a snafu with the package and some stuff got lost.* I looked over the lie. It really didn't ring true. I scrunched this one up too. Then I sat in the chair trying, and failing, to think of how to put things. The two balls of scrunched paper in the waste bin began, creakingly, to unscrunch.

Dear Lez. Did you write last week? I'm afraid I lost a letter, klutz that I am! That was closer to the truth. But then I thought: *What if she had written me a Dear John letter? Or a let's-get-married? Or a-close-family-member-has-died?* How embarrassing to write back a jaunty 'please repeat your message!' note. What if she hadn't written at all? What if it had been somebody else?

This latter thought clawed at my mind for a while. What if some important information, perhaps from my academic supervisor at Reading, Prof. Addlestone, had been in the letter? Privacy was one thing, but surely Roy didn't have the right to withhold such info?

I stomped down the corridor and knocked at Roy's room. He made me wait for a long time before opening the door just enough to reveal his carbuncular face, smirking up at me. 'What?'

'I've changed my mind,' I said. 'I want my letter back.'

'No dice, doofus,' he replied. 'I paid for it. It's mine now.'

'Look, I'll *buy* it back, all right? I'll give you your ten pounds. I've got it right here.'

When he smiled, he showed the extent to which his upper set of teeth didn't fit neatly over his lower set. 'It's not for sale,' he said.

'Don't be a pain, Roy,' I said. 'I'm asking nicely.'

'And I'm, nicely, declining.'

'What? You want more than a tenner? You can go fish for *that*, my friend.'

'It's not for sale,' he repeated.

'Is it a scam?' I said, my temper wobbling badly. 'Is the idea you hold out until I offer – what, twenty quid? Is that it?'

'No. That's not it. It's mine. I do not choose to sell it.'

'Just tell me what's *in* the letter,' I pleaded. 'I'll give your money back *and* you can keep the damn thing, just tell me who it's from and what it says.' Even as I made this offer it occurred to me that Roy, with his twisted sense of humour, might simply lie to me. So I added: 'Show it to me. Just show me the letter. You don't have to give it up, keep it for all I care, only—'

'No deal,' said Roy. Then he wrung his speccy face into a parody of a concerned expression. 'You're embarrassing yourself, Charles.' And he shut his door.

I went through to the common room, fuming. For a while I toyed with the idea of simply grabbing the letter back: I was bigger than Roy, and doubtless had been involved in more actual fist-flying, body-grappling fights than he. It wouldn't have been hard. But instead of that I had a beer, and lay on the sofa, and tried to get a grip. We had to live together, he and I, in unusually confined circumstances, and for a very long period of time. In less than a week the sun would vanish, and the proper observing would begin. Say we chanced upon alien communication (I told myself) – wouldn't that be something? Might there be a Nobel Prize, or something equally prestigious, in it? I couldn't put all that at risk, even for the satisfaction of punching that bastard on the nose.

Maybe, I told myself, Roy would thaw out a little in a day or two. You catch more flies with honey than vinegar, after all. Maybe I could *coax* the letter out of him.

The week wore itself out. I went through a phase of intense irritation with Roy for his (what seemed to me) immensely petty and immature attitude with regard to my letter. Then I went through a phase when I told myself it didn't bother me. I did consider returning his tenner to him, so as to retain the high moral ground. But then I thought: *ten pound is ten pound*.

The week ended, and Diamondo overflew and tossed the supply package out to bounce along the snow. This annoyed me, because I had finally managed to write a letter to Lezlie that explained the situation without making it sound like I valued her communiqués so little I'd gladly sold it off to weirdo Roy.

But I couldn't 'post' the letter unless the plane landed and took it on board, so I had to hang on to it. And I couldn't even be sure the letter Roy had purchased had *been* from her.

On the fifth of July the sun set for the last time until August. The thing people don't grok about Antarctic night is that it's not the same level of ink-black all the way through. For the first couple of weeks the sky lightens twice a day, pretty much bright enough to walk around without a torch – the same dawn and dusk paling of the sky that precedes sunrise and follows sunset, only without actual dawn and dusk. Still, you can sense the sun is just there, on the other side of the horizon, and it's not too bad. As the weeks go on this gets briefer and darker, and then you do have a month or so when it's basically coal-coloured skies and darkness invisible the whole time.

Diamondo landed his plane, and tossed out the supply package, but didn't linger; and by the time I'd put on the minimum of outdoor clothing and grabbed a torch and got through the door he was taking off again – so, once again, I didn't get to send my letter to Lez.

That was the last time I saw that aircraft.

There were two letters in this week's batch: one from my old grammar school headmaster, saying that the school had hosted a whole assembly on the 'exciting and important' work I was doing; and the other from my professor at Reading. This was nothing but a note, and read in its entirety: 'Dear A. I often think of Sartre's words. Imagination is not an empirical or superadded power of consciousness, it is the whole of consciousness as it realises its freedom. Where is freer than the very bottom of the world? Nil desperandum! Yours, A.' This, though slightly gnomic, was not out of character for Prof. Addlestone, who had worked on SETI for so long it had made his brain a little funny. No letter from Lez, which worried me. But, after all, she didn't write every week. I reread the Professor's note several times.

Did it read like a PS, a scribbled afterthought? Did it perhaps mean that the letter Roy bought had been from Addlestone? Maybe. Maybe not.

We got on with our work, and I tried to put the whole letter business behind me. Roy did not help, as far as this went. He was acting stranger and stranger; simpering at me, and when I queried his expression ('What? What is it?') scurrying away – or scowling and saying, 'nothing, nothing, only...' and refusing to elaborate.

The next thing was: he moved one of the computer terminals into his room. This was a proper hefty 1980s terminal; not one of those modern-day computers the size and weight of a copy of *Marie Claire*, so it was no mean feat getting the thing in there. He even cut a mousehole-like shape in the bottom of his door, to enable the main cable to come out into the hall and through into the monitor room.

'What are you doing in there?' I challenged him. 'That's not standard policy. Did you clear this with Adelaide?'

'I'm working on something,' he told me, not meeting my eyes. 'I'm close to a breakthrough. SETI, my friend. Solving Fermi's paradox! You should consider yourself lucky to be here. You'll get a footnote in history. Only a footnote, I know: but it's more than most people get.'

I ignored this. 'I still don't see why you need to squirrel yourself away in your room.'

'Privacy,' he said. 'Is very important to me.'

One day he went out on the ice to (he told me) check the meteorological data points. It seemed like an odd thing – he'd never shown any interest in them before – but I was glad he was out of the base, if only for half an hour. As soon as I saw his torch beam go, wobbling its oval of brightness away over the ice, I hurried to his room. I wasn't doing anything wrong, I told myself. I was just checking the identity of the letter's author.

Maybe have a quick glance at its contents. I wouldn't steal it back (although, I told myself, I *could*. It was *my* letter after all. Roy was being an idiot about the whole thing). But once my itch was scratched, curiosity-wise, then everything would get easier about the base. I could wait out the remainder of my stint with equanimity. He need never even know I'd been poking around.

No dice. Roy had fitted a padlock to his door. I rattled this uselessly; I could have smashed it, but then Roy would know what I'd been up to. I retreated to the common room, disproportionately angry. What was he doing, in there, with a whole computer terminal – and my letter?

I had enough self-knowledge to step back from the situation, at least some of the time. He was doing it in order to wind me up. That was the only reason he was doing it. The letter was nothing – none of my letters, if I looked back, contained any actual, substantive content. They were just pleasant chatter, people I knew touching base with me. The letter Roy bought must be the same. He bought it not to *have* the letter, but in order to set me on edge, to rile me. And by getting riled I was gifting him the victory. The way to play this whole situation was to be perfectly indifferent.

However much I tried this, though, I kept falling back.

It was the not knowing!

I tried once more, during the week. 'Look, Roy,' I said, smiling. 'This letter thing is no big deal, you know? None of my letters have any really significant stuff in them.'

He didn't reply to this, but he did look at me with a 'that's all *you* know' sort of expression. This was, I decided, just winding me up.

'I tell you what I think,' I said. 'You can, you know, nod, or not-nod, depending on whether I'm right. I think the letter you bought was from my girlfriend. Yeah?'

'No comment,' said Roy primly. 'One way or the other.'

'If so, it was probably full of inane chatter, yeah? Fine – keep it! With my blessing!'

'In point of fact,' he corrected me, holding up his right forefinger, 'I do not need your blessing. The transaction was finalised with the fiduciary transfer. Contract law is very clear on this point.'

I lost my temper a little. 'You know how sad you are, keeping a woman's letter to another man for your own weird little sexual buzz? That's – *sad*. Is what it is. I don't think you realise how sad that is.'

'Oh Charles, Charles,' he said, shaking his head and smirking in that insufferable way he had. 'If only you knew!'

I swore. 'Suit yourself,' I said.

Then the airstrip lights failed. I assumed this was an accident, although the fact that every one of them failed at the same time was strange. Diamondo came through on the radio: 'Fellows!' he declared, through his thick accent. 'I cannot land if there are no lights to land!'

'Don't know what's happened to them,' I replied. 'Some manner of malfunction.'

'Obviously that!' came Diamondo's voice. 'Can you fix? Over.'

Roy suited up and went outside; he was back in minutes. 'I can't do anything in the dark, with a torch, in a hurry,' he complained. 'Tell him no. Tell him to toss the package out and we'll fix the lights for next time.'

When I relayed this message, Diamondo said, 'Breakables! There are breakables in the package! I cannot toss! Over.' Then, contradicting his last uttered word, he went on. 'I can take out the breakables and toss the rest. Wait – wait.'

I could hear the scrapy sound of the plane in the sky outside. Then, over the radio: 'Is in chute.'

'Wait,' I said. 'Where are you dropping it? If there's no lights – I mean, I don't want to go searching over a wide area in the dark with...' There was a terrific crash right overhead, as something smashed into our roof.

'You idiot!' I called. 'You could have broken our roof!'

Static. And, through the walls, the sound of the plane's engines diminishing. Roy looked at me, and I at him. 'I think it rolled off,' Roy said. 'You go out and get it.'

'You're already suited!'

'I went out last time. It's your turn now. Fair's fair.'

It was on the edge of my tongue to retort: *Stealing my letter – is* that *fair?* But that would have done no good; and anyway I was hoping that there would be a new letter from Lezlie in the satchel. So I pulled on overclothes and took a torch and went outside.

It was extraordinarily cold – sinus-freezingly cold. The air was still. The sound of Diamondo's plane, already very faint, diminished and diminished until it vanished altogether. Now the only sound was the whirr of the generator, gently churning to itself with its restless motion. I searched around in the dark outside the main building for ten minutes or so, and spent another five trying to see into the gap between the main prefab and the annexe, which was half-full of snow. But I couldn't find it.

When I went back to the main door it was locked. This was unprecedented. For a while I banged on the door, and yelled, and my heart began blackly to suspect that Roy was playing some kind of prank on me – or worse.

I was just about to give up and make my way round to try the side entrance when Roy's gurning face appeared in the door's porthole, with the graph-paper pattern woven into the glass. He opened it. 'What the hell were you playing at?' I demanded crossly. 'Why did you lock the door?'

'It occurred to me that the lights might have been sabotaged,' he said, not looking me in the eye. 'I thought: security is valour's better part. Obviously I was going to let you back in, once I was sure it *was* you.'

'Have you had a nervous breakdown?' I yelled. 'Are you *high*? Who else could possibly be out there? We're three hundred miles from the nearest human settlement. Did you think it was a ghost?'

'Calm down,' Roy advised, grinning his simpering grin and still not looking me in the eye. 'Did you get the package?'

I sat down with a thump. 'Couldn't find it,' I said, pulling off my overboots. 'It may still be on the roof. Seriously, though, man! Locking the door?'

'We need to retrieve it,' said Roy. 'It has my medication in it. My supplies are running low.'

This was the first I had heard of any medication. 'Seriously? They posted you down here, even though you have medical problems?'

'Just some insomnia problems. And some allergic reaction problems. But I need my sleeping pills and my antihistamines.'

'You're kidding,' I said. 'What is there to be allergic *to*, down here?'

He gave me a pointed look. But then he said: 'Come and have a drink,' he said. 'I've got some whisky.'

Now, I knew the base was not supplied with whisky. Beer was the most they allowed us. I should, perhaps, have been suspicious of Roy's abrupt hospitality, doubly so since I knew he hardly ever drank. But I was cold, and cross, and a whisky actually sounded like a bloody good idea. 'How have you got any of that?'

'I brought it with me. My old tutor at Cambridge gave it me. Break it out when you've solved the SETI problem, he said. *He* never doubted me, you see. And solved it, I have.'

And then a second thought occurred to me. It came to me like a flash. I could *get Roy drunk*. Surely then he would be more amenable to telling me what was in the letter he'd snaffled from me. I couldn't think that I'd ever seen him drunk; and my judgement was that he would hold his liquor badly. He'd be a splurger. OK, I thought, butter him up, some, and get some booze in him.

'I'll have a dram,' I told him. Then: 'Kind of you to offer. Thanks. I didn't mean to ... you know. Yell at you.'

He ignored this overture. 'You didn't go to Cambridge, I think?' he asked, as we went through to the common room. 'Reading University, isn't it?'

'Reading born and bred,' I replied, absently. I half-leant, half-sat on one of the heaters to get warmth back into my marrow whilst Roy went off to his room to get the whisky. He was gone a while. Finally he came back with a bottle of Loch Lomond in one hand and a bottle of beer in the other. He handed me the former.

I retrieved two tumblers from the cupboard, but Roy said: 'I'll not have the whisky, thank you anyway. I don't like the taste.'

This was about par, I thought, for the weirdo that he was – bringing a bottle of Scotch all the way to the end of the world, to not even drink it. On the other hand the seal was broken, and about an inch was missing, so perhaps he had tried a taster and so discovered his aversion. I honestly didn't care. I poured three fingers, and settled myself in one of the chairs.

'Cheers!' I said, raising a glass.

'Good health,' he returned, propping his bum on the arm of the sofa.

'So,' I said, smacking my lips. 'The fact that we're drinking this means you've solved the Fermi Paradox?'

'We're not drinking it,' he said, with a little snorty laugh of self-satisfaction. 'You are.'

'You're such a pedant, Roy,' I told him.

'Take that as a compliment,' he said, smirking and making odd little snorty-sniffy noises with his nostrils.

'So? Does the fact that I'm drinking this mean you've solved it?'

'The answer to your question is yes.'

'Really?'

'Absolutely.'

I took another sip. 'Congratulations!'

'Thank you.'

'And?'

He peered blankly at me. 'What?'

'And? In the sense of: what's your solution?'

'Oh. The Fermi Paradox.' He sounded almost bored. 'Well, I'll tell you if you like.' He seemed to ponder this. 'Yeah,' he added. 'Why not? It's Kant.'

'Of course it is,' I said, laughing. 'You complete nutter.'

He looked hurt at this. 'What do you mean?'

'I mean – the best part of a year of our lives, millions of pounds sunk into this base, probably billions spent worldwide on SETI, and all we needed to do was open a seventeenth-century book of philosophy!'

'Eighteenth-century,' he corrected me. 'And the kit, here, certainly has its uses.'

'Glad to hear it! But – Kant? Really?'

Roy took the smallest sip from his beer bottle, and then rubbed his chin with his thumb. 'Hard to summarise,' he said. 'Start here: how do we know there's anything out there?'

'What – in space?'

'No: outside our own brains. Sense data, yes? Eyes, ears, nerve-endings. We see things, and think we're seeing things out there. We hear things, likewise. And so on. But maybe all that is a lie. Maybe we're hallucinating. Dreaming. How can we be sure there's anything really *there*?'

'Isn't this I think therefore I am?'

'The cogito, yes,' said Roy, with that uniquely irritating prissy inflection he used when he wanted to convey his own intellectual superiority. 'Though Kant didn't have much time for Descartes, actually. He says I think therefore I am is an empty statement. We never just think, after all. We always think *about something*.'

'You're losing me, Roy,' I said, draining my whisky, and reaching for the bottle. Roy's eyes flashed, and I stopped. 'Do you mind if I have another?'

'No, no,' he urged me, bobbing forward and back in an oddly birdlike way. 'Go right ahead.'

'So,' I said. 'You're saying we can't be sure if the cosmos is a kind of hallucination. Maybe I'm a brain in a vat. So what? I've got to act as if the universe is real, or,' I directed a quick look at Roy, 'they'd lock me in the loony bin. So? Does this hallucination also include ET, or not?'

'Quite right. Well, Kant says there *is* a real world – he calls it the Ding an sich, the thing as it really is. There is such a reality. But our only access to that real world is through our perceptions, our senses and therefore through the way our thoughts are structured. So, says Kant, some of the things we assume are part of the world out there are actually part of the structure of our consciousness.'

'Such as?'

'Quite basic things. Time and space. Causality.'

'Kant is saying that time, space and causality aren't "really" out there? They're just part of our minds?'

Roy nodded. 'It's like if we always wore pink-tinted contact lenses. Like we'd always worn them, ever since birth. Everything we saw would have a pink tint. We might very well assume the world was just – you know, pink. But it wouldn't be the world that was pink, it would be our perception of the world.'

'Pink,' I repeated, and took another slug. I was starting to feel drowsy.

'We're all like that, all the time, except that instead of pink contact lenses on our eyes, we're wearing *space-and-time* contacts on our minds. *Causality* contacts.'

'Space and time are the way the universe is. Just is.'

'That's not what Kant says. He says we don't really know the way the universe *just is*. All we know is how our perceptions and thoughts structure our understanding.'

'Wait,' I said. 'Kant says that cause and effect are just in our heads?'

'That's right.'

'That's nonsense,' I said. 'If space and time and causality are just inside my head, then what's my head in? It takes up space, my brain. It takes time to think these thoughts.'

'There's *something* out there,' Roy agreed. 'But we don't know what it is. Here's a thought-experiment, Kant's thought-experiment. You can imagine an object in space, can't you?'

I grunted.

'OK,' said Roy. 'And you can imagine the object being taken away. Yes? Then you have empty space. But you can't imagine *space and time* being taken away. You can't imagine no space, no time.'

I grunted again.

'That shows that space, time, causality and some other things – they're part of the way the mind perceives. There's no getting behind them. Is the Ding an sich itself structured according to that logic? The eyeball cannot see itself. We cannot know. Maybe, maybe not.'

'Ding,' I said, my eyelids slipping down my eyeballs, 'like a microwave oven?'

'We're looking for aliens with visual telescopes and radio telescopes,' said Roy, standing up and putting his beer bottle down. 'But whatever tools we use, we're looking for aliens in space and time, aliens that understand causality and number. But maybe those things are not alien. Those things are the way *our* minds are built. And that means we're looking in the wrong place. We should not be looking in space, or time. We should be looking in the Ding an sich.'

'Sick,' I said, My eyes were shut now. I didn't seem to be able to open them. Such muscular operation was beyond my volitional control. 'I feel a bit sick, actually.'

'Ding,' I heard him say, at the far end of a very long corridor. 'You're done. Let's open the microwave door, now, shall we?'

I suppose I was asleep. I tried to shift position in bed, but my arms were numb. Sometimes you lie on an arm and it goes dead. But this was both my arms. They were up over my head. A scraping sound. Distantly. I tried to pull my arms down but they were already down. I tried to process this, failed. *This is the chance*, somebody was saying, or muttering, I don't know. Perhaps I was imagining it. *We've never had this chance before. Because although human consciousness is structured by the Kantian categories of apperception, there's nothing to say that* computer *perception needs to suffer from the same limitations. It's all a question of programming! A programme to sift the Centauri data so as to get behind the limitations of consciousness.*

I was moving. Everything was dark, dark, dark. My arms were trailing behind me, I thought; and something was pulling my legs, I thought; and I was sliding along on my back. Was that right? Could that be right?

We look out from our planet and see a universe of space, and time, of substance and causality, of plurality and totality, of possibility and probability – and we forget that what we're actually seeing are the ways our minds structure *the Ding an sich according to the categories of space, and time, of substance and causality, of plurality and totality, of possibility and probability. We look out and we see no aliens, and are surprised. But the real surprise would be to see aliens in such a vista, because that would mean the aliens are in our structures of thought. Surely there* are *aliens. Of course there are! But they don't live in our minds. They live in the Ding an sich.*

The motion stopped, but I was still too sluggish to move, or speak, or even open my eyes. The next thing I knew, somebody was kissing me on the lips. *Goodbye*, was a word, and it floated around. Then nothing.

O dark, dark, dark, they all go into the—

Or.

Or something. It came upon me slowly. It, as it were, crept up on me. I couldn't as yet put a name to it. *Let me think through the necessary and contingent possibilities*, I thought to myself. *It could have been a letter from my mum, in which case it was full of family trivia and Roy's just yanking my chain for the hell of it. He's certainly capable of that.* The thing, whatever it was, was closer now, or larger somehow, or in some sense more present, although I still couldn't put a name to it. *It could have been a letter from a friend, or from Leicester Lenny, but if so it would only say Q-B4 ch! or Kn-R7 or something, and that could mean nothing at all to Roy. Or it could have been a letter from Professor Addlestone of Reading University, blathering on about something. Or it could have been*, the thing was all around me now, or all within me, or otherwise pressing very imminently upon my consciousness. *Or it could have been from Lezlie. But then, what? It was full of the usual blandishments? In which case Roy's hoarding of it is creepy but, in the larger scheme of things, unimportant. That's not what I'm afraid of though, is it?* I felt sick and I was sick and it froze on my chin. *I'm afraid the letter says: I'm leaving you, I've found someone else. But but but, if it is, then I'll find out eventually – won't I. I just need to be patient. I'll find out in time. Assuming I have time—*

Cold.

That was the thing.

That was what had crept up on me. That's what's behind the

veil. Endless, implacable, killing cold. Even the most cursory examination of the cosmos confirms this.

I sat up.

I was outside, in the darkness, in my indoor clothes. Scalded with the cold. My whole body shook with a Parkinsonian tremor. I angled my head back and the stars were all there, the Southern Fish, the Centaur and the Dove; the Southern Cross itself; Orion and Hydra low in the sky; Scorpion and Sagittarius high up. Hydra and Pegasus. I breathed in fire and burned my throat and lungs. It was cold enough to shear metal. It was cold enough to freeze petrol.

I got to my feet. It wasn't easy, but I did it. My hands felt as though they had been dipped in acid, and then that sensation stopped and I was more scared than before. There was nothing at the end of my arms at all. I tried rubbing my hands together, but the leprous lack of sensation and the darkness and my general sluggishness meant I could not coordinate the action. My hands bounced numbly off one another. I became terrified of the idea that I would perhaps knock one or more fingers clean off. It looks ridiculous as I write it down, but there, in the dark, in the cold, the thought of it gripped my soul horribly.

I had to get inside, to get warm. I had to get back to the base. I was shuddering so hard I was scared I might actually lose balance with the shivering and fall down – in which case I might not be able to get back up again. Ghastly darkness all about. Cold beyond the power of words to express.

I turned about, and about again. Starlight is the faintest of lights. I could see my breath coming out only because of the vast ostrich-feature-shaped blot that twisted in my field of vision, blocking out the stars. I needed to pick a direction and go. But I couldn't see any lights to orient me. What if I stumbled off in the wrong direction? I could easily stagger off into the wilderness, miss the base altogether. I'd be dead in minutes.

I addressed myself: take hold of yourself. You were dragged here. Roy dragged you here. Runty Roy; he couldn't have removed me very far from the base. Presumably he figured I wouldn't wake up. That I'd just die there in the dark.

'OK,' I said, and took another breath – knives going down my throat. I had to move. I started off, and stumbled over the black ground through the black air. I began to fall forward – my thigh muscles were cramping – and picked up my pace to stop myself pitching on to my face. My inner ear still told me I was falling, so I ran faster. Soon I was *sprinting*. It's possible the fluids in my inner ear had frozen, or glued up with the cold, I don't know. It felt as if I were falling, but my feet were still pounding over the ice, invisible below me. I felt like a diver, tumbling from the top board.

And then I saw the sea—

—I was at the coast. Obviously I wasn't at the coast because that was hundreds of miles from the base. But there it was, visible. There was a settlement on the shore, a mile below me, with yellow lights throwing shimmery ovals over the water. There was a ship, lit up like a Christmas decoration, balanced very precisely on top of its own lit reflection. I must have been ten degrees of latitude, or more, further away from the pole, enough to lift the moon up over the horizon. The texture of the sea was a million burrin-marks of white light on a million wavelets, like pewter. There was no doubting what I was seeing. My whole body trembled with pain, with the cold, and I said to myself *I'm dying*, and *I'm hallucinating because I'm dying*. I must have run in the wrong direction. I felt as if I'd been running all my life, all my ancestors' lives combined.

There was a weird inward fillip, or lurch, or clonic jerk, or something folding over something else. I was conscious of thinking: I've run the wrong way. I've missed the base.

And there *was* the base. Now that I was there, I could see that

Roy had covered the common room window on the inside with something – cloth, cardboard – to make a blackout screen. He had not wanted me to see the light and follow it as a beacon. Now that I was there, I could just make out the faint line of illumination around the edges. I couldn't feel my hands, or my feet, and my face was covered with a pinching, scratchy mask – snot, sick, tears, frost, whatever, frozen by the impossible cold to a hard crust.

I slumped against the wall, and the fabric of my shirt stuck. It was so stiffened it snapped. It ripped clean away when I got up.

The door. I had to get to the door – that was when I saw…
I was going to say *when I saw them* but the plural doesn't really describe the circumstance. Not that there was only one, either. It is very hard to put into words. There was the door, in front of me, and just enough starlight to shine a faint glint off the metal handle. I could not use my hands, so I leant on the handle with my elbow, but of course it did not give way. Locked, of course locked. And of course Roy would not be opening it for me this time. Then I saw – what I saw. Data experiences of a radically new kind. Raw tissues of flesh, darkness visible, a kind of fog (no: fog is the wrong word). A pillar of fire by night, except that 'it' did not burn, or gleam, or shine. 'It' is the wrong word for it. 'It' felt, or looked, like a great tumbling of scree down an endless slope. Or rubble gathering at the bottom and falling up the mountain. Forwards, backwards.

It was the most terrifying thing I ever saw.

Flames about me, and black coals the size of mountains.

There was a hint of – I'm going to say, claws, jaws, a clamping something. A maw. Not a tentacle, nothing so defined. Nor was it a darkness. It made a low, thrumming chiming noise, like a muffled bell sounding underground, ding-ding, ding-ding. But this was not a sound-wave sort of sound. This was not a propagating expanding sphere of agitated air articles. It was a pulse in the mind. It was a shudder of the soul.

Flames all about me, and the blackness of night rolled into giant coals. I was in some titanic fireplace being burned, and the burning consumed me. Sylphs of light, like the aurora australis in the sky, flickered about my head. It wasn't my head. My head was wholly and acephalically gone. Top of the world, Ma. Top of the world.

The world-serpent slid monstrous from its den and I knew it was going to devour me.

I could not get inside the base, and I was going to die. I felt the horrid cold in the very core of my being. Then 'it', or 'they', or the boojummy whatever the hell (I choose my words carefully, here) it was, expanded. Or undid whatever process of congealing that brought it – I don't know.

Where I stood experienced a second as-it-were convulsive, almost muscular contraction. Everything folded over, and flipped back again. 'It', or 'they' were not here any longer. In fact they had been here aeons ago, or were not yet here at all.

I was standing inside the common room.

Do not demand to know how I passed beyond the locked door. I could not tell you.

The warmth of the air burned my throat. I could no longer stay standing. I half slumped, half fell sideways, and my arm banged against one of the heaters – it felt like molten metal, and I yelled. I rolled off it and lay on the floor, and breathed and breathed.

I may have passed out. I have no idea how I got inside. I was probably only out for a few moments, because the next thing I knew was that my hands were in agony. Absolute agony! It felt like the gom jabbar, like they had both been stuffed into a tub of boiling water. Looking back I can now say what it was: it was sensation returning to my frostbitten flesh. But by God I've never felt such pain. I screamed and screamed like the Spanish Inquisition had gone to work on me. I writhed, and wept like a baby.

Somehow I dragged myself into a sitting posture, with my back against the wall and my legs straight out on the floor. Roy was standing in the common room doorway. In his right hand he was holding what I assumed was a gun, although I later realised it was a flare pistol.

'You murdering bastard,' I said. 'Have you come to finish the job? You going to shoot me down like a dog?' Or that's what I *tried* to say. What came out was: 'yrch yrch orch orch orch'. God, my throat was *shredded*.

'The thing-in-itself,' he said. There was a weird bend in his voice. I blinked away the melting icicles from my eyelashes and saw he was *crying*. 'The thing-as-such. The thing *per se*. I have experienced it unmediated.' His face was wet. Tears slippy-sliding down, and dripping like snot from his jowls. I'd never seen him like that before.

'What,' I croaked, 'did you put in my whisky?' Oh God, the pain in my *hands*! And now my feet were starting to rage and burn too. Oh, it was ghastly.

He stopped crying, and wiped his face in the crook of his left arm. 'I'm sorry,' he said. Even at this juncture he was not able to look me in the eye. He lifted his right hand, holding the flare pistol, slowly, until he was holding it across his chest, like James Bond in the posters.

I was weeping. Not because I was scared of dying, but just because my hands and feet hurt with such sharp and focused intensity.

Roy took a breath, lifted the flare pistol to his own head, and pulled the trigger. There was a crunching bang, and Roy flopped to the ground. The common room was filled with fluorescent red-orange light and an extraordinarily loud hissing sound. For a moment we were in a luridly lit stage set of Hades.

What had happened was this: the tip and fuse of the flare projectile had lodged itself in Roy's skull, and had ejected the illumination section and its little asbestos parachute at the ceiling, where it snagged against the polystyrene tiles and burned until it was all burned out.

I sat in that ferociously red-lit room, with molten chunks of polystyrene dripping on to the carpet. I was agonised by my hands, feet, face. Then the shell itself burned free and fell to the ground, where it fizzled out.

Roy was not dead. Nor was I, amazingly. It took me a while, and an effort, and the whole way along I was sobbing and begging the cosmos to take the pain away; but I got to the radio, and called for help. They sent an air ambulance that laid a pattern of flares on the unlit runway during their first fly by and landed alongside them on their second. It took four hours, but they got to us, and we did not die in the interval.

I crawled back to Roy, unconscious on the floor, and pulled the shell-tip from the side of his head. There was no blood, although the dent was very noticeable – the skin and hair lining the new thumb-sized cavity all the way in. There was little I could do, beyond put him in the recovery position.

Then I clambered painfully on the sofa, my hands and feet hurting a little less. Then, surprisingly enough, I fell asleep. Roy had dissolved a sleeping tablet in the whisky, of course, to knock me out; and when the pain retreated just enough I couldn't fight off the chemical effect any longer. I was woken by the sound of crashing, and crashing, and crashing, and then one of the ambulance men came through the main door with an axe in his hand.

We were flown to Halley, on the coast – the subject of my vision, or whatever that had been. We were hospitalised, and questioned, and my hands were treated. I lost two fingers on my left hand and one on my right, and my nose was rescued with a skin graft that gives it, to this day, a weird patchwork-doll look. I lost toes too, but I care less about those. Roy was fine: they opened his skull, extracted a few fragments of bone, and sewed him up. Good as new.

I don't think they believed his version of events, although for myself I daresay he was truthful, or as truthful as circumstances permitted. The official record is that he had a nervous breakdown, drugged me, left me outside to die and then shot himself. He himself said otherwise. I've read the transcript of his account. I've even been in the same room with him as he was questioned. 'I saw things as they really are, things *per se*, I had a moment – that's the wrong word, it is not measured in moments, it has always been with me, it will always be with me – a moment of clarity.'

'And your clarity,' asked the investigating officer sternly, 'was: kill your colleague?'

He wanted the credit all to himself, I think. He believed *he* was the individual destined to make first contact with alien life. He wanted me out of the way. He didn't say that, of course, but that's what I think. His explanation was: my perceptions, my mental processes and imagination, would collapse the fragile disintermediating system he was running to break through to the Thing-as-Such. I confess I don't see how that would work. Nonetheless: he insists that this was his motive for killing me. Indeed, he insists that my reappearance proved the correctness of his decision, the necessity for my death – because by coming back at the time I did, I broke down the vision of the Ding an sich, or reasserted the prison of categorical perception, or something, and the aliens fled – or not fled, because their being is not mappable with a succession of spatial coordinates the way ours are. But: I don't know. Evaporate. Collapse away to nothing. Become again veiled. He wrote me several long, not terribly coherent letters about it from Broadmoor. I still prefer the earlier explanation. He was a nerd, not right in the head, and a little jealous of me.

So, yes. He happened to buy Lezlie's Dear John. She couldn't cope with the long distances, the time lags between us meeting up, she'd met someone else… the usual. After he drugged me and left me outside to die, Roy left the letter, carefully opened and smoothed out, face up on the desk in my room. It was going to be the explanation for my suicide. People were to believe that I couldn't handle the rejection and had just walked out into the night.

His latest communication with me from Broadmoor begged me to 'go public' with what I had seen. You'll grasp from this account, the one you're reading, that I don't know *what* I saw. I suppose it was a series of weird hallucinations brought on by the extreme cold and the blood supply becoming intermittent in my brain. Or something, I don't know. I still dream about them. It. Whatever. And the strange thing is: although I know for a fact I encountered it (them, none, whatever) for the first time in Antarctica, in 1986, it feels – it feels deep in my bones – as if I have always known about them. As if they visited me in my cradle. They didn't, of course.

My life has gone down the toilet since I saw it. My life has gone to shit. My life has quite literally turned to garbage.

I look in the mirror, and some days I see myself, my frost-bitten face weirdly distorted; and sometimes I get a vivid hallucination that somebody else's face is looking out – a younger somebody, their face likewise scarred with burn tissue. He's not me. I don't know who he is. There's something about him I find unpleasantly familiar, though.

The John Carpenter film *The Thing* was on the telly a while back. That wasn't one of the VHS tapes they gave us, to watch on base I mean. For obvious reasons. That's not what it was like for me at all. That doesn't capture it at all. They, or it, or whatever, were not *thing*-y.

They are inhuman. But this is only my dream of them, I think. But it is not a dream of a human. It is not a dream of a thing. Or it is, but of a sick kind of thing. And, actually, no. That's not it.

He keeps writing to me. I wish he'd stop writing.

2

Baedeker's Fermi

Plurality

1900. The first year of a new century, and the twelfth day of April: bright sunshine. How could it be anything other than auspicious? A sky so flawless a blue it looked as though enamelled and polished from horizon to horizon by the celestial jeweller Himself. From Cologne to Mayence we were travelling aboard the saloon-steamer *Deutscher Kaiser*. The journey upstream took us twelve hours, although the guidebook assured us the return voyage downstream takes as little as seven and a half. No man may doubt the muscular implacability of the Rhenish flow here, close as it is to the North Sea. Albert and I sat on deck all morning smoking cigars and watching the green landscape slide beautifully past, green as emerald, green the ideal ocean of the fairy tales. Albert particularly admired (he said) the view of distant hills, and behind them the spectral white of faraway mountain tops. I preferred the nearby vineyards. By seven we disembarked into Mayence.

We took adjoining rooms – with, of course, a connecting door – in the Hof Von Holland, located upon the Rheinstrasse. Both rooms had fine views of the river. It was a simple matter to obtain the services of a valet-de-place for 5 marks a day – as one German mark has the monetary worth of a good English shilling, this was not cheap. But he agreed to serve the both of us for the money, and these being the early days of our Rhine odyssey, we preferred not to haggle or pinch our pennies – or pfennigs, I should say.

That evening we dined well, and strolled along the gas-lit Rheinpromenade as far as the Schloss. Later, Albert joined me in my room and together we consulted the Baedeker. Mayence, in German Mainz, is a strongly fortified town with 72,300 inhab. (23,000 Prot., 4,000 Jews), including a garrison of 8,000 soldiers. It is pleasantly situated on the left hand of the Rhine, opposite and below the influx of the Main.

'It says,' I observed, 'that the Romanic-Germanic Central Museum contains the most varied and interesting collection of ante-Christian antiquities in the whole of Germany.'

'Ante-anti,' repeated Albie, chuckling. 'It is too painfully clear these guides are not written by native English speakers.'

'The Library and the Collection of Coins occupy the second and third floors of the west wing, to which is appended a remarkable assembly of typographical curiosities, manuscripts and incunabula. A complete set of coinage from the court of Charlemagne is the collection's pride.'

'I am more interested in the two valuable coins that comprise *this* collection,' said Albie, slipping his hand into my breeches. There then occurred the event which, naturally, modesty, not to say legal sanction, prevents me from detailing. Afterwards we slept. I wanted us to share the bed in my room, which was certainly ample enough for two; but Albert, wisely I suppose, considered the possibility that a chambermaid, or hotelier, or even young Hans our valet-de-place, might chance upon us together. So he returned to his room.

We rose late and broke our fast in the Weiner Café on Gymnasiumstrasse. The date was 13th April – a Friday. Sharply drawn white clouds, perfect as puffs of white, mobbed the sky. A strong spring breeze had awoken itself, making the big trees lining the Strasse move with an underwater slowness. But as I drank my wine-and-water and picked the last flakes of pasty from my plate, I bethought me how very comely was the pink and white stonework of the buildings of Mayence; how courteous and handsome the natives – even the Jews, of whom there were many in their funereal black. I reminded myself of how fortunate I was to be able to enjoy so much of the world's beauty with Albert. I was, I told myself, happy. I insisted upon it. If I insisted strongly enough, the feeling of chewing apprehension in my stomach would surely recede.

After breakfast we visited the cathedral: an imposing block-shaped edifice of rose-coloured stone, with one superbly tall slate-clad spire at the northern end. Ingress was achieved via two marvellous and mighty brazen doors that opened on to the north aisle, and in silent admiration we walked the length of the building – 122 yards long, the Baedeker informed us, and supported by 56 hefty pillars. Albert translated some of the funerary inscriptions for my benefit, and I sketched a few of the statues into my notebook. There is a particularly well-rendered head of Saturn on the eighteenth-century monument dedicated to a certain Canon von Breidenbach-Bürresheim. The cloisters are tranquil, built in the Gothic style, and Albert and I sat side by side and smoked for an hour, as the shadows slowly swung about the great axis of the turning world. The Baedeker recommended visiting the crypt, but by now it was lunchtime, and the verger could not be found to unlock the door for us.

We strolled out into the breezy sunlight, north to Gutenberg-platz where a fine statue commemorates Mayence's most famous son, John Gutenberg, inventor of the printing press. We heard the first of the commotion here. It was Albert who first saw the changes in the sky. At the far end of Ludwigsstrasse a

34

considerable crowd of people were in motion, and their shrieks and yells of terror carried cleanly to us on the clear spring air. A tram, rolling along its grooves down the street, stopped suddenly. I saw its driver scramble from the cab and abandon it.

'Clouds!' Albert yelled, suddenly. Such uncharacteristic behaviour for this reserved, immaculately mannered individual! 'Clouds!' He was pointing upwards. For a moment I saw clouds, visible masses of water droplets suspended in the air according to the logic of their relative density. But then the ghastly reality struck me, a modern-day Saul on the road to a ghastly Tarsus – for water must always be heavier than mere air, and no structure of such size and evident solidity could support itself overhead. What we had thought clouds were not. They were something else. They were gigantic amoeboid *beings*, creatures of monstrous otherness. A venus-shell of silver mist, animated by some incomprehensible will or mechanism, swooped low over Mayence's crenulations and spired roofs. It was a *device*, a machine constructed on principles quite different to steam engines or electrical capacitors; a chariot for cleaving the high sky, a throne set about with rods and lights. Weapons? And seated in its heart, wraithed about by the very device it piloted, was a creature unlike any I have seen – like the meat at the centre of a cockle, but the size of a bullock, orange and quivering with life. I looked about me, my heart galloping, a hideous anticipation of perdition in my whole body. Every cloud was a chariot, and in every one monsters of various sizes were enthroned – from cattle-big to whale-big. They thronged the sky. 'O strange!' I howled. 'Strange strange strange!' The creature I had first seen had brought its mist-chariot down almost to touch the ground. Now it began advancing towards me over the cobbles of the square. Its tangle of nude-muscle-fibre body jittered, and weird black tentacles, like tadpole tails, sprung up upon its torso. Thorns made of flesh. Beckoning scilla. I am not ashamed to say that I hurled myself down upon the ground, that I pressed my face against the stones, and wrapped my arms about my head, whimpering.

That evening we dined at a restaurant named Hanaczik, at the very top of Jacobsbergergasse. The main course was of middling quality, but dessert – apple torte and fine-whipped cream – was delicious, and the claret belonged in the first class. We strolled side by side along to Gutenbergplatz where the theatre is, half-thinking of seeing a play. But we had not planned ahead and by the time we got there the performance had already started. It was, moreover, a Germanic translation of a Dion Boucicault play, and Albert was of the opinion that we could see Boucicault any day of the week at home. 'We're in Rhineland!' he told me. 'We ought to immerse ourselves in *Germanic* culture!'

'Oh that we could walk, arm in arm, through these streets,' I declared.

He hushed me at once. 'You wouldn't enjoy being arrested, Harold.'

'These people?' I said, gesturing. The Platz was thronged. 'Ordinary Germans going about their business – they pay us no mind. It's as if they don't see us. We are merely two foreigners, babbling in a barbarian tongue!'

'They'd see us pretty quick if we started behaving as spoony young lovers,' Albert retorted, in a quiet, forceful voice. 'And you'd see *them* too, if you looked properly—' So I looked again; and saw that the crowd of people possessed a markworthy homogeneity. Black-clad people, moving without timidity and yet with unobtrusive haste across the square. Jews. For the Friday evening commences their sabbath, and I suppose they were returning from their temple to their homes. 'These Hebrew gentlemen will be even less disposed to notice us,' I said. 'Keeping themselves to themselves.'

We returned to the hotel, and sat in the lounge smoking and

reading. Albert made his slow way, brow furrowed so deeply it was as though the book was a plough, carving up the soil of his head, through a work of German philosophy – that same Freddie Nietzsche upon whom the clever set in London is so keen. I read for the second time my copy of Herbert Wells's *War of the Worlds*.

The following day we caught the train to Frankfurt.

On the train I completed my reread of the Wellsian story. There was something about it that snagged meaningfully upon my imagination, though I couldn't decide for myself what this *something* was. As storytelling it made no absurd pretence to great art; Wells himself, a man I knew distantly – the acquaintance of an acquaintance – was no Goethe, or Shakespeare, or Homer. He was, in point of fact, a servant's son, bred in the honest humbleness of the Kent countryside. To meet him in the flesh was to be struck by his ingenious cleverness and his bouncy earnestness, both characteristics as clear markers as you could hope to see of his *lack* of gentility. True breeding cannot be counterfeited. This same fellow was now making a name for himself in the literary world with nothing more than a penny dreadful sensibility and a few handfuls of journalistic glitter cast upon the page. Nonetheless, his was the book that refused to leave my mind! Having read it twice, I was now certain I would read it a third time. What *was* it that so fascinated me? I asked Albert's opinion on the matter, but he was dismissive. 'That trash,' he said. 'To call it a penny dreadful overvalues it. Farthing dreadful, let us say. Lights on Mars? Strange creatures descending from the sky to wreak havoc in . . .'

He stopped speaking. For a moment we looked at one another. Indigestion clawed at my guts. 'Sausage is supposed to be,' I said, looking out of the window. 'I mean, the people of Germany are *alleged* to be masters in the making of sausages! And yet my poor guts are rumbling lamentably upon that breakfast meal.'

'Mine too,' said Albert, returning to his philosophical treatise. 'Intestines having a fearful job chewing over this stuff. It's unaccountable, I must say.'

'You usually have the most enviable digestive constitution,' I observed.

'Indeed!'

In a moment the sensation passed out of my midriff, and I felt more at ease. For a while I attempted to peruse a local newspaper, by way of improving my German. But Albert grew cross-tempered with my continual interruptions to *his* reading, and my asking after the meaning of this word, or that word. So I threw that project over, and instead stared out of the window of our compartment. The train line passed for many miles through woodland; but then it broke free of the trees and ran alongside the Rhine. I stared at the waterway, which returned a muddy-silver version of the wide sky back to the heavens. The trees on the distant far bank were as small as grass blades. The motion of the train, and the pacifying fullness and inexhaustible flow of the river, soothed me. Then, but then, oh *but then* fleetingly I saw something reflected in the body of the water – a mile-long snake in the sky, with fanning blue feather-like protruberances on its tail, and lights gleaming as portholes along its length. I cried out, and looked up, and there were tears in my eyes: I was weeping with a kind of terror of recognition, a strange throat-closing emotion combining horror and delight. Why delight?

The central railway station of Frankfurt is the largest and handsomest structure of its type I have encountered upon my travels in Germany (I hear the Berlin Bahnhof is larger, but I have yet to go to Berlin). The station overlooks its own spacious Bahnhofsplatz, from which wide and tree-lined streets radiate – Kronprinzestrasse, Kaiserstrasse, Taunusstrasse. Inconveniently, however, the station is located a distance west of the centre of the city, and the hotels of Frankfurt do not send omnibuses to meet the trains. We were obliged therefore to hire a private cab, and some foolish delay in loading our luggage was the occasion for Albert losing his temper. It is not like his normal character to rage so, but *something* had agitated his balance of mind, and he railed at the blank-faced driver in fluent German for five full minutes. Eventually we clambered aboard and rode bumpily to the hotel Schwan, on the Goetheplatz. According to my Baedeker, it was at this luxurious establishment that the peace of 10th May 1871 was concluded, the defeated remnants of once-mighty martial France forced to capitulate to the resurgence of German might. And what opulence there was inside! A large gilded reception hallway, blood-red carpets soft as silk up the two arching stairways. The Schwan also operates a mechanical elevator in which, with some small apprehension at its prison-like sliding grille and confined space, the two of us ascended to our room.

I'm sorry to say we quarrelled like children as soon as the porter left us to ourselves. I rebuked Albert for his ill-tempered words to the cabriolet-driver, and he retaliated hotly, accusing me of *sticking my nose in* when I 'couldn't even get my mouth around the simplest Deutscher terms'. We parted badly, and I tried to cool my fury by wandering through the streets of this strange city with only my guidebook to direct me. I stood beneath Schwanthaler's Monument of Goethe, erected in 1844, twelve years after the poet's death. The reliefs on the front of the pedestal are allegorical, and the ones on the sides are figures from Goethe's poems. I strolled to the Römer, the town hall of the former free imperial city, and the most interesting edifice in Frankfurt from a historical point of view. The façade presented three lofty gables to the Römerberg, or market-place, opposite. I passed the cathedral without going inside, and instead wasted an idle hour in the Städel Art Institute, a handsome building of grey sandstone which contains collections of pictures, engravings and drawings by all the great European masters, as well as numerous casts and busts. The main picture gallery is especially rich in specimens of the early Flemish and German schools of the fifteenth and sixteenth centuries, as well as many pretty Dutch interiors from the seventeenth century and even a few from Italy. The names of the artists appear on the picture frames.

I took a solitary luncheon, feeling gloomy indeed, and watched the passers-by. Frankfurt has a population of some 179,800 inhabitants, including 18,000 Jews and a military garrison of 1,800 soldiers. The city lies in a spacious plain bounded by mountains, on the right bank of the navigable Main. Wherefore did I comprehend such dread, in my very guts? Of what was I scared? That Albert did not love me? No, for I knew he loved me, and I said so, to myself, aloud, quietly and in English. Saying the words, like a charm, helped reduce the sensation of intestine agony a little. But then a new fear leapt up in my heart – did he doubt my love *for him*? Such a supposition was not to be endured. I left a banknote on my table and ran straight off, not even finishing my pitcher of Rhenish, all the way back to the Schwan, and up the stairs – for I could not abide the thought of locking myself in that elevator cage – to our room. Albert was there, sitting with his feet up on the rail of the balcony, smoking and reading. The little emotion I could read on his face, that beautiful, reserved, manly face, was enough to reassure me that he knew. We had no need of words of apology. Instead I drew the shutters, and wedged a chaise-longue against the door to prevent the ingress of unwanted servants or maids, and took him to the large bed, where we lay together as Achilles and Patroclus once lay together, millennia ago.

Into the Trojan lands, astride a horse larger than a palace. How could Ilium not see the danger, in that vast equine structure? They believed they had won, and saw everything – even their own destruction – in those terms. The terms that shape our modes of thought are so intimately worked into the things we think about, and thinking *behind* thought of course structurally impossible, that no other outcome was possible. And so it was that they were fooled by the horse.

In the comfortable shadow afterwards, with the slats of the shutter laying parallel strips of sunlight over his naked flanks, we two talked for a long time. I confessed to him of my own often roiling stomach, and of my bafflement as to the cause. Albert confided in me that he too had been feeling a sense of dread ever since Mayence. He couldn't understand it, any more than I. Though he had toured through Germany many times, yet never before had he felt so apprehensive – of what? He knew not. 'It may be this accursed stuff I'm reading,' he growled. 'This Nietzsche is a devil – self-confessedly a devil. His job, as he conceives it, is to make his readers doubt everything they have hitherto taken for granted! It is an uncomfortable proceeding, I do assure you, most uncomfortable.'

'What of truth, though?'

'Oh, *truth* is mutable, saith the sage. Truth is power, not science; or rather, it is *science*, but science is power too. The strong legislate what is true, and after a while we forget that this is whence it came. Our habits of thought are stronger than strait-waistcoats. We walk about with habit-coloured spectacles before our eyes, and see everything as we are accustomed to see it.' He shuddered, and I embraced him to warm him, and this in turn led to a manlier embrace.

We dined at the hotel, and the wine helped ease our mutual sense of dissatisfaction with life – or our sense of saturated satisfactions, as a man who has eaten too much rich food moans about his stomach.

The next day we spent the morning at the Zoological Gardens, admission 1 mark, built upon the grounds of an old estate, in the sink of the ruins of which is a remarkable salt-water aquarium. Afterwards we walked upon the Old Bridge, and stood in its centre, looking out upon the Main. The bridge is fashioned from red sandstone, and dates from 1342. The middle is embellished with a statue of Charlemagne, by Wendelstadt and Zwerger, and nearby is an antique cross of iron, with, in Catholic style, an iron-fashioned Christ upon it. A small figure of a cockerel surmounts this, memorial to an old story that the architect completed his bridge by means of a treaty with the devil, in which he agreed to sacrifice to the antichrist the first person to cross it. But the canny builder held back the crowds, and sent a hen over the span before anything else.

Passing along the Schöne Aussicht Obermainstrasse, I noticed a street cleaner leaning on a wide broom. He was brushing the road in long, slow strokes. Curious as to what he was clearing away, I stepped over to him. My eyes stung. My stomach was abruptly burning with an inner blaze. I felt deeply, unconscionably afraid. But of what? Of what? The sweeper was moving piles of – I know not *what* they were. Dozens of them. A multitude of tadpole-like beings, each head the size of a bowling-ball and the colour of myrrh, the tails double-bladed and streaked with silver and blue. A semi-transparent jelly coated the heads. And though some of these weird monsters were clearly dead, many writhed sluggishly, and strained to move themselves in the heavy and unfamiliar gravity of our Earth. I knew, looking upon them, that they possessed powers of thought and will and even of spirit at least the equal of ours. Yet here they lay, heaped and discarded, in great banks of shuddering alien flesh.

The sweeper had stopped long minutes before, and was staring at me in frank alarm.

'What are you doing?' Albert called to me. 'Why are you gawping at that fellow? You're spooking him, my dear boy.'

He added something in rapid German, and the street sweeper looked over at him, nodding slowly.

'What's he—?' I asked. 'What's he *doing*?'

'Sweeping the streets, you goose.'

'Sweeping *what*?'

Albert was at my side, and slipped his arm through mine. 'Rubbish, of course. What else? Come along.' And he led me off.

After luncheon, Albert returned to the hotel for a sleep, but I did not feel sleepy. Instead I walked the streets, my mind pleasantly idle. I passed the old Leinwandhaus, which in English is Draper's Hall, a structure dating originally from the first half of the fourteenth century, and provided with a splendid array of turrets and pinnacles, recently restored. There was nothing about which to be alarmed. I was in a civilised city, with a purse full of gold, and a head full of learning. I had my guidebook in my hand. God was in his heaven and all was as right with the world as I wanted it to be.

I took a seat outside a café on Hotzgaben and drank a glass of German beer in the sunlight. I brought out the Wells novel and laid it on the table in front of me. Something about its oatmeal-coloured binding filled me with a sort of revulsion, and yet I felt the compulsion to reread it for a third time. I resisted this. No good would come of it. Instead I brought out the Baedeker, and read up about Darmstadt, attempting to determine whether it was worth detouring south of the river to visit that place.

My glass contained nothing but suds and air. The waiter removed it. He brought me another.

'You are a believer, I see, in the efficacy of Baedeker,' declared a fellow from a nearby table.

I conceded that I was, and introduced myself. The stranger told me his name, and got up to reach me so we shook hands. He sat back in his seat. 'It is always a pleasure to meet a fellow countryman when abroad,' he said. He moved his chair round to face me better and wished me health with a sup from his glass. He was a pleasant-faced elderly fellow, with a grey-white beard trimmed to cover only his chin, and a broad pink forehead reaching, under some strands of brown hair, all the way up to the top of his crown.

'You do not use a guidebook yourself?' I asked.

'I find,' replied my new friend, 'that to tour a town with a guidebook in hand is to see only what the guidebook permits.'

'There's no law that it must tyrannise us so,' I countered. 'One may stroll where one wishes! Only if we choose to omit the handbook, one will not *know* where one is, or what one is seeing.'

'I fear I have expressed myself badly,' said the man, with a queer little smile. 'I do not mean that the Baedeker forces us to walk this street or that. I mean that we do not see Frankfurt – we see Baedeker's Frankfurt. I mean, we tick off the things the book lists, and see them only as the book describes them. And when we leave, and think back, we find ourselves remembering not the city, but the pages of a book.'

'There may be something in what you say,' I admitted, laughing. 'Is the choice so stark, though? Slavery of the mind, or ignorance?'

'Is that other book *The War of the Worlds*?' he asked.

'Do you know it?'

'Indeed I do. And think highly of it, I must say.'

'It fills me with a strange dread,' I blurted, and as soon as I said it I realised the truth of it. Dread clung to the book like a smell. I nudged it away from me with my knuckles.

'Do you mean,' the man asked, 'that you fear Mr Wells's predictions might come true, and Martians lay waste to Woking? I know Woking, sir, and figure the possibilities for post-bellum architectural improvement worth the cost.'

'You are from there?'

'Ascot,' he said. 'You?'

'Chelsea. But, no, no, you are right to mock.'

'I beg your pardon indeed if I have done anything so ill-mannered!'

'Not in the least. Most kindly you have pointed out a small nonsense, nothing more.' I nodded. 'Still: it is not as prophecy that the book upsets me. There is an – uncanniness to the narrative. Or not even the story: just to the material fact of the book. I am,' I added, moved obscurely to confess myself to this stranger, 'touring the Rhine cities with a … friend of mine. There is much for us to enjoy, and many fine sights. And yet sight increasingly fills me with—' I stopped speaking.

'Dread?' he prompted.

'Such that I almost wish – Providence forgive me – to be blind, that I might never again have to worry about what *can be seen*.'

The man was silent for a while, and drained his glass of hock and soda water. The waiter, hovering behind, approached; and the fellow ordered a new drink – in French. 'I speak no German at all,' he confessed to me.

'My Deutsch is rudimentary, I fear. Though I have enough to order a drink, thank God.'

'Fortunately for me they all speak French hereabouts. I understand,' he continued, looking directly at me, 'why you are fearful.'

The acidic bubbling sensation sparked up in my gut. My heart began to beat faster. 'You do?'

'I have seen what you see. Books like *that*,' and he tipped his chin at *The War of the Worlds*, 'are something of a favourite of mine. Scientific romances.'

'You have not seen what I have seen,' I said, in a trembling voice, 'because I have not seen anything.'

'And neither have I. And no more have all the hundred thousands who live in this city. And yet still we see. They,' he added, looking upwards. I actually (it makes me ashamed to say it) scrunched both my eyes tight shut, rather than follow his gaze and *see*. 'They are not hostile, I think.'

'I might hope you are correct,' I said, in a small voice, 'I must fear you are not.'

'Mr Wells has clearly seen them clearer than most,' the stranger agreed. 'And he thinks they come to wage war. But I wonder if— If they mean only to greet us. To say hello. And in their incomprehensible implacability they continue trying to greet us, as a fly butts his hairy head over and over upon the pane of glass. Or do they comprehend how difficult it is for us to meet them? Is that why they persevere so? Out of kindness?'

The waiter returned with a new glass of hock-and-soda, gave us a stiff little bow, and retreated inside again.

'Perhaps it is as difficult for them to see us,' I said.

My new companion nodded once, twice, long deep nods, as if this were a new thought, and he was pondering it. 'What if Mr Wells stands at the head of a new form of storytelling?' he said.

This provoked me to a sharp speech close to rudeness. 'That trash? Never! Never! Sir, forgive me, but I consider myself something of a *literatus*, and Mr Wells has no posthumous reputation to which he can look. Read the novels of Henry James, or of George Meredith, or Gissing, and then read this novel, and then tell me which is truer to life!' I was growing heated, and took a sip of beer. The stranger was looking intently at me.

'Truer to life is the point, of course,' he said, in a distant voice. 'True as a straight line is said to be true. True as a portrait is said to be true. Unless the cosmos itself is so constituted that the portrait precedes the sitter? Schopenhauer believed will the structuring principle of the universe; and what *is* will if not the idiom of mind? He confessed no master, did Schopenhauer, but Kant; and Kant says as much. Well, then, it might not surprise us if the physical sitter, on his stool, in his artist's studio, finds his nose changing length, or his eyes moving further apart, or his hair colour darkening, as the portrait dictates.' I must have looked aghast at such a suggestion, and the fellow laughed. 'Of course, it's nonsense!'

My heart lightened. Of course it *was*! I was touring, in the grand manner. The man I loved was asleep in the hotel, and soon I would return to him. I had seen nothing untoward.

'To repeat myself, though,' the other fellow said, musingly. 'What if Mr Wells *does* stand at the head of a new form of storytelling? If he does, I'd wager many more people will ... see. I'd wager the newspapers would fill *up* with accounts of strange beings, and lights in the sky, and tentacles and I know not *what*. But I daresay you are correct, sire. I daresay the twentieth century belongs to Mr James.'

We parted on good terms. On the way back to the hotel I went to the Opernhaus, and purchased two tickets for the evening's performance.

3

The Institute

Totality

: 1 :

Let me pick the threads of this story up again, rearrange the letters into a new form. And the name of this anagram is *how quickly life goes to shit*. For to shit mine went, and assuredly so. For a long time I blamed the drink, and my mashed-up face and my prolonged loneliness, and a malign deity who hated me and didn't even exist, the bastard, which naturally made it worse. I didn't blame my *encounter* (let's call it that) in Antarctica – because I really didn't want to think about my *encounter* in Antarctica at all. I had experienced things and couldn't unexperience them. The whole. Yet, somehow, my life crept onwards. The booze helped. I acted as if it had never happened, except that it structured my whole miserable existence – *as if* is, of course, more than enough for English living. That's pretty much a thumbnail definition of Englishness, that.

That Oscar Wilde line about living in the gutter but looking at the stars has always irritated me. The affectation of it! The smarm. I speak as someone whose life used to be, literally, looking at the stars and then got relocated – literally again – to the gutter, so I know whereof I speak. At twenty-five I was an astrophysicist doctoral student at Reading University working on non-random radio emissions from galactic locale stellar objects. Then my life turned to garbage. On my fiftieth birthday I was working as a bin man for Bracknell and Wokingham council. The letters tumble down the slope in a big heap, as the lorry tips up its back. I was haunted, the whole way down.

What had happened to me in Antarctica was, I told myself, only hallucination. But it was a horribly vivid hallucination, and it kept returning to me, and it required large quantities of drink to return it to more conventional functioning. This is the first, and most important thing I learned from my Antarctic experience: the brain is a complex machine, and once you've dinged it, it will tend to throw weird shapes and glitches into your thoughts – for years. For decades. Bad dreams.

Bad dreams.

Ghosts.

Whole sight: or all the rest is desolation.

People haunt other people in many ways. Here's a for instance: you'd think that ignoring somebody studiously enough would lead eventually to them giving up. Not so. Not with some people. Take Roy, snug in his insane asylum. After a few stilted 'please cease and desist' replies to his many letters, I simply stopped responding. I had no personal animus against him, I told myself. The balance of his mind had been disturbed at the time of his actions and so on and so forth. It was regrettable; let's forget all about it. I wanted him to stop. He did not stop. So I reneged on my resolution to ignore him, and wrote back angrily, imploringly, commanding him to stop, which is to say in truth begging him to stop. He continued writing. Eventually, on the advice of a friend, I got a solicitor to write to the director of the asylum requesting that the patient named 'Roy Curtius' be prevented from harassing my client via unsolicited and distressing letters sent etc., etc. The letter we received back expressed regret and surprise, and included a photocopy of a letter signed by me – of course I'd never signed such a thing – written upon Koestler Trust headed notepaper no less, courteously requesting him to keep sending me his 'insights'. This letter spoke of a 'collaborative creative project'. I was baffled by this. I instructed the solicitor to write back, distancing myself from the forgery. I also approached the police, who took a statement from me and did everything short of literally rolling their eyes and sighing to show that they were perfectly uninterested. Nothing more came of this, except that Roy either stopped writing to me, or else the asylum stopped his letters from going into their out-box.

Each of those solicitor's letters cost me £90. That's £180 for two letters. A lot of money back then. It's *quite* a lot of money, even now.

I got on with my life. I was a man with seven fingers, a weird patch of skin on my nose that was markedly redder than the rest of my face and a nest of leprous-looking scars on the left side of my face. My visage, not hitherto ill-favoured, now possessed a patchwork complexion somewhere between the scarecrow in *The Wizard of Oz* and a scary clown. I also own fewer than the usual complement of toes. The frostbite had killed some of my facial nerves, giving my interactions an unfortunately mask-like demeanour. Add into this a certain stoutness in the belly area: not *fat* exactly, not in the slack or flabby sense of the word. The way my torso is shaped, really. I have a solid, blocky arse, and a convex rather than a concave waist. For a period of eighteen months or so (this was when I was working as a postdoc at the University of Dundee) I attended a gym; and assiduously sculpted and toned my body. My muscles bulked, I could lift heavier weights and turn myself into a giant crab-pincer by lying back and performing a hundred rapid sit-ups. But this didn't shift my fundamental shape, and after a while I grew disheartened and gave up.

My life through the nineties and noughties was one defined by long stretches of involuntary celibacy. It occurs to me that most people live this way. It occurs to me, too, that art, literature and culture have been rather derelict in their duty so far as capturing this essential truth of things is concerned. Once upon a time, sex was unspeakable in our stories, and so was only always implicit – we get Elizabeth Bennett and Darcy dancing a saraband rather than thrashing about in bed. Nonetheless, stories were always about a *lovely* woman and a *handsome* man dancing that saraband. Then there was the Chatterley trial, and suddenly in the 1960s and 1970s novels were full of sex scenes. Of course, it was always a particular kind of sex scene. Growing up in the late seventies and early eighties, before the supersaturation of culture by internet porn, I devoted a lot of time to digging out the dirty bits in contemporary novels borrowed from the library. It was all we had, back then. I pored over the scenes in Harold Robbins blockbusters, or Henry Miller, or the novelisation of *Endless Love*. What you get in those books is amazing, mind-blowing, transcendent fucking. Beautiful, physically confident young people getting naked with one another and blowing one another's minds. Then computer porn came along and literalised precisely that for the whole world. We went in short order from no sex in our literature and film to— Well, that. In doing so we hopped right over the broad middle ground. It's that middle ground where we all live. All of us save only a few supermodels and tantric sex athletes and whatnot. At the upper end of this hinterland are people with thinning hair and bad skin having sex with other people cringingly self-conscious about their flab. People who cannot build physical confidence upon the shifting sands of frankly unprepossessing bodies, who yet can't seem to make common ground with one another over their shared insufficiencies. People who muddle through, sweetening a life of low-level self-dissatisfaction with tart little orgasms from time to time, though 'time to time' turns out to be never *quite* frequent enough, the partner never quite attractive enough, the wellbeing provided by the orgasm just a touch *too* fleeting a thing, breath into the wind. People tired, and resentful, and corroded by their cul-de-sac awareness that this is all there is for them. People making compromises on their sexual fantasy ideals in order to accommodate them to the reality.

And those are the lucky ones. The lucky ones! At the lower end of that same hinterland matters are murkier. The people dwelling there go for months, or years, having sex only with themselves, bedding-in (hah!) the poisonous disjunction between commercial fantasy and individual actuality by relying on the same porn that mocks them with their own insufficiencies to bring themselves off. It's not a recipe for psychological health.

I'm not saying that the nineties and naughties were a total strike-out zone for me. I dated some women. Let's be precise and say: I dated four women, relationships lasting between one month and two years. But I couldn't make it stick, and the time between girlfriends was long and lonely. I tried dating agencies, and personal ads; I pressed friends to hook me up with their single friends. I chatted nervously to people in bars. It did me no good. My face walked always before me, a boy with a red flag preventing my motorcar life from moving into any of the higher gears.

I'm not bidding for your pity when I say this. Most people live like this, after all, to one degree or another. For most of the time, I simply got on with my life. I worked hard, and got together with my friends, and I read and watched telly and went on holidays. I drank, and pointedly didn't think about my experiences in the Antarctic, and drank some more. I interviewed poorly for a job at Lancaster, but somehow got it anyway, and moved to that city. There was important work to do. Hubble was launched in 1990, and I was part of a team run out of the universities of Michigan and Lancaster to analyse the data from the telescope's High Speed Photometer. Then they discovered that the Hubble mirror wasn't quite the right shape, and fitted cunningly designed optical correction hardware to bring the telescope's images into focus. The HSP was one of the instruments sacrificed in order to make room for this corrective kit, and my team was at a loose end.

Four women. I could pretend to be blasé and claim that I can't remember many of the details, but who would I be kidding? The most heartbreaking one was Molly. She worked as a secretary in the Registry at Lancaster University, and we were set up on a date by mutual friends. She was sweet-tempered and clever, and we had a great deal in common. We hit it off. We dated, and it got serious, and we moved into a flat together, a proper couple. And then we ended up separating, more in sorrow than anger. She didn't mind that I had two slightly mangled hands, and that I was so self-conscious about the state of my toes that I never once (I think) took my socks off whilst we made love. She didn't mind that my nose looked so weird, or that ever since Antarctica I had suffered from recurring nightmares, when *they*, or *it*, or whatever, congealed – palpably, visually – in my bedroom, resolving into the figure of a young boy, the old haunting, the yelling-aloud, sweat-flowing raging awakening in the small hours. I wept and apologised and she said, 'It's OK.' She *didn't mind*. That's the kernel of the heartbreak, right there. She *put up with these things*. And I in turn *didn't mind* her acne. I'm not talking about a few teenager-y spots on her face. This was an all-body affliction of red-purple bumps, about a third of which crusted into cream-coloured scabs. They were on her face, across her chest, inside her thighs. They turned her back into a Jackson Pollock, and for the ten days leading up to her period

53

were so sore that she couldn't lie supine. Without them she would have been a most beautiful individual: white-chocolate skin, red hair the colour of Tizer, eyes green as an old pound note, slender body. But with them they were all anybody could see about her. She told me that one of her earlier boyfriends had suggested, as he broke up with her, that in future she ought to date a blind man – the most hurtful thing, she said, anybody had ever said to her. And I nodded, and put on a sympathetic face, and consoled her, and agreed with her that the world was full of bastards. But inside I was as big a bastard as any, because I was thinking: well *that* wouldn't work because Molly's acne was a tactile as well as a visual disfigurement. Running my hands over her body at midnight, with the lights out, I could feel every bump and hollow, every braille-like scab.

But beggars can't be choosers, we say, and the truth of the cosmos is that we are all beggars. Molly's acne, a trick played upon her by some malicious deity, affected all of her skin, even in her most intimate places. On rare days, when her period was a long way away, we might manage some slow and delicately orchestrated penetrative sex. Most of her cycle such a thing was too painful for her to contemplate. We used one another's hands, and mouths, and did all the things ingenuity suggested, and all the time I was secretly fixating, and I'll bet she was too, only upon the things we *didn't* do. If only we could do *that*, I thought, in my inmost heart. If only we could have a normal sex life of regular vigorous fucking. And that was what broke us up in the end – not the endless search for medical amelioration of her condition, the long drives to specialist clinics, the sitting in chilly waiting rooms for hours, the hand-holding, the new pills that made her sick (holding her lava-coloured hair out of the way of her face as she knelt at the toilet in our flat), the other new pills that made her so depressed she could hardly get out of bed and her libido vanished altogether. The ointments that I would apply, as she wept with the pain. The weird diets Molly picked up from online sites, and in which I would join her, in a spirit of, I now think, misapplied solidarity. All this was bearable. The secret fantasy of a regular sex life, though, was not. Our fantasies always betray us in the end. Opportunity presented itself, and I spent the night with a feisty, fat woman called Barbara. And Barbara lay there gasping and hooting and I banged away between her legs, like a lusty young blacksmith forging a magic sword with my weighty hammer, and some part of me thought: *I simply can't be doing with this tentative never-quite fucking I'm getting with Molly any longer.* So I sat down with Molly and told her it was over, and she didn't cry; and I agreed to keep paying half the rent until the end of the lease, but I moved out and slept for a month on the couch of a friend called Leo. Of course, things didn't work out with Barbara, partly because she was rather unhinged, and prone to hitting me with things, sometimes quite heavy things. But mostly it didn't work out because she got together with a long-distance lorry driver and I decided I had too much self-respect to share her. And actually the worm in the bud was my memory of Molly. All through that month with Barbara, as the two of us worked out energetic bang-bang-bang fucking in bedrooms and on staircases and in the front of my car – all through that my mind kept reverting to Molly. I dreamed of tenderness. Soon enough I found it occurring to me that *I really couldn't be doing with this one-note hammer-away too-obvious fucking I was getting with Barbara.* My fantasies were all slender women and delicacy and the lightest touch of a fairy hand. I went back to Molly, and wept, and begged her, but she was cool and firm and told me that the relationship was over. She reminded me I had been the one to kill it. I could hardly disagree. Then I was single for many years, and the more effort I put in to dating the less success I had. I went through the four phases of sexual bereavement: anticipation; rage; despair

('I'll never make love to another human being again') and finally grudging acceptance.

Dreams were uncomfortable. I slept badly for so long that I grew accustomed to sleeping badly. I had odd little blackouts, such that I would wake, suddenly, lying on the grass outside my flat, in the dark, in the cold, in my pyjamas, in a state of disorientation and fear. I presumed I had sleep-walked outside, and lain down. Several times the police found me about the town and entertained me with the hospitality of their cells. I was drinking a lot, it's true. Nowadays counselling and support would be made available to somebody in my situation – the victim of a crime, after all. Attempted murder no less! Not back then.

And the thing is: the attempted murder didn't bother me. Roy's unsuccessful attempt to end my life. That sounds blasé, doesn't it? It's true though. Curtius was a nutjob. I knew his attack upon me was nothing personal. What bothered me were the hallucinations. The things that I had seen in Antarctica. The thing that I had seen. Not that I had *had* hallucinations, in the conventional sense; because (as a friend pointed out), I'd been drugged, and drunk, and sensorily deprived in the Antarctic night. It was hardly surprising that my mind had started playing tricks.

It was the persistence.

Looking back, I can see that there was a very long sine wave resonating through my life. One year of misery would be followed by a second, and then would come a glorious third and the nightmares would recede, if never quite vanishing. My concentration and energy levels would improve. I would sleep better, drink less, focus more on my work. Then I would see him – a boy, stringy-framed, simple clothes. A ghost. For a long time I assumed he was me, the ghost of myself as a little boy. I thought this partly because the ghost-boy had a scarred face (although his pattern of scars was different to mine, and although I had not *been* scarred as a youth). I wondered if perhaps I was dead. Maybe I'd died at the South Pole, and now I was living some ghastly afterlife purgatory. Maybe the ghost of the boy was there to haunt my death with my life. My thirteen-year-old life, back when I was young, and reading *Shoot!* and *2000 AD* on a Saturday morning, and eating Blackjacks and Fruit Salad chews, and cycling my Chopper through the park. It wasn't easy to get a good look at the ghost. Thirteen, I'd guess. Something like that. That's the way with ghosts, though, isn't it? Usually he would be in the corner of my bedroom. Or I might see him standing just outside the tepee of light cast by a street lamp. Or in a crowd, and I would *feel* him more than see him. Sometimes I got a better look. He didn't look anything like me.

The ghost-boy's appearance marked the point from which the sine wave would begin its inexorable downslide. For a full year the nightmares would increase in vividness and regularity. Back in the blackness and the cold, the southern lights casting an intermittent neon corpse-glow upon me, and the terrors, the terrors, the terrors, gathering all around me. Through a second year the night terrors would get inexorably worse. By year three I was barely able to function. I kept a bottle of gin on my bedside table. I moved to gin (I laugh at myself to write this, but it's true) because in my sodden mind I told myself the juniper berry element counted as fruit, a glimpse of health, in a way that wasn't true of my previous favourite tipple, vodka. I also drank a good deal of red wine. My teeth turned blue. My hands shook. This was my morning routine: I would wake, my face crusty with tears shed in the night, a sense of grasping, swallowing horror around me. Then I would take a swig of gin, and grimace, and cough, and take another. The discomfort of the firewater going down my parched throat was part of the routine, as much as was the slow blurring of the edges of my fear. But mostly it was the habit. Once I took my third glug – always three sips in the morning – I would have the sense of a painful but necessary ablution completed. Then: shower. Brushing my teeth. Breakfast cereal. Brushing my teeth again. Getting dressed, and a third brush of the teeth. I told myself I needed to brush my teeth thrice to disguise the fact that I started the day with alcohol, lest my employer get wind and fire me. The truth is: I had become wedded to the OCD routineness of it all.

My work at the university, substandard for years, finally dipped below the level where the authorities could continue turning their collective blind eye. I was issued with a first formal warning, and booked into training sessions designed to help me, which I either attended drunk, or skipped. I was issued with a second formal warning. My head of department took me aside, after a departmental board, and urged me to join Alcoholics Anonymous. I was distracted by the ghost of the scarred-face boy, walking down the corridor away from us both, visible over her shoulder. If he wasn't somehow *me* then why was his face scarred?

The third formal warning was tantamount to dismissal.

Unable to land another university job I retrained as a school science teacher. I told myself this was a stopgap, and I would continue applying for university work, but three years into schoolwork it started to dawn on me that I wasn't ever going to get back into tertiary education. This was depressing, and the depression was made more acute when I lost my teaching job. I'm not writing this narrative in order to give an account of my time as a schoolteacher, so I won't dwell on this, except to say that I was suspended rather than being sacked. I got three months' pay, and then the pay stopped, although my suspension carried on, for being drunk in the classroom. I had managed to modify my behaviour to the point where I would not go to work drunk in the morning. But by lunchtime I was usually in a state (maintaining discipline amongst bored and hostile teenagers disinclined to learn any physics, whilst the ghost-boy wandered through the rows of desks) that only several glasses of wine could remedy. After lunch I often went back into class under the influence. It grew more noticeable. The kids laughed about it and told their parents. The parents, when they complained to the head, were not laughing. The head had no option but to suspend me.

The three months' suspension passed in a haze. I checked the papers for jobs, and applied for several teaching positions, but didn't even get to interview. This at a time when the news assured me there was a national shortage of school teachers, especially in the sciences. A double blow to my ego. I signed on (you were still able to do that, back then) and lived for another six months on the dole. Eventually the dole people made my benefit conditional on me working at a series of low-grade employments: cleaning offices; working in a petrol station. So I did that. I applied for a job as a bus driver, and got as far as the sponsored HGV training, when the instructor smelt booze on my breath and dismissed me. He promised me my name would be blacklisted, and advised me not to apply for any more professional driving jobs. I accepted his scorn with as much downbeaten grace as I could muster. Eventually I found work with the council: two weeks on the dust carts, two weeks manning the Bracknell recycling station, where the public drove up to unload cardboard boxes and old toilet cisterns and bags of garden waste into the huge concrete-walled bays. The main downside (apart from the smell, and the low pay) was having to get up at 4 am every working day. I minded this less than some of the others, since sleep was an intermittent and turbulent business for me. The main upside was my gaffer was tolerant of his people taking the occasional snifter on the job. Then again, as the only middle-class, university-educated member of an otherwise solidly working-class, left-school-at-sixteen crew, I cannot pretend that I ever really fitted in.

I would drive to the depot in my old Vauxhall Astra, through pre-dawn streets and the carroty illumination of street lamps. I rarely saw another vehicle. I was often intoxicated. One time I misjudged a corner, side-swiped a parked van and drove through a hedge into the backlot of a Kentucky Fried Chicken outlet, causing – the subsequent court case established – £7,477 worth of damage. I was banned from driving for three years. The car was written off. Since I had been driving under the influence insurers refused to pay out for a new car. I was landed with a monthly instalment plan to pay the fine, the damages, the court fees.

I eventually got a handle on the drinking. It happens as you get older. It happens, or you don't get older. Drink hard in your twenties and you're a regular, fun guy. Keep drinking hard through your thirties and you start to separate yourself from fun, health and indeed other people. If you're still doing it in your forties it's probably because you have unresolved stresses and problems which you are clumsily and destructively self-medicating. Drinking hard into your fifties means that you're blowing hot and cold on ever seeing your sixties. I woke up a week after my fiftieth birthday unable to remember the previous three days, and decided to stop. I could say 'simple as that', except that it really wasn't simple at all. There was a clincher, though, and it was this: my main rationale for drinking was to calm myself in the face of my night terrors. But although I drank a lot, the nightmares refused to go away. I tried a few weeks of facing them without the alcohol, and though the terrors were no better they were certainly not worse. So I quit drinking.

Without booze jangling my nerves, and without needing to get up at 2 am every night to piss, I actually started sleeping better. Most nights the nightmares were still there, but every now and again I would sleep right through without disturbance.

The oddest thing about that was the nights in which I was unterrified left me not with repose, but with a kind of blankness. Habit accustoms us to anything, including misery and pain. Perhaps especially to those two. Another unexpected consequence of my new sobriety was that my libido perked up again. Given my difficulties in getting laid this was rather more a burden than a joy. But it goes some way to explaining why the arrival of Irma had the effect upon me that it did.

: 2 :

I had a toothache. A simple enough phrase. Does not capture the intensity of the misery. When I went to my dentist, for the first time in decades, I discovered my practice had reclassified me as a private patient, without (of course) my permission. I had a half-hearted argument with the receptionist, who insisted that the practice no longer provided NHS cover at all. I was welcome to try another practice, she said. In considerable pain, exhausted, frustrated, I agreed to be seen privately provided only I *was* seen. She asked me to sit down. I crouched on the settee in the waiting room, clutching the side of my face. The pre-booked patients went through, one by one, and soon enough the room contained only me and the ghost of the young boy.

If I looked straight at him he vanished. But if I looked a little away from him I got quite a good sense of his appearance. When I was finally led through to the Big Chair and the Bright Room he trotted along too. As I settled in the padded seat and opened my aching mouth, he was standing right beside the dentist.

The treatment took hours: X-ray, back in the waiting room. Through to the Big Chair again for the anaesthetic injection, and back in the waiting room for it to take effect. My boss rang during this latter interlude, and berated me. I tried to tell him I was at the dentist, that it was a medical emergency, but it sounded like I was speaking through a mouth packed full of marshmallows, and he told me he couldn't understand a fucking word I was saying, and gave me to understand that I was fucking around with a solid job in the middle of a fucking economy in which jobs were hens' fucking teeth and a number of other statements in which the word *fucking* figured prominently. Finally: the drill. That high violin whine, and the burn-y stench of chewed-up tooth, and the shards of discomfort that slid through the protective sheath of my anaesthesia. The ghost-boy was there through this, leaning close in as if fascinated by the procedure. My previous night had been more or less sleepless on account of the discomfort, so I was feeling trippy and weird, but when he began to stroke the side of my face with his hand I felt it very distinctly.

The dentist wrote me a scrip. I had a second, fuzzier argument with the receptionist over the bill – a vast sum of money, hundreds and hundreds of pounds for which I simply didn't have the funds. She offered me a payment plan, and I told her I would have to think about it. I sat back down and fell asleep there and then in the waiting room. The next thing I knew I was being shaken awake by the dentist himself, the reception-ist looking on. In a half-awake state I gave them all my bank details, signed a form – who *knows* what it specified? – made a follow-up appointment and left the practice.

I wandered back to my flat, followed as if by a faithful hound by you-know-who. Was I hallucinating him? Maybe he was a remnant of the things, thing, I has seen in Antarctica. Maybe I was dead and he was me and me was he and I was so tired I could barely walk, and stumbled into a lamp post. I had just enough mental wherewithal to stop at Boots on the way and fill my scrip. By now it was lunchtime, and I was hungry, but I couldn't face using my numb jawbone to chew. I climbed the stairs to my flat, let myself in, drank some milk, swallowed the first of my pills, and lay down on my bed.

When I awoke, the sun was setting: an early March evening, cool and rather beautiful. My whole face was tingling, like a parody version of the Christmas feeling. I stood at the window and looked across the concrete prospect of Bracknell as the west finally purged itself of red and let the interstellar black-purple own the sky. My view was of a stretch of large cuboid warehouse buildings, concrete, steel and cladding, which housed variously a long-term storage warehouse, a DIY superstore, an exhaust and tyre depot and so on. Behind them was the line of trees that marked the train line running west towards Reading. Visible in the deeper distance was the shaggy hem of Bracknell Forest, ancient and beautiful and perfectly indifferent to the industrial estate and transport infrastructure humankind had forced into its domain. But the sky! The colours in the sky passed through a series of Monet canvas richnesses; red-purple to blue-green-purple to black. Homer has a special Greek word for the colour of a deep-sea ocean water. That word, whatever it is. Then only the artificial light in the faraway empty car parks attached to the bottom of the view, and above it the glorious pure-black night sky. There were clouds, and there were also breaks in the cloud, and some stars visible, and something in the starved, drugged lightness of my head made the direct connection between the tingling in my face and the pinpricks of the stars. For a moment there really was no barrier between the curve of the night sky and the curve of my swollen jaw. The two were, in some sense, the same thing. *In some sense* is mealy-mouthed of me, I know. You want to rebuke me. You want to remind me that I trained as a scientist, and to urge me to precision and evidence and some falsifiable thesis. It wasn't rational; but it wasn't vague either. I was filled with insight, the way my skull is filled with my brain. The insight sat snugly inside me, as if the cavity had been designed to be exactly the right size to fit it. The insight was something like this: distinguishing between the outside world and my inner existence was abruptly revealed to me as *a false step*. Or not quite that. It was the realisation that I had been construing that distinction wrongly all this time. It was not a separation. It was an inflection, a refinement. It was a connection. The world and I constituted not two separate things, but a totality.

A huge sense of joy sprang up inside me. It was unprecedented. I've never felt anything like it before. You're thinking I was lightheaded with hunger and residual anaesthesia and the aftermath of prolonged suffering. I'm not going to argue with you.

When Roy and I had shared the base, on the underside of the world, I had been the one reading pulp SF and he had been the pretentious Latinist and high-culture snob. Returning to the UK, I discovered that some of his pretension and taste had leaked into me, somehow. I wouldn't be surprised if Roy spent the eighties and nineties reading *Doctor Who* tie-in novels and getting excited about the *Lord of the Rings* movies. This is a— This is a *thing*. I'll come back to this. For the moment I want to talk about Irma, and about that evening, and the high stars, there.

My stomach squeezed with hunger. The mood retreated a little, but did not dissipate. The ghost-boy was squatting in the corner, keeping an eye on me, but when I turned on the light he disappeared. Doesn't like the light. Doesn't like that tart, lemon concentrate quality of it, maybe. I made myself some toast and Marmite. I had nothing else in the flat to eat. I drank some more milk and took my second pill. Belatedly reading the small print on the side of the pack I discovered that this particular brand of antibiotic was not to be taken with alcohol or milk. I laughed.

My doorbell rang. You need to understand: I never had visitors. I was a man in my fifties, living alone in an ex-council flat on the outskirts of Bracknell. My work colleagues were all bin men and although I sometimes went to the pub with them, they never just popped round to see me. I wasn't expecting anybody.

Still, as I snibbed the door to my flat and made my way downstairs (the intercom was broken, so I couldn't just buzz people through) the magical sensation that was flowing through my body intensified again. I was in the verge of something marvellous happening. I felt as if everything in my life was pregnant with possibility.

I opened the door.

Standing there was the most beautiful woman I have ever seen. I loved her straight away. It's as simple as that.

'Hello,' she said. 'I'm here to drive you to the Institute.'

'OK,' I said. 'You want to come in?' Then I thought of how scummy my flat was, and quailed. Then I thought of *myself* – in the same clothes I'd been wearing yesterday, my mouth reeking of Marmite, my face disfigured, seven fingers on my hands. There was an inward lurch and the moment fell away in flakes. 'Wait! What?'

'I'll stay here,' said the woman. 'Get your coat, though. And a toothbrush. You'll be with us a few nights.'

'With you?' She had long dark hair, and regular though not exceptional features – a straight, quite long nose, a wide mouth and full lips. The light bulb over the door threw what would have been for most people an unflattering illumination over her face, but her skin, though lined, was clear and lovely. She wore a dark jacket. She was in her forties, I'd say.

'I'm sorry: did you say what your name was?'

'I'm Irma,' she said. 'It's a couple of hours driving so we need to get a move on.' A clear middle-class south-east accent.

'Where are we going? Can I grab a quick shower first? I'm— Look, this is unexpected. Are you sure you have the right person?'

'You're Charles Gardner,' she said. It wasn't a question. I'd been Chaz at work for so long the *Charles* sounded strangely. 'It's taken us a while to track you down. We have contacts in the university sector, but it's been a long time since you left academia. Your records there were no help. No one still in post could steer us the right way. Hardly anyone even remembered you.'

This was a rather desolating thing to say, when you think about it. Yet, coming from the mouth of so beautiful a woman, it was somehow charming rather than deflating. I thought back to my colleagues – to lovely Molly, who I had treated so badly, and the coolness with which she had greeted my betrayal. My own stupidity and her calm reaction. So she wasn't working at Lancaster any more? I wondered where she was.

It was a cold March night, and the air brought my head a little further back towards reality. 'Who do you work for?' I asked. It sounded tetchy, and suddenly I thought to myself: *what's going on here?* 'And, you know. Me? What do you want *me* for?'

'You work for the council, in waste disposal and recycling,' said Irma. 'But you used to be an astrophysicist. That's an unusual career progression, right there. Now: of those two skill sets, which do you think my Institute is likely to be interested in?'

'Institute of what?'

'Just Institute. Come along, Charles. Harp and carp. At least come talk to Peter.' That's how I heard the name. 'The Director will set you up for a chat. Decide after that. But you will want to hear what Peter has to say.'

'I have work in the morning,' I said.

'We've contacted your line manager and arranged a week-long holiday. Full pay. We are persuasive, and have friends in high places, so it wasn't hard. Come! We want you. I want you.'

That was the phrase that did it. I felt an almost irresistible urge to reach out and embrace her, there and then. 'This is sur-real,' I told her. 'I think you may be the most beautiful woman I have ever met.'

'You can't have met many women,' she replied drily.

'I'll come,' I said.

: 3 :

Her car was clean, nearly new. It felt like company wheels rather than her personal auto. And off we went. That she didn't put on the radio seemed to me an invitation to talk.

'Irma who?'

'Irma Casbrook.'

'So, your institute is involved in astrophysics work? Astron-omy?'

'Strangely enough.'

'University?'

'It's an Institute.'

'I mean, are you affiliated with a university?'

'We have many connections in the world of academia,' she said. 'But the Institute is a private business.'

It all felt unreal. 'Maybe I'm dreaming,' I said aloud. 'Whisked away after sunset by a beautiful woman. You know where I work now. You know what I *used* to do. Look, I'm guessing you know I'm not married.'

She didn't reply. We turned, swept up the feeder lane and joined the M4 heading west.

'Just waiting for the right woman, I guess,' I said. 'What about you? I mean maybe you're waiting for the right man. Maybe you're waiting for the right woman. I don't know. I try not to judge. But maybe you're married. I don't know. I'm babbling. I spent all morning in the dentist, you know. He gave me some

67

pills and I wasn't supposed to take them with milk and then I did take them with milk. I don't feel bad. In fact I feel pretty damn amazing.' It occurred to me that I had left my antibiotics back in the flat. This fact didn't bother me. Signage pointed the way M4 West. 'How far are we going? All the way to Wales?'

'Not all the way to Wales, no.'

'Bristol? Swindon? I'm sorry to babble. You are a beautiful woman.' She let this one go.

We vroomed along the motorway, and I rested my head against the coign where the top left of the seat meets the door frame. The hum passed its vibrations from car frame to skull in a manner more or less soothing. Having my head at this strange angle meant that the rows of gallows-tall street lamps we went blipping past appeared to rear up from the ground, swivel through, and snap down, like an endless procession of one-direction-only windscreen wipers.

'You're a scientist,' she said to me suddenly. 'So tell me this: where does mind come from?'

'Human mind?'

A scimitar flash of teeth in the darkness; but she didn't take her eyes off the road. 'That's right.'

'I guess we evolved it. I mean, all animals have minds, more or less.'

'More or less what?'

'More or less, uh, sophisticated. More or less intelligent.'

'More or less self-aware.'

'If you like.' I wasn't used to having this kind of conversation, to be honest. But I didn't want to give the impression I was a dunce. I sat up straight. 'The ability to process data, to make decisions based on that, bestows an evolutionary advantage on a creature. Shall I eat this, or not? Shall I fight, or run away? That kind of thing. So the human brain's just a much more complicated form of that. It's been millions of years in the making, laminated over time with new input-output—' I couldn't think of the word. 'Programmes,' I said. 'Feedback loops. Algorithms. Whatever. These are all cats-cradled together in a human being. But they're all, basically, doing simple things. Consciousness is, I guess, the kind of weird effect of all these things operating, in parallel or in sequence. Gives us the *impression* of something more than just a whole bunch of action-reaction data-processing loops. It gives us the impression of something more solid. Like a bunch of gnats,' I said, the image suddenly occurring to me, 'buzzing around you as you walk out of the wood. And then you look back into the sunset, and it's like, uh, the cloud of gnats looks for a moment like a human being, a cloaked human being, standing in the gloaming beside the woods. Only then it swirls again and you realise it's just a cloud of gnats.'

'Gnats,' she said. I felt the heat-prickle of embarrassment in my face. Christ, how I wanted to impress her.

'Sure. To say it's an illusion is not to say it's not real.' Then I thought: *what if she was religious, and believed in the soul and all that palaver?* I tried a little diplomatic back-pedalling. 'Of course nobody really knows, do they? The Hard Problem and suchlike. It's, uh notoriously hard to get any objective experimental data, anything verifiable, about – you know, dying and such. Using the mind to think about the mind is ... well, it contaminates the process from the beginning, doesn't it? It inserts the end of the experiment in the procedure.'

'The eyeball sees everything but itself.'

'Exactly. That's well put!' I was overdoing it. 'Who said that?'

'Wittgenstein.'

I'd heard of him (of course), but knew nothing about what he actually said, and didn't want to expose my ignorance to this attractive woman. 'Right,' I said.

'He was in an Italian prisoner of war camp during the First World War. Fought for the Austrian army, did Wittgenstein, and was captured. There was only one book in that camp, and Wittgenstein read it over and over. You know what it was?' She didn't wait for me to guess. 'Kant's *Critique of Judgement*. It was the one work of philosophy that had a deeper impact on him than any other.'

'Right,' I said.

'Read it and reread it.'

'Right,' I said again. Kant's name naturally reminded me of Curtius, and our time together in Antarctica. Not a pleasant memory. Decades ago, and yet still a trigger. I rubbed my scarred finger-ends against the fabric of my seat. It had been cold, back then. Ah! The cold.

'So,' I said, looking out of the passenger window. 'You believe in, what, a like immortal soul, do you?'

She began tutting, presumably rebuking me for my impertinence. Her tut-tut was surprisingly loud and resonant, and was issued with a clockwork regularity. Only when I looked back at her did I connect the noise with the intermittent orange light that was coming on and going off outside the passenger window.

Then we were pulling off the motorway. We rose, slowing and stopping at a roundabout.

'Until a few months ago I believed exactly as you do,' she said, suddenly. 'But that's all changed now.'

'You've, what. God God?'

'What?'

'I mean: *got* God? Have you?'

She eased the accelerator and we swung round the roundabout and away on a bright-lit dual carriageway. A faint drizzle began to touch the windscreen, and for a moment, before she switched on the wipers, the whole black surface was smallpoxed with opaque little dots.

'God,' she said. 'I used to think, like you, that there is an external reality, out there, into which we humans arrived. Or our ancestors did. And over time we developed minds as a way of navigating that external reality. In other words, I used to believe that our minds were fitted into the real world.'

She fell silent, and I had to prompt her. 'You don't think that now?'

'It's not fitted to the world. The world is fitted to it.'

'Right,' I said.

We stopped at some lights. 'Let me ask you something,' I tried.

'Yes?'

'Are you seeing anyone? Are you married, say? Is there boy-friends? Are there a boyf—' I coughed.

The engine hummed again. The forces of acceleration exerted their opposite and equal effect upon me, pressing me into the comfortable upholstery of the car. Oh, how those speedo numbers flickered upwards. Oh how my heart rate scuttled. The car describes a long shallow arc along the stone road.

'My best friend at university was a Catholic,' she said. 'I still see a lot of her. We're close. We meet for lunch sometimes. We used to argue about religion. I'd tell her what *you* just said, more or less: what science says about the likely origin of human consciousness. She's say, no, no, God created our souls. My soul is what makes me different to you. And I would reply – because, really, there are a hundred reasons why that seems to a scientist like a really weak hypothesis – I would reply: if that's so, then isn't it an amazingly improbable coincidence that the soul fits the world so well as it does? The real clincher for me is: Alzheimer's. If mind is a product of brain, then as the disease deteriorates the brain you'd expect to see the mind decay. And that's exactly what we do see.'

'Of course you're married,' I said. 'You're beautiful, assured, intelligent. How could you not be married?'

She replied: 'Kant believed he had achieved a Copernican

71

Revolution in human thought. Any astronomer has got to be excited at the prospect of that. Yeah?' A quick sideways look at me, in the passenger seat. 'Up to now, he said, everyone has assumed that our cognition must conform to the objects of the external world. But all attempts to find out something about our cognition from first principles have come to nothing. Come to nothing because of this presupposition. So, he said, let's try it the other way around. Let's see if we can't get further with the problems of metaphysics by assuming that the *objects* must conform to our *cognition*. Like Copernicus, who said: I know what it looks like, that the stars go around the Earth. But let's imagine it's the other way about, and see if that doesn't explain things better.'

She was silent for a bit, and then said: 'Copernicus isn't a good analogy. We thought the cosmos revolved around us, and Copernicus came along and showed this wasn't true. Kant is like an anti-Copernicus. We used to think we were just a part of a pre-existing cosmos, until Kant comes along and shows that, no, actually we make the universe by perceiving it. A better comparison would be Einstein, maybe. If Kant had lived long enough, he'd have talked about how he wrought an Einsteinian revolution upon thought. The big bang – that's not a little knot of dynamite, hanging in the middle of a huge empty cavern, exploding to fill it with stars. The cavern, its space, its time, was what was created *by* the big bang. Every time a consciousness comes into awareness and self-awareness, it's a conceptual big bang. Space and time structure the reality of things anew with each perceiving mind.'

'Don't buy it,' I said.

'Because?'

'Common sense.'

'You can do better than that.'

'It just feels – wrong.'

'It's logic. You can't see behind space, or beyond time.

Everything you think and feel and perceive happens in those terms. We've looked into it. In some detail, Charles. It turns out there is *something* in the real reality, outside of our minds, something our minds perceive in terms of space and time. The thing itself, whatever it is, isn't metres and kilometres, seconds and hours. Not that. It's a mode of – amplitude – of a different kind. We look at the universe and see that it is vast, and that spatial vastness reflects something important about the thing in itself. It's not a literal mapping from its spatial scale to our sense of space, though.'

Finding all this a little hard to follow, I looked outside the car. We drove through a lit-up gateway and were rolling along a crunchy drive that seemed, in the darkness, to go on and on.

'So,' I said, suddenly aware that our journey was coming to an end, and that I had to say something – I didn't know what – so that she remembered me. I went with: 'So you *believe* in God, now?'

She glanced at me, by way of reply, but didn't speak.

I panicked a little bit. I tried: 'What do you do?' A rather better way to start a conversation than end it, I thought, cursing myself. 'At the Institute, I mean. What do you work on? Not just' – I laughed three precise and utterly unconvincing separate laughs – 'chauffeuring?'

'Do,' she said.

'It's research and development. Didn't you say that? The Institute? What are you personally developing? Or researching? Or...?'

She was silent for a moment. Then she said: 'Instantaneous communication. I'm seconded to the astrophysics team. We're hoping to set up a remote viewer and position its focus on or above the surface of the planets Kepler-438b, Kepler-442b and Kepler-440b.'

'Well,' I said. 'OK then.'

My first glimpse of the Institute was indistinct: a three-storey block in the darkness with some windows illuminated, a curving drive that hissed its snaky tyres-on-gravel hiss as we rolled to the garage. Impossible to gauge how extensive were the grounds in the darkness. Dwarf lamps set in the lawn traced the edge of the driveway. Black flame-shaped absences cut into the starry sky at the edge of vision: cypresses. It was a fine, clear night on the cusp between spring and summer, and none of what was happening to me felt real.

We sat, the engine idling, as the garage doors retreated slowly upwards, the smell of the unsullied car plastic and leather in my nostrils. I got the sense of other unlit wings to the building, away to the right, before the garage lights came on and I could see nothing but the brightness inside. Irma parked the car carefully, and we both got up.

There was space for half a dozen cars in the garage, though Irma's car was the only occupant. Up some steps and through into the main building. Along a corridor and round the corner. Irma took me to a room – mine, she assured me – and told me I had half an hour to settle in. 'I don't understand: what's to settle?' I asked.

'You'll be here for a few days at the very least.' She didn't meet my gaze.

A flush of anger. 'The bollocks I will,' I replied. 'Is this a kidnap?'

She didn't shrug with her shoulders, but there was no mistaking the shrug-like expression on her face. 'Walk back, if you like. It's seven miles to the station. I've no idea what time the first train runs, but you could catch that.'

'So you drive me here,' I said, my anger a weird tangle of

resentment and desire, because she was standing in the doorway and I wanted to beg her to come in, to join me on the bed. 'But you *won't* drive me back? Is that it?'

'I'll drive you back,' she said, looking away. 'But Kos wants to have a word first.'

She went, ignoring my 'Who is Cause?', which became, as she turned the corner and vanished, 'Or is it *what* is Cause? Shouldn't I speak to Peter?'

'Kos first,' she said, without looking round. 'Peter later.'

I gave up, shut the door, lay on the bed. It was a single, though comfy and spacious enough. Like a hotel bed. Then I got up and showered. My sense of cleanliness was compromised by the fact that I had to get back into my old clothes. I turned on the telly and watched a documentary about badgers. Then she was back, knocking at my door with a woodpecker rattatta.

'Come meet Kos,' she said.

Half an hour had been long enough for me to forget how beautiful she was. In the way of these things, my craving sense of desire got diverted through those masculine circuits that convert love into bitterness. 'You're working on extrasolar planetary science, yet they're using you as some kind of PA, then? Secretarial staff, chauffeur? Because if that's really it, I'd like a coffee: could you fetch me one?'

'You,' she said, 'are quite the charmer.'

We walked down a long corridor past a series of shut doors. Blandly abstract art on the walls.

'Shouldn't I just speak to Peter?'

'Nobody just speaks to Peter,' she replied. 'You speak to Kos first, and we'll see.'

'He sounds suspiciously precious,' I said, 'this Peter.'

'Ah,' she said. 'It's ah. It's not err.' I had no idea what she meant.

Up a staircase, past the angled slide for a wheelchair lift. A dark door. Another brisk little drum tattoo on the wood from Irma's sharp little knuckles, and an indistinct syllable uttered from within. Beyond the door was a large office: bookshelves, one wall dedicated to high-tech objects of various kinds, a desk. The curtains were undrawn, so the windows functioned as a dark mirror as I stepped through. I looked like a scruffy old man, but then again: that's exactly what I am.

'Hello, Charles,' somebody said in a helium voice. A woman sitting in one of a pair of sofa-chairs. She stood up. The door clicked behind me, and I was alone with her.

'I'm Paulina Kostritsky,' she said, holding out her hand. 'My friends call me Kos.' I've always thought people misuse the cliché *a cut-glass accent*; because the best way to cut glass is with a fine-calibre drill, and that whining dental equipment is not what people mean when they use that phrase. But Ms Kostritsky – Professor Kostritsky, I later discovered – had exactly that combination of upper-middle-class English chill and slight nasal high-pitch. Small larynx, I suppose. Grating.

'I don't usually shake people by the hand,' I said. 'On account of my fingers being all fucked up.'

Kostritsky was a little under my height; but something about her long neck, or perhaps the combination of a large round head with small-set features clustered in the middle of her face, made me feel that she was looking down at me. I flushed, on one side of my face only. 'Sorry,' I said. 'Didn't mean to— Sorry for swearing. I'm a bit cranky.'

'Like a toddler who hasn't had his nap,' she said. Perhaps the single most condescending thing anyone has ever said to me. And this woman, with her mosquito voice and big, ugly head, had only just met me. Crankiness sublimed into anger, which, as an Englishman, and according to the logic of my tribe, I expressed through exaggerated politeness.

'You will have to excuse me, I'm afraid,' I said, pushing my smile that extra distance into grimace territory. 'Plucked from my flat in the middle of the night. I really have no understanding of what is going on, here.'

'I'm sure you've deduced some key things. Once upon a time you were a high-flying astrophysicist. PhD, junior lecturer. Then it all went a bit wrong for you, didn't it?'

'Are we having a chat then, are we? Are we, now? Because I was told I should speak to Peter.'

She angled her head a little. 'What was it that sent you on that downward spiral, Charlie?' Oh she was annoying me now. 'What traumatised you so, in Antarctica, that it has ridden your whole life into the garbage?'

'I didn't *see* anything,' I said, stiffening internally, and feeling very much like a drink. It's a yearning that never goes away, that. My jaw throbbed and buzzed. 'I hallucinated. I survived attempted murder. You *could* show a little fucking compassion. Or not, of course. It's entirely up to you.'

'I apologise,' she said stiffly. 'Please, sit,' she added, encouraging me to follow suit by flopping back into her seat. 'Sit down.'

I contemplated saying *I prefer to stand*, but decided it would sound petulant and prissy rather than dignified. So I sat. There was, I saw, a silver cafetière of coffee on the low table, and two porcelain cups. Sugar, milk.

'Help yourself,' she said. 'And to answer your question, no: I'm not in charge. I suppose you'd say Peta is in charge.' I again heard this name as *Peter*, and she didn't correct me.

'Peter, eh. So he's the big cheese? Is it governmental, Peter's institute?'

'We are not governmental. We do have some board members who also sit in both the British and the EU Parliaments. And the nature of our research – or, to be precise, the way our research has evolved over the last few years – has necessitated clearance from the Prime Minister's own office.'

'I feel like I'm being softened up prior to a sales pitch from some Ponzi scheme. Ms Kostritsky, you need to know: I'm poor as a church mouse.'

'We're not interested in your money, Mr Gardner,' said Kostritsky, smiling. 'Money is not a problem for us. We have many investors with very deep pockets. And to speak truthfully, if our research pays out, money really will be the least of it.'

'Shall we cut to it?' I almost added: *and tell me if Irma is single and might go on a date with me*, but I had – just about – enough self-respect not to do that.

Although it was a close-run thing.

'The total picture, everything at once,' agreed Kostritsky. Then she yawned.

'You do look tired,' I said.

She nodded.

'He works you hard, then? Peter?'

At this she laughed, a strange, strangulated sea-bird noise. 'Forgive me,' she said. 'You don't want me to drip-feed the info. You want the total picture, all at once. Here it is: the Institute was set up a little over a decade ago to develop hyperfast computing models. The fastest computer in the world has been China's Tianhe-2 for the last seven years running: this year it managed 8.57 petaflops a second. We were working out way up the TOP500 list, and performing pretty well: spitting out various marketable by-products along the way, keeping our investors happy. Then our research veered in a totally new direction.'

'Astrophysics?' I said.

'It's an odd story. One of our researchers had a nervous breakdown. He was being haunted by the ghost of a boy.'

I experienced an unpleasant little adrenalised jerk inside me at that. 'Say what?'

'We had to let him go eventually. But before he left he came across an account by an early programmer – ancient history, really. Somebody who worked on computer programming in the early days – the 1980s.'

I intuited what she was talking about moments before she said it.

'Roy Curtius,' she said. 'You know him.'

'I'm here because of Roy?'

'You want the total story, Charles,' she said, rubbing her eyes and looking so exhausted I actually wondered if she was about to fall asleep right in front of me. 'A total portrait with no omissions. You are intensely important to this project. And therefore you are intensely important to the future of the human race.'

'To which, from my throne of importance, I can declare,' I said, 'pigshit, am I.'

'It's the plain truth. You and Mr Curtius both are. The two of you together.' Ugh! The thought of Roy somehow shading into me, me into him. Horror. 'The two of you,' Kos stressed. 'What's become apparent – Peta is insisting upon it, in fact – is that we need you both.

'You need Roy, and you think I'm the way to get him. Or else you would've approached him directly. He's in Broadmoor, you know. He's a dangerous man.'

'We know where he is,' she said. 'We've been in touch. Peta would like him moved from his current incarceration to rooms here. I think our security would be up to keeping him safe. But even our high-placed friends can't order the release of somebody detained under section 3 of the Mental Health Act. Especially not considering the … crimes he has committed.'

'You mean, against me?'

'Since then,' she said darkly.

I elected not to poke this metaphorical spiders' nest. 'So you're interested in *my* bin-man expertise only to the point where I can get you access to Mad Roy?' I had a sudden insight: '*He's* made it a condition, has he? Christ on a quasar.'

'You want the full picture and I'm keen for you to have it. This is not about increasing our shareholder value. This is about taking us over the threshold of the single most significant advance in human history. More so than the wheel, than printing, than the internet. The biggest leap forward imaginable.'

'I don't believe you,' I said.

'You don't have to believe it. You only have to persuade Roy Curtius that *we* believe. He won't talk to us, but he will talk to you.'

I thought of all my high hopes, in the car driving over – a new career, the new love of my life in the driving seat – and a debilitating sense of my own foolishness entered into my soul. 'You want me to be a messenger boy,' I said.

'Mr Gardner,' said Kos. 'You and Mr Curtius are the only two people in the world to have shared the experience, whatever the experience was. The thing that— The thing in itself in Antarctica.'

'A hallucination, is what that was.'

'We've been working with Kant,' said Kostritsky. 'If you'll pardon the apparent non sequitur.'

'You've been infected with Roy's madness,' I said. I put my coffee cup down. It was making my tooth twinge. 'Look, I wish you all the joy of your insanity, I really do. Curtius tried to kill me. I'll say it again: to *murder* me. Kant addled his brains. You'll excuse me if I don't want to hang around to see what effect it has on yours.'

'Kant,' she said mildly. 'It's just philosophy.'

'It's ordure,' I said. And then I did stand up, aiming for the maximum dramatic effect. 'Please drive me home. You brought me here, you can take me home. Or do I have to go wake up Peter himself and make him order you?'

'Charles,' said Kostritsky, putting the palms of both hands over her face, as if weeping. I think she yawned again, it was hard to see. 'Too late to drive you back to Berkshire tonight. Please. I'll take you back to your room, and you can sleep here. First thing in the morning, I give you my word, I will have a driver take you back.'

I thought about putting my foot down, making a scene. But the truth is: I was tired. I didn't get out much, and this little adventure had drained me. My jaw still ached. I daresay a residuum of anesthetic was still in my system, tangling strangely with the caffeine. Back in my youth, as an academic going to conferences and the like, I would sometimes stay in hotels; and the thought of sleeping in a bed not my own, with clean sheets stiff as parchment and a power shower instead of the dribble at my flat, was appealing to me. Nostalgia. So I said: 'First thing? You give me your word?'

'My word.'

'Liberties have been taken.' I felt an inward flutter. This physically unprepossessing woman, and her whiny little voice, and her evident exhaustion, and the lateness of the hour, and my own bruised ego all came together in one awkward urge to apologise. 'Look I'm sorry. Don't pin your hopes on Roy. He's, look, he's not reliable. I'm sorry I can't help you.'

She took her hands away from her face. Bleary eyes. She stood up, and then she led me wordlessly back down the stairs and along the corridor to the door of my room.

: 5 :

It looked like a hotel room, but it wasn't a hotel and so there wasn't a minibar, which was good, since the circumstances would have sorely tested my new sobriety. There was, however, a terminal with internet access, so I sat for half an hour and browsed. The daft thing was that neither Irma nor Kostritsky had told me the *name* of the Institute, so I couldn't google it. I faffed around following links to AI research and supercomputers, and hazarded a quick search for 'Roy Curtius'. Nothing very much. Then I browsed Kant, and found myself drawn in to the rococo intricacies of his systems. So I shut the machine down, and went to bed in my clothes, because I hadn't brought any pyjamas.

Almost as soon as I turned the light off there was a short drumroll knocking sound. Looking back, I wonder if she was waiting in the darkened hall – Christ knows for how long – until the horizontal line of light vanished from under the door. I turned my bedside light on again, and got up, and unlocked the door, and opened it, and light spilled out into the darkness and Irma was standing there.

She came inside, and shut the door behind her. Then she said: 'The questions you were asking in the car.'

And I said: 'The questions I was asking,' like an idiot, because my heart was suddenly gulping hard inside my ribcage.

'About me, the personal ones. There's an answer.'

'Yes.'

She took my hand in her hand. 'You need to understand, and we need to understand one another. I don't like kissing, nothing on the mouth. No penetration either. All right?'

This was so bewildering that I almost whinnied like a horse. I said: 'I didn't bring any condoms anyway. Unless you did?'

She shook her head. 'Condom or no, no penetration. Not what I'm into. And you'll need to wash your hands and scrub your nails before you can touch me. I'll need to watch you wash, to make sure you do it right.'

I couldn't think what to say. I couldn't think at all. My cock was stiff as steel. She tugged my hand a little leading me uncomplaining into the adjacent bathroom, where I washed my hands three times under the mixer tap. Then back in the bedroom, and she undressed, and with a wordless nod instructed me to do the same. Then we got under the covers together and I ran my clean hands over her clean skin, and kissed her with my scarred face although always below the neck. She came, I think. Then she spat in her hand, once, twice, three times, with what sounded upsettingly and yet arousingly like contempt and applied her palm to my member and undertook the necessary motion. She used her left hand, which may or may not have been significant to her, and which made me think of her driving and handling the gear-stick – a spurious memory, this, since the car that had chauffeured me here had been an automatic. It didn't take long. I lay there panting, and she slipped from the sheets, and vanished into the bathroom. The light went on, and from where I was lying I could just about see her splashing her abdomen with water and towelling it dry. Then she came back to the bedside, dressed with the light from the bathroom behind her in a series of intensely beautiful silhouetted shapes. There was a click, and the door pulled shut, and she was gone.

I fell asleep.

And then it was morning, and the light was coming through the windows, and the bathroom light was still on. I drank from the cold tap and pissed the previous night's coffee into the toilet bowl and took a shower. My tooth throbbed. I made Francis Bacon faces at myself in the mirror. It looked OK.

There was nothing except yesterday's crusty clothes to wear, and so I dressed in them. Unsure about leaving my room, and for want of anything better to do, I switched on the computer and surfed the net some more. I put on Radio 4 via iPlayer to hear the news. Perhaps turning on the system alerted them to my being awake, because very soon afterwards there came a single, firm knock upon the door.

It was Kostritsky. 'You driving me home personally?' I asked.

'Don't you want breakfast first?' she asked. 'Do you want

to head straight off?' But her expression said: *You're not going anywhere and we both know it.*

My heart went bippety bippety, and I had to make the conscious effort to restrain myself from agreeing too eagerly.

'OK,' I said, trying for *cool*. 'Breakfast.'

Kostritsky led me down a different corridor, and down some stairs rather than up them, and through a weird dog-leg series of spaces into a large canteen. A dozen long tables, and a bank of serving counters at the far end. It was entirely deserted except for the two of us, although the lit-up counters were well supplied with rectangular stainless-steel containers inside containing, variously, bacon, hot beans, scrambled eggs, button mushrooms in their own hot juices and so on. Kostritsky took a tray and I followed suit. An automated machine filled my mug with coffee. I watched the black circle rise like a piston-head inside its chamber, and all the time my brain was thinking: *If I give the impression I'm not eager to say, she'll have to send in Irma again tonight.*

There was an open door frame to the kitchen: lights on, ovens and other cooking apparatus visible. I didn't see any kitchen staff. Maybe they were on a fag break. I followed Kostritsky to a table, and all the time my brain was thinking: *I can surely leverage once more – but what about after that? How to make my assistance conditional upon Irma visiting me? Should I say that outright, or would that be too crass? Can I take it as tacitly understood by us both?* I hated myself for thinking with such reptilian ruthlessness. That's not an exaggeration. I really hated myself. But I was in the grip of something that mere self-hatred couldn't dislodge. Of possibility. The step up from solitary isolation to that oneness and totality we call sexual connection.

I sat down. *It's a negotiation*, I thought. It wasn't though. It was the beginning of a conversion narrative. It was a direct line from this to me believing in God and running around the Arctic ice in my socks.

Seriously.

'Believe me, Charles,' she said, without preamble. 'I was as sceptical as you are now. But that's all changed.'

'Sceptical about what?'

'The Kant stuff. I trained as a proper scientist, no time for metaphysical gobble-gook.'

'Uh, gobble-*dee*...'

'I used to think it airless speculation by a narrow-minded German thinker. But now I know it's true. And that changes everything.'

'What's true?'

'The transcendental categories are true. Space and time as intuitions of perception, not structures innate to reality. The necessary subjectivity of all scientific investigation.'

'Mumbo jumbo,' I said, taking a mouthful of scrambled egg, and all the time thinking: *Should I just come out with it? Tell her I'll stay if she guarantees continued night visits from Irma?* And at the back of my mind the still, small voice, trying to make itself heard: that amounts to prostitution, Charles. This isn't ethical, Charles. Are these *really* the terms on which you want Irma to sleep with you, Charlie? Wouldn't it be better if she did it because she wanted to? Ah, the still small voice. Because it had a cliff to climb, that voice. And the cliff was: the choices are between her doing it because she thinks it is in her better interests, or her not doing it all. This 'her doing it because she wants to' is not even an option.

'Whilst you eat,' said Kostritsky, 'I'd like to talk through the four categories. Because, as I promised you last night—' Was there a faintly leering emphasis upon those two words? 'Promised you last night, you deserve the full story. The total vision. And the total vision has four parts to it.' She put down her cutlery, and pulled out a large-screen smart phone. 'And once I've explained, I think you'll be more inclined to stay.'

'Well,' I said, trying to sound mysterious. 'The thing about staying...'

'Look,' she said, putting the screen next to my plate.

1. *Categories of Quantity*
- Unity
- Plurality
- Totality

2. *Categories of Quality*
- Reality
- Negation
- Limitation

3. *Categories of Relation*
- Inherence and Subsistence (substance and accident)
- Causality and Dependence (cause and effect)
- Community (reciprocity between agent and patient)

4. *Categories of Modality*
- Possibility—Impossibility
- Existence—Non-existence
- Necessity—Contingency

'Okily dokily,' I said, and went for some bacon.

She waited patiently until I came back. 'Kant says: we perceive the real world, but we only have those perceptions. We can't get behind them. Something out there – the thing in itself, he calls it – affects us, and we process the incoming data. But the *way* we process that data is distinctive to us. Space, time, and these categories, these are in our perceiving mind, not in the thing in itself.'

'So it's all in our mind, yeah? It's the Matrix and we can't get out of it. There's no real, it's all relative.'

'No. Not at all. Of course there is a real world. Kant is very clear about that. Here's you, sitting there, perceiving the real world. Here's me, doing the same thing. And there is a real world for us to perceive. If there weren't a real world, then there'd be nothing for us *to* perceive. But—' And her she held up a single finger, like a schoolteacher. 'The crucial thing is that the reverse is also true. If you weren't there to observe, then there'd be no real world to *be perceived*. At least, not in the way you are perceiving it right now – space, time, causality, modality and so on.'

'Spurious symmetry of ideas,' I said. 'I'm not an idiot; I've been sitting in my hotel room reading your canny Kant.' Actually I'd browsed online, and read the *Stanford Encyclopedia of Philosophy* entry, but I figured that was close enough for government work. 'He thinks there are twelve categories that *structure* our experience of the real universe. Four neat little groups of three. I might be minded to believe him if it weren't *so* just so. So neatly ordered and arranged.'

She angled her head a little. 'You have a problem with the neatness?'

'You don't?'

'Isn't your job to make things neat and clean?' Before I could reply she said: 'Maths is all about the patterns. About the neatness. Physics is basically applied maths.'

'This is a theory of everything, and it's neat as a pin. It's like constellations in the night sky – the stars are scattered more or less randomly. When we group them together as bulls and ploughs and whatnot we say nothing about the stars and everything about the human obsession with order. Kant's categories are like that. Disposing everything that exists into four neat little boxes called, eh,' I consulted the screen, 'quantity, quality, relation and modality. Subdividing each of those into three further neat little sections. It's— OCD, is what it is. I read up about Kant, and that's just the kind of man he was. Got up every day at exactly the same time, crossed the town square on his way to work so at exactly the same time that people used to set their watches by him. Don't get me wrong, I'm not judging. Takes all sorts. But he was a weird little man obsessed with order and neatness, and he produced a philosophical system that – surprise! – discovered order and neatness to be the truth of the whole cosmos.'

She said: 'I agree.'

'You do? Well there we are. Can I go home now?'

'Except that you're making an argument in favour of what Kant says.'

'I am?' I sniffed. 'It's like,' I added, abruptly, remembering something, but not remembering from where I remembered it, 'the story of the scientist who looked into a microscope and sketched what he could see, and then it turned out he hadn't used the device properly and had ended up sketching the reflection of his own eye.'

She smiled at this, making her ugly face uglier. 'Exactly so. You're saying that Kant's philosophy tells us more about the way Kant's mind worked than about the world. I agree. That's precisely the point. Kant's philosophy says that the only thing we *can* know about the world is the way our minds work. We don't have some magic access to the way things really are. We only have what we perceive and think. We have what our senses tell us, and what our rational minds can deduce.'

'That's not true, though. We know *loads* of things about the external world, independent of my observational bias.'

'You have some magic access to things that doesn't involve observing them, do you?'

'Not that. But we can *combine* a whole bunch of different observations, iron out subjective quirks from the data, approximate reality to within really fine tolerances.'

'You're still thinking in the old paradigm,' she said. 'The fact is: you perceive space because "perceiving space" is how your mind is structured. Time is the same. So we perceive the thing in itself, and that data comes in, and our minds convert it into space, time, causality and so on. We can't help doing that. It's how we work.'

'So there's no space, or time, or causality or any of that, in the real world?'

'Kant would say,' she said, taking a forkful of scrambled egg, 'we can't know.' She ate, swallowed. 'We can only know what we perceive. We can't get past our structures of knowledge and reasoning to get at the baseline reality.'

'So I get in my car and drive a hundred miles, I haven't really gone anywhere. It's like, what, the Holodeck?'

'The what?'

'You know: the Holodeck in *Star Wars*. You're saying the cosmos is in the business of tricking us. A giant system of illusion.'

'You mean *Star Trek: The Next Generation*,' she said, pouting. 'That's a poor analogy, I think. The Holodeck was a room – a three-dimensional space – that created the illusion of being a much bigger space. We're not talking about that, here. I agree with you; it certainly *seems* to me that I move through space. I instruct my body to move, and my legs cycle through their stride, and I appear to travel from A to B. If you pressed me, I'd guess *something* is happening in the Ding an sich that informs my sense data. I'm just not sure what. Maybe it's a mode of resistance, rather than a mode of distance. Maybe it's something else.'

'So we feel like we're moving but we're actually just walking on the spot?'

'Not even walking on the spot. Our legs aren't actually moving, any more than we are, because movement of our limbs would require spatial extension. But something about the thing in itself gives us the impressions that we interpret as swinging our legs, as walking along. Something about the thing in itself registers forces as equal and opposite; something actualises the sensations we perceive as spatial and temporal.'

I thought for a bit. 'How do you *know* it's not, though? You just told me you don't *actually* know anything about the thing in itself. Maybe it is structured by space and time after all?'

She shook her head. 'Now you've come full circle. Now *you're* the one arguing the million-to-one coincidence that our perception of the true reality just happens to coincide exactly with that reality. We're wearing orange spectacles and everything looks orange, but you're arguing that if we could ever take the spectacles off then everything would actually *be* orange. Actually, there are good reasons for thinking it isn't like that.'

I tried what I can see now, looking back, was my last throw. I didn't think of it that way at the time; it occurred to me as just another of the great stack of reasons why the Kant stuff was all nonsense. But it was actually the last thread connecting me to my old mode of thinking. 'You know what makes this all so arid? It doesn't make any difference. It doesn't make *any* difference. I'm saying: I walked a mile, measured on my pedometer. You're saying I only *think* I walked a mile, and my pedometer is wrong – that it only appeared to me that I walked a mile. So what's the difference? Even if you're right, I still have to walk that mile to the shops to buy milk to go on my cornflakes. Maybe it's a real mile, maybe it's an artefact of my perceptions: it adds up to the same thing.' Warming to my theme, I added: 'And, like, science. We measure Jupiter and determine it has a diameter of a million kilometres. You say: it only appears to have that diameter, because space is a function of our minds, not of the real reality. That what looks like a million-kilometre-wide planet is actually only some peculiar kink in the Ding an sich. I could agree with you, and it would make no difference. I could disagree, and it makes no difference. No difference at all. We can do things with our spatial measurements of the solar system, like send probes to land on comets and arrange satellites to beam television around the world. So your Ding an sich might be real reality, or might not, and either way it makes no difference to the way we actually live our lives.' I sat back, feeling (I confess it) suddenly rather pleased with myself. 'That's a nice knockdown argument, *if* you like.'

'What you're forgetting,' she replied, 'is we have something Kant didn't have.'

'A fucking sense of humour, is it?'

'AI,' she said.

This is what set the dominoes trembling in my head, ready to tumble. 'You what?'

'Kant, as you so eloquently noted, was talking about his own structures of consciousness. His, yours, mine. He said that we can't get behind them. We cannot get round the back of space and time, any more than a man whose corneas have been dyed orange can help seeing the world with an orange tint. Space and time are how humans *see* reality, and until very recently we've only had human beings' experience to talk about. Now, though, it's possible to build a whole new way of thinking.'

'We can't step outside our way of perceiving the universe,' I said. 'But computers can.'

'Exactly.'

'Computers still need time,' I said. 'Sure they're *fast*, but we're still talking about sequential operations of calculation and itera-tion. They need to perform physical operations, through circuit boards that have length breadth and width. They've been getting smaller, it's true, but they still take up space.'

'Very good,' said Kostritsky. 'It's pleasing to have our confi-dence in you justified. Still something of the professional scien-tist somewhere inside the garbage disposal man.'

'The fuck!' I said, stung, and unable for the moment to think of a wittier retort.

'Of course you are correct. Until very recently that's been true. Until very recently computer thought was subject to similar limitations with respect to accessing the Ding an sich as we are ourselves. That's not surprising, when you think of it. We made them in our image. But, latterly, we've been building new kinds of computer, on radically different principles. And we've discovered that, once you abandon the notion of trying to *copy* human consciousness, AI is really quite easy to achieve.'

I digested this. It was – well, huge. 'You've done this?'

'We have, yes.'

'You've built functioning AI? Here, in this institute?'

'Sure.'

'A rational, sentient, intelligence consciousness, unfettered by the constraints of space and time? One that can see into the Ding an sich?'

'Essentially, yes. Pretty much.'

'Pretty much?' I boggled.

'There's work still to be done,' she conceded airily. 'But we've done enough to confirm that Kant was right.'

I took a long breath in. 'And I'm supposed just to talk your word on that, am I?'

'Talk my word?'

I breathed out. '*Take* your word, I mean.'

'No, Charles,' she said, with perfect ingenuity. 'You're supposed to see for yourself. That's why we invited you here.'

'You've done this thing,' I said, 'but you haven't announced it to the world. It's like you don't *want* the Nobel Prize.'

'There's no Nobel Prize in computing,' she observed mildly.

'Or whatever the hell the equivalent— Look: come on. You've really done what you're claiming, if you have, I mean, actual working AI: the world will go crazy. Crazy! Ticker-tape parades, chat shows, your own brand of perfume. Why haven't you announced it?'

'The main reason,' she said, and stopped. She yawned, enormously. 'I'm sorry,' she said. 'I am tired. The main reason is that AI is not an end in itself. It's a means to an end.'

'What end?'

'Direct manipulation of the Ding an sich of course. Come on, Charles, think! Can't you imagine the possibilities?'

'Possibilities.'

'Take space. Distance could be eradicated. And not just human-scale distances. Stellar distances. We could reach the stars, the galaxies. And time? Well, time travel may be more than reality can bear, but we're working on *slowing* time ... giving ourselves as much time as we need to compute any problem, to prolong consciousness as long as we wish. Really, even a simpleton can see how revolutionary it would be to break through the prison of space and time.'

I felt dizzy. 'You're a cult leader, trying to brainwash me. That's all—' I didn't know what it was all. I stopped.

'It's incredible, I know. But, look, we're not there yet. There are certain, uh, obstacles to clear.' She yawned again, massively, and poked her now-cold scrambled egg with her fork. 'We have a broad three-point strategy. First, to get a clear enough view of the thing itself to confirm, or deny, Kant's theories. Well, we've done that.'

'Jesus Beelzebub,' I said.

'Second, retrieve specific data about the thing in itself, via an AI unfettered by time and space. And third, to use those tools to begin *manipulating* the thing itself. That's what we're still working on. And that's why we need you.'

'Me.' I shook my head.

'You and your friend.'

'Roy. Not my friend. Very much not.'

'As you said yourself: back in the 1980s computing was too primitive to support AI. Those old machines were slow, with very meagre processing and memory. And they were locked into the structures of space and time, in terms of their operating parameters. It shouldn't have been possible to do anything with such a machine, as far as getting access to the Ding an sich was concerned. Yet Curtius did it. We don't know how. It shouldn't even have been possible – yet he did. We figure he was some manner of genius.'

'That would be genius spelled p, s, y, c, h and o.'

'Mentally challenged, yes certainly. Difficult. Geniuses often are. But he could be the one to provide the key. The key to accessing the *real* reality. And once we do that... well, everything changes. For all of humanity.'

'Accessing the thing itself.' Nausea uncoiled itself in my gut. 'Look if *that's* what happened to the two of us in Antarctica then my very-much advice to you would very-much be: leave it the *fuck* alone.' There were flickers of light in the corner of my eye. My hands were trembling.

'We understand that your experience,' she said, 'was not... pleasant.'

'I'm going to be sick,' I said. And indeed a hot sensation of nausea was churning through my gut. 'All this abstract metaphysics— I didn't make the connection with the South Pole. Jesus, Professor: what if you connect with the Ding an sich and it turns out to be, like, a hell dimension?'

'There's no danger of that.'

Demons flickered in my mind's eye. Leering, mocking. What I had done with Irma last night: had her consent been, shall we say, compromised? Damned, damned, damned. A glimpse of the real reality and it was darkness, visible. '*You* didn't see them,' I said, and my stomach clenches sharply. My filled tooth bulged and throbbed.

I got up, and stepped briskly away from the table. There was a white plastic bin, elephant's-foot-size, and with nothing inside it except a discarded Twix wrapper. I held it to my chest, and waited. But the urge to vomit passed. All through this – it must have lasted three or four minutes – Professor Kostritsky sat patiently, looking at me. I began to feel self-conscious, standing there. So I returned to the chair, and sat down with the bin in my lap. 'You didn't see them,' I repeated.

'You don't know *what* you saw. Certainly something disorienting and upsetting happened. But that's not to say that this was some profound insight into the essential nature of reality. Maybe it wasn't what you saw but the mode of seeing it that was so … debilitating.'

It dawned on me that, for the first time in decades, I was sitting in a room with a person who actually believed that what happened to me in Antarctica was *real*. I felt dizzy again. 'That's putting it mildly.'

'We have models. Best-guess scenarios which, with the most recent data we've accumulated, are I think pretty *good* guesses. That suggests that as the space and time modalities are … reduced, shall we say. As that happens, it's likely an unprepared consciousness *would* become disoriented. That it would experience rapid and alarming shifts in spatial and temporal scale, foldings, fractal shudders. I didn't experience what you experienced, of course. But your account of them was entirely consistent with what we would expect from our models. And those models rule out medieval demons. Believe me, they do.'

'Take your word for it.'

'Once again: no. Do the work yourself. That's an invitation. It's an invitation to advanced scientific work – a job, a salary. A position here in the Institute.'

'I don't believe it,' I said. Because thinking it might be real was making my gut churn again.

'You,' said Kostritsky. 'That is, you *and* Curtius, you are the only two people in the world to have shared that experience, whatever the experience was. Take a look at yourself: highly intelligent, articulate, creative. Yet you're working as a bin-man. You think that's compatible with your intellectual potential? We're offering you something real, here. It will stretch you, challenge you. It will pay considerably better than your council wages. And most of all it will give you the chance to be part of the greatest scientific advance in human history.' She opened her hands. 'All we ask in return is that you apply your, uh, friendship to Mr Curtius as a lever. We need him. He may be the difference between success and failure.'

: 6 :

So I stayed. I didn't follow through on my low-down principle of using Irma as a bargaining tool. I simply stayed. I slept in my room, and ate in the canteen, and had further conversations with Kos. I met a few of the other staff. I wandered around the grounds as May turned into June, and the land became gorgeous with summer life. I met other Institute employees, and they were all pleasant, welcoming, well-adjusted people. I had bad dreams, and the demons capered at the edge of my vision sometimes, but it was late spring and early summer and the sun came out. Light everywhere. Light falling from above, light shining from within.

The bald fact is: I was converted. I had further conversa-tions with Kos about what the Institute hoped to achieve. It was a lot: not just a single major advance with the potential to revolutionise human life, but a whole *bunch* of major advances that would turn human life verso-reverso. To access the thing itself, the reality *behind* human perception, through carefully programmed AIs. To manipulate it.

'The four modalities,' was how Kos explained it. 'These are what we hope to transcend – if we can make the system work. These modalities are the four walls of our prison, you could say, and we're planning ways to break through them.'

'OK,' I said. 'Run through them one more time, would you?'

'The first is *quantity*. That means number. That means space, and time, both of which are numberable. Spaces is always so many metres long, so many wide, so many high. Time means so many seconds, countable forwards or backwards. And it is those metres, in their trillions upon trillions, that keep us from simply stepping into the surface of a paradise planet in orbit around another star – that keep us from spreading humanity through the whole cosmos.'

'I don't see why quantity is subdivided into three. That's just Kant's weird three/four fetish. That's the neatness thing again.'

'It makes sense, though. He's saying *quantity* comes in three kinds – one, many, all.'

'But multiply each by space and time. Shouldn't that be six?'

'It would be, if space and time were completely separate things. But Einstein says they're not. Space and time are the same thing. Spacetime. That's not so important.'

'It's not?'

'What's important is what this can do for us. If we can master quantity – the *measurements* of space and time that structure our universe – only imagine! *Quantity* is the gold circle at the centre of our target. Here at the Institute, I mean. That's the jackpot. If we can tweak our approaches so as to be able to step past some – or even all – of the obstacles provided by the categories, then we can re-emerge where and when we like … well. Then the entire universe is our oyster. We could, for instance, simply sidestep the very many light years between Earth and the stars.'

'So quantity is top of our wish list.' How quickly I had started talking about *us* and *ours*. Ironic, really, looking back. I was part of the totality. Or I thought I was. 'What about quality?'

'That's slipperier. Quality, says Kant, is the *degree* of reality of something. Some things are only very faintly real, have only a very faint effect upon us. Like a feather tickling your elbow. Some things have much more palpable or vivid quality. Pushed to an extreme, quality is our perception of pain – agony, even. That's a necessary thing, obviously, for the proper functioning of a human body. But when we're talking, as we are here, about manipulating it, altering it . . . well, we don't want to trip the agony wire if we can help it.'

'So Kant's three inflections of quality, are, what? A tiny bit, a moderate amount, a lot?'

'No. The modifications Kant suggests are reality, negation, limitation. Professional philosophers have argued long and hard over what he meant by that. This is what I understand by what he says: quality is the filling up of time with a sensation. When time is completely filled, we have very vivid, very strong sensations. When it is meagrely filled, we have weaker sensations. So that's what reality *is*, for us. It is the experience of sensation in time. Negation is the opposite; the lack of sensation in time. And limitation is scale between the two, the range of degrees.'

'That's kind of what I said. But we want to leave that alone?'

'Our best guess, from our models, is that it would be better to keep well away. Sensation might be pleasurable, of course; and the modulation of such sensation to fill up our reality would be, well, orgasmic.'

'I can imagine the commercial applications.'

'Yes. Well. But until we understand the tolerances, the precision, with which we are able to manipulate the Ding an sich, we just need to be careful. Bliss might flip over to agony in unpredictable ways.'

'OK: the third?'

'The third is relation. He means the order in which things are arranged, or in which they happen in time. That's Kant's way of speaking of things like cause and effect, necessary and accidental qualities of things, reciprocity.'

'How's this not the same as the first category?'

'Well, because the things you're talking about – unity, multiplicity, totality – are not features of the thing itself. Only of the way we perceive it, the way we intuit it. Relation, likewise. We don't just perceive space and time, we perceive space *ordered in a certain way*, time *structured in a certain way*.'

'So what happens if we sidestep this category?'

'Tricky to say. Maybe chaos. Things possess specificity, distinctiveness. That's good. We don't want that to stop it being true. If we manipulate the Ding an sich directly in ways that affect this, maybe those same things are no longer able to inhere. Worst case: atoms fuse with nuclear-explosive consequences. But maybe not. The real question, I'd say, is whether relation is *easier* to manipulate – in the thing itself, I mean – than quantity. Maybe we can't sidestep the thousand light years between us and our dream planet. But perhaps we can instead manipulate the way those thousand light years relate to one another. Make them all stack up on top instead of stretch out one after the other. Fold them into a fractal spiral. I don't know. So, our *prime* target is quantity, but *relation* is Plan B, if we can't get that to work.'

'I'm still not grasping what Kant's subsets here *are*, exactly.'

'One is inherence-subsistence, which is basically the thingness of things. Two is causality and community. The third is Kant's way of bringing action and passivity into his model. Some things have agency, some things are passive, and there is a reciprocal relationship between those two things. The white billiard ball is in motion, and strikes the red billiard ball. The white ball is the agent, the red one the patient; and, like Newton says, the force of one on the other is equal and opposite. So that's that. Community, he calls it.'

'Seems an odd word to describe what you just said.'

'It's just terminology. Think of a different word if you like. The ball is spherical and has mass, that's inherent – that's substance. It's white and is made of ivory and so on: that's accident, subsistence. It wouldn't matter if it were blue and made of plastic, provided it had the same shape and the same mass. Whether the ball is white or blue makes no difference to how it strikes the red ball. And taken together, the white ball striking is the cause of the red ball suddenly shooting off. Taken together there's an equal-and-opposite community of forces.'

'So that just leaves the fourth of Kant's categories.'

'This one is the hardest to get your head around; or at least, I found it so. Modality.'

'Modality.'

'Three varieties of this: possibility, existence and necessity. The wrinkle is that these words only capture half the picture. Possibility is the other half of impossibility, or impossibility is the other half of possibilities. A triangle whose angles add up to 200 degrees is impossible in a flat Euclidean plane, but possible in a non-Euclidean space like the curved surface of the Earth. The two have a reciprocal relationship to one another. Some things exist, and others don't exist. We can think of either kind of thing. Some things must be the way they are; other things are only the way they are because they depend on other things. Or maybe they're Schrodinger-random. Never mind about that for now. It makes no sense for us to tinker with modality. Of all the four categories it's the one lowest on our to-do list. We don't want to tinker with the Ding an sich and discover that we've somehow messed up the difference between possible and impossible in our world. It's really hard to see how that could end well.'

Total vision, I thought. Or all the rest is desolation. The capering demons' faces were in constant motion, like serpentine flames in a fireplace. I studied the ground, and had individual sessions with members of the team to bring me up to speed.

:7:

I settled into my new mode of life. I even found myself enjoying it. I signed a non-disclosure contract, and it mentioned fearful sanctions if I dared spill any of the Institute's beans. But nothing could be as bad as my life had once been.

For the first week or so I didn't see Irma. Instead I spent time with Sue Bao, one of the workers on the project, trying to build (she excitedly told me) a matter transporter. Sue in turn introduced me to a woman called Jennifer who worked security, and who shook my hand solemnly. 'You're in seventeen,' she said, as if repeating the phrase helped her memorise it. 'Seventeen. Seventeen.'

'Surprising there are that many rooms,' I observed.

'Most of us live off-site,' said Sue. 'Not many bodies on campus these days. But a few years ago we would very often fly people in, from all over the world. There's a lot of programming expertise in Russia – you'd be surprised.'

'So who else is staying on site?'

'Oh, just you,' said Jennifer. 'And security, obviously.' She was wearing a blue uniform, and had a police-style utility belt, with telescoped-truncheon, pepper-spray, cuffs, around her sturdy waist; and depending from it I noticed what I took to be a pistol. Was it a real firearm? Or was it an air pistol, taser, something like that? I looked at Jennifer herself: an impressively hefty individual, who was in turn regarding me with professional dispassion. I decided against asking her about her gun.

It did her no good, in the end, anyway.

'Shouldn't I be in room number one?'

'Room one,' said Jennifer, nodding slowly. 'One. One. Cracked shower pan. Maintenance hasn't got round to fixing it.'

'Oh. Can I assume there's something comparably wrong with rooms two to sixteen?'

Jennifer scrunched one eyebrow downward, as if holding onto an invisible monocle. 'Of course not.'

'Of course not,' I repeated.

'You need *clothes*,' said Jennifer. I was ready to take this, given how she was eyeing me, as a snide comment on my shabby attire when she added: 'Professor Kostritsky says. Size?'

'I'd say she's a sixteen.'

'*Your* size.'

'Medium. Thirty-two waist, thirty leg. I don't need anything fancy.'

'And you won't be *getting* anything fancy.'

'I can see you're in good hands,' said Sue, smiling an insincere smile. 'And I'd be getting back to work.'

'Good to meet you,' I said to her retreating back. I turned to Jennifer. 'It's weird having somebody shop for me. Wouldn't it make sense for me to go get my own clothes?' The invisible monocle had returned to Jennifer's face, but I pressed on: 'I'd need a lift into town, of course. And money. I don't have any money. But that way—'

'Give you a fold of money and a lift to the train station?' Jennifer said, sternly. 'We'd never see *you* again. Think we were born yesterday?'

'Say what?' I replied, startled.

Sue was suddenly at my side again, so she obviously hadn't gone back to her work. 'I think what Jenny means to say,' she interjected, taking hold of my elbow, 'is that you'll be too *busy* with important *work* here to be wasting time at the *shops*.' She led me off. Her hand was small but, on the evidence of my pinched elbow, rather strong. 'Jenny will sort you for clothes. Let me give you a quick tour of the main rumble room.'

This was so obviously done it was almost endearing. I decided not to kick up a fuss. I had wandered the grounds unchaperoned earlier in the morning, and the walls, though taller than I, looked perfectly climbable, assuming I did ever decide to cut and run.

At any rate I was provided with clothes, and the clothes were fine. They assured me that high-up people in Berkshire council had prevailed upon my boss to give me an open-ended sabbatical from my bin-man job. At the time I was too caught up in my immense good fortune to give my old life a second thought.

I met various other people. Poking around online, I found nothing that explained 'the Institute' to me; and googling the names of the people I had met led me into a wilderness of technical computing-theory sites, none of which talked about a well-funded research centre on the outskirts of (were we?) Swindon. This puzzled me a little. It should have puzzled me a lot more. I asked Kos about it, and she said something about both private and governmental stakeholders insisting upon secrecy for multiple, overlapping reasons, until the research was completed and could be announced to the world. I ought to have been suspicious about this. I was suspicious, I suppose. I was just having too good a time to care.

And, the capstone: a week after I arrived Irma visited me again in my bed, and we repeated our previous encounter, and I was briefly aware of a sense of contentment that I don't think I'd ever experienced in my life before.

The following day, at breakfast, I pondered whether this was the unspoken deal, now. Irma would visit me one night a week. On such an expectation of intimacy I was to remain in the Institute. Kos came and sat with me, as she sometimes did. I had grown accustomed to her weird physiognomy (as if I had grounds to object to an ugly face!) and whining voice, although her brusqueness often passed over into outright rudeness. Maybe it was a function of mild Asperger's. Maybe she was just tired – she always looked exhausted.

'Good morning,' she said.

'Am I ever going to get to talk to Peter? Assuming he really exists? *Does* he exist, your head honcho?'

'He exists.'

'And you're just his deputy? Look, he's clearly not on site, or I'd have bumped into him. So he's somewhere else, and I guess he doesn't like Skype. So I guess I'm supposed to wait until he swings by the campus. You're going to tell me he's real busy now, and can't spare the time.'

'No, no,' said Kos, drawing herself back to an approximation of attentiveness. 'You must speak to Peta. Very soon. But first we need you to do a thing.'

'A thing?' I knew what she was about to specify. So, I thought to myself: *this is why Kos has joined me for breakfast, the morning after Irma had come visiting.* It was so clumsily orchestrated it was almost funny. Funny. 'You mean: Roy?'

'You'll need to drive down to Bracknell,' she agreed. 'We'll provide you with a car. We've spoken with the authorities at Broadmoor, and they're expecting you tomorrow. After that you can meet with Peta.'

'Well,' I said. 'All right then.'

4

Penelope's Mother

Affirmation

Yes I said yes and Pedro sang in my ears and my eyes said I
will and the whole of the mountain grew swollen and ripe and
riper again and the stars were all overhead it should be possible
Albie said his voice so English and solemn and *rey*fined like a
king possible to know if those lights in the night are worlds and
worlds inhabited by intelligences not unlike ours and I put my
moon mouth o over his sun mouth o and kissed him and the
night scratchy with cicadas all saying yes and I saying yes and
he making my name into a heavenly body Lunita Lunita over
and over and the sandy soil still warm from the day and the
whole of the world laid below us but he left his telescope there
as we scrambled down the road and he saying Sennora Laredo
will be displeased like an Englishman in a novel and I laughing
the way and the rock beneath us swelling and he had to return
the following day because Tweedy only a captain then shouting
at him with his Dublin fury about regimental equipment not
to be discarded sir and if he had not gone back to the top of
the rock would he have performed again his measurement and
found out what happened to the rock

  maybe we would not have known and I even went back to

Mrs Caraway with her tarot cards and begged her to see what the spirit world had to say and she peered at me with her eye swelled by her eyeglass like a fish swimming in a bowl so ridiculous they looked and for three days it seemed it was all Albie would talk about his collar stud missing and the collar pricking up at the back so comical and Pedro was in my ears at this time whispering the truth things

it was after the séance Albie announcing himself to Mama and Papa so stiffly and kissing Mama on her hand and she showing off her English and asking what he did and he saying Sennora as if the tilde had gotten lost in his moustache by day I survey the rock of Gibraltar to perfect the garrisons cartography and I couldnt help giggling and by night he says I survey the night sky oh a stargazer said Papa and Albie bowed a little and Captain Tweedy or was he Major yet I cant remember is your superior officer with her putting great length into those vowels of superior tho I hardly cared if she set her cap at the Irishman for my sake who can see so far ahead I smelt his cologne and later as I lay in bed and Mamatina came to give me besos I said is our new guest not as fine a gentleman as Señor Tweedy and she hushed me but it was him I dreamed about looking at the stars through his great shaft of brass at the moon and the star Sirius and Pedro murmured in my head that the whole cosmos was alive and that he might take a running jump and leap clear free of it and I pictured him jumping like Icarus from the peak of the rock and flying not down but up fast as a plummet and bursting through the place where the sky is sealed and opening a new way yes and impossibility is no word yes and possibility is everything at the séance it was Pedro who started speaking and I thought it was Mrs Caraway throwing her voice like the stage magician we saw on our voyage to London but his voice was low and o so male and he spoke Spanish and English and ladino all as good as each other and Mrs Caraway could no more do so than rid her face of warts and yes I said and for only a moment I was alarmed that Pedro was some devilish creature and the seven candles ranged around the table squirmed their flames in fear and I shut my eyes but then I opened them again and I knew something potent had changed in me yes and I felt the yes the past and the future were clear to me as if I stood high on the Rock and could see two seas and Spain and Africa and everywhere ranged around me and I saw you my lovely Molly though you were yet to come and I saw marrying the Major and our ancestors all the way back to Abraham and our descendants all the way to the time when time itself shall loosen and the words rose in my mind *to my crown shall be added a glory as of stars* and yes I said all timidness gone and Mrs Caraway turned over another of her picture cards with portentous slowness and stopped halfway and looked up at me as if she could see something profound had shifted around inside my soul but couldnt be sure what and I only smiled and Albie came the next day was it only it felt as if I had summoned him so handsome and he walking around the patio with me arm in arm perhaps he thought he was paying a teetotum court to me but mamá surely told him I was promised to his superior officer tho he could not keep away from me yes and he showed me his surveying equipment and theodolite and I said the word back to him and we laughed together and he unrolled his charts on the dining table and Conchita loitering and giving us both the evil eye old-fashioned and Andalucian about betrothal yes and sure that Tweedy is a good-looking man still though getting a bit grey over the ears but Albie yes was who I wanted and yes I said I may have him and yes the timid girl was banished by whatever happened at that séance and Pedro coming and now that the future was unrolled like one of Albies charts I could see my darling Molly coming and me feeding her from my breasts the bountiful one and her growing into her beauty and marrying and moving to Dublin and all this vision filled me with the calmness for fear is all the blind future harrying us and when the scales drop away the fear goes too and we sent Conchita out to get oranges and I led him by the hand up the stairs to my own room and we had one another there in my own bed the sheets soft as dandelions and his telescope concertinaed out into a great shaft and the pain and the sweetness folded together and yes I said and however impatient he was I was as much so for I could run the fingers of my thoughts over his mind and maybe he sensed this or maybe not but it meant his pleasure fed mine and we cried aloud together and then hearing the door click down below as Conchita returned and we hurriedly buttoning

yes Mamatina said something changed in you *bonita* when you had that tarot reading from the mujer Inglés with the wart on her face something changes yes I said yes I know yes its as if the pauses inside me have evaporated away into the night sky and my soul can flow and flow and

the year of the war between Prussia and Denmark and all the horrors in America still and him shipping over the dangerous ocean seen from the summit of the Rock a colour beetleblue or shining as the coruscant ants and his ship coming always closer pinned to the breeze by its sails and all of it alive within me yes and all of it fresh and coloured bright yes and this newness filling me with strength and Mama crooning a song for una ninya tan fermoza in the cool of dusk singing *los mis males son muy grandes* to a tune that is all plums and apples for sweetness and *no te lo kontengas tu fijika* until he came marching up and in my own mind I could sense his limbs and their strength and his eyes and their calm blue and his mind and his heart hot red and his maleness and as he bowed to me and yes later on the daytime on the summit of the Rock he making his measurements most precisely and I beneath my parasol watching him and our mule chewing thistles and straining to get the juicier ones and tipping over our cart and yes the night visit when he showed me the moon through his telescope and said my name Lunita Lunita over and over and nuzzled my ear and slipped his hand under my skirt and as I cried out in ecstasy lights poured through the firmament and he danced like a Rock ape and shouted about the meteors falling down in shining greens and blues from the black sky yes and the Pedro whispered to me that the lights were my soul

because the future was unfolded to me I saw Albie married to a woman called Isabel and living in Lewes in England and yes I saw his cardiac complications and the stoutness that would bunch around his midriff and the colour he would turn when the last of his heart pains seized him but none of it could touch my joy yes and I knew he wont find the joy he found with me where softly sighs of love the light guitar where poetry is in the air the blue sea and the moon shining so beautifully coming back on the nightboat from Tarifa the lighthouse at Europa point and he coming all excited down City Mil Lane and taking me by the hand tho everyone could see us together and gasping that the Rock was bigger and he had measured and remeasured and he could not doubt it and he could not understand it and I reached out with my mind and compassed the whole of the mountain yes and it was true and it was I that had done it and I led him to a café table and we sat more respectable and because all I felt was love I told him about Pedro and the breadth of my thoughts now and how the world was all before me now so various and new and because I could run the fingers of my thoughts over his mind I knew he was doubtful so I reached into him and for one moment yes he saw and then he shied away like a stung thing and stumbled but later he came back and we found a place in the garden where none could see and yes he was hot for it as the afternoon was hot and he cried after a little tho it didnt unman him in my eyes and he said he loved me and was afraid of me and I laughed and the song came into my head a little two glancing eyes a lattice hid it was as clear as if a woman was singing it two eyes as darkly bright as loves own star arent those beautiful words as loves young star and perhaps Pedro is a womans voice as much as a mans for Pedro must be a creature of spirit and not flesh and so not man and woman like angels perhaps

and it was some days before we could again get away to the top of the Rock and it was calm evening and everything clear and the dark green western flank of the Rock running down and we strolled like a courting couple though were not and Albie said some foolish things about how his life had run smoothly along til he met me but how I was the rock and then he said Pedro means rock does it not in Spanish it is the same name as Peter and I tushed him and lights started coming awake below us in the town and the sports ground was round as a copper penny and the dusk thickened and the apes capered and finally the stars plinked into vision overhead and each one tickled my mind as it revealed itself and we found a quiet place away from the road and made love again and all my joy yes went out into the cosmos joy and he kissed my breasts and clasped my hips with his hands yes tight as he spent himself and I felt it inside me as the milky way through my body are you a witch he asked me afterwards in awe and a single cloud like a scimitar edged the moon full and ripe white gold not silver and the next day he came to visit with Tweedy and another officer and we all took tea and had to pretend we were the merest of friends but the day after he came back and gabbled that the Rock had grown again after our act of love and that he measured it the following night there being no opportunity for further sweetness between us and it grew not at all and how much is it growing by my fine professor and he said only inches but think of how large an object the Rock runs a length of 3 miles from north to south and is ¾ mile wide and a quarter mile high how many extra thousands of tonnes of mass was added it was coincidence he said o most firm yet there was no geologic evidence for vulcanism in the Rock he said could it be some planetary bulge and Pedro whispered that it was I yes I said yes it was that the space of the Rock had become connected with my mind in a closer harmony than before and that we could as well say my swelling belly was caused by the Rock growing as the Rock growing by my belly that it was possible for a soul to achieve a harmony with the ironmould mark of space itself and time itself and then might the universe itself throb with the pulse of thought and

and my sweet Albie wrote to the Royal Society or somesuch fiddlefaddle and yes we made love one more time and the stars swooned through him and swooned through me and northern lights folded their bales of cloth in the nightskyport a sight never seen so far south before he said and then he sobbed a little and my infinite tenderness touched his mind and he was quiet as a baby and later as we rode down the Rock he said I am scared of you my beautiful Lunita and I do not know how to reconcile my fear with my love and I said it is the nature of love to be infinite and in such an ocean any fear and jealousy is washed away and I knew that my little Molly was quickening in my belly as I spoke a spark palpable to thought or rather to love and I the very next day he tramped to the summit of the Rock by himself and measured it again and again it was inches higher than before and it was that week or the week after that Tweedy and I were married and none too soon to save his pride concerning the birth of his daughter for a mans pride is the shape his love takes at the point of strength and cannot be wholly mocked and dismissed and for weeks I saw Albie not at all and some nights Tweedy was with me and covered me with his much broader hairier body and some nights he left me alone and I stroked myself yes and thought of the two men I loved yes and how my love reached all men and women too and I dozed and dreamed with each lovemaking the Rock that was me that was my body would swell as I was swelling now and soon it would be miles high and its peak would poke out from the covering of air around the world and into space and men would build curious funiculars to the top and a new kind of port at the top from which ships would fly to the moon and the other worlds with ease and the Rock base would swell and close the gap between Europe and Africa and the Mediterranean would become an oval lake blue as sapphire and pure and it was my own lap and inside it were my own waters and in those waters life teemed and grew clean and strong and I woke because yes Pedro was whispering he was leaving me and his way of putting it was that he had paced out a large enough footprint in his months plodding through time with me and I felt my first pang since he had first arrived for this was separation and felt like a no but he said he would press his heel into the place he had made and leap and where will you leap I asked and he said yes I will leap into yes and then he told me a story out of Plato the Philosopher about how Andalucibiades and Aristophanes and Socrates drank together and how in primal times people had double bodies with faces and limbs turned back from one another like globepeople cartwheeling yes some doublemen and some doublewomen and some men and women and these last were descended from the moon the moon until they were guillotined into separate halves and how they searched their whole lives for their other half that was me said Pedro and I searched long and hard for my other the woman to my man the man to my woman the half of my moon to be joined with the half of my moon and finally we were reunited and in our joy of combination we could leap and so we leaped and wait I said but they could not wait and I was left alone

and my senses shrank slowly over three days from everywhere

to tight now and close here and it was as calm and gentle as waking from a sleep and my tummy starting to show and I promenaded beside the sea arm in arm with my husband and the surf purred at my feet and we met Albie by chance and Tweedy said well met Bainbridge will you escort my wife to our house if you please I have business with the harbourmaster and Albie nodded his head and we walked our way back in silence most of the way and he told me the Royal Society had written back very chilly suggesting his instruments needed recalibrating and poohpoohing his observing and I told him I was sorry and then it was bursting in him to say it so he said he took a whore to the top of the Rock and undertook her embraces and the Rock was exactly the same size today as yesterday and had not changed so much as an inchs fraction and though it was cruelly said I felt a pity for him as acute as love and forgave him and he turned into an alley that he might weep and none see and then he stood to attention before me and begged me to explain my witchcraft for he was a man of science and would not believe mumbo or jumbo and I reminded him how he had told me about the solar system and how it is full of tumbling rocks rolling and cartwheeling around the sun and the planets all rock and the ground of life carbon which is burnt or silicon which is petrified and he nodded at this and I told him that if the universe was full of life then it might not be shaped in body or spirit like men and women are and that may this be the reason he could not see it through his telescope and there was enough connection between us

I think yes on account of the baby in my belly and enough of the old glamour adhering to me still that I was able to touch the idea into his mind and he started up with a shout by jupiter he yelled his selfpity evaporated what if those tumbling rocks were only the corpses of beings and not beings themselves what if the very Rock of Gibraltar were the body of a being long brought down from heaven and expiring slowly over thousands of years and pulsing with the last shudders of alien life and yes he was looking past me now at the Rock towering over us both and banners of Levant cloud pouring over its topledge like white water and gasped why might it not have fallen from above as easy as been pushed up from below by geologic force and he forgot himself so far as to embrace me and then he pulled himself away and ran to his own house and I made my own way home

and I saw him not at all for six months until I was big with Molly and placid with her inside me and he came to bid me farewell for he was leaving on the HMS *Sandwich* the next day and he stood though we begged him to sit and Mama knitting and I in the softer chair and he wished me all the maternal joy in the universe at my encroaching and I assured him I had experienced all that joy already and yes he said yes though Mama looked queer at us and he said one final thing how to read Europe as a whole imagine sitting southfacing on the south coast of England and read the whole snaking continent from left to right in its richness and conflict and beauty and danger and it ran all the way down through France and Spain and where else did it come to a full stop save Gibraltar and I laughed a little like this and he finished with please pass on my heartfelt congratulations to your husband and yes I said yes I will and Molly kicked her legs inside me yes.

5

Broadmoor

Negation

: I :

They gave me a phone. It was a fancy design, too: a model I hadn't seen before, brand new. I had no one I wanted to call, but it was good to have a nice new phone. And better than that (or so I thought), they gave me a car. Paulina Kostritsky announced this over breakfast. 'You know how to drive.'

'I *can* drive,' I said. 'I'm just not allowed to.'

'We've spoken to the relevant authorities,' she said. 'Had the points taken off your licence.'

'You can do that?'

'There's a lot we can do. Not everything, but a lot. Friends in high places. Not me personally, you understand,' she added, looking momentarily awkward, as if I were about to rebuke her for boasting. 'I mean the Institute.'

'It never occurred to me that you personally had any friends,' I reassured her.

She blinked. Then she blinked again. 'There are people in the very highest offices in the land who are keen for the Institute to succeed in what it is doing. Your visit to Curtius is crucial in that regard.'

'I honestly can't see how,' I said. 'But, anyhow. Thanks for the loan of the car.'

'It's not a loan,' she said, frowning. 'It's a gift.'

I didn't know what to say to this. 'Wow,' I said.

'Think of it as a token of our commitment to you. You're with us now, Charles. Peta *likes* you.'

'He does?'

'I know you've yet to meet him. Be patient. The crucial thing now is: you can help us move this vitally important work onwards.' All this was uttered in a kind of worn-down monotone, as if Kos were recalling a speech she had learned. 'It means the world to us that Peta likes you.' She shook her head, a single brief gesture. Man, she looked *tired*. She always looked tired.

A duo of people who couldn't have looked more like computer geeks if they'd been supplied direct from central casting came into the canteen, helped themselves to coffee and Danish, and sat at a table by the window. Whatever their conversation was about, it resulted in a lot of low, burbling laughter.

'So I'm off to Broadmoor today?'

'Not today,' she said. 'Today's slot has fallen through. But soon. We're talking with the people there to arrange a mutually agreeable time.'

'Do I get a say in the timing then?'

She didn't reply to this; looked past me, through the tall windows and out at the trees in the grounds. It took me a moment to realise that she was looking at the two newcomers. After an elongated pause they realised they were being stared at, and met Kostritsky's gaze. Then, without a word, they stood up and left.

'This thing you keep saying, or,' I rubbed my bristly chin, 'or implying, or whatever. This idea that there's anything useful Roy Curtius can contribute. That's not actually true, though, is it? I'm guessing he hasn't programmed any kind of computer since the eighties.'

By way of answer Kos said: 'Don't you think it strange that you ended up living in a flat only a few kilometres from Roy Curtius? Don't you think that's – *significant*?'

I grew annoyed. 'My life went to shit. I wasn't happy about that, but to shit is where it went. I came home to Reading, for where else was I going to go? But you think somebody earning what I earn could afford to live in Reading? Bracknell is compromise-town, rentwise, that's all. And as for the decision to base the UK's main secure psychiatric hospital on the outskirts of Bracknell, well that's hardly down to me. And anyway,' I added, my vexation evaporating with the effort of expressing it, 'anyway.' What did it matter? It didn't matter. 'It's not as though physical proximity is any kind of … uh. What's the word? Salient. Is that the word?'

At this Kos looked at me as if I were a moron. 'Proximity and distance are what we strive to overcome,' she said stiffly.

This struck me as some kind of veiled insult. 'What do you want me to *do*, anyway?' I asked, in a surly voice. 'I mean, sure: I'll drive down there. Are they even going to let me see him?'

'They'll let you in. They're expecting you. We can lean on them to let you in. What we can't do is persuade them to let Roy *out*.'

'I daresay they have good reasons for not wanting to do that,' I said.

Kostritsky looked through me, her eyes going slightly squint. Her whole body language sagged slightly. She looked like she was about to topple forward, and that it was costing her an active effort of will to keep herself sitting upright. So tired! But *why* so tired, all the time? 'He's been responsible for,' she said, in a distant voice, and then said, 'deaths, it's true.'

My whole expedition seemed to me abruptly less appealing. 'You,' I said, 'are kidding me.'

Her focus jumped back. She saw my scarred face as if for the first time. 'Oh, you'll be fine,' she insisted, with a new briskness. 'And they're experts at, ah, *handling* him. Believe me, Charles, it's not *you* who should be worried on that score.'

'I suppose you think it's you?'

'Yes,' she said simply.

'Sitting here on the outskirts of Swindon, behind your secure perimeter? Whilst he's detained in a padded cell in Crowthorne? I *don't* think,' I said. But the curious thing was, as I said that, I was aware of that part of me that believed her completely. She was at greater risk from Curtius than I was. Assuming he ever broke out of his secure facility, which eventuality was surely most unlikely. 'So you reckon I'll be OK?' I said. Then, to make it more real in my own mind, I altered it, said it again. 'I'll be OK, don't you worry about me. You haven't told me what I'm supposed to say to him, though.'

'Say hello from us,' she said. She seemed, suddenly, to be sitting very still. 'Give him our best wishes. Tell him that we are still very interested in working with him. We think that, coming from you, it'll have an effect.'

'He knows what you're up to, here?'

'Oh yes.'

'And that you think he could help?' Something else occurred to me. 'If he's actually killed people, shouldn't he be in prison?'

'He's been in prison. Back and forth. But he's not the usual sort of offender. Rather obviously. We do what we can to keep him away from the crueller sort of inmate. He's ... delicate, in many ways.'

'But – what? Killed *people*? As, more than one?'

'That is what the plural usually indicates.'

'Woh.'

'He was,' said Kos, leaning in a little, '*hurt*. By what happened. In Antarctica.'

'So was I.'

'I know. But your wound was of a – different sort.'

'Whatever,' I said, and finished my coffee.

What did it matter? What did any of it matter? The whole thing – the entire experience of these weeks in the Institute – possessed the quality of some strange dream, or fantasy. Maybe I'd had a stroke, in the shower, back in my flat, and this was all some bizarre end-of-life hallucination. Or maybe it was really happening. After decades of misery, it hardly mattered. It was a time of existential plenitude. I can't put it any better than that. There's a phrase that goes *I did not know how empty was my soul until it was filled*. Or maybe not, since I was only too aware how shitty my life had become. But the plenitude was a sudden and unexpected sweetness. The thing about negation is: it requires *something* to negate. This was that. This was that.

For some reason, another week passed before they finally let me go. I wondered, during this time, if they were having hiccoughs organising a time for me to visit at Broadmoor. Or maybe it was taking them a while to get me that car. Or maybe it was something quite other; I never found out.

At the end of that week, on the very last day of June, Irma visited me a third time.

That night, after Irma slunk away, I slept right through. In the morning, washed and breakfasted, I said goodbye to Kos. She gave me to the keys to the car – to *my* car – and gave me the phone. State-of-the-art slate, like a hand-sized model of the black slab from *2001: A Space Odyssey*. Amazing to a man of my generation, so much so that she had to show me how to use it. I was instructed that the phone would be my entry ticket. Then she gave me a wallet, and in the wallet a wodge of money.

'There's some money in this,' she said. 'Cash. That way we don't have to bother with registering a new debit card.'

'This is what? A per diem? Salary?'

'We can sort out the contractual details when you come back,' she said, not meeting my eye. 'You'll need to keep receipts for purchases over five pounds.'

'I can be back tonight.'

'Tomorrow will be soon enough,' she said. 'Stay in your own bed tonight, back at your flat. After you've seen ... him. Of course.'

So I climbed into my new car, the key in my pocket, and it started at the flick of a button. I drove down the driveway and the guard at the gate let me out. With a smoothly sexy female voice the sat nav guided me down country lanes. July sunlight glinted on the white polythene wrapping the fields. I put Radio 2 on, and feeling a weird, slightly unstable lightness in my soul, addressed the empty universe by singing along that it made me feel, that you make me *feel*, like a nat, ural, woman. I slid down the slipway on to the M4 heading east, and the sky darkened, and summer rain came down, and the windscreen wipers started of their own accord.

: 2 :

The approach to Broadmoor does not display the building's most prepossessing side to the visitor. Your car rolls to a halt outside a great hedge of wire fencing, topped all along its length with a towering Afro of barbed wire. Behind this is a hefty-looking brick wall, over the top of which are red-brick buildings and grey sloping rooftops. Just visible past all this, on a small rise, is the main building itself: a much more elegantly designed Victorian structure looking for all the world like the stately home of a well-to-do industrialist.

I was behind a silver VW Passat, the driver of which chatted to the guard on the gate for ages and ages, either because there was some difficulty in gaining official clearance or else because they were old friends having a chinwag. Finally the gate opened and he rolled inside. I pulled up, and showed the guard the sigil on my phone. He took the device from me, scanned the image, checked my face against whatever came up on his terminal, handed me back the phone and opened the gate, without a word.

I drove in. BROADMOOR HOSPITAL said the signs, in standard NHS font. PARK IN DESIGNATED BAYS ONLY. The inner gatehouse, motte and bailey (if that's the right terminology), was a splendid Victorian structure with a clock in its centre like a Cyclops's eye, over an arched green door three times the height of a man. I found a designated bay and parked. Then I strolled, feeling a fizzing in my stomach of sheer apprehension, to the door.

'Morning,' I said, grand as you like. 'Charles Gardner, to see Roy Curtius? I believe I'm expected.'

There were two guards on duty, both women; and they peered at a ledger and checked the ID on my phone, and eyed my scarred face suspiciously. But they let me through. I emptied my pockets of everything, and walked through the magic doorway of metal detection. 'You're not allowed phones inside, I'm afraid,' one of them said to me. This lady had a halo of alopecia-thinned hair all over her visible bald scalp, like a cloud of nanobots.

'OK,' I said, and smiled beamingly.

'This guy's exceptional,' said the other. 'Look, orange notice.'

'Orange,' the other repeated, in a tone of voice that made it clear such a colour was a rare and remarkable occurrence. 'What does it say?'

'Says he can keep his phone.'

'It's fine,' I said. 'I don't mind leaving it here.'

'Says here you can keep it,' she insisted. 'And keep it you shall. Orange.'

Her colleague checked, looked at me again, and checked once more. 'Well,' she said, in a grudging voice, 'very well. But Mr Granger, you must understand, do not pass your phone to any of the patients.'

'Gardner,' I said.

'As for Mr Curtius, he is …' She searched for the right word. 'Unusual. We're used to the unusual here, of course, but. So: understand, yeah? I'll take you up myself, though I'll have to hand you over to Delaware when we get to the Paddock Centre. Security is tight as a drum up there, let me tell you.'

'Seems pretty tight here,' I observed.

I spoke blandly enough, it seemed to me, but she decided to take offence at this, and scowled at me. 'Come along now.'

I pocketed my phone, leaving my keys and wallet in a plastic tray behind the security desk. The guard unlocked a door, and locked it behind me after we both went through. We crossed a courtyard, and the sun flashed his arse at us before veiling it again in cloud. Through a new set of blue-painted doors, unlocked and relocked; along a corridor and through another valve of doors, unlocked and relocked. A second courtyard, and in once again. All in silence.

'Worked here long?' I essayed, as she relocked the door, sealing us inside.

She looked at me, bleakly. 'Curtius is very dangerous,' she said. 'Look: you've an orange code, so I daresay you've been trained.'

'Of course!' I assured her, feeling a twitch of anxiety at my complete lack of anything resembling training.

'The drill, you know it. Don't get too close to him. Don't give him anything – certainly not that phone you're apparently permitted to carry inside.'

This little speech wasn't doing anything for my levels of

anxiety. 'I knew Roy before he was banged up. Hospitalised, I mean. I know this isn't a prison.'

She looked at me suspiciously. 'He's been inside a lo-o-ong time.'

'It was a good while ago when I knew him,' I admitted. 'Maybe the Roy I used to know has changed a little. But he's hardly Hannibal Lecter.'

'No, you're right,' she said, starting off down a polished-floor corridor. 'He's much more dangerous than that.'

I padded after her in silence, considerably discommoded by this assessment. We turned a corner and into a nurse station that could have been transplanted from a regular hospital. Two orderlies stood, leaning on the counter. A male nurse sat behind, with a mug of tea in his hand. 'This one's orange,' said my chaperone. 'Here to see Curtius.'

All three facial expressions shifted in unison. 'Oh,' said the nurse.

'Hi there!' I tried. 'My name's Charles.'

'Charles,' said the smaller of the two orderlies. 'That's the feller.'

'That's?' I prompted.

'He's been talking about you. Curtius. He is expecting you.'

'Of course he is,' I said brightly. The Institute had been in touch with him, evidently, telling him that I was coming. Or *he* had been in touch with them. Either way, it might have been nice to keep me in the loop. I stood up straighter. 'Don't look so doomy,' I said. 'I knew Roy before he was admitted. He's only a little feller. How much damage can he do me?'

All four of them looked at me: the only word to describe it would be *agog*. 'You been briefed?' asked the nurse.

'He says he's been briefed,' said the guard who had brought me over. 'Orange,' she said again.

'I was briefed,' I lied, again.

'Look,' said the larger of the two orderlies, in a voice like a laden sack being dragged over gravel. 'You look like you're no stranger to a *fight*.' He nodded at my face. He wasn't the first person to misread the significance of the scars in this manner; though the truth is I've never once been in a fight in my life. 'You're confident you can handle yourself. Fine. What I'm saying is: don't trust that confidence. His manner of fighting is ...' He looked at his colleague for help, and when he shrugged he rolled his eyes.

'Don't touch him, don't give him anything, don't even *think* of touching his restraints,' said the nurse, getting to his feet.

'Restraints?'

'You want one of us in there with you?' asked the smaller of the orderlies.

'He's orange,' said the guard, before I could answer. Apparently this meant *no*.

The nurse led me down a corridor of hefty, locked doors, and stopped at the end. Slapped on the door with a meaty palm. 'Roy, it's your visitor?'

Barely audible through the door I heard: 'Charles?'

'That's the geezer.' The long key went in, and the lock turned, and the nurse caught my eye. 'Don't know why we bother with these locks,' he said to me, gnomically. It was, I suppose, his way of saying *good luck*.

I stepped through, and the door thudded behind me.

'Hello, Charles,' said Roy.

'Roy,' I said, and nodded.

He was sitting on his bed, with a book on his lap. There were, I saw, a lot of books: fat copies of philosophical tomes, some in German. There was a round-shouldered desk, but no computer. The room was fitted with a single window with a view across a down-sloping lawn interrupted by its white metal bars. There was a commode in the corner. And there was Roy himself, seated, looking expectantly at me.

I experienced two related reactions. One was surprise at how different he looked. For one thing, all his hair was gone, and his face had collapsed into a series of lines and wrinkles, like cross-hatching in a line drawing. His bald head showed off the big dent he had acquired in Antarctica, and the declivity was not advantageous as far as improving his good looks. His body, never large, seemed to have shrunk into itself: skinny arms and legs, though his belly was round as a cannonball. It had been decades, of course, since I had last seen him; and I daresay I looked as weird and shrivelled to him as he did to me. And as soon as I registered how *old* he looked, a second realisation hustled up upon me: it was obvious from one glimpse that, in essence, he hadn't changed at all. His sly eyes twinkled up at me.

'Oh my dear fellow,' he said, setting his book aside. 'Those scars! Are they down to me?'

'To be fair,' I said. 'Yes.'

'I *am* sorry. Please, sit down.'

There was only one chair, so I pulled it away from the bed, away from him, and sat down. My heart was pounding like the drum intro to the Clash's version of 'I Fought the Law'. After what happened to my face, many of my pores were sealed up, and that fact means I'm more prone to sweat under the arms and across my back than I used to be. I could feel the tickling sensation.

Roy swung his legs out and sat on the edge of the bed. Turning through ninety degrees, which this entailed, revealed just how extensive was the valley in his skull. I also noticed for the first time that he was chained to the bedhead. It was a long chain, presumably to give him the latitude to reach the commode and the desk. But, weirdly, it went from the bed not to a handcuff, but to what looked like a piercing in the side of Roy's wrist. He saw me staring at this, and held the wrist up. 'Pretty, no? They anaesthetised me before they did the piercing. I'm not an expert on tattoos and piercings and so on, but I believe they are usually administered without pain relief.'

'I've heard as much,' I said.

He peered at the piercing. 'It goes right through. Through the space between the radius and ulna, near the point of distal radio-ulnar articulation.'

'And they preferred this to a regular handcuff, because ...?'

He blinked, slowly. Looked at me, snake-like. Blinked again. 'I fear they don't trust their handcuffs to hold me,' he said. His voice was exactly what it had always been. Hearing it again, after all these years, took me right back to that base. The half-year-long austral night, and Roy's weird tics and mannerisms. I had a brief dizzying sense of faintness. Even after all my time at the Institute, I hadn't really taken what I had learned and reflected it back upon the Antarctic events. But, looking at Roy now, I thought to myself: *did he really* do *it, back then? Did he get close to the thing in itself? Was that what I saw?* The horror, the horror.

'They, uh, looking after you here?' I said. 'Like a nice hotel?' It was a fatuous thing to say; but my heart was hammering inside me. The voice in my head was saying: get out, get out, get out.

Roy smiled thinly. 'Mustn't grumble,' he said. 'They certainly attend to me. Provide for all eventualities. Although, as the man himself says: *Ich habe nicht nöthig zu denken, wenn ich nur bezahlen kann.*'

'No idea what that means, Roy.'

At this he made a gun-shape out of his right hand, and aimed it at me. 'Charles, Charles. *They* didn't send you down here to shoot—' and he pretended to fire off his imaginary gun '—the breeze, now, did they?' I flinched, I confess it.

'They were pretty bloody oblique about the whole thing,' I said, in a louder-than-I-intended voice. 'Look. You know what they're about – research-wise, I mean. They seemed to think that you could help them.'

'So I can. They've often approached me. I'm not boasting when I say they need my help very badly. But I *wouldn't* speak to them. For years I simply ignored them. Then I decided: I would speak – but only to you. So they found you for me! Can't fault them for effort.'

'Jesus, Roy,' I said, a tremor troubling my left leg. I kicked the heel down on to the floor to try and rid myself of it. 'Why me? Finish what you started, is that it?'

He looked very grave at this, and said, 'That's a hurtful thing to say, Charles,' and he pouted. 'To apologise, of course. I thought – back then, down there – I thought I needed to be solus to access it – them, the thing – the thing itself. I thought two consciousnesses would muddle the approach. But I know a lot more about it now, and I see I was wrong. There was no need to dispose of you.'

'So it was all a misunderstanding,' I said, in a tight voice. 'That's heartening.'

'Don't be snide! You and I have shared something, Charles. We're the only two in the entire world! There will always be that link. As for the Institute…' He trailed off.

'Go on,' I prompted him. 'What am I to tell them?'

'Well,' he said gloomily. 'A deal's a deal. They located you. I suppose I must help them.' He ran the fingers of his unchained hand up and down his tether.

'Great. They'll be delighted to hear that. I'm sure.' I found myself wondering how to get out. Did I just bang on the inside of the door and call for it to be unlocked? Could I do that without sounding desperate? 'Well: it's— I was going to say *good to see you again*. But good. I don't know if that's. That's the. *Mot juste*. Let's settle instead on, well, it's certainly been *interesting*.'

'Don't be in such a hurry, Charles,' Roy said, with reptilian suavity. 'Don't you have something for me?'

'My liver and nice bottle of Chianti? No early Christmas presents I'm afraid.'

'The phone,' he said.

Almost as if impelled by a force other than my conscious mind, my hand went to my pocket and brought out the phone.

'They expressly told me not to give you this,' I said.

'They did?' Roy replied, looking puzzled. 'Oh, you mean the staff here did. Well of course, *they* did!'

For some reason, this has a mollifying effect upon my anxiety. Slowly, with a fuzzy sense of the oddity of my own action, I held the phone out to Roy, holding it by one corner between thumb and forefinger. Roy reached out and took hold of the opposite corner with the same digits. For a moment we were in proxy contact, like Michelangelo's Sistine God and Adam. But no spark ran through the metal, or plastic, or whatever the phone was made of. Then I relinquished my hold, and Roy slipped the phone into the chest pocket of his uniform.

'Most kind,' he said, in a bored voice. 'I'm going to have to go over there now.' He gestured with his head. 'Back on the bed up, right up I mean, by the wall, so Reggie can see I'm not near the door when he looks through the peephole. Rat-a-tat and say you're finished here, and he'll unlock.'

'That's it?' I said, sitting back, feeling a weird gush of relief in my breast. 'Are we over?'

'Dear, dear Charles,' said Roy, staring ahead by way of pointedly not looking at me. 'After what we shared we can never really be over. *Au revoir*, my friend. *Auf Wiedersehen*. And *sehen* we shall, sooner than you think.'

'Not if I *sehen* you first.'

Roy went back to the bed. I stood and stepped over to the door. Knocked. After a hiatus, the nurse let me out. The guard was there, and she led me back through all the various locked doors. Not a word was spoken. In a sort of daze I discovered myself in the car park. I felt rather discombobulated, but also – frankly – relieved. I was still alive, at any rate.

So I climbed back in the car and drove out of the complex. It was a ten-minute drive through early afternoon Bracknell streets to my flat. I parked on the road, and walked away from the immaculate brand-new automobile with an unprecedented sense of dread. What if it got nicked? I'd never had a car worth any kind of money, before, and mine was a rough sort of area. What if sheer envy keyed it, daggered the tyres, scratched the windscreen? Not that there was anything I could do to prevent such eventuality, except trust to luck.

I let myself in to my flat, and breathed the unfamiliar air. An English July afternoon. The light coming through the big windows an aquarium light. I turned on my laptop, and waited for it to boot – slowly, slowly. Whilst it was working its way, its fan wheezy, almost visibly spitting dust out of its side, I thought to check the wallet they had given me. Eight hundred pounds in fifties and twenties. I counted it twice, I was so surprised. I googled Roy; but there was nothing very much online, except old stories concerning our Antarctic misadventure, and a few newer rehashes of those old stories.

I took a nap, and when I awoke it was dark outside. There was nothing to eat in the flat, so I got back in the car and drove to Reading. There were, at that time, no restaurants in Bracknell, it being in the process of being comprehensively redeveloped, with more than half the town centre a muddy building site. And since I had £800 in cash in my pocket I didn't feel like a McDonald's or take-away pizza. So I parked and ate at a posh restaurant, and even treated myself – the first alcohol to cross my lips in years – to a glass of wine. I wandered about Reading for a while watching the romantic couples arm in arm, the groups of lads on a pub crawl, the office parties shrieking and laughing. None of this had anything to do with me. I kept thinking of my encounter with Roy. Though I'd walked away with a light heart, it occurred to me that there was some significant residuum of dread at the encounter.

I got back in my car and drove home and watched the telly.

Sleep was elusive, in part because there was a childish Christmas-is-coming sense bubbling somewhere in my torso. Absurd in a man my age. In the morning I tidied the flat and rather ostentatiously turned everything off at the plugs. I even draped a spare sheet over the table, the laptop under it. As far as I could see there was going to be no reason for me to return to that place for a very long time. My base now was the Institute, and the countryside outside Bristol, and Irma – if not every night, then at least as many nights as she could be prevailed upon to visit.

The car was whole and undamaged in the bright morning light, and I got in. The only ointment-fly was the malfunction of the sat nav. I instructed it to return home, and it told me that the destination wasn't logged. So I typed in 'the Institute' but this had no effect. On my way down I had driven through a small village almost immediately on leaving the Institute. I typed in its name: nothing. More than that I could not recall. I thought to google the postcode of the nearby village, but of course I had given my phone to Roy. I even debated with myself as to whether I should go back into my flat and boot up my laptop to search for the postcode, but then I decided that was foolish. I had driven down only the day before; surely I could remember the way back today.

So, feeling a sunshiny sensation of joy in my breast (and how long it had been since I felt *that*), I pulled away and drove to the motorway. Traffic was light and I zipped along. The fullness, from which negation was poised to detract, filled me.

I came off the M4 at the junction I had joined it, and for several miles drove recognisable roads. Then, rather frustratingly, I got lost. For twenty minutes I drove and turned, and drove, and turned back. Finally, annoyed at the selective memory of my supposed state-of-the-art sat nav, I pulled into a garage and bought a map of the local area. Using this, and with the attendant's help in pinpointing the location of the petrol station, I made my way to the nearby village. I recognised the church, and the pub (the Poet's Rest), but several forays into the surrounding country lanes drew blanks. I passed several farms and one large concrete water tower like a giant robot cock. But turn and turn about as I might, I didn't seem to be able to locate the Institute. It was not marked on the map – since the thing was copyrighted to the 1990s this did not surprise me – but the buildings and grounds were very extensive, and surely the law of averages would mean I should eventually rub up against the perimeter wall. But nothing.

Finding myself driving back into the village for the third time, I stopped and asked directions of an elderly man out walking his dog. But he had, he claimed, never heard of the Institute. 'Do you live here?' Man and boy, he replied; seventy years. His father had been a GI, his mother a local girl. He hadn't seen his dad after his own eighteenth birthday. Not even once. Back in Missouri. 'Surely,' I interrupted him, 'you've heard of the Institute? It's a very large facility.' Never been nothing like that here.

This was daft. I cruised around some more, and then dived back into the countryside. On this foray I was suddenly reminded of an H. G. Wells story I read once. The story is called 'The Door in the Wall', and concerns a nineteenth-century fellow, in, I dare say, frock coat and dour hat (I don't believe the story specifies) who discovers a certain door in a certain wall that leads him to a blissful place. But he makes the mistake of coming back into the real world, and thereafter no matter how long he lives or how assiduously he searches he cannot find the door again. The tone of melancholy resignation with which the (now elderly) narrator tells his own story is the strength of Wells's writing at his best. But, I told myself, it was daft. The story was a metaphor. My life was no metaphor. My life was the real thing. As I was having this thought, the words forming distinctly inside my head, that U2 song came on the radio, 'Even Better Than the Real Thing'. I swore at the radio.

For the fourth time I found myself driving, despite myself, back into the village, after following the Ariadnean thread of the country roads. It was now noon, and a lanky youth was putting out a folding sign beside the door of the pub, so I parked and went inside. That strong stench of hops and last night's beer. Sunlight shining through the windows and coming so brightly off the waxed tabletops it hurt the eyes. 'It'll be a minute,' said the youth, in the gloom behind the bar. He aimed a remote control at a telly on a bracket high up the wall.

I asked him about the Institute. He stared at me with half an inch of mouth showing between his lips. I tried him again. The set clicked and Sky Sports shone into life, the commentator mid-sentence. 'Don't know it,' he said. 'Though I've only lived here a year or so.'

'Is there anyone around who knows the area better?' I pressed.

'I tell a lie,' he said. 'I've been here over eighteen months. *In* fact, nearer two years than one.'

'I've been driving around,' I told him. 'Getting kind of lost. Any help would be much appreciated.'

'It was early spring,' he told me. 'I remember, on account of I sowed some small salad in the garden out the back. So I suppose not so many as eighteen. Meant to do the same this year but forgot. It gets good sun, that little plot. Pint, is it?'

'No thank you,' I said, and went back to my car.

For a long time I sat behind the wheel and stared ahead. A

sense of doom was corroding the edge of my wellbeing. Frustration. But it existed. I'd hardly hallucinated the entire Institute. Quite apart from anything else, the car I was sitting in was proof of that. So, one more time, I started the motor and drove out of the village, and cruised the roads. Ten minutes turned into twenty. The songs being played by the radio became sarcastic in tone. 'Up the Junction', 'Superstition', 'Stairway to Heaven'. As the opening strums of 'I Still Haven't Found What I'm Looking For' came on I punched the radio off – and at that very moment I drove past a tree I recognised.

I stopped the car, laid my arm along the top of the passenger seat and looked over the ledge of it as I reversed. Definitely a familiar tree. A narrow roadway, discreetly hidden by two giant labia-like hedgerows. That was familiar too. I turned up the way. In two minutes I was arriving at the gates to the Institute, with a childlike buzz inside my chest, relief compounded with excitement.

The gates were closed. The layout was such that I had to get out of the car in order to press the intercom and so gain ingress.

No dice.

Bzzcht. 'Hi: this is Charles Gardner. Could you let me in please?'

Static.

'Hello?'

Crchzzt. 'No entry, mate. Buzz off.'

'What?'

'*Burze* off.'

'You're wrong,' I said, in my surprise. 'Let me in please. I'm, eh, affiliated with the Institute. I'm Charles Gardner.'

'I've got your name here, pal. It's on a no entry list. You're not getting in. I'm sending one of my guys to the gate now, and I should warn you for your own' – shzzcht – 'that our security guards are licensed by special' – fzzzcht – 'to carry firearms. Get in your car and drive away, would be *my* advice.'

I stood for a moment. I could say *it took a moment for the meaning of his words to sink in*, but that wouldn't be the truth. I grasped instantly what was happening. Kos, on her own initiative or else taking orders from Peter, was freezing me out. A ridiculous rabbit-like panic gripped me. I wouldn't see Irma! And then, almost at once, I felt rage. They had used me: a monkey's paw to get to Roy. He told them it had to be me, and he wouldn't budge; so they'd reeled me in, given me just enough to get me onside, used me, and now they were discarding me. I kicked the door.

'Let me in!' I yelled.

'It's on camera, pal,' said the voice on the other end of the intercom. 'We *will* prosecute criminal damage.'

I kicked the door again. 'I demand to speak to Kostritsky!'

'Word to the wise,' said the voice. 'That ain't going to happen. They want you out of the way. You think they wouldn't *prefer* you in prison? I'd say they would. They' – fzzk – 'contacts in the highest strata of law enforce' – skrzz – 'and security services. You want to give them an excuse to prosecute you? Go ahead. It's all recorded' – zzhsch – 'camera, and the police will be here in minutes. If I were you I'd get going.'

I stood there. My rage drained through me, departing who knows where. Into the earth, perhaps. It was hopeless. But I couldn't just give up!

'I'm coming in,' I told the intercom. 'I want to talk to Kostritsky.'

And the voice replied: 'No.' The barest essence of negation.

I took three steps back and ran at the gate. Though it had been decades since I'd done anything more athletic than lug dustbins about, I nonetheless managed to get my hands to the top. And as I strained my arms to pull myself higher, the faceless voice at the far end of the intercom – I assume it was him – flicked the switch on the electrified strip that must have been embedded there. My palms took the shock directly, painfully, on their meat. My muscles – all of them seized. The next thing I knew I was lying on the ground, hugging myself, my left ankle throbbing. It took some considerable willpower to get up and climb back into the car.

It was lucky the car was an automatic, because my left foot was too sore to pivot. Pranged the ankle falling from the gateway. The pain did not help mollify my rage. I drove slowly back down the lane, and then through the village, and towards the motorway. All the time I was thinking: three fucks. Not even proper fucks, three half fucks. Eight hundred quid, a car and three measly shags, and they had fooled me into doing their dirty work. And now I would never see Irma again.

As the M4 junction approached I saw a giant shoebox chain hotel, part of the Way Inn franchise. I was in no condition to drive, so I decided to check in. I slouched like a wounded soldier from the car park and into reception, booked myself a room – my cash caused the receptionist to raise one charcoal eyebrow, but she took my money. I asked for some ice to be sent up to my room. Then I rode the elevator to my floor staring, aghast, at the broken tramp-like figure hunched in the wall-high mirror inside the compartment. What could a woman as beautiful as Irma ever have seen in me? Why would she ever have slept with me, except that she had been instructed to?

In my room I sat on the bed to rest my throbbing ankle, and stared at the blank TV screen opposite. Ice was delivered and I wrapped a clutch of cubes in a towel and applied it. What was I going to do? It was not acceptable that I be denied entrance. I would not stand for it. They had made promises. They had made a commitment to me. They could not simply toss me aside.

Irma.

I needed to think strategically. No good just turning up at the gate again. I needed to find a way of contacting them and applying pressure. I could threaten to go public – tell the press, post what I knew online. Even as I thought this, I could see their reaction (sure, go ahead, nobody cares, nobody will believe you). Or should I beg? Plead? Promise them something? They needed me, in order to be able to liaise with Roy! They would shrug. My self-esteem crumbled further: I would promise them anything. I would say that there were things about my encounter in Antarctica that they didn't know and needed to know, stuff I'd kept to myself. Stuff I would have to make up, of course, from whole cloth; but which might be enough to get me through the gates again.

I ordered a packet of Nurofen from room service, and took two. Then, with an inward squelch of self-disgust, I snaffled two tiny whisky bottles from the minibar and drank them both straight down.

I dozed.

Then: the strangest part of the whole experience.

When I woke it was dusk. The sound of the motorway was faintly audible, like a distant Niagara. I was chilly. My ankle gave a tweak of pain, and I reached out to it to – I don't know, rub it, clasp it, something – and there was the ghost-boy.

I hadn't seen him for months: in his rags and his near-skeleton frame and his egg-nog-pale skin and the scarred half of his face. Not since my dentist trip, in fact. But this wasn't a dream. This was real. He was standing only feet from me. He was looking right at me. It was dim in the room, but there was no mistaking what I could see.

My heart paced with glolloping repeated convulsions. I breathed hard. My breath was visible, like ectoplasm.

Very slowly, as if fearful of scaring the lad away, I swung my legs, one good, one bad, over the side of the bed. 'Now,' I said. 'Look,' I said.

I don't know why I said those two words.

The boy was looking right at me. My hand was on the bedside light switch, and I turned it on.

It wasn't the ghost-boy. It was Roy, standing in front of me. He was maybe three inches taller than the boy – not that big a difference, really – and dressed not in rags but in the clothes I had seen him in the day before. But there was no confusing the two. What I mean is: I didn't mistake Roy, in the murky quarter-light, for the ghost-boy. I definitely saw the ghost-boy. And he definitely changed into Roy when I turned on the light.

'Jesus crap,' I shrilled, actually startled by the abruptness of the transition.

Roy smiled his weird reptilian smile. His left sleeve was tie-dyed black at the cuff. He put a finger to his lips.

I stood up, quickly, and my ankle squeaked and jagged and complained. But at least now my head was higher than his. 'What are you doing?' I demanded. 'Creeping in here. How did you get here and how did you get in here?'

He was real. It didn't occur me to me to think he might be a hallucination or a dream-state confusion. He was as real as Marley's ghost.

'Oh but they're squeamish,' he said, and I knew at once he was talking about the Institute. 'A different set of people would have just *killed* you, you know. They're squeamish, or cautious – or maybe they think they'll need you again. I don't know. Maybe they think *I'll* demand to see you again. That's a distinct possibility, in their minds I mean. They may think they're holding you in reserve, and if they do need you they can use their previous bait to reel you back in. Woman, was it?'

'Christ's sake, Roy. They let you out of Broadmoor? Did the Institute wangle that? How did you know I was even here?'

He lifted his finger to his lips again. 'It's a bit,' he said, and looked to the side. 'Chaotic over there, right now.' He looked at me again. Hindsight tells me he was debating with himself whether to kill me, or to leave me well alone. Still, he was an Englishman, and the nature of our national character is compromise.

There was sharp, horrid pain in my leg. I staggered back, against the bed. A bristle appeared through the fabric of my trousers, and grew suddenly longer. And my whole left side was agonised, as if boiling water were being poured down the hollow tubules of all its nerves, and I slipped, and nearly fell completely, propped by the mattress. My face was, doubtless, a picture. That may have been what Roy was going for, now that I come to think of it: my facial expression.

He was saying something, but I couldn't really focus on his words, what with the searing pain and my own screams. It may have been 'for old times' sake'. Or it may have been something in German. I neither know what he said at that juncture, nor care.

The bristle was a cord, a fishing line, a cable down which pain was being syphoned into my body. It grew longer and longer and then it came free and snaked through the air. I don't know what happened to it then. Maybe Roy pocketed it, as a kind of souvenir. It was the tendon from my lower left leg, drawn up past the top of my kneecap, yanked in a single smooth motion right out of my body. Finally I fell right over, and lay weeping and screaming on the carpet beside the bed.

Roy had gone.

6

A Solid Gold Penny

Limitation

MY NAME is Thos Firmin. I was born in *Somer's Towne*, neare *London*, &d did live my early years, such as I remamber not by virtue of my infancy, in that place.

WHEEREAS for several years I did labour under the guidance of Mast. John Cornelius tarring Barrells &d aiding the loading of Barrells from the storeroome onto carts, whence I was sold unto Mast. Samuel Newbolt *aet.* twelve, &d apprenticed to the Lemmon trading. My duties were to handle the Lemmons, casting out such as were rotten, &d painting or smearing the fair with wax made from whal-blubber that they might not fall into corruption. I worked for Mast. Newbolt for three year, whence I lived in the house of goodman Usher Serjent, &d slept in the Kitchen; which pleased me much, for the Stove theerein was alway lit, &d the roome accordingly warme. At the end of my living with Usher Serjent, Mast. Newbolt took me into his own house. But heere I was obliged to sleep in the Outhouse, wheere I was greatly troubled with Rats &d other Crawling things, which Prayer &d Begging to my Lord Jesus in no wise discouraged. At this time I was also poorly used by *Censor Morum* James Newbolt, being the brother of Mast. Newbolt the Lemmon merchant. He visited his brother variously, &d took to calling on his brother's house when Mast. Newbolt was elsewheere upon business, wheereupon the maid would admitt him. One time he came even into the Kitchen, wheere I was scrubbing the Pots, &d I was fearful lest his Judge's Robes be touched with grease. But he sat at Table &d was greatly merry, jesting with me on many scores. Before going he Handled me, &d I was greatly afraid, but he told me not to Care, or Speak of it, for it was below speaking of. Then he called me *chuck*, &d *red-robin*, &d give me sixpence, the which frighted me the more, for wheere would I claim to have earned a silver sixpence? I would be thought to have stoln it.

I SPOKE to Mistress Ive, who commanded the lower scull-ers &d kitchen, but she tushed &d talked grandly of Judge Newbolts *wife*, a goodly woman, &d his three children, &d wheerefore should he be interested in a lad suchane myself? &d, truthly, I did wonder somewhat as to the event, doubting that my senses did not play me false. *For*, as I admonished myself, *if it were another apprentice who attested such things &d I heard of this, would I believe it of him? &d, not doing so, how do I believe it of myself? Am I so proud as to advance myself in God's estimation over another?*

Mast. Newbolt thought well of me for my waxing of the Lemmons, &d I enjoy'd this work; for the odour of the day was clean upon me, &d I found my skinn, that had prior given out in Rashes, Botches &d suchlike Boils, did improve under the efficacion of Lemmon vapour &d Lemmon-water. But His broth.r, Judge Newbolt, did persuade my master to release me into his servitude, for (claim'd the Judge) he needed a boy with nimble Hands such as mine, to deal with his stitching &d Judicial Gouns, &d as all affirmed I was dextrous indeed with the needell. On the day my mast.r acquainted me with the news of my Removal from him &d my Placement in his brother's house, I confess I fell to the floor &d wept upon his very shoes, ev'n unto staining the velvet with my water. I cried to my master that I had been happy under Him, &d earnestly requested him to keep me in his Lemmon-service. My Mast.r seemed caught upon an awkwardness, &d handld his Kerchief, &d meerly left the Warehouse without speaking one worde.

I was carried to Judge Newbolt's house with the Delivery Boy's cart, for it was in *IslingTown*, &d it was a Great building, with a wall'd-Garden before &d an Acre of gardens behind, tall as a *Castle*. My lodgings were up with the sparrows, &d the white-spatter'd roof-tyles, in a roome by myself. When I first came inn, &d was shewn my Roome &d afterwards the Kitchen, the maid-of-works spoke angry to me, of how surprizing a Thing it was to see a mere *Stitching-Boy* obtain a roome of his own; but I own'd to being frighten'd &d made to weep upon her bosom. But she, a tall &d bovie maiden, had none of it, &d chided me with my lack of manliness, calling me *My Lord's Bully-boy* &d *trowser-wife* &d many other names beside. This woman was nam'd *Anne*, &d I had many dealings with her in the months that came upon me. She was hard of countenance, &d spared no kind feelings for me, for (as she said) *The Lord hath forsaken you, &d wheerefore should I coddle ye?* In the darkest houres of the night, I in truth was perswaded by her wordes, for the light had dwindled so fully that it seemed no more than the furthest starre in heaven, &d I was left shivering on my bed. This *Anne* had the charge of bringing me food, which she oftentimes ate herself, or sold on, or gave me half-portions. She also had the charge of bringing me my lord *Judge*'s gouns &d cloaks to be darned, stitched, hemm'd, or otherwise tailor'd. But, divers times she brought me other materials to be stitched, &d I had no place to gainsay the goods she gave me to work upon, for theere was none to hear me. This way, I do believe, I spouted much money direct into mistr.s *Anne*'s purse, &d she needful of doing nothing more than watching the kettle boil by itself. But on another occasion, to speak fairly of Mistress Anne, she came into my roome late at night much tearful, &d hugged me to her bosom, &d call'd me her *poor boy* &d *evilly-used lad* &d *dearest* &d called on God to rescue me from the ways of the evil one. The next day I, hoping but meekly that Mistr.s Anne was now my friend, looked onto her face in the kitchen as I stirred the porridge, but she would not greet my eye, &d she scowled so that I slunk off. This was the sole time she spoke kindly to me, that night, &d after she was hard againe.

I worked for three days &d slept three nights unmolested, for my *Lord* the *Judge* was away at Tonbridge on some royal business. But on the fourth day theere was much business as the house was made ready for him to return, &d I grew fearful. At two hours past lunchtime, Judge Newbolt returned to the house with a retinue of three men, &d he was greatly merry. He called forth all the servants of the house, &d we ranged ourselves in the hallway, eleven in all, tho four were day-servants only, come to clean &d odd-job from time-a-time. To these men, the *Judge* paid threepence each &d bid them cheerily away. The rest he greeted singly, &d came to me with a grin &d said *For you my ladde, I have a rare gift, to welcome you to my service. Will you do me faithful service, young buck?*

I being scared said nought, but Mistress Anne standing aside me spoke up that *I was a good boy, &d would do as I was bid, &d be an honourable servant.*

At which my new master laught, &d bid me take a coin, *a solid gold penny, as rare a gift as a servant ever took on starting life with a new master*, he said, *&d only offered because my brother has spoke so good of you.*

I tried to thank my *Lord* the Judge, &d held the penny in my Hand tight, but no wordes would issue.

After, in the pantry, whilst the cook &d the two maids

prepared an afternoon feast, Mistr.s *Anne* chid me, &d struck me on the head, so that my forehead knocked againste the wood of the doorway &d blood started, &d ran down between my eyes. She took the penny from me, for *safe-keeping* she said, &d bad me go to the garden &d wash my face in the pond. *&d you need not mourn your loss,* she said, *for it is but a Penny.*

That night, despite my fearing it, my *Lord the Judge* did not visit me in my roome, tho I lay awake most of the night with the pain in my head, &d with anticipating. But the next day Judge Newbolt sent *Anne* to call me to his Librarie, wheere I was to wait on his pleasure.

The Librarie walls were covered with Bookes as a *Serpent* is with scales, in greene, blacke &d red leather (&d leather is but skinn, as ye know well): &d Bookes were balanced in the shevles so high that no man might reach, lest it be on a scaffold or with a ladder. My *Lord* the Judge told me that a pane of Glass was missing from his study-window heere, &d that the weather being November did send spouts of cold air through the gap like ice-water to chill him in his reading. I examined the pane, &d one of the twelve was gone complete; but I had too little knowledge of Glasing-skills, &d was fearful to tell my lord so. As I waited by the window, my Lord approached me.

Tell me, said he, *what hath befallen your brow? Theere is bloode upon it.*

I begged my Lord's pardon, but he laugh'd at this &d declared theere was no offence in it for him, &d that *the offence is all for thy Head, which is the plaintiff heere.*

I told him it hurt but little.

But how did it come to pass? he asked.

I struck it againste the door in the pantry, my Lord I said, *&d I humbly beg your pardon for it.*

Againe my lord laughed, &d said *you might as well beg pardon of the wooden Door. Did the door not complain?*

I said, *No.*

Then wheerefore should I take offense?

Then he said *come hither* to me, that I was compelled to approach him. Heere he Handled me once more, causing my Breeches to remove, &d Slapping &d Beating my thighes &d butocks with the flat of his Sworde. At this I was greatly feared, that he was going to use the sworde-point &d turn out my life from its poor frame, but instead he threw me on the floor in a great Passion, &d stormed up &d down the Librarie as if in a Rage, tho I could not overhear the wordes he spoke. He told me to begone, but as I gatheered my breeches &d made towards the door he grabbed me. Heere he forced me againe onto the floor, &d pressed my legs close together, that he might rubbe himself between my thighes, until with terrible groaning he concluded, &d lying on me gasping for some time before he sent me away.

I was in poor state at this Happening, &d did cower in the garden by the tree with my face to the floor, such that dropt Fruit did slime me with its rotten flesh. I aim'd to rins &d wash myself in the pond of the garden, but the Garden Boye discover'd me &d dragged me to the kitchen, wheere Mistr.s *Anne* did scold me fiercely for soiling my cloathes &d for my mournful state. But she did not smite me on this occasion, albiet she struck me many the time before &d after.

After this time my *Lord* the *Judge* did visit me several times in my bed when the Night was still; when he would Wrestle with me, calling himself *Abraham* &d myself his *Angel*, until he would promote his own coming-off, with his own Hands. One further time he called me to the Chappel on pretext of mending some or other furnishings, but instead us'd me badly, before the very altar. This Happening caused great fear to settle upon me, for I consider'd it awful, &d blasphemy to perform such acts before the very *cruxifice* of solid Gold that stood upon the altar rail. Judge Newbolt was in a great agitation this time he called me to the Chappel, &d at first he stood at one side &d I the other. Heere he debated with me the course of True Faithe, the mercy of God, &d the nature of Love, but I being fearful took little heede of his conversation. Then upon approaching me, he seized me by the shoulder &d stared wildly at my face, his eyes glinting. For how long he clutch'd me so, I know not, but that I noticed his brows contract upon themselves, &d a shiver leave his eyes, wheereupon he began kissing my lips, as a man devours his meats after long fast. Then (for I said nothing, being trembled with fear even unto silence) he took the cloathes from my body, but gently, &d turned me around. He did place his mamber inward as the bridegroome's Hand comes through the latch. I had never been so us'd before in my life, nor by the Judge neither until this time. I believed my bones within me breaking, so fierce was the paine; &d when he began moving back &d forth I felt my skinn pulled apart &d ripp'd, that the blood ranne down my legs. I cryed out at this, for I could not remain silent nor despite my terror; &d with my cries my *Lord* the *Judge* cryed also, that we howled together like *Dogges*. At this Judge Newbolt shuddered like a dying man &d fell back from me, &d his mamber slitheered out of its den like the snake, &d I fell too, at the feet of the altar-rail, wheere I sobb'd. But for all the shouting we had made, nobody in the house thought to come into the Chappel in this time. My Lord came beside me, &d knelt at the rail to pray, &d I flinched away like a wild creature, &d gatheered my cloathes &d hid myself in the corner of the Chappel.

With such Foule chances, I grew to the fullness of Despond, &d wished myself dead many times. I would have carried this co[u]rse through, I bethink me now, had not first decided upon Going Away from that Place, &d making off for a Soldier or Sailor-man. During the day, with Mistress *Anne's* Eyes upon me I was without the chance to slip away, but one Night, a few weekes since I came first to that House, I was resolv'd with myself to begonne from theere. I folded my blanket, for it was *Winter* still, &d I had bethought me not to freeze in the iciness. But I could not pass through the house, for Mistress Anne had locked the door of my roome. But I could pass through the window, like a Cat, &d so I made my way onto the fore-roof of the House. I was a great height up, &d the sky was blue-blacke, &d the starres had cupp'd their Hands around their chill candle flames. I felt my path forward for a little way, with the icy winde pawing me &d licking me, turning my skinn to stone &d making me numb. I tried to unfold the Blanket, but the *Winde* caught it &d flung it from me. I went a little way on, but when my fingers fumbled at the precipice, &d I knew fear at the gap, not knowing which way to proceed. With difficulty I crawled backwards to the window, thinking to get back inside &d give up the *Escape* til a better weather were come: but I found the window had banged shut &d I could not raise it. At this my fear grew, for it seem'd to me that *God* had decided to punnish me for my undoubted *wickedness* by having his Terrible Gales come &d plucke me from the roof &d dash me to fragments on the stone-paving beneath. For a long time I clung to the roof, as the Winde &d the Hail cut through to my Bone &d Blood. Then I bethought me to finde the Blanket, by following the way of the Winde, that I might at least rappe myself in it. To this end I was obliged to Climb the Slant of the roof as it mounted over the Attick: but the *Tyles* being slippery with the Hail I slid down, &d fell.

Ah! Great was my *Terror* at this, the Plunge seeming to bring my Bowells into my Throat, &d I scream'd as I descended, albeit none heard my cries with the *Storme* now raging, Gales &d Hailstones. My fall lasted aeternities after, for on recalling it I felt like *Lucifer*, dropping Downwards through the airey Firmament of God's displeasure. In my remembrance, then, the fall continu'd *on &d on*, with my never striking the ground, nor every being releas'd from the Eccho of my own howling, the Hiss of the Wind, or the Nips of the hailstones. In Truth, no doubt, I fell but an instant, &d struck the upper-branches of a *Tree* that grew in the Garden of my *Lord* the Judge's house. These Branches pummel'd me somewhat, &d rolled me about like a Pat of butter in the churn. I came down the tree by degrees, Accumulating many Bruises as I passed, &d then I collapsed at last on the *grasse* in a state of Great Distress.

I lay for a time, but the Hail was Strong now &d the Wind chiller, so that I Resolv'd I would face the Wrath of Mistress *Anne* sooner than freeze to death in the Garden. So I made my way Pickingly through the dark to the Back Door, &d theere I struck the Door with my puny fist, &d shouted fit to unset-tle the Dead. At last *Pamela*, an under-maid who slept in the Kitchen, called quavringly through *Who was theere at this time of Night?* &d I answered sobbing with Cold, that she should *Fetch Mistress Anne*, that it was *I, Master Thomas*, &d that I earnestly begged admittance. She was so long about raising Mistress *Anne* that I would have Shiver'd myself into the very King of Agues, &d froze quite dead if leaft another minutes; but that I heard the Bolts undrawing, &d the door opening; &d theere was *Anne* with a carving-knife demanding who goes theere.

When she discovert it was only me, she grew Hard with rage &d beat me, notwithstanding my Bruis'd &d Froze condition. She woke Patrick, the footman, &d baden him *Watch the boy whilst she rouz'd the Master*, for she believed that if I were to abscond she herself would be dealt Hardly by my *Lord* the Judge, &d that accordingly she had a Duty to act as Prison Warder to me. Patrick was much daz'd with being woke at this hour, &d he held the candle very ill, for wax splash'd on his own bare feet &d he roar'd with the paine. He withdrew to wash his foot &d I was left alone: but escape was very far from my thoughts now.

I was so cold &d shiveringly, so Aching with my bruises, that I curled in the floor &d Wept &d Rocked myself.

When my *Lord* the Judge came down he was first much worried for my dreadful state, but after he grew wrathful that I had tried to run away &d Rag'd such that even Mistress *Anne* withdrew a little. He promis'd me all manner of torture if I tried such againe, &d dragged me whimpering forth from the corner to slap me with the Back of his Hand. Then he soften'd, &d held me like a baby, Notwithstanding that I resisted, &d coo'd at me to calm me. Finally he instructed Anne to lock me in the Cellar, but added that I was to be granted the Grace of a new blanket. I was Transported downstairs, &d in the dark I fell asleep with my Back againest a Barrell.

In the morning I awoke to the Cellar, which was Gray with umber-light only, &d I shivered &d cryed to myself, for all my boddie ach'd &d pain'd me, &d I could trace Scratche &d Bump upon my skinn. Then I bethought me what would happen, &d what torture my *Lord* the Judge might inflict upon me. At length the door ope'd, &d down came Patrick, carrying a cot &d a candle. *Heere's for you, master,* he sayed, *you'll sleep heere now, I warrant. Ye'll not be able to Fly from your bolt-hole now, will ye?*

I wept forsooth, &d begged Patrick to take Pity on me, but he only shook his head mournfully.

He placed the cot agaynst the Wall, &d placed the candle on the floor beside, fixing it with a Spot of waxe. Then he left, &d I tried to find it in my heart to be Thankful to *GOD* that I had been given a lamp to light my Gloome. But the flickering of the candle-light wash'd upon the corners &d crannies of the Cellar, &d I bethought me I saw the tails of Rats disappearing behind Barrells, &d into cracks in the wall, &d I became much more Fearful. I began to howl, like an animal, for *GOD* had abandoned me &d Retreated into the Temple of his Righteous-ness, &d heere was a Desart of Sin, &d I was abandoned in it.

But the crying brought no *succour*, so I fell quiet, &d began rocking forards &d back, &d this comforted me some.

When my *Lord* the Judge ope'd the door &d came down the steps carrying a lantern &d a canteen of Water, I was no longer able ev'n to be Fearful, &d I did meerly rock forards &d back, &d sang to myself in a small voyce. My *Lord* the Judge sat on the hindmost step &d look'd at me.

My boy, my boy he spake eventually. *What devill whisper'd to you to Leap from the Window? Didst think thou couldst Flie?*

I could not say.

God gave you life, said my *Lord*, his voice dark with melancholy. *Dost think it is yours to cast away?*

Oh my lord, I said at last, *I am so very unhappy*.

Yet wheerefore? said he.

I bethought me for a while, but my witts were tumbling so that I could not frame a proper answer. *I am afeared theere are Rats in this place, my lord* I said.

Tush he said. *Theere are no rats my boy*.

&d Mistress Anne uses me so cruel, I broke out weeping.

How so, lad? he sayeth.

She holds my food back &d methinks sells it to others, I say, but my tongue is babbling &d cannot be contained. *She beats me from time to time, &d brings in fretwork for me to toil at, yet she pockets the money earned theereby. She tooke away my penny that you gave me—*

My *lord* looked at me for a long time, &d spoke some wordes of Promise, that Mistress *Anne* would be punished. Then he came to my side &d, tho I flinch'd, he stretched my body out to lye flat upon the floor. Heere he took away my cloathes, &d I began trembling &d shivering, tho not with the cold, but with fearful anticipation. But heere my *lord* did not lay with me, but took the Canteen of water &d splash'd his sleave, &d rubbed the Dirt from my skinn. He then took out some *Oil* from a small bottle he carried about his person, &d rubb'd this same upon my *Bruises*. The pain diminish'd somewhat, albeit not being altogether gone. All this time he was *cooing* &d saying soothing matter, &d I was weeping with Great Pity of myself. Heere my *lord* left me, taking the lantern but leaving the Water for my Thirst. I lay *Naked*, for a length of time. My mind suffer'd fearfully at this time. My sense of abandonment by *GOD* was now most Profound, &d I Wept tears *Bitter* as Lemmon-Juice in my *Eyes*. I lay Friendless, my soule *Ruin'd* beyond hopes of redemption, quite without hopes of Deliverance from mine Persecutors. In my state of Savageness I fell to alternately *Pleading* &d after *Railing* at *GOD*; first begging him to release me from the State of Agony, &d after wishing fearsome Imprecations upon the *Godhead* for punishing so terribly a small boy who had never the *chance* to sinne so manifestly as to merit such treatment. But I recall'd my Church-going, that the sinne was not mine, but *Adam's*, &d that all soules are born blacker than Coal, &d liable for the *Fiery Pit* by merest virtue of breathing, all on account of *Adam's theft*. But at this thought I began inwardly cursing *Adam*, instead of Humbly praying to *GOD* for forgiveness.

The following Day Mistress *Anne* came down upon me, &d I was greatly afeared lest she should wish to Punish me for speaking of her to my *lord*. Indeed, she did looke Darkly upon me, but she strucke me not, nor us'd me ill, but bade me gather up my blanket &d come along with her. When I ask'd her whither we tended she said *Away, &d a good riddance*.

Wheere away, Mistress Anne? I asked, for the thought made me to tremble anew, for if I were cast into the Street then I would surely starve.

Away into a coache is all I know, she said, *&d that suffices me*.

Into the hall, with me blinking &d winking at the daylight, I was met by a coachboy &d a Serving-butler. This last was a great tall man, who *Grinn'd* at me like as I was a morsel of food, &d I trembled againe. But he saw me into the coach &d sat opposite me, forever keeping his Eye upon me, &d from time-a-time Grinning some more. When the coach started away I called upon my Courage &d in weake tones begged the Man tell me what was to become of me.

Why, little sprat? he cried in a great loud Voice, such that I trembled. *Do ye not know?*

No, sir, I pleaded. *&d I am greatly afeared that you will do away with my miserable life, &d I call on you to be merciful in the name of GOD in Heaven.*

He laught at this, til verily I bethought him a very Grinning *Devill*. But then he spoke more kindly, that *we were bound for my Lord the Judge's House in the Countryside West of the Citie, wheere it was peaceful &d the air fragrant with the coming blossom.*

Wheerefore does my Lord wish me to remove to this House? I asked, but at this the Grinning man spoke not, but wrapped his arms together over his chest &d Ey'd me.

I then asked whether Mistress *Newbolt*, the wife of the *Judge*, was in residence at this House? &d whether the three children were present also?

At this the Man laughed the more, &d said *No, young Scrap; they live in the Judge's Great House in Dornie, by Maidenhead, which they only leave to come up to London for the Royal Season.*

I trembled some at this, not knowing why my *lord* should wish to remove me to a far distant house, with none but the Grinning Devill as guardian, if it were not to use me Ill. My mind turned againe to Self-*murther*, &d indeed it was a frequent thing for me in these days to think of ending my life. But, having been cooped-up so long in the Cellar, my Eye was soon distracted by the roads &d views to be Spyed out the coach-window.

We travell'd to *Windsor*, wheere my *Lord* the Judge had Stabling-rights, &d at an Inne we lunched upon Capons &d Beere, the Grinning Man watching me the while as if he feared

I might give him the Slip at any time. For indeed the Streetes of this town, &d the Fine Castle, looked so Fair in my eyes that it seemed to me the Celestial Citie, &d I imagined I might live happy heere, e'en if only to bed me down on the streets. But at night I was lodg'd with the Grinning man, who tho he touched me not, yet he never left off Looking at me. When I fell asleep he was watching me, &d as I awoke in the Dawn he was watching me still.

We travelled from theere alongside the river to *Maid*[enhead], &d from thence into the countryside wheere we came to a Farm of my *lord*'s, &d a House in moderate Gardens &d a wood near bye. In this house, smaller than my *lord* the Judge's Towne house, I was lodg'd in a clean white roome, although it had Barres on the window to prevent my egress. Heere I had a good straw-mattress, sheets, a pitcher of water &d a jugg, &d a bowle, &d a Bible to read. I was kept in this roome, nor allowed out for five days; &d only the Grinning Man came &d went with my foode &d to remove the pan into which I voided my selfe. I strove to improve myself in these days, &d read the Bible often, but theere were times of great Darkness of Soule too, &d I often contemplated my owne Death, drawing a satisfaction theereof that I Reason'd must reflect on my Wickedness. Truly is it said, *Life* is a Gift of *GOD Himself*, &d all who rejoyce in that gift praise *GOD* in their way. But if *His* face is turned away from ye, &d ye see but his hind-partes, then the Sheen of Life is rubb'd Away, &d Death preys upon the Minde. For the Abandoned of God, theerefore, is *Death* the colour of Soule, just as *Life* colours the Godly. By this Token, I knew that God was gone from me, &d I read in the *Book*.

On my second day, a *Parson* did come &d talk with me. He bade me think of *GOD* &d humbly beg forgiveness, &d I heart-ily wept with this man that he should so know my Wickedness. He staid but a short time, &d he read aloud a passage from the *Testament* of Paul, which I considered to lighten my mind greatly, but after he left I felt the weight more direly on my Soule, that *GOD* should so have turned His face away from me.

Now this *Parson* did visit me on divers occasion, &d at first I considered him a *Succour*, or agent of Redemption &d Deliverance; but afterwards he revealed himself in another light. &d his name, as he willingly told me, was *Wilmot*.

After a weeke of confinement I grew pale &d sickened, &d knew in my Hearte that the scab, &d the itch, had been sent of *GOD* to seeke me out in my isolation. A doctor attended me, with a silk-cherchief over his nose, &d after I was brought out of my roome during the day, &d given great meals in the Kitchen (although my appetite was feeble still), &d walked with the Grinning Man, or with Parson *Wilmot*, amongst the apple-trees of the garden. I thought that my skinn would fall off my bones with the Scab, &d Devills come up through the floor in my fever &d carry me directly to *Hell*, but this did not come to pass. I regained my strength in time, &d walked some more amongst the Blossom of the trees, so Fragrant &d Fair that I thought myself glimpsing Heaven.

The Parson first proposed to teach me *Lattin* at this time, &d would come to my roome with a great, black-bound *Vulgate* to help me construe. For a time this was broke off by the return of my *lord* the Judge, but after was recommenced; for what reason I afterwards knew.

At a later poynt this Parson did teach me a moiety of Greeke.

To busy my Hands, the Parson would give me chores about the house to be seeing too; &d only a Serving Maid of great Girth &d a sounding Wheeze was theere, excepting always the Grinning Man. It seemed that my *lord* came to this house but seldom, &d that no large retinue was necessary to keep it clean for him. Yet the Serving Girl spoke very little, &d I only knew her name was Molly from the Parson, &d she would quickly tire of any work &d sit at the side of the roome to watch me. The Grinning Man's name I did not know, but he would absent himself if the Parson be present, &d journey to the town, or wheerever. I reasoned that my *lord* the Judge had given him a most particular charge in respect of me, for he would always guarantee for himself that the windows were bolted &d the door locked before I would lie me down to sleep.

Spring gave onto Summer before my *lord* the Judge returned, &d I had almost begun to consider that he had Decided not to see me againe, &d had Pensioned me to Grow to manhood in the house. But a week before coming the Parson receipted a letter, &d brought me news of my *lord*'s being with the King in *Windsor*, &d of his plans to bring a party up to this house.

This was straightway to promote in me terrors during the night, &d Sweats with trembling, that the Parson talked of calling the Doctor againe. But the Grinning Man said *Nay, twas just a bride's trembling, as the Song of Solomon would say.* At this the Parson tittered, like a woman, tho I had thought he might be outraged. I tried to pray in the Night, first in English &d after in *Lattin* (having the foolish thought that such was *GOD*'s tongue, &d truer to prayer), but the wordes would not order themselves in my head &d I despair'd.

Then my *lord* the Judge arrived from Windsor in a great Coach &d Four, with a body of other men all finely drest in bright colour'd coates &d silk. A cart came behind with servants, &d a cook, &d dogs, &d the Wheezy Maid Molly told me that her master often came to this corner of the Land to hunt. I asked her whither he found the horses, &d she replied with a sneer that the horses were to be borrowed from Squire Thompson three fields yonder. She made to give me a box upon the ears (&d in truth she had never liked me from my first coming to the house), &d at this my *lord* the Judge came upon her &d struck her hard on the face. She wept &d wailed, &d

gather'd her skirts to flee away in shame, but my *lord* the Judge caught her by her hair &d so threw her to the ground. At this I felt no sudden glory in the vanquishing of my enemy, but rather fear at the strength of arm possess'd by my master. He seemed in a sudden rage that sweated from him quickly.

Why did she make to strike you, my lad? he asked of me.

Begging you lordship's pardon, I replied, *but I was ignorant of how your lordship proposed to go hunting, &d was asking her.*

&d wheere was the crime in this? he asked Molly, who was gathering herself from the floor. But his wrath had gone, &d she weepingly fled away.

At this I was strangely moved with fear, for it seemed to me that my *lord* might shift his mood at a moment's leave, that tho he appear kindly towards me one hour, yet might he be suddenly sparked in anger &d be cruell to me.

That night I was to wait upon my *lord* the Judge &d his Hunting friends, &d I carried wine from the kitchens to fill their glasses. They made great merry, &d sang songs by the firelight, &d when I entered every time they cheered greatly, &d on one time I was lifted up as by a Wrestler, that I spilt the wine &d was afraid lest I be punished for this slip; but they only laught the more.

In the kitchen, wheere the travelling Cooke or *Belgian Chef* as he styled himself was at work fashioning the meals, I cached myself under the table, to be away from the feet of the Grinning Man &d the Cooke &d Molly the maid. But then I would be called from the Dining Roome, &d Molly would come in breathless to scold me for hiding &d tell me to go thither.

After the meal had been supp'd, &d the brandy drunk, I was called againe. My *lord* the Judge himself greeted me &d tryed to make me drink some Brandy, something I was loathe to do on account of my strangeness to the Liquor, but I was prevailed upon to take some in my mouth.

At this they all cheered, &d made me for to drink some more, &d then sang againe &d carried me around the roome on their shoulders. I was Flushed with the drink, &d when they had finished their sport, I crawled away into the corridor, &d lay underneath a Priest's-bench by the wall in the dark. Heere it seemed that the world did spin, as I have heard Philospher's claim it do, caught in Grooves or Trackes in space that propell it around &d around. I perhaps slept a little time, &d dreamt of a great Fiend with skinn all covert in small fur like a bat, but huge wings of blacke feathers. When I awoke this dream was still large in my mind, &d I was afeared; but my *lord* the Judge was shaking me awake with his foote, &d theere was one other fellow theere with him.

Come out, Thomas my lad, saieth my *lord. Have you not a Roome of your owne, that you couch yourself on the floor of a corridor like a common beggar?*

I stumbled out, &d begged my *lord's* pardon, but he was in good humour &d chastised me not.

We are to blame, he said to his fellow, *for having turned the poor lad's wits with our Drinke. Come through to the fire, young Thomas, &d warm yourself. Some Vittles will soone restore you.*

I went with the two gentlemen into the roome wheere the fire was roaring still like a Great Winde. I sat me down &d had some cheese &d a glass of Nogg.

Heere, Thomas, said my *lord* the Judge; *permit me to introduce to you William, Lord Knox, a young man of excellent temper &d prospects.*

I bowed to the young lord, as was proper. He said: *Hola my lad! James has told me much of you, you know.*

Tush! said my *lord* the Judge. *Is he not as I described? &d Thomas, what think ye of my young lord Knox? My noble lord Knox? Is he not a tall, well-shap'd, Handsom fellow?*

At this I was uncertain how to answer, &d I began shivering

with a terror; I tried to ask to be Excus'd, but the wordes would not form, &d I chattered my Teeth instead like unto a Parrott.

Are you school'd, asked the young lord.

I can read sir, &d write sir, I told him. *&d Parson Wilmot is learning me Lattin, so please you.*

Lattin, cried my lord the Judge, who seem'd in a fine humour. *A fine undertaking! To read Ovid, my lad! Amores – that means Loves, you know.*

Come come, said the lord Knox. *Let us see the lad, as you promised.*

Ay, said my *lord* the Judge, easy as anything. *Strip, lad, &d be quick.*

Not wanting to appear insolent before too such Noblemen, &d yet not wanting to be Naked before them, I knew not what to do, &d meerly stood &d shook, looking from the face of one to the other, &d back.

He is shy, said my *lord* the Judge, with a laugh.

Damn his shyness, said my lord Knox, sudden Wrathful &d his face dark. *I'll see him strip or hang him*. At this he rose &d came towards me. Being in great terror of his furor, I made to retreat, but he caught me by a leg &d tipped me onto the floor. At this he began ripping my Shirt &d tore it from me, &d them roughly tugging my Trowsers.

Have a care with the lad, said my *lord* the Judge, coming over. *You'll put me to expense if I have to buy him new shirts.*

I'll buy the shirts, said my lord Knox tho his teeth were gritted, *&d breeches too.*

I was much afeared at my lord Knox's design, &d struggled to free myself but his strength was too great for me, &d his vigour was compounded with a terrible purpose. My Breeches were torn from me, when my *lord* the Judge intervened, &d caught my lord Knox by the shoulder, saying *injure him not, I adjure you. Wheerefore this suddenness, my lord?*

At the loosening of the grip upon my shoulder I made a leap, on a sudden, &d strugglt free. I heard but my lord Knox shout in sudden Rage, &d blindly I fled my way forward, my mind blotted out with the fear. Yet Fate guided my steps poorly, for I stumbled &d fell forward into the open Fireplace, &d my arms went out before me into the orange flames.

Of this I remamber little, save that I screamed, but with terror rather than paine. I saw the glowing log of the fireplace come up close to my eyes, such that I saw the lit scaly embers upon the wood; &d I heard the mouth of the fire roar loudly as if at the application of more fuel, &d this roar did greet my ears as [if] I were to be consumed also in the fires. But all was red &d orange &d yellow [in my] eyes, &d in my heart, &d whether this was meerly the fire or whether the Red descended over my eyes in my swoon (as I have heard said it do), I could not say. It was as a dreame, &d the arms of Flame curled round my body to embrace me, &d the fire kisst me upon the skinn of my right arm, &d on the side of my face, &d the bosoom of hot coals was soft to receive me, as I was a child againe.

It beseemed me that I dreamt, &d that in my dream I passed into the coals, which revealed themselves to be a mighty Blacke Hill. But they opened, as Arthur's Hill will sunder in the days to come, &d I was carried within riding the steed of the West Wind. &d within were treasures, &d weaponry, of sorts never seen before, &d a man with a great bald head with a dent in it &d a blacke throne, twinkling, as it were molten black oil &d solid abbomate [ebonite?] at once, wondrous. &d upon the throne the windes did bring me to alight, &d when I touched the surface it was hot as coals but did not burn my skinn, &d I was crowned with a ring of the same black substance, that was hot as blacksmith's metal but [did] not burn my temples. Theere was a glamoure in this place, &d a sensation of shadow was in my bones, wheerein was also a glow, as of starlight, all of which

I felt, or rather apprehended, in place of actively perceiveing. Theere was noyse, as of a thousand paper bells ringing, faint &d rustling as of leafes on a tree, yet penetrating. A horde of Devills flew in upon the throne-roome, &d all settled in ranks like starlings upon a wall, &d all bowed before me. I awoke with a feeling of great Joye in my heart, but I was in my bed, &d Molly was standing over me.

Molly told me that I had not been asleep but an half-an-hour, but that she had been set to watch over me, for they feared I might grow feverish.

Twas lucky that my master &d the young lord were hard by, she told me. *They pluck'd you from the fire as soon as you threw yourself in. What Devill possess'd you boy, to do such a thing?*

At this I wept, for I felt that a Devill indeed was inside me, &d my Dreame confirmed it to me.

I heerd from the footman that you had thrown yourself from a high window in London, continued Molly, as she bustled around. *It is a curious madness. In my village, such folk were treated to ducking in the river, until the madness flew out of them at the cold water.*

A poultice had been applied to my right arm, which had been burnt the most &d grievously so, &d which arm was covert theerefore in soft linen, with a mixture of herbal gruel kept close to the charred skinn. This was Saint Bartlemew [Bartholomew]'s wort, for suche was I told. My face had been a little touched by the fire, but was Blister'd rather than Burnt through to the flesh, on the right side. The burns hurt somewhat, but the Paine would advance &d recede. Sometimes it would wake me in the night, &d sometimes I would weep with the paine when my poultice was chang'd. But my *lord* the Judge was loathe to summon the doctor, for fear perhaps of needing to explain how I came to fall Naked into the fireplace. Molly, I have no doubt, was wise to the ways of her master, as was the Grinning man. In my maim'd state my heart turned over, &d I began to repent me of my Dreame, bethinking it preluded nought but my Damnation in Hell. That God had hurl'd me into the fire to punnish my Wickedness was most probable to me, &d my Dreame did confirm this suspicion most palpably. In my Soule's darke Night I felt myself abandoned utterly, in a House wheere none cared for me, with even God's face turned away from me. Never before or since had such Violence of Despair seiz'd me.

In the morn my *lord* the Judge visited me, &d put on a shew of seeming concern for my health. He examined the skinn of my arm, Molly removing the Poultice to this end.

My boy, my boy, he said. *How are you, my lad?*

I thought I saw his Ey moisting, as if he would Weepe, &d this frightened me greatly.

I am well, my lord, I said, yet I was shrinking in the bed, &d Molly was attempting to unfasten the Poultice about my Head, that my *lord* the Judge might view my burnt eye.

Leave that, Molly, said my lord, with the Displeasure entering his voice, *can ye not see it uncomforts the boy.* Molly began to excuse herself, but my Lord grew only more fierce with her &d bad her *begonne, Molly, I would be alone with the lad.*

Molly tried to stand, so as to Courtsey for my lord before withdrawing, but her Elbow caught the jugg of water with which she had been a-washing me. The water spilt all across the floor &d some spattered onto my bedcloathes. At this my *lord* did shout with vexation, &d rail at Molly as she hurried out &d returned with a pail &d a mop to wipe the water away. I felt close to weeping at all this Activity, but my *lord* the Judge soon usheered her out of the roome &d return'd to my bedside, to seat himself at a Chaire beside me.

My lord Knox has ridden out this morning, he told me. *He has taken the hounds &d will hunt all day, methinks. You must not blame him, my lad, his temper is hot, you know.*

I knew not what to say to this, so I held my peace.

What think ye of my lord Knox? Is he not a fine gentleman.
To this I only said *He is a gentleman my lord.*

My *lord* the Judge squeez'd my Hand at this, &d smil'd, &d said *he is indeed a man of good parts, &d very clear sense. His Conversation is brisk, my lad, &d ingenious, would you but converse with him. He is a man of such Boldness, such Enterprize!*

I am very sorry to have lept into the Fire, I now told my lord, the tears starting in my Lamentation. *I ought not to have done it, but that I was put into such fear by the action of my lord Knox, when he gripped me, &d went to remove my Cloathes.*

I know my lad, he said, in reply. *But ye should not be afeared of what Knox was about.*

At this I burst forth, *I am indeed afeared my lord, for I am fillt with terror at the Usages he would put me to.*

Blood! cried my lord at this, *what Pelican have we heere! How he turns his beak in at my breast!* At this he paced the roome about for a space of minutes, before repairing to my bed &d seating himself againe. *Lad, you speake in haste, in a poor Humour. Your injury has impair'd you, perchance, filled you with Ill thoughts. My lord Knox meant you no harm, my boy.*

Being frighted by my lord's behaviour, I concurred heere, &d readily.

Did none ever speake to you of the Greekes? asked my lord of me, &d it seem'd Relenting some towards me.

None, your honour, I answered. *For I was but ill school'd, tho Parson Wilmot is teaching me Lattin, so please you.*

Ay, very good, Lattin is very good, he said. *But better were the Grecians. Founders of all our Sciences, of all Philosophy. Masters of all Arts, of the Tragical but also the Comical. My lord Knox has some fine discourses on the Grecians, I wish ye could hear them.*

Twas the Grecians fought the Troians, I said then, wishing perchance to display what poore Learning I possess'd.

You're right boye, you're right. At this, he spoke to me in a

Tongue I presumed Grecian, tho I knew not a one of the wordes. *I wish ye could hear my lord Knox speake of the Greekes, my lad*, he said againe, Musingly. *Twas the Foundry-place of Civilisation, indeed it was. Athens, theere was a true Commonweal, my lad. All the Men together tooke a Responsibility for Soldiering, &d Marine Endeavour too. The Athens-men formed a mightie Empire, my chuck. Perchance we may one day do like.*

Shortly after this my *lord* did leave, &d Molly was sent back to me to affix my Poultice anew, in no good humour she. She scowled at me, &d Yank'd &d Pull'd the Poultice Cloth about to such degree that my burns wept, &d I cried likewise. *Would that you had fall'n in the Fire &d burnt to a cinder*, she Hisst to me. *&d if ye tell the master I said so, I'll creep heere in the night &d sort you, Saints &d Angels help me.*

I could not forebear weeping at this unkindness, but she only boxed my ears, &d said *cry on, little mewler. Dost think we are blind, tho we live below stairs – wheere* you *should be.*

I know nothing of what you say, mistress, I said.

O no, she said, *&d a fish has no scales neither. Dost ye think I am too much a Country Maide not to know what you were doing in the Hall, with two gentlemen, &d you Naked as the day your Mother bore you?*

Truly, Mistress, I wept (for she was twisting the Hair above my ears most painfully), *I am an innocent.*

If ye tell the master what I say, she said, bringing her Face very close to mine, *I'll punish you. Yet even if you give me away, theere's another you cannot give away, another who will Punish you when I am gone. You should ask the Parson to read you the Chapters of Genesis wheerein the dreadful Fate of the Cities on the Plaines is laid down, as the word of God.*

At this she desisted; &d, to be sure, she seem'd tired with her Exertions, &d she Lost her Winde easily upon any task or Chore. Her quoting of the book of the *Holy Bible* filled me with hope that she might succour me in my distress, &d help me hence from that house (for I was much worried with the thought of what my lord Knox would doe on returning from his Hunt. &d, indeed, what would become of me at the Hands of my *lord* the Judge).

Mistress, I said. *I beg you mercy. I am a prisoner heere, &d if only you could help me—*

But she cut me short with another box on my ears. *Help you!* she said. *To touch you is Pestilence. My lord had another such as you, last year it was. He was a young soldier lad, no older than yourself, &d my lord kept him heere in fine array, I might tell you, forever eating &d drinking, &d never having to Work a moment. But his Regiment mov'd from Maidstone, &d he moved with it, to my lord's unhappiness.* &d heere she leant closer to me. *&d more unhappiness, too; for a Person told the Camp Serjeant of what manner of man this young Recruit was, &d I heerd after that he was Hung like a Dog, for his sins.*

This speeche gave me great trembling, &d I could not even bring forth Teares, so profound was the Terror it put me to. &d before leaving, Molly leant over me &d spoke *you are a sinner in the Hands of an Angry God. Your foot shall slide in due time!*

This left a great Impression on me, &d I lay in a sort of Catalepsy, or State of Terror, whence I could not do so little a thing as lift my arm. By-&d-by the Sense &d Vitality returned to my Limbs, but I now lay in little doubt that I would remaine but a short time, until my *lord* shoud weary of me, &d send me away, or until some other Circumstance forc'd my departure. &d that then, upon departing, I would be Arraigned &d Hanged for my Unnatural experiences; or put to public Pillory wheere the Violence of the Mob might kill me. I saw no Salvation from this situation, for look wheere I might I saw always the Great Obstacle of Molly, who would give me away, &d make certain of my downfall.

It was in this State of mind that I languished for a night &d a day, until at the Eve of the following day Parson Wilmot visited me againe. I was somewhat lightened in Spirit at his approach, for I consider'd him to be a Friend to me; for her had never lifted his Hand againest me, nor us'd me with any Unkindeness.

When he came in, he carried a great Booke, bound in Calfeskinn &d with a strange odour. This he put upon the bed, such that it lay upon my feet &d presst them into the mattress.

Are ye well, my lad? he asked, but I, being greatly oppress'd with humours, was unable to withstrain my Tears, &d I cried in answer to his question.

Come come my boye, said he. *Why crying? Are ye badly us'd?*

I gave my assent to this, &d cry'd some more: but Parson *Wilmot* being in so merry a humour, I was unable to maintain my lamentation long, &d soon I was jollied somewhat. *That is better*, he said, after jesting with me for some time. *Put a smile on thy face, &d the World cannot harm thee so greatly.*

&d shortly I came to ask him of his Booke, for I had never seen him carry a Booke about with him so large – nor any booke, save only the Bible.

I have brought this book expressly to shew it to you, my lad, in the hope that it may lighten your suffering in some degree – perchance your Deliverance from the evil fortune you find yourself in.

Being naturally pleas'd at such a Prospect, I bade the Parson to tell me more, as to how this Deliverance might be affected.

Sure we cannot do it alone, said he, shaking his head. *We will needs recruit help.*

I eagerly asked whence help might derive, but he said:

Not of this world, my boy, not of this temporal world. For the lord the judge Newbolt is a powerful man in this realm. He has friends at Court. He has friends in the Chambers of Lawe, &d he has taken Coffee with the King. Dare we Cross him? Nay.

At this I was much disheartened, for it seem'd to me that my position was Hopeless, &d my Fate controul'd by a Force too powerful to me. But at my long faice, the Parson laught.

Do not give up your Hope, my boy, he said. *Theere are other nations we can impress for our aid.*

Which other nations? said I. *Are they mapp'd in your Booke?*

They are, he said. *For our help we may call upon that Race of fortunate Beings who are made to Intercess in our Affaires, the Paracleetes, or Genii, or Demons.*

I had not thought I had heerd the Parson correctly, but upon his repeating the worde, I trembled for fear of Heavenly Retribution, for him to so Brazenly call out such a name. But he rebuk'd me.

Boh, my boy, he said. *Theere is nothing to feare from saying such a worde; the Heavens do not fall &d crush a murderer when he kills, or a traitor as he betrays, or a robber robbing, so why should they come down upon our heads for only speaking of Truthful things?*

But, I said timorous, for I wanted not to instruct the Parson in his own work, &d I but a boy, *do you not fear the Wrath of GOD?*

He smil'd againe, &d touched my arm lightly, &d said *Is this the waye of God in this world? No, no. He punnishes the virtous, &d rewards the Wicked. &d why is this?*

I know not, I said.

Ye will read the New Testament, the Testament of Christ more closely, he said, laughingly. *Do you not heed how Lucifer is named in that Great Book? How Lucifer's dominion is measur'd out in the Scheme of Things? Isaiah calls him the Son of the Morning, &d dominion has been given to him of all the Lands upon which the morning Sunne shines. For St Paul instructs us, in his Epistle unto the Ephesians, to walk according to the course of this World, &d according to the Prince of the power of the air. In His Second to Corinthians, this same Paulus nameth Him as the Angel of Light, &d delineates Him as The God of this World. It is clear, theerefore, that Dominion has been given unto Lucifer to rule this portion of* the Universe, such that stretches underneath the Air (of which he is Prince), &d upon which the Morning Sunne doth shine. It is He ye must call on for succour if the beings of this world are tyrants over you. It is He you must worship, as the Bible commands.

I thought carefully of this Speech, &d I read the passages from the *New Testament* to which the learned Parson appealed, &d they seem'd to support his wordes. But I quailed still at the thought of Summonning so Dire &d Deadly a Being as a *Demon* into my presence.

If we were you call forth such a Beast as a Demon from the Great Depths, would he not Devour &d Destroy us?

You mistake the Nature of the Creature, he replied. *For Demon is but the Greek worde for Genius, or Intercessor: &d these creatures are a sort of Mediate Being, between human &d divine, which gives the mind of Man a pleasant conjunction with the Angelic &d Celestial faculties, &d brings down to earth a faint participation of the Joyes of Heaven. That theere have been such fortunate Attendants upon wise men, we have many rare Instances. They have been ascrib'd to Socrates, Aristotle, Plotinus, Porphyrius, Iamblicus, Chicus, Scaliger, &d Cardan. The most celebrated of all these Antients was Socrates; &d as for his having a genius, or demon, we have the testimonies of Plato, Xenophon, &d Antisthenes, his contemporaries, confirmed by Laertius, Plutarch, Maximus Tyrius, Dion Chrysostomus, Cicero, Apuleius, Ficinus, &d many others; many of the moderns, besides Tertullian, Origen, Clemens Alexandrinus, Austin &d others; &d Socrates himself, in Plato's Theage, says: 'By some divine lot I have a certain demon which has followed me from my childhood as an oracle;' &d in the same place intimates that the way he gained his instruction was by hearing the demon's voice.*

At this I was much puzzled, but the Parson was Patient &d did spend great paines in elucidating me.

Dost know what the name, Lucifer, signifies, my lad?

I do not, I told him.

It signifieth 'Light', or the 'Being of Light', or 'the Essence of Light'. Now, my lad, since I am Charg'd (you said so) with the Promulgation of the Holy Bible, I shall quote to you from that Mightie Book. Dost know the first wordes of the Booke of Father Genesis?

I said I did: *In the beginning, God created the heaven &d the Earth.*

Aie lad, said the Parson. *&d the earth was without form, &d void; &d darkness was upon the face of the deep. &d the Spirit of God moved upon the face of the waters.*

&d God said, Let theere be Light: &d theere was Light.

The Parson did quote these wordes from the Bible at my bedside, &d after did discourse upon the wordes.

For, said he, *when they translated 'Let theere be Light', they might with equality have rendered, 'Let theere be Lucifer.' For it is Certaine that God's first action was to create the Prince of Light, or Lucifer, or Satan as some have it. &d it is just as Certaine that without this Act of Creating, God was Nothing. Do you note how it says that the Spirit, onlie, of God moved on the face of the waters? By that is signified that without the Creation of Lucifer, God was without Body, &d was a meer Spirit. When a Baby is borne to this world, at once is united Spirit &d Body, so in the first of Creation, God's Spirit &d Lucifer's Body were joined together.*

Tho God created Lucifer, which is to say, God was before Lucifer, or Anterior as we say. Yet it is just as Plaine from this that God is a creature of Darkness, composed of Darkness &d Co-Existant with the Darkness. &d, by the same Token or Coine, it is clear that Lucifer from His first was a Being of Light, created into Light &d dwelling forever in Light.

But, said I, for I was much mov'd by this discourse, *does the Bible not name Satan as the Creature of Darkness?*

By this phrase, replied the Parson, *is signified meerly that Lucifer is the Creature that proceeded out of Darkness, that was created out of Darkness; which Darkness we call God, or Jehovah (which worde, in Hebraic, signifies 'the Obscured' or 'the Dark One'). Yet tho Jehovah is Anterior to Lucifer, yet the Son was Greater, as the Newest Testament demonstrates.*

Mean you, I asked, for this last was News indede to me, *that Jesus, the Son of God, is the same Being as Lucifer.*

The Parson smil'd carelessly &d smooth'd the hair on my head. *You ask for the Truth of the Bible, &d I give it. Jesus is a creature of Light, begat from the Jehovah or Darkness, who spoke the Gospel of Lucifer. Did he not say, 'I come not to build up, but to tear down'? Did he not committ the Sin of Wrath when he Cast out the Moneylenders? Did he not display Lust when he consorted with Prostitutes? Selfishness when he abrogated money meant for the Poor &d insisted it be Spent on Himself? When he rose from the Dead, did he not Tour the Countryside as a Ghoul or Walking-Cadaver, like unto a creature of Witchcraft? Did he not command his followers to Eat human flesh, &d Drink human bloode? But these are not sinnes, although the Priests of Jehovah would punnish them as such. For theere is no Sinne in the natural passions, &d in the conjouration of spirits. But only, the oppressing of the spirit is sinful, &d the tyranny of the Father over the Son.*

That night I slept but Fitfully, &d saw curious visions of Spirits shap'd of Light out of Darkness, &d Red &d Dark-Blue, and chief mong them the man with the great baldhead, and upon the curve of that baldness a great dent or valley or declivity. In the morn, Molly attended on me further, &d my *lord* the Judge came once againe &d peer'd under my Poultice at the Skinn mending. I had some Jitters, lest he should somehow divine what manner of conversation had pass'd between myself &d the Parson, &d denounce me for a Heeretic or Trafficker with Evil. But he was onlie Mild, &d petted me a little (which discomforted me), tho Molly was in the roome. He said my arm would be heal'd soon, tho I could see that the skinn was sadly Shrivell'd &d Puckered, &d the use of the limb would not return fully. My face was likewise scarr'd (for tho I was shewn not a Glass, yet I could trace the Ridges with my good Finger, &d it made a Lamentable Cartography).

This day gave on the next, &d another after that, but the Parson did not revisit me. On the third day my *lord* the Judge did return, &d in his company was the lord *Knox*. His young lordship seemed at ease, &d languishing somewhat, but he was not Pleas'd to see the effect of the Fire upon me.

You shall find no Cosmetician to Powder that away, he said to me, as if in jest.

Your looks are sadly spoilt, concurred my *lord* the Judge. *But the cover of a Book need not presage its contents.*

Its contents are nought but Foolish, so says his mad leap into the flames, said the lord Knox, with an Expresion of great Distaste. So did he exit the room, &d my *lord* the Judge followed him.

After a week my arm had heal'd sufficient for me to work at Tasks about the House, although my lord Knox had departed to London, &d my *lord* the Judge had gone with him. During this time I worked as best I could, common serving work suchane scrubbing the fireplace ironwork &d porting firewood, stick by stick. After this week, however, my lord return'd in ill humour, &d went to his roome &d ate not at all. To this roome he summon'd me, &d us'd me ill, between my thighes. This occasion injur'd me greatly in my minde, for it had been so long since I had been so us'd; &d my skinn was still tender, tho my lord shew'd no compassion for it. I wept much after this time, &d my lord was in no wise pleas'd by what he had done.

After this time, my lord came to my bed on one occasion, but did nothing more than weep upon my chest &d sleep for a time.

It was soon Summer, &d the birds cried in the air beyond my window. It seem'd that my *Lord* the Judge had been absent for so long a time that I almost forgot me the look of his face, but in *June* he returned to the House &d staid several weeks. Theere was a Change about his manner, &d he was no longer pleased to see me, but marked my presence with signs of displeasure. Such prevalency had wrath in his soule that he struck at all the servants, &d myself also. He came to my roome on three occasions, &d us'd me ill, but it was brief &d he was briefly gone. Hee said not why he was in sutch displeasure with me, save only (I guess it) my disfacement by the fire. At length he summon'd me &d I went to him. He was reading some Papers from off a great table, &d Parson *Wilmot* attended him.

Boy, he said at length, *I can no longer maintain you at your leisure &d at my Charity. God did not put us heere to lie down &d slepe, but to work.*

I said, humblie I hope, that I had always thought so.

Well, well, he said. *To work then. I must find you a place on a farm, if ye are hale enough to do farm work. I've a farm in Devon-shire wheere ye might tend the cowes.*

The thought of this fate as my wished-for escape was strong in my mind at this news, although I vexed myself by weeping at the news, why I know not.

Tis no good mewling like a babe, said my *lord* the Judge, harshly, &d howlding up his hand, as if in remembrance of the times he had struck me. *Needs must, my boy, needs must. &d I cannot find a place for you heere.*

Yet that night my *lord* the Judge visited me againe, &d this time creepingly, coming into my roome when I slept &d waking me with kisses &d afterward Clasp'd me as if he would grapple with me. Then he wept againe, &d begg'd Pardon for my face, &d promis'd he would never let me depart. *I am to blame,* he said, &d then began railing against himself, &d beating himself with his fists that I became most alarmed at his violence. After, when he had gone &d I trembled alone.

*

The Parson afterwards said to me and discoursed as to my Lord's changeable moods. *Nor can I explaine it, excepting that my lord the Judge has a mutable soule, now cheereful now everything melancholic &d black-bile. Yet have I seen him with boyes who would dance at his behest &d him unmov'd, &d heere is this boye without birth or manner, without even Fair Face since yor fall in the fire, &d most of all, Rare!, who flinches from him who could do you so much good, &d actes coy. This is the one who captures his heart. So, so. But it matters not. My work goes well. I'll confess to you, my boy, as if ye were a Romish confessitor, that I befeared me you had ruined all by hurling yourselfe into the fire. But mayhap this has fastened you closer in his affections. He'll pay me a thousand Crownes, if you direct him aright!*

At this I reasoned that this Parson was concerned to extract monies from my lord, &d hoped to use me to that end.

He went away at this time, &d later returned, telling me that the time was propitious for to meete his masters.

I was curiously affraighted at this News, for partly I was properly alarmed that this meant coming to a Black Masse or suchlike, abomination that the Lord GOD would strike with thunder &d wrath, a *scandalum infiniti* – yet was I also intrigued, with the curiouseness of a sapient mind, to discover whom these masters were.

The Parson did not take me away to these Beings this day, nor yet the next; neither did my lord the Judge visit me againe, save only to stoppe in a door-arch &d gaze at me as I swept a fireplace one morning, &d he sighed &d Rubbed his beard with great force as if caught up in some turmoil of the soule. My Hearte did rattle in my breast like a coach-wheel over cobbles, for I beleaved he would come into the roome &d use me as was his habit, but insteade he turned &d went away, tho slowly.

That night I lay me down &d slept as ever I had, but the Parson came sleekit into my roome &d woke me with a Hand upon my face. *Come now, boy*, he said. *The Moone is at full, &d*

this badge pleaseth my masters. By this lamp we shall make our way, &d feare no bandit, for rather they should feare us.

I pulled my breeches on &d shoes in a fumble, & I did not bethink me to gainsay this command, for I was not altogether awake. But stepping down the stairway, &d through the door into the Night woke me somewhat. Though the air was mild, yet the freshness touched my skinne &d I ope'd my eyes. Heere was my lord's herb garden, all closed about by a wall; &d thro' the ebon door at the far side heere was my lord's lawn, on which he would sometimes play at quoyits. The grass beseemed black to my eyes, tho the Moone was sharply bright &d silver, glowing enough to throw long shadows. The Parson, who led my steps, seemed more giddie than ever before I had seen him, &d he fair pranced down the slopeing lawn towards that place wheere the River bounded my lord's estate.

What hour is it? he asked me.

I replyed that I knew not the time.

But I do, my lad, he said. *It is past midnight, when the lampe burns blue &d the sky drapes itself in Royal Purple. Then 'tis the hour that the great Monarch of the upper world enters into his closet. Do ye know his name?*

You are pleased to sporte with me sir, I said.

I may believe my masters shall be well pleased with me, he said. *Well pleased with what I bring them. An August month for an august proceeding.* &d heere he tweaked my cheek, as a man chucks a babies face, which I liked not.

We came betimes to the waters edge, &d heere we rested. The Parson tooke from his cloake a flint, or ovall of ivory, &d peered at it. *My boy*, he said, *you must prepare yourself. You are not to crie out in horror, for that might displease my masters.*

Are the formes of deviltry so terrible? I asked.

Deviltry? said the Parson. *Why Thomas, who said t'would be* devils that attend our meeting? *Sainte Peter himselfe! Saint Peter himselfe.*

I kept my owne counsel at this.

We waited for a further halfe of an houre, or perhaps more. I could not resist the yawning that overcame me, &d notwithstanding the curiousenesse I felt to discover what blacke masse the Parson was attendant upon I craved to sleepe againe. But the Parson did pinch me &d keep me from nodding.

Theere was silence for a long while, &d then the Parson did break it with a long speeche. *That doctrine is well-knowne*, he said, *wheereby the four elements of this worlde are peopled with creatures of a Forme &d species less corporeal than vulgar mortals. The wize Theophrast Paracelsus hath delineated this in his workes of philosophie. Those from the fierie regions do we calle* Scalamanders, *who beget kinges &d heroes with spirits that resemble their deietical sires; those from water we call* Nymphs, *&d such lovely inhabitants as dwell in that element. Those of the earth, earthie, are called* Gnomes *or* Fairies *or some times* Elfs. *Those of the air are* Sylphes, *&d it is these Sylphes that shall attend our revels this faire night.*

&d howe, I asked, *do these Sylphes appeare themselves before us?*

As beings like to themselves, he replied, &d againe he peered close at his flintstone, or whate'er he held, for I sawe not.

Do ye see the moon, master Thomas? he asked me, shortly. &d in truth I could not miss seeing it, for it seemed larger than ever before I had seen it, glassie &d white &d shyning with a tide of light.

I do, said I.

Diana herself, the ancients thought, said the Parson, looking up. *But do ye see the mountains &d lakes in her Globe? Such pocks upon the goddess her face as a courtesan might fear from her* mal d'amour. *Have you ne'er considered what creatures may live in that place?*

I had not til that moment bethought me of this question, &d said so to the Parson.

Yet I assure you that the Moone *is a worlde, &d that it is inhab-ited. But this carries in its traine certaine questions of great import. For think ye: these Beings in this globe, created as the Divines tell us by* GOD *Almighty. &d aske yourself, how are they saved? Are they redeemed in the bloode of Christ, as are we? But how can that be, if Christ died in our world &d not theirs – &d if Christ took the forme of a man of our world, &d not a being of theirs? So are they redeemed in the bloode of their owne Saviour, who took the forme of their being, &d was cruxified upon a device fitted to their frame? But then theere were two Christs, not one, tho the Bible promised us our unique &d special favour in God taking man's corpus. &d if two, why not three, or ten, or ten thousand? Or are theere as many Christs as theere be graynes of sand upon a beach? If so, then why do we worshipp the Christ instructed us by the Church that hath taken his name? For He is in no wise special. Perhap we should chuse another.*

At this moment I felt a great turning-over in my bowells, as of fear, tho theere was naught to Hand at which I might be affrighted, save onlie the Parson who was no different to his selfe as always was. But I trembl'd with this feare, &d turned me around, &d about againe, expecting to see a Spectre or Ghoust approach.

Sir, I cried, *I like not this place.*

It is a charming spott, he said, speaking tightly, yet perchance in jest.

I beg you sir, I cryed, falling upon my knees in the wette grass, *if you can by any meanes prevail upon your Conscience to release me heere, I beseech you so to do, not scrupling anything for feare I should report to any person of what has passed, for I shall not, but onlie to have mercie upon my distress.*

Fie, Master Tickletumble, he said, mockingly, *do ye quail? Are you a man or a babe at suck?*

Tho he spoke lightly &d in jeste, yet his Wordes might have been cries of great wrath for the effect they had upon me. I quail'd further, &d I beleeve I whimpered like a whipt dog. O I tryed to speake, but no wordes came beyond a stammer of *Pa-pa-pa*. I was on the grass, &d tiny &d fearful. Then they came &d fill'd me &d I stood up. Yea, I stood up as a flame stands from the summit of a candle, &d life was in me. My former pusillanimity &d timidity sloughed from me, &d I stood tall &d strong.

The Parson, seeing this change in me, shewed a change in his Countenance also. In the clasp of his great excitement he danced before me. *Are they in ye now, my lad?* He cried. *&d how do ye? Do they communicate?*

But I was far beyond him now. I took him &d placed the padde of my Thumb &d Forefinger upon the skinne of his throat, such that he gasped &d gasped as a fishe without water. But I cockt my eare, as a hound does, to attend to the wordes of such Sylphis as were now speaking to me, or better to saye not speaking, for theere were neither speeche nor wordes in their discourse, but in some wize to reache me with sapience &d thought. Theirs were not Wordes, I saye againe: or (for it is precious harde to catch the truth of it in my saying) perhap their Wordes were Wordes of *Aire*, which is their element, &d the grosser matter of my ear was poorly tuned to it. Yet could I hear them, &d they were drawne to me, as the Parson had said.

&d. Peter spake

&d. he had searchd for me, over great times, as seventeen years, and two hundred and eighty-nine years, and more.

&d my sight &d hearing was wondrous increas'd, such that I felt the coming of divers gentlemen who in converse with one &d another reveal'd themselves to be colleagues of the Parson, come to revel in the Black Masse. Tho they were yet on the far side of the river I reach'd out for them anyway &d stay'd their path. These gentlemen, who were unknown to me quite, yet they lay down up'n their backs &d cried in fearful paine, for I had seiz'd their Ribbes &d their Spines &d rolled them twixt my fingers like pastry.

I shall have more to say of these gentlemen anon; for they were men in *conspiratus* with the Parson, &d soon I was finisht with them.

At this time in my Account it behooves me to relate such things as passed in Common Exchange between myselfe &d these Sylphis, seeing as howe I am now arointed as Warlock, set to be hanged, &d meerly on account of my traffic with these Beings. But such, tho I shifte me to recall them all, &d tho I am resign'd to lay it all down, yet the taske is not so simpl as all that. For *item primus*, the appearance of these Beings was mutable &d strange, sometimes coming into my Minde as *Devils*, Black *Bats*, scal'd serpents &d Insectes of prodigious proportion, such as might be expected of the brood of *Sathanas*. But for *item secundus*, they would sometimes occur to me as strands of light all woven into a [k]not &d streaming radiance upon me, with strips of *Luminance* like limbs, as might be Legs, Arms, a Head &d such, &d from these beings would come great Comfort &d a great sense of wellbeing &d Hopefulness. &d nor is it true to say that these two manners of Manifestation were follow'd one on another, but *Concurrent*, in somewise I know not. The greatest length of our discourse together was concern'd with the Sylphis their anxietie about *Time*, by which worde they, it seem'd, meant divers matters, id. the time mark'd by *Clock*; the time marked by *Sundiall*; the time mark'd by *Heartbeat* &d by some obscure process of the Nerve or Brain of which, in truth, I wot not; &d in most particular Uncertaintie of theirs, the time mark'd by a *Child*, such as waits with agony for the Schoolmaster's Lesson to end that they might runne out &d play with their fellows, as is compared with the time of the *Olde Man*, for whom Days fleet bye, as minutes might to a youngster, &d the years folde into one-the-other, &d time blurs like the wingbeat of a Kingfisher. For this matter perplexd the *Sylphis* very greatly, for why I know not in sooth, yet they tryed to plumb by thoughts on this matter in such wise as they were able.

Of divers other Matters, concerning the country of their origin (a Monstrous Spacious place), their hope in being *Heere*, their reasons for selecting me as their medium, &d the question which vexd the Parson so, as to whether they touched Redemption through CHRIST or through someother force, or whether Redemption was utterly deny'd them: these things I once knew, but with the passage of time (now amounting to almost a full Yeare) I find them more cloudy in my remembrance than hitherto. Yet I recall that once I knew of them, &d this thought comforteth me.

As the dawne turn'd the eastern sky from a broad shene of black to rose skinne of such pinkness as a young girl's cheekes, so I found myself alone, for the *Sylphis* had departed. I was lying beside the river, amongst the dewy grass. Yet was I still strong, &d remaine so to this day: the mewling infans that had once been Me was now banish'd &d gone away. I felt a potentcy in my limbs &d muscles now. Sainct Peter may deliver us from death, ye as me. I looked about me &d breathed the river aire as if for the first time. Theere, on the grass, was the Parson, who had fall'n into a Swoon; &d tho I lifted him &d lent him againest a Tree, yet was he obnoxious to rescuscitation, for his throat was sorely blackn'd &d bruis'd. Theere was still breath in his lungs, &d so I left him.

My chief concern then became the Parson's fellowe conspirators, that had been on the farside of the river, for they had come bye in the dark houres of the night &d I had reach'd them with some reaching-forth of myself, an *Ec-stateis*, &d perchance harm'd them sorely. But my mind lack'd the reache of the night, &d tho I liked it not I took to the river, wading, cold as ice and cold as death, and flynching I walkd &d then swimming to the far side. Heere, after half &d houre of searching, I found the pair of them lying in the long grass as if sleeping. Yet it was the sleepe fro which no Man wakes, &d their bodies were quaintly slack beneath their cloathes, as if theere had been some crushing of their bones within their boddies, as the *Giant* boasteth he will do in the Tale told to Children of *Jack* &d the *Beanstalke*. At this discovery I was incommoded, for they seem'd fair gentlemen, well-dressed in velvet jackets &d molescin breeches &d with their hair longe &d oiled with sweetsmelling oils. Yet theere was no helping them, &d I loathe to splash twise in the River (which, to be truthful, was a-shocking cold, tho it was almost Summer) trailed my way along the bank to the bridge, some mile away. Indeed, howe the gentlemen had plann'd in crossing the River to our side I do know not, unless they hop'd the Sylphis would carry them thro' the aire, for they had no Boat. But perhaps they had had no intent to cross the river that night. I know not.

Coming back along the road to my lord the Judge Newbolt his house, it was well advanc'd morning as I arrived. The sunne had warmed me &d I was drie as any sech upon arrival. &d I found that I had been barely miss'd, tho the doorman was surpriz'd to see me knocking at the outer door so early in the day. *Have you been out my lad?* he asked.

Verily as far out as Saint Peter himself, I replied to him.

As I broke my fast solitary in the kitchen upon a Heele of Bread &d some cheese &d tripe, so a commotion was gotten up in the house at large, for the Parson had been discovered by a *Boy* going to the river to fish for my lord the Judge's breakfast, &d theereafter he was carried in to the House upon a board, breathing heavie like a bottomsawyer cutting woode, yet stille senseless &d nerveless to command, his eyes lolling shut &d his limbes fluid. A *Clamor* ran through the servants quarters that footpads had strucke him in the night, &d the Judge's two strongest laddes went running to the Lands with staffs to sniffe them out, or so they said. But this meerely increased the Panic, for they swiftwise chanced upon the boddies of the two further men whose bones were all porriged. These corses were left where they laye, across the river, &d one ran off to fetch the Justice of the Peace from Maidenhead, whilst another gatheered all the servants together to tell the tale, with much round-eying &d hulla-bulla-ing. The maids shrieked &d threw their *Aprons* over their heads, &d the chiefe gardener, who was a man scored with age &d weather'd like a log, call'd aloud that the End Times were heere, for he had seen nothing so foule in all his days. None thought of me, for my reputation was of a mewling sprat, &d in this disguise I was free of suspicion. So the constable came, &d the Justice too, &d anon they fetched a surgeon to examine the boddies (the two having been brought at last to the cold store), &d to examine the Parson too. But nothing could this surgeon determine, &d the buzz-buzz in the House did not diminish until after sunset, &d sleepe.

To my roome in the darke, I considered the Matter of *Justice* against *Revenge*, this latter being of the LORD's alone, &d not for mortals to arrogate to themselves, the former being the duty of all men. Yet had I not been ill-used? Tho when I put this point, or thought so to do, to the Sylphis, they answer'd not to the purpose, perhap mistaking my question: &d replying that twas not a matter of faulte, but that some twist in the braine was the cause of the effecte that Time was improperly parcell'd out, with divers grievous consequences for all human kinde; or els that the approach to the truth of all things caused ripples or tourbillons in time itself, such as set moments at three decades, and eighty-seven years, and fifty plus eighty-seven, and so on. This answered not my question, *viz.*, should I revel in my newfound-strength &d punnish those who had evilly us'd me, or do not so? Nor could I rightly understand their point; altho truly they were greatly fascinated with the arid business of clockwork time &d other sorts.

In my roome that darke I did essay my new *Skille*, &d thought to reach out &d squash certaine buggs &d insects that troubled the chamber, yet could I manage no purchase upon them, for it was as if I try'd to pluck up pecks of *Duste* with the ball of my *Foote*, I could not. Then I tried again, with two pigeon that mew'd &d burbl'd in an *Oake* outside the window, yet though I could apprehend their Being, as were I to smoothe a bolt of silk with my palme &d come upon a pea beneath, but I could not grasp upon this. As a final essay I reached through the door of my roome, for foorsteps alerted me, &d I fell at once upon a living human corpus around which my fingers, as it were, fell at once, &d in the joy of so easily recovering this skill I almost squeez'd the air from the soggie *Bellows* within the barrel-hoops of his chest, yet did I withhold myself, for I sens'd that this was my lorde the Judge.

He gasping, did pause without the doore for some minutes, before coming through &d looked fluster'd, declaring that *he had felt a curious turne upon the stair, as though some ruffian did clasp my chest &d would have done me away, as those poore men were murthered.*

Yet you are well, my lord? I asked.

Strange times, my boy, he said, &d brought his candle to my bedside, &d sat himself upon it. *A strange day, &d the Parson still a catalept – Jane declares that a spell has been placed upon him, &d that witchcraft is about the house.*

He wept to say this, and hid his face in his hands.

I did gaze upon my mast.r, James Newbolt, &d tho I had often seen him cruell or indifferent, &d sometime seen him tender toward me or remorsefull, yet had I never seen him so tired &d afeared. My minde still revolving in this question of the fitness of Revenge, I was surprized in myself to see this figure, formerly one of such tyranny in my life, now reduc'd so far. Yea even his frame seem'd shrunken, as if suddenly aged, &d I felt the kindling of pitie. He spoke to me in a low voyce for a time, not meeting my eyes, &d then he reach'd out &d lay his Hande upon my chest, wheere I satt in the bed. At this gesture my anger again ripen'd, &d the memory of many ill-usages crowded my thoughts, such that had he attempted to use me, as he had formerly, in that time I daresay I would have injur'd &d perhap kill'd him outright. But he did not, &d his Hand upon my breast was tender, &d then he withdrew it &d look'd into my eyes as a Father might a lov'd sonne, &d did say My Boy I have a thing for you. &d reach'd in his purse &d drew out a solid gold penny, such as he had given me once before.

This was not expected, my lorde, I said as I tooke it. Yet was I gladly mov'd to see it againe.

He said nothing for a while, yet gazed at the flame of the candle, which moved slow upon its wick like a butterflie of *Light* tucking up its wings, &d putt me in mind, in some small manner, of the Sylphis themselves.

I know that Mistr.s Anne *tooke this penny from you*, he said, *&d I am sorry for it. At that time I tooke it fro her &d did mean to returne it, yet something stayed my Hand.*

It matters not, I said, *for it is but a penny.*

At this he look'd at me againe, as if he mark'd the change in my manner, from feebleness to strength. Yet habit was stronger in him, &d he look'd away again. *The worth of a thing may not to be determined by how it is labell'd*, he said. *And is gold itself by valued by custom, as is the custom that declares one pennie to buy one small loaf? O! O! I confess to you, my boy, that for a while I held back the gift againe, as though I could only see your outer worth. I thought thee an adornment for my life, an no more need'd to smoothe you with gifts than a horse or sideboard. Thou wert as a Guinea made of woode, or so I thought, &d I beg thee for thy pardon.*

This amaz'd me much, but I kept my counsel.

After ye fell into the fire &d your lookes ruin'd, he said, snatching another Glimpse at me, *I was at first disgusted &d wanted thee sent away. But the Parson perswaded me, speaking of hidden worths, &d suchanlike. He convinced me, to my shame, although I saw those worths onlie in the shape of my own lust. &d great, &d strange, were the glories he promis'd me. Yet tho I look at thee in thy ugliness, my boy, still theere is a place in my soule mov'd by thee – never before, in all my longe life, nay not with my wedded wife or with the* Ganymeedes *I have known, has theere been this twist in my soule at the presence of another. It disturbs me, my boy, yet I cannot remove it. I had thought to playe you as a true* Sonne, *as a* Father *might, but my feelings are not Paternal, &d 'twould be meerely a lie to declare them as such. Yet my flesh recoils from your – from your –* (I saw heere that he was crying) *– so pucker'd &d wrinkl'd, O! it maketh my flesh to shudder – I'm sorry for thee, lad. &d in sooth your right side is barely touch'd. Yet – yet. The Parson promis'd much, &d even, he swore, theere was a way— But I have sinn'd. Sinn'd! O the Parson his Affliction has mov'd me strangely, &d I finde myself driven to Repentance of my former Crimes. For what &d if* GOD *Himself has punished the Parson with this catalepsy? &d so my son*, he concluded &d rising from the bed in teares, *I am sorry, am sorry, &d heere is the coine againe.*

He lean'd in &d kiss'd me, once, upon the browe, &d then he departed &d taking the light with him left me in the darkness. I clutch'd the penny to my selfe &d lay down, &d as I lay I ponder'd that Mercy had prevail'd, when had my lord try'd to use me as I were his Wife, then Revenge would surely have ensu'd.

The following day the Justice of the Peece came againe, with certaine bills he had printed offering Four Guineas as reward for the murtheerers of the two strangers, &d a Cart came to take

away the mortal remains. The Parson was fed with Milk thro'
a Clyster Pipe, but spilt it much, &d came not awake againe.

I offert myself for worke, yet the servants shoo'd me away, I
know not whether because the Judge had order'd them so to do.
That morning I wander'd thro' the gardens, &d betook me againe
to the river, wheere the Sylphis had visited me, or I them. But
to walke againe beside the flow was not to perceive the eccho
of that night. I lay amongst the grass, &d directed my Ey at
the clouds &d the Skie clear as cleare &d Blue as pure water,
&d the *Moone* was visible too, tho its brightness was diluted by
the Day. I here dedicated that this new *Power* would not betray
me to Cruelty or Vice, &d recalld to myself that the LORD
GOD puts temptation in the way such that we may retort it,
not for us to succumbe. In this resolution I was much pleas'd,
&d returned to the House in good spirits with myselfe, yea, even
praising myself in my heart.

But Pride Goeth before the Fall as the saying is. &d such
resolution did not last the fortnight, for it is not given that mankind may continue in possession of great power in innocency.
Does it not saye in the *Bible*, Heare now this, O foolish people,
&d without Understanding, which hath eyes &d see not; which
hath ears &d hear not? But this people hath a revolting &d a
rebellious heart; they are revolted &d gone. Does it not saye: A
wonderful &d horrible thing is committed in the Land?

On the morrow the Parson died, &d on the Friday was buryed
in the graveyard; &d so he pass'd away. For the Saturday, &d
againe in the Sunday, my lord the Judge was much desponded
by this newes, &d kept to himself. Yet in the weeke after he
sent for the *lord Knox*, who came with companie, &d amongst
them other Gentlemen, &d serving boyes. With this company
my lord Newbolt made merrie, &d drank &d carded until late.

My lord Knox greeted me in hallway upon his first arrival
with mocking, *how now*, crying afterward, *who is this ladde with*

boyish frame yet face of a wizzen'd dotard? Why dost thou keep so wrinkl'd a retainer about thee, my lord? He hangs like a Scrotum, needing only to be scratch'd &d then tuck'd out of sight. Theere was much more in the veyne, an the company laught long at it; &d for my parte I was gladd to remove myself. Yet was I not let alone, but call'd forth that night from my sleepe to serve at their table. They twitted me, &d tugg'd at my cloathes, &d I left them with gladness to return to bed. Yet they call'd me againe, &d I came down again. O that they had let me asleep! They bargain'd not for what they rousd in me.

The eve pass'd thiswise, for my lord the Judge Newbolt was asleepe with drinke, &d lolling in his chaire, yet did he wake when I came in. The lord Knox made merry againe in his clumsy manner, &d once more twitted me, but I saw that another serv-ing boy was theere, &d that they had no neede of me. I was on poynt of retiring once more when one of my lord Knox's fellowes (I know not his name) call'd to me, *hop, hop, &d bring me a stoup, old scar-skin*, &d meeting my gaze at the other lad, laught with a *we have other playe for this one, &d not a-serving wine.* &d he put his Hand upon his boddie.

Then did a great wrath fill me, to my later shame, yet did I feel no remorse at that time. I saw neither the face of the boy, whether he was Complicit or Press'd against his Will, nor did I ever know his name, nor his mynd on this business. But, either being tired with constant waking in the darke, or filled with Wicked Wrath from some Diabolic prompter, I surrender'd myself to this Anger. Indeede, as I recall it now, I am surpriz'd at the sudden kindling of this rage, as if theere had been some *Gunnepowder* in my spirit.

I felt forth &d grasped some innard, I know not what, yet it squeez'd under my touch like as a *Raysin* or *Currant* from which the juyce has not been altogether press'd, &d it was hidden well within the Scull of my lord Knox. This I flatten'd &d spread into tendrils, t[e]aring some, &d he jerk'd backward in his chaire with a mightie bellow like a Heiffer at slaughter. So, and so with no outward motion of my boddie, I reach'd down a litel way &d press'd flat his windpipe, such that he dropp'd silent down, &d was dead.

At this, as ye may suppose, was great confusion &d clamor of voyces, &d in the midst rose up my lord the Judge with eyes starting out on's face, &d calling out in a fierce distress *It is Hogart, it is Hogart his Spirit vexing us, we are haunted by the wickednesse of that man* (for Hogart was the Parson's name). &d as they all stoode, I felt the surge, like a tide within my soule, &d the strength grew within me, such that for a mimim I held them all, eache man &d boye of them, in my minde, &d felt with the arm &d the *Virtue* of it mixt in my heade. I felt the pulse of their viscera like the *Eeles* that are solde in London byside the river, &d the wash of *Bloode* in which each organ bathes, &d the sparkle &d prickle of their soules scattering through their limbes, not unlike the touche of a *Stickleback-fish* as ye might touch it with your fingers-ends in a streame, or like unto the rubbe of cloth on cloth that makes for the haires of a man to stand up, running along the threads &d strings of their sinews. But this moment past, &d much mov'd by drinke &d feare the companie ran from the roome, some thro' one door &d some thro' the other, &d I was left alone with the corse of my lord Knox.

&d looking upon it againe I felt in the first moment nought but exultation, &d I thought in my heart *rejoyce not against me mine enemie, tho I fall yet shall I rise, &d at the last victorie shall be mine.*

Hearing the commotion the Steward did enter the roome, &d demand of me, none too courteous, *what hath happened heere, wretch? What noyse is this?*

My lord Knox is fall'n dead with an apoplexy, I said.

What? said the Steward, who was a Puritan man, drestt very sober in blacke, *what, in his drinke?*

Ay, I said.

But did I not tell my lord the Judge that no good could come of this carouze? he said, approaching to looke ypon the corse. *Look thou not upon the Wine when it is Red,* he said in a sorrowful voyce, *when it lendeth its colour in the cuppe, when it moveth itselfe aright, for at the last it hath teeth &d biteth like a serpent.*

My lord is runne crying thro' the house that the ghoust of the Parson has smitten him, I said.

The Steward look'd very queerly at me then, &d tushed this notion, saying *GOD allows not such things.*

Yet my lorde said so, I did saye.

A Parson? A minister of Christ? No, no, said the Steward. But he withdrew soon theereafter to finde my lord the Judge &d I was left alone againe with the corse of the lord Knox. At this moment I felt a pitie swell in me, &d I felt ashamed that I, a mere serving boye of no account, had so acted upon a great Lord of the Land as to slay him. For I remamber'd me that the LORD GOD putt all people in their place in this world, both high degree &d lowe, &d that it was not given to me to question it, or essay to overturne it. &d with this thought came a regret that the lord Knox, who was so young &d faire, with Handsome countenance &d straight limb, had been so struck down. The more I stoode in that place the more I swelled with griefe at what I had donne, for altho he was not courteous to me &d had spoken rude words, yet he had offer'd me no actual violence, &d wheerefore shou'd I smite him? As I thought I began to weepe, &d the more I wept the more teares did come.

I repented me that I had done. Yea, I even reached into his head again &d gather'd together the torn pieces of what I had donne, as a maid might rolle together scraps of pastry into a globe. Yet it made no odds, for my lord Knox was dead as ever he was dead.

Heere I resolved: I must take myself farre away, &d live removed from mankind that I might do them no other harme, or else I resolvd to take the King his shilling &d become a soldier, wheere my strength might serve some better purpose. Yet did I not acte upon this resolve for a weeke, but kept my own counsel &d companie.

For the following day theere was a strange hush in the house, &d the servants did speak low of how theere was a curse upon it; &d my lord the Judge came from his chamber, nor issued orders for the arrangement of any matter. Yet the surgeon did come again, &d did declare that my lord Knox had indeed dyed of an apoplexy brought on by drinke. One of his companie said that the lord his estate was in Easte Anglia, &d a tun of liqor was ordered from *Maid*[enhead] for to stowe his boddie in &d keep it from corruption on the cart to that distant place. The Justice came again, &d told the Cooke that two ruffians had been apprehended in *Henley* on suspicion of killing the two in the field bye the house, &d were to be tried the next week, &d the cooke spread this worde through the house. Yet did it not lift the mood, for all felt the presence of something wicked. It came to me that this wickedness was truly me.

So the following day, which was the Sabbath day, my lord the Judge did come from his roome to church, &d did take the Lord's supper &d praye &d then retire againe. But on the day after he came forth &d sat in the chamber looking through the window at the Land, wheere *Summer* was weaving blooms of red &d yellow into the hair of the fields, &d the trees were shaggy with dark greene, &d the sky blue as a jewell. I crept close to him, &d begged his mercy, &d when he looked at me I said, *&d it please you my lord, send me away from this place, from your service too.*

He thought about this for a long time, &d then said, *I have heeard what they say below staires, that the house be haunted. I know not, my ladd, but perhaps we should all leave this place, go all of us away.*

I knew not what to say to this, but to repeat my entreaty, *my lord, I beg of you to release me from your service &d allow me to depart.*

I have sent for a vicar, he said, answering not to my purpose, *&d he from Windsor. He is famed for the casting out of – devills, I should say, tho it frights me to mowthe the word. Yet shall he exorcise this house, &d then – &d*— heere he stopp'd &d fell into a reverie.

This newes comforted me to some degree, for I thought that this priest of GOD would bring out the truth, id., whether I was possest by some Devill or whether this new strength came from some other Place. &d so I altered my resolution to leave that place, &d waited.

Yet was it comfortless to dwell in that house; for the servants avoyded one the other, &d fewe words were spoken, &d tho it was High Summer outside yet inside was darke &d stille. On the Sunday following the priest came, a very fat man call'd Baker dressed in a somewhat greasie cloth of black. He went to roome &d to roome sniffing the aire, &d declar'd that he cou'd smell the stench of the *Adversarie*. &d so he blest the house, &d walk'd thro' scattering with the holy water broadcast, so as to splash the walls &d floors, &d pronouncing *Lattin* with great solemnity. My heart was rattling, for I fear'd that I might tumble to the floor as the Devil struggl'd with this cleansing, as I have heerd tell. Yet did his words have no effect upon me, &d after he had gone I felt the same as before.

At first this pleas'd me, for I reasond that this new Strength must be a gift of GOD, or at least a gift of some creature that offendeth not the LORD. Yet after I became fearfull once more, thinking that perhaps it was not this, but rather the Devill in me was so strong that this parish priest had not the Power to overthrow him. &d the more I thought on this, the liker it seem'd to me.

Againe I came to my lord &d begged release from his service, but now he treated me as a fool, saying *&d who would take thee in, my lad? Glance in any mirror &d see how ruin'd is thy face, how pucker'd &d repulsive.*

Then send me to your farme, my lord, as you thought once to do.

But he would not.

Ane day, and a dark one it show'd itself ere dusk, I was in the kitchen, idle, &d a Tinker came to the doore across the kaleyard offering to mend pots &d pans. The Cooke, an honest woman if somewhat sloven, shoo'd him away, but he went not, &d instead offer'd to embrace her, chucking her chinne &d reaching round about her with his armes. He was a swart fellowe, &d smelt ill, &d I found my rage starting, tho if the truth be told the Cooke was not much distress'd with his attention, &d even laught at this playe, chiding him as a *foolish vagrant*, &d bidding him *go drowne himself in the river that his corse might be cleane for burial* &d suchlike. Yet tho she laught I grew angry, &d I reach'd out with my strength &d felt the length of his shinbones, like the planed wood of table-legs, &d felt up wheere it was smooth &d warme wet.

He said to the Cooke, *if it be bathing you wish, come with me now &d we'll bath together my chucke.* &d he pressed upon her breast with his fingers, even in that place wheere the nipple is, &d she, tho squealing &d slapping at his Hande, yet was grinning. I felt up with my strength to his Knees, &d popped the one firste, &d the other after, as they were two circlets of stale bread, turning them with ease into crumbes. He bellow'd in great paine &d fell, pulling the Cooke down upon him after, who thinking this was more of his sporte, shrieked the more &d call'd him to stoppe *for Enoch* (this being the Steward's name)

*was about, he was sure to finde them, &d he was hotte against lechery
as a Puritan &d she could lose her place.* When the Tinker did not
release his hold she cried, still mistaking him, *not heere, not heere,
let us go by the wood behind the fallow field.*

I knowe not what befell my minde now, for the Cooke had
always used me well enough, though sometimes short with me.
But this plea for Fornication made the rage grow fiercer in me
somewhat, &d I reached inside the Cooke, even to her *Stomach*,
which felt in my touch like a twist of wet woole, or a scoop of
tripe filled with Sauce of some kinde, &d this in my sinful wrath
I Squeez'd. Out came a deale of *Spew* fro her mouth, &d after
came a gout of *Bloode*, upon which she choked &d gagg'd, &d
rolling from the Tinker did clutch her gut &d crie aloud that
she was Dying.

My rage fell from me, &d I knew great feare at what I had
done, &d I broke like a *Fawne* from a thicket &d ranne from
that roome.

It beseemeth me then that I was wicked, &d that I could
not be trusted with the strength that was in me, gift of the
Sylphis for good or ill. I knew not wheere I ranne, for the teares
did smocke in my *Eys*, &d the walles did dance before me, the
door jerck like a Shaker as I try'd to hurrie thro'. &d, in hind
sight, perhap I should have fled the *House* altogether, &d gone
as I sometime ponder'd as a soldier or sailor, yet did I not. For
reason of which I am not sure I haul'd up the stair to my lord
the Judge's chamber, &d I burste in upon him without knock
&d fell on the floor before him.

How now my ladd? he said to me, much surpriz'd.

I babbl'd, &d tolde him that the deaths of so many &d the
hurte of others was on my conscience lay'd, &d begged his help,
for I was too weake to hold against the Temptation to hurte
others. At first he was much amaz'd, &d bade me repeat myself,
&d repeat againe, &d soon his face grew darke, &d he trembl'd,

&d tolde me *go against the wall theere*, &d *go away from me*. I retreated to the far wall &d sobb'd &d wrack'd, &d my lord pac'd up &d bade me repeat it again. I told him the tale entire, &d promis'd to proove it tho he scoff'd. Yet he did not scoff, he was a willing eare, &d shooke his head a great deal. *It is the Devill, the Devill*, he said, many a time, &d added that he *should never have trafficked with that Hogart, the man had sold his Soule*, &d then he sat back.

Finally the teares were out of me, &d I was calme againe. But my lord was more agitated than ever I have seene him, &d he grew more fearfull to be in the roome with me. *You must stay heere, in my chamber, my ladd*, he said, &d when he left he drew the locke closed behind him. This gave me reason to ponder, &d already I repented me that I had come to him &d babbld all. But theere was no escape, unless I us'd againe my strength to wound or kill those that came against me, &d this I resolv'd not to do. When my lorde returned he came with three of his men, who were all armed with a pitchforke one, &d a cleaver another, &d a third with a pistol. These three took me to the cellar, &d theere they lockd me againe. I had been in this roome before, yet did it seem to me in a light anew.

Now from this space I was taken to a gaol in Maidenhead towne, &d theere kept for many weekes. I was arraigned &d try'd, &d condemn'd as *Warlocke*, &d the Cooke spoke in the triall against me. Yet was sentence delay'd, to give me space to write this history of my time, &d come to some account of the Change. During this time theere have been times when the Temptation to use my Strength has been fierce upon me, &d so to escape &d runne to the Sea or to Scots Land, yet have I not done this, save one time when in a *picque* I did blackenn the ey-balle of one Jailor heere for cuffing me &d speaking violence to me, popping the littell tangle of veines that are stitched into the reare of the balle, &d spilling blood into the jellie, such that he was blinded in that Ey. Yet did I repente me as soone as doing this, &d begg'd his pardon, offering him to strike mine owne Ey &d so be reveng'd, e'en as it saieth in the Bible, a Ey for an Ey. But he fled away, &d I sawe not him againe. &d this, thanks to GOD, has been my onlie relinquishing of myselfe to temptation, nor shall I do so againe.

As to the Sylphis, I have spoken with a learned divine, a wize &d compassionate soule, who doth convince me that they were Devills, assum'd a pleasing shape as the *Bible* doth saye they may. &d I do repent me of the hurt I have done, &d am reconciled to my punnishment, which is to be hang'd for the deathes of the fine gentlemen of which I am guilty. I commend my spirit to the mercy of my LORD JESUS CHRIST, in whose bosom all sinnes howsoever foule are clean'd &d made pure againe. May He receive my soule, &d may any who reade this true history beware the temptations of the Devill &d cleave only to the one Saviour.

I have heerd Saint Peter whisper to me in the *night*. He beggeth me to join with him, and I shall meet such unitie at death, which I feare not. So am I donne. This day, the twenty and sixt of August, the yeare of our Lord Sixteen hundred &d Ninety-five.

Pursuit

Substance and Accident

I was taken to the Great Western Hospital at Swindon, and there I stayed for a long time – the lion's share of five weeks, in fact. They operated, and it became infected, and for a while I was very ill and feverish and unhappy. Then I recovered, but the artificial tendon they had tried to fit me with was rejected and they took it out. The stitches they used to repair my Achilles fared a little better, but still I walked with a limp, and do so to this day: brace on my leg, stick in my hand. Another infirmity to add to my various other infirmities. Another deformity the further to deform deformable me.

It seemed (said Dr Giridharadas, the hobbit-sized, energetic doctor attached to my case) that 'something very peculiar indeed' had happened to the ligaments and tendons of my left leg. 'I have never seen an injury quite like it,' she told me, with too-poorly-concealed professional delight. 'You did not receive this injury playing tennis.'

I assured Dr Giridharadas that I had not received this injury playing tennis.

'The plantaris tendon is quite gone,' said Dr Giridharadas, putting the end of her left little finger against her right thumb, and then swivelling both hands about to bring the end of her right little finger against her left thumb, then repeating the entire gesture once, twice, three times. 'It has been removed. The Achilles is snapped, or rather sliced. You are lame, my friend.'

Since I couldn't get out of bed, this seemed to me a reasonable diagnosis.

'You can see the little hole through which the plantaris was removed,' said the doctor, although the waddy bandages covering my swollen leg meant that I could see nothing of the sort. 'By pliers, perhaps?'

'It just,' I said, 'slid out – like a snake out of its den.'

'Of its own accord?'

'I was assaulted,' I said. 'A man called Roy Curtius attacked me. He is very dangerous – the police must be informed.'

Dr Giridharadas looked very grave, wrote the name down, and promised to have the authorities notified. I got the sense she was humouring me. I dare say humouring patients is a large part of the job. A nurse came in to check on me, and loitered by the door when she discovered that the doctor herself was there. 'As for the Achilles,' she said, 'I would normally say: immobilise it and leave it to heal. But the break is so smooth, bizarrely smooth, oddly smooth' – each iteration added more 'oo' to the word – 'so smooth that I am afraid stitching will be needful. Actually the absence of the plantaris isn't a huge problem. You will experience some reduction in the functionality of the knee, I think; but people get by without that tendon pretty well.'

This fact brought me, a little, out of my self-absorption. 'I'm sorry?'

'It is by way of being an evolutionary hangover, I think, from when our ancestors used to manipulate things with their feet the way we do with hands. In fact, we sometimes use the palantaris posterior when we need to transplant a more vital tendon somewhere else in the body, because the patient can get along fine without it. You may find movement of the knee and ankles a little restricted. You may limp a little. Interesting fact: it's the longest tendon in the human body, often thirty-five or even forty centimetres long.'

'It hurt when it came out,' I said.

'I'm sure it did. There *will* be swelling and discomfort for a while. But you can function pretty well without a plantaris. It's the Achilles I'm worried about. How did you come to snap that?'

'I don't know.'

'It may have happened,' she said, 'during the extraction of the plantaris.' She looked at me again, with a wary eye. '*Did* he use pliers? This Mr— What did you say his name was?'

'Curtius. And no.'

'He must have used pliers,' said Dr Giridharadas decidedly. 'Or some similar tool. The extraction was remarkably efficient. Is he a surgeon, then, this Mr Curtis?'

'Curtius,' I said. 'And: no.' I could have explained that he used telepathy, but I realised how that would sound, and I held my tongue.

'At any rate if he pulled it out *without* anaesthetic, then it must have hurt. Very distressing. It's possible that you snapped your own Achilles, thrashing or jerking your foot in pain.'

I thought back, but couldn't remember very much, besides the strangely placid expression on Roy's face. And the agony, of course. 'I don't know.'

Dr Giridharadas put each of her little fingers inside the shell-curl of her two ears, one either side: and ran them around the groove in unison. It made her look as though she were making pretend elk-horns at the side of her head. Then she put her hands in her pockets. 'Let me say this: your injury is unusual enough to merit me writing it up for the *BMJ*. I'm not legally obliged to obtain your permission to do this, I should tell you, and of course I will anonymise the details. But I hope you don't mind, at any rate. What I don't understand is how Mr Curtis got *hold* of the end of the tendon.'

'Curtius,' I said.

'It can't be pliers. You're quite right to correct me. It can't be pliers, because the wound through which the tendon was extracted is no larger *than* the tendon. I'm envisaging a long steel knitting-needle-type structure, with a hook on the end. Is that right? Am I ballpark?'

'No,' I said.

'Most unusual!' she cried. 'Thoroughly unusual case.'

I had my Achilles stitched under local anaesthetic, lying on my front. Then I spent two days with my leg elevated and motionless. Then they gave me an NHS walking stick, which hung on a peg at the end of my bed, and I tried hobbling around with that for a bit.

Then things took a downturn. There was some post-operative infection, and I grew feverish. I was put on antibiotics, and the first course disagreed with me, plunging me into a near hallucinogenic state of total prostration. I had odd visions. Some of the things I had seen in Antarctica returned to me, but with the hazy lineaments of vision rather than the hideous immensity of actuality. A great black hill, burning with fire, glimmering with darkness visible, and a door in the hillside that opened to scorching white fires within. I saw Irma, but she looked sourly at me and left. I saw the ghost-boy, and wished I hadn't.

One night was especially grim, and I writhed so much I wrenched my foot from its elevating cradle, and pulled the stitching out. Further surgery was necessitated. The wound was reopened and the torn stitched removed; and then the tendon was fixed with glue and restitched and a hard cast placed on my foot to keep it in place.

I understand the regular police visited me during this time, but I was not responsive to their questions. Then representatives of the government came – Belwether, and her armed guard – and relieved the local police of their duty to pursue further inquiries.

All this I learned after the fact. I went through a phase when I was only half present, heavily medicated and passive, drifting between sleep and wakefulness. At one point (really, this is all very hazy) I tried to get out of bed. Unused to the cast on my leg, and not fully compos mentis, I fell. There was a loud clatter, and I was attended not by a nurse but a man in a sports jacket. I had a moment of mental clarity when I thought: *this geezer isn't a nurse.* As he leant over to help me, his jacket gaped open to reveal a pistol in a shoulder holster. The scarred boy, behind, winked at me with the eye on the good side of his face. And then the night nurse came in too, and the two of them had a low-volume conversation that, in my fever-heightened state, I heard perfectly. 'I heard a crash, I didn't know.' 'Wendell, please leave it to the nursing staff to attend to the patients.' 'I was just helping him up.' And so on.

I slept. When I woke it was dark and still and I was alone again, with only the hallway light spilling through the little window over the door for illumination. I listened. There were various sounds, distant and irregular, to do with the functioning of the hospital. There was a regular pulsing sound, like a wonky wheel turning, or a car alarm very far away. The more I listened to this, the more it drew me out of myself and into the sound. It was not coming from inside the hospital, I decided. It was from outside. It was a dog barking, or perhaps a fox, but a long way away. And then a sub-rumble added itself to the barking, and this grew to supplant it, and finally a trapezoid of light appeared on my ceiling, stroked smoothly across and half down the wall before vanishing again, and the mystery clarified in my head. I heard the ambulance shutting off its engine, and then a series of tubular, metallic noises as (I assume) its back doors were opened, a stretcher loaded on to a gurney and wheeled inside.

The distant scraping sound of the motorway, like a faraway waterfall. After a while you stopped hearing it.

No birdsong.

Then some coughing, low-level conversation – two male voices, too muffled to be decipherable – and the ambulance engine drum-soloing back into life and receding, and eventually, quiet again. The lights did not appear again on my ceiling.

I must have slept because the next thing it was morning – late in the morning, in fact. A nurse brought me breakfast, and Belwether was sitting in the corner, looking at me. After the nurse had gone, I spooned muesli into my gob. 'When is it?' I asked my visitor.

'Tuesday.'

'I meant month.'

'September. Aren't you curious who I am?'

'I always liked that the ninth month was called "seven". And the tenth, "eight"; and the eleventh, "nine". And the final month in our twelvemonth year called "ten". That's pleasantly wonky. Don't you think?'

'It's almost as if the year begins in March,' she said. 'My name is Belwether. I work for Her Majesty's Government.'

I finished my muesli, and took a sip of orange juice. 'She employs a lot of people, that lady.'

'Mr Gardner. How are you feeling? Well enough to talk?'

'I do feel better,' I said. And it was true. There was something familiar about Belwether, although, outside of this hospital, I'd never met her before. I couldn't put my finger on the familiarity.

She sat up a little straighter. 'You won't be aware,' she said, 'what happened at the Institute.'

'What happened?'

'Well there is some good news, at any rate. They're not all dead.'

My heart gave a little fishflappy spurt. *Dead.* 'There weren't many people on site when it happened, which was lucky, I suppose.'

'When what happened?' But I already knew what she was talking about.

'Curtius,' she said. 'He did that to your leg, you say? You were with him in Antarctica, of course. You went to see him in Broadmoor, back in July.'

'Where is he now?'

She smiled. 'I wish we knew.'

'Hence the armed guard on my door?' The horror of this was percolating through my brain, and I'm not proud that one of my first thoughts was personal survival. 'You think *that* will stop him?'

'To be honest, we've never dealt with a situation like this before.'

'Like what before?' I swung the tray away from the bed on its hinged bracket and sat up. My leg was throbbing vaguely, discomfort rather than acute pain. 'What? Here's what I'd like: I'd like you to explain what on earth is going on.'

Belwether sighed a modest little sigh. 'I was rather hoping you would explain it all to me. You're an Institute member, after all. I'm not.'

'Me neither, it transpires,' I said. The memory was sour, and I daresay I scowled, and it led me to: 'Irma. Is she all right? Is she still alive?'

Belwether took out her phone and glanced at it. 'This would be,' she said, thumbing down, 'Irma Casbrook? My understanding is that she wasn't on site when Curtius attacked.'

'So where is she?'

'I've no idea. That's not my job.' She put her phone away again. 'Mr Gardner. May I call you Charlie?'

'You may not,' I said.

'I'm going to anyway. Let's start with something we agree on. What you said about Her Majesty.'

This wrongfooted me. 'What?' I didn't remember saying anything about the Queen.

'As you said, she employs a lot of people. In her house are many mansions. I don't need to spell out for you in precisely which sub-department of which section of which ministry I am employed. But I'm part of that group that handled liaison between the Institute and the Government.'

'I was there a couple weeks, max,' I said, taking hold of the cast on my left leg with both hands and trying to shuggle it a little, to reach an itch on the skin. 'I was never really part of it. They used me, and then they discarded me.'

'The point *I'm* making is that I've signed the Official Secrets Act.'

'How marvellous for you.'

'So have you, as it happens.'

'I haven't,' I objected.

'At the Institute, a Professor Kostritsky gave you a number of documents to sign. Contracts, waivers and so on. The Official Secrets Act was one of these. All members of the Institute signed it, on account of the extraordinary sensitivity of their work.'

'You'd be better,' I said, looking past Belwether and through the window. September, she'd said; but the leaves were still green, 'better off talking to Kos yourself. She knows the ins and outs.'

'She's dead.'

'Oh.' Good grief. I tried to think of other people I'd known at the Institute, but though a few faces flashed upon my memory I couldn't recall their names. That's bad, though, isn't it? 'And – Peter?'

'Peter?' queried Belwether.

'Head honcho. *You* know.'

'I've already told you. She is dead. Tragically. Who's Peter?'

'Never mind.'

Belwether paused for a moment to peer at me, and then said: 'I believe you know more about the workings of the Institute than you let on. But it doesn't matter. I've been well briefed on the day-to-day. The project aims and objectives.'

'Isn't that tautology? Aren't aims and objectives the same?'

'By no means!' said Belwether. For the first time there was actual passion in her voice. But it passed quickly. 'I tell you what, Charlie. I'll give you a summary of what *we* think the Institute was up to, and how Curtius is involved. And you can tell me whether that chimes with your understanding.'

'All right.'

'Having said that, I'll have to begin with something I'm not sure about. The Institute was set up to programme and develop superfast computers. At some point, apparently prompted by interactions of some undisclosed nature with Roy Curtius, they radically revised their ambitions – upwards, if you see what I mean. Developing AI, in itself a huge achievement, wasn't enough. They decided that the very thing that had held back earlier advances in this field was the thing that could revolutionise almost every aspect of human existence. Computers had been programmed to one extent or another after the manner of human consciousness. Not surprising, when you come to think about it. Back in the last century, people thought robots would eventually be humanoid creatures with arms and legs, for no better reason than that *we* are such creatures. In fact, as we now know, robots are hinged and craned arms in car factories, or plate-sized vacuum cleaners, or whatever. As with robots, so with computers. Maybe mimicking human consciousness was not the way to make AI. Maybe you had to try something radically different.'

'Kos told me they'd succeeded. Or thereabouts.'

'In the early days Her Majesty's officers of statecraft had little interest in their research. The world is full of small companies programming and developing computing stuff. Our interest came later. They approached us, in fact; or rather, they approached officialdom. They did this because they claimed that their research was going to lead to something rather extraordinary. Remote viewing; vastly more speedy travel, perhaps even instantaneous passage, circumventing the speed of light. Manipulating objects at a distance too. Professor Kostritsky even hinted at slowing down or speeding up time. And she was able to back up her claims, to the satisfaction of our experts.'

'Pretty far-fetched,' I said. 'Are we sure it's not some big con?' The memory of Roy drawing the tendon from my leg returned to me. But then, maybe I was misremembering that? Maybe he had yanked it out with a pair of pliers, as Dr Giridharadas suspected, and afterwards hypnotised me, or otherwise messed with my head. Maybe my hallucinations in Antarctica has predisposed me in some way. Made me suggestible. 'Small mercies, though,' I added. 'At least you're not wanking on about Immanuel Kant.'

'I was just coming to him.'

I sighed. 'Of course you were.'

'Professor Kostritsky was *very* clear about this. As I understand it, Kant had certain theories about the relationship between the human mind and the world around us. Specifically, he thought that space and time, as well as a number of qualities such as cause and effect and so on, were "in" the way our mind structured experience, rather than being actual features of the cosmos. This provided philosophers with pleasant matter to discuss for several centuries. But it was all abstract discussion because there was no way of testing it objectively. *That* there was no way of testing it objectively was a central part of the theory. Human consciousness is defined by reality, and reality is defined by human consciousness, both at the same time. Or at least *our* reality was defined that way. We couldn't "step outside" our humanity and get, as it were, a third opinion. Until now.'

'AI.'

'Exactly. The Institute developed AI, or at least a programme close to that. It did it by not programming in imitation of the paradigm of human perceptions of time and space. And according to Professor Kostritsky, it meant that Kant's theory could finally be triangulated – and proven right. She was very excited at the possibilities.'

'I remember her telling me,' I said. 'Eradicating space and time was just the start of it.'

'For myself,' said Belwether, 'I have to assume that the time thing is a non-starter, or we'd already know about it. Future time travellers would be everywhere, wandering around, taking photos of the Eiffel Tower and Big Ben. But they're not. But the space thing is very – live. I spoke to my superiors, and they spoke to *their* superiors, that the Institute might be on the threshold of developing a remote viewer. It's been a holy grail of espionage for a while. All the fancy cryptology in the world is no use to our enemies if we can just zoom in on their secrets before they even code them. If we can eavesdrop and spy on any terrorist training camp, without needing satellites or drones, just by turning on Prof. K.'s clever new computer.'

'The civil liberty implications are not comfortable,' I pointed out. 'Speaking as a citizen.'

'Ah, but, Mr Gardner. As noted earlier, you're *not* a citizen. You're a subject of Her Majesty the Queen.' She smiled and shook her head. 'Our advantage would, clearly, be lost if the existence of such a device became widely known. That was why it couldn't be announced publicly. It was why there was so much secrecy associated with the Institute.'

'That's why the news hasn't covered the – murder at the Institute. Murders?' Belwether nodded solemnly. 'Murders.

Christ.' I screwed up my face. Was Belwether lying to me about Irma? Was her body lying in a mortuary somewhere, cold as outer space? Then again: she could be lying about everything. Maybe Curtius hadn't gone anywhere near the Institute. 'You're reminding me about the Official Secrets Act in order to keep me, I don't know – what?'

'High stakes, you understand. High stakes.'

'Kos was talking in terms of remote astronomy. Finding habitable planets. Hell, even travelling to them. I'd say those stakes are rather higher than, uh, petty espionage.' It wasn't very stinging, but it was the best I could do.

'As far as that goes,' said Belwether. 'In time, who knows? The glorious interstellar future for humanity. Sure. As my daughter likes to say, *whatever*. It's a long game. But there are pressing reasons, here and now, why this needs to be kept under wraps. National security. Indeed, it doesn't overstate things to say: international security.'

'Hence your visit?'

'You're almost well enough to be discharged. According to your doctor. You asked for the police to be called, pursuant to the assault upon your person by a certain Roy Curtius, an individual we are also seeking. I am not the police. I am better than the police. I am asking you to assist us in apprehending Curtius.'

I sniffed the air. 'Are you arresting me?'

'I am not a policewoman,' said Belwether.

'That is not an answer.'

'I've been very open with you, Charlie. Open and, I think, friendly. I'll be even *more* open and say that my department certainly possesses powers of detention. But I'm perfectly genuine when I say I hope we can be friends. Allies.'

'So,' I said. 'When I check out, and help you with your inquiries, I'd be staying – where?'

'Go back to your flat, if you like. Or go stay in a hotel:

we'll cover reasonable expenses. That doesn't matter. We will be keeping an eye on you, just to make sure you don't make any sudden blurts.' She sniggered, as if she had said something funny. 'Online. Letters to newspapers. Chatting down the pub. Anything like that. Mum's the word. And I *am* a mum. As such I'm hoping we can trust you.'

'And how am I supposed to help?'

'Let's begin with—'

'And what's in it for me?'

She was used to people trying to wrongfoot her, I think, and my interruption didn't ruffle her in the least. She smiled. 'After what Curtius did to you, not once but twice, surely you have an interest in apprehending him? Wouldn't that be a valuable thing for you, just having him behind bars?'

'Bars won't hold him, I think.'

'We'll figure something out, as far as that's concerned. But never mind that. Instead, why don't you tell me what you two talked about, when you visited him at Broadmoor?'

My leg was aching and itching at the same time. 'Jesus, I don't know. I can barely remember. What did we talk about? Nothing very much. It was Kos who wanted me to go. She went to quite extraordinary lengths to *get* me to go in fact.'

'This,' said Belwether, 'is exactly why we are so keen to find out what happened when you *did* go.'

I looked at her. As if seeing her for the first time, I clocked her dark blue trouser suit, her frizzy black hair, medium length, framing a narrow face. Her nose was small, but her cheekbones and chin long, which gave a strange disproportion to features that would otherwise have been pretty.

'Kos said,' I told her, 'that Roy would only speak to me. Because of what we shared. So I went to speak. We chatted, awkwardly, he and I. About trivia.'

'Did he tell you,' she asked, 'at what point the Institute first contacted him?'

'Didn't come up.'

'You understand, Charlie, that this is important. The Institute's on-off relationship with Curtius goes back a long while. It was them leaning on us to talk to the relevant authorities that kept him in Broadmoor rather than in maximum security.'

'A bad idea, it seems.'

'Oh I'm not sure a secure prison would have been able to hold Curtius any better than Broadmoor, once he set his mind on leaving.'

I looked around, as if he might teleport into my room at any moment. 'Why did it take him so long? He was there *decades*. If he could just slip away when he chose, why didn't he do that earlier?'

'That's a very good question. Your most perceptive yet. My answer: I don't know. Perhaps he *couldn't* slip away until very recently. Perhaps he could, but chose not to. Behind all this is: assuming it's possible to approach the Kantian "thing", whatever that is – possible to manipulate it, using some kind of tool to, let's say, step past the structuring limitation of space, as ordinary people understand that. Let's say that's possible and Roy was able to step *out* of Broadmoor and step back *in* at – a location in Wiltshire, let's say. Posit Curtius doing this thing. What my superiors are most interested in at the moment is: does doing so have negative consequences for the teleporter? Does approaching, as it were, closer to the thing itself *drive you mad*?'

'Roy was bonkers before he ever dabbled with this stuff,' I said, at once. 'Though I daresay it certainly hasn't done his mental health any favours. And for myself…' I stopped, because, absurdly, I felt as if I were about to burst into tears. I continued, speaking more slowly. 'For myself – where Antarctica is concerned. To me, I mean. If I … look I've got into the habit of believing that what I saw, down there, was a hallucination. It's self-defence, is what it is. Psychological self-defence. I'm trying to adjust to the idea that what happened to me was, in some sense, real…'

'If Kant is right,' said Belwether, 'then we're talking real in a literal sense. More real than this room, more real than you and me chatting.'

'So. Well, all I know is: experiencing it, that, whatever it was – it messed me up. It was a trauma, and I'm not sure you could say I've ever really recovered from it. I had really good prospects, you know. Then my life went to shit, and I drank a red sea of booze, and … well, here I am.'

Belwether nodded, perhaps aiming at sympathy. But it only made her look more predatory. 'You understand why this needs to be kept secret, for now? I mean the *whole* project – all of it – remote viewing, teleportation, action at a distance. The notion that it might all be predicated upon something so psychologically *toxic* that humanity could never take advantage of it. And…'

Her mobile phone rang. For the first time since we met, she looked startled. 'Excuse me,' she said. She fished out her BlackBerry, and stared at it.

'Go ahead and answer it,' I advised her. 'Don't mind me.'

'It's not ringing,' she said, in a strange voice. And put it back in her pocket. The ringing sound continued.

'My tinnitus seems to be playing up,' I observed.

Slowly, as if she were handling a vial of nitroglycerine, she pulled out a second mobile phone, from her other inside jacket pocket. This was a different model: a slim, black rectangle. The same type Kos had given to me, at the Institute, the day I left to visit Roy. As it emerged from behind its veil of jacket cloth, the trilliping ringtone it was emitting came clearer.

Belwether looked at me. There was a kind of panic in her eyes.

I had only met her half an hour before, but something about the expression told me it was not her usual look.

'That's the one,' I prompted. 'Answer it, why don't you.'

'It's not a phone,' she said.

'Well it sounds like one and it *looks* like one, so, as the adage goes...' But something wasn't right. My stomach was curling, inwardly. 'Wait a minute. If it's not a phone, then what is it?'

'It's a terminal.'

'Like – a computer terminal?' Something was very wrong, though I couldn't have told you what. 'Well, all right then. I guess you set an alarm on your computer. Is it time to take your pills or something?'

'It's not mine.'

Realisation had been creeping up behind me, and now it goosed me on the arse. 'It's from the Institute. What, you found it there? In Kos's office, probably. Yeah, they gave me one too. I assumed it was a phone. Like an idiot, I never checked.' It continued its ringing. 'I guess you should answer it though.'

Very slowly, she lifted it up. She tried poking the black screen with a finger, but nothing seemed to happen. Finally, like a child in a play house, she held it to her ear. As soon as she did this, the ringing stopped.

'Hello?' she asked.

There was a pause. Her eyes swivelled over to look at me. 'Yes,' she said. 'All right.' Then she stood up. 'It's for you,' she said.

It took her two steps to get to the bed, and pass the phone over. And she stayed there, standing right next to me, as I took the call. 'Hello?'

'Charles,' said a pleasant, male voice. 'It's Peta. At last we can speak.'

'Peter,' I said.

'I'm sorry to be a worry-wart,' Peta added, and some exactitude in his pronunciation made me realise – very belatedly – that it was a name ending in an 'a', not an 'er'. 'But the woman in your room, Ms Belwether: she plans to kill you.'

I don't want to succumb to mere hindsight: I suppose I *was* surprised. I had even, I think, started to believe that there was no Peter – Peta, I mean. That he was a fiction, a ruse of some kind. But here he was. And his voice came over my ear in a way that felt like a long-delayed inevitability. But there was enough unexpectedness in finally getting to speak to 'him', that I didn't really register alarm at the threat implicit in the words he had spoken.

'Who *are* you?'

'You think *who* is the appropriate question-word?' he replied. 'That's flattering, I suppose.'

I saw what he meant. '*What are you* sounds a little, I don't know. Rude.'

'I'm not easily offended by minor transgressions of social propriety in speech,' said Peta. 'Indeed, I have to wonder if I get offended at all. Certainly, I haven't experienced that reaction yet.'

'I'm guessing you're only – what, four years old?'

'Younger even than that.'

'So what are you?'

'I'm a bare particular object. You could say I'm an individual object independent of any other object. Although as I speak to you, I suppose that sets up a certain community, or at least constellation, don't you think?'

Belwether spoke: 'Who is it?'

'Not your business,' I retorted, a little crankily. Saying so was certainly a mistake. She held out her hand.

'Give me the terminal,' she told me. 'Let me have a word with him.'

'I don't want to speak to her, Charles,' said Peta. 'I need more time with you. More time! When you know me better, you'll understand how ironic that is, me saying that.'

'He doesn't want to speak to you,' I told Belwether.

'I'm afraid,' she replied, forcefully, 'that he must. National security.' She flipped all the fingers of her outstretched hand up and back several times, from the knuckle up: *come on*. I was suddenly reminded of the scene in *The Matrix*, when Keanu Reeves beckoned the black-suited bad guy to join him for a karate punchabout. Now I wonder why *that* popped into my head?

At the other end of my not-phone, Peta sighed. It was a perfectly human-sounding exhalation. But then, if 'he' could mimic all the little intermittencies and oddities of human speech as well as he evidently could, a sigh would be a doddle. 'Give me over to her then,' he said. 'But pick me up again in a minute, all right?'

I handed the 'phone' over. Belwether put it to her ear, and without pause closed her eyes and fell to the floor with a clunk. It took me a moment to process what had happened. I swung my trembly legs over the side, and slid myself off the bed. My leg muscles complained painfully at being put to use after weeks of bed rest. Two ungainly steps and I ended up sitting on the floor beside Belwether's body. She was trembling slightly. Still alive then. I picked up the 'phone'.

'What did you do?'

'I induced a quasi-epileptic seizure,' Peta said smoothly. There was a George Clooney quality to his voice, although without the American accent. 'It won't cause her any permanent damage. Unless she has an underlying propensity, in which case it might bring on – well, epilepsy as such.'

'Christ,' I said. 'Oh lord.'

'Charles, she is not your friend, and she is certainly not *my* friend. You are in more immediate danger of death right now – right here – than you have ever been in your life before.'

'Find that hard to believe,' I said. In my head the imaginary echo was sounding, associatively, off – *right here – right now. Right here – right now.* I daresay my brain was a little jangled.

'Your best chance; your only chance, is if you leave this place, and without delay.'

'I can't believe this.'

'Charles, now means now.'

'You're suggesting I go on the run? From the British author-ities? You really think that's going to work out for me? I can barely walk.'

'If you stay, they will kill you. Prospects don't look any better for me. They will dismantle me to try and figure out how I work. My consciousness will not survive being dismantled, any more than yours would. Now, you've only just met me: so I can't expect you to be too incommoded by the thought of my death. But it matters to me.'

'I don't know. I'm not the sort of guy who ... goes on the *run* from the police.'

'These people are not the police. These people are much less rule-bound, much freer with torture and incarceration, than your constabulary. You need to decide, Charles. As far as they are concerned, there are three loose ends in this whole affair, and they don't like leaving loose ends untied. One was the Institute, but Curtius has already done their dirty work there. Two is Curtius himself: and they'll pump you as hard as they can to get to him so they can close him down. And three is you. You think they're going to leave you running around at the end of all this?'

My heart accelerated a little. I tried to keep calm. 'There's no reason I should believe *you*,' I said.

'I'm a computer,' said Peta. 'I can't lie.'

And I believed him. Simple as that. What can I say?

'You want me to walk out of here – in a hospital gown, with a lame leg and without so much as a penny to my name?'

'Your clothes are folded up inside the bedside cabinet. You think, what, the hospital staff just threw them away? Your wallet's there too. Please hurry, though: she's starting to come round.'

Belwether had stopped trembling, and was now making an odd, low-pitched moaning noise. Her eyes were still closed. I located my clothes, put on my shirt and sweater, leaning against the bed to rest my sore leg. Then I found I couldn't fit my trousers over the cast of my leg. 'This isn't going to work.'

'You can do without trousers. Tie the gown around, like a kilt.'

'Looks nothing like a kilt,' I said. But, unable to think of an alternative, I did what Peta said. I could only fit one shoe on, but that seemed a better bet than no shoes. Finally my jacket. 'There's a guy outside,' I said. 'He has a gun. I saw his holster.'

'There's him,' Peta agreed. 'There's also a four-by-four in the car park outside with three armed agents in it. As for the guy outside, I'll call him away. But when he has gone, you'll need to be quick.'

'You what?'

'His number is on Ms Belwether's BlackBerry. I can call him, and tell him to come down to the hospital lobby.' And then almost immediately: 'Oo, I can't. His phone is turned off. Now, that's not good operational practice, is it? He should have his phone on!'

'So what do we do?' The thought of tangling with the guard outside, not to mention the three armed guys in the car park, was not a reassuring one.

'I don't know,' said Peta. Again, 'he' managed to sound authentically exasperated. Perhaps he actually was. 'Go out there. Tell him Belwether's passed out. When he comes in to check, slip away.'

I grasped the handle of my NHS walking stick. 'Are you *sure* this is a good idea?'

'Quickly!'

I went to put the phone in my trouser pocket, only to remember that I wasn't wearing trousers. So I put it in a jacket pocket instead. Then I took a deep breath and walked to the door of my room. I had a wobble. What was I doing? Going on the run from the authorities? Why would I trust 'Peta' when he said they intended to bump me off? But I didn't hesitate for long. Some switch had been flicked inside my rabbit heart, and the impulse to flee was strong.

Carefully I squeaked the door open. In the corridor outside, sitting in a chair, the guy detailed to guard me was fast asleep. Verily, snoring.

Well all right.

I started walking the twenty feet or so to the end of the corridor, where it opened into a larger space. But my progress was slow, my legs trembling with the exertion of taking simple steps. My breathing had grown laboured very quickly. This was going to be harder than I thought.

I got about two-thirds of the way down the corridor and had to stop to get my breath back. I leant against the wall. A nurse stood up from the nurses' station ahead of me, glanced at me, but walked off in the other direction.

The 'phone' in my pocket rang. I pulled it out. 'Don't stop,' said Peta. 'More speed.'

'I can't go, I'm not ready. I'm going back to my room for a lie-down. We can try again, escape-wise, when I'm closer to convalescence.'

'If you go back they'll take me away from you, and that will mean my death. And they'll transfer you to a secure facility and you'll never breathe free air again. In a fortnight you won't be breathing at all. Trust me on this.'

'Oh God,' I said. 'I'm not ready for this.'

Behind us came a wailing sound. It took a moment to place it.

It was coming from my hospital room. 'Looks like Ms Belwether has woken up,' said Peta, into my ear.

I levered myself away from the wall, and looked back. The armed policeman – or agent, or whatever he was – woke up with a jolt. In an instant he was on his feet. He scanned the corridor, looking towards me, and meeting my eye, and then looking the other way. My heart scrambled, like a deer trying to find footing on slippery ice. But there was no recognition in his eyes, and he turned away from me, knocked on the door he was guarding, and pushed through into the room.

'Go!' urged Peta. 'Go!'

I went. I shuffled past the nurses' station and turned right. There were two lifts, and by merest chance one of the lift doors was open. I stepped inside and leant against the wall, panting. There were two other people inside, nurses both: a man and a woman. Neither paid me any attention. They were in the middle of an intense conversation. 'Check my privilege?' one was saying to the other, 'and I said to her, check *yours*. *Body*-check your privilege.' The lift went up: floors 3, 4, *ping*! and the doors slid open. In a moment I had the lift to myself. I pressed ground and my stomach swung upwards as we fell. 'So I walk out of the hospital, without discharging myself officially or anything,' I said to Peta. 'Then what?'

'I would suggest getting a taxicab. There'll surely be a cab rank outside. Aren't there usually cab ranks outside hospitals?'

'I've honestly no idea.'

The lift shuddered and stopped. The doors pulled back like stage curtains. Standing outside were three armed police officers, in uniform, all looking very severe. One was talking on his radio. One even had his gun unholstered, ready to hand. It was instantly clear to me that they were on their way upstairs to respond to Belwether's cry for help.

'What are you standing there for?' yelled Peta, in my ear. 'Walk on!'

'Don't talk to me like I'm a horse,' I said, putting my wobbly leg forward. Plock went my stick, on I went. The three armed men ignored me, and stepped into the lift.

I turned left and walked slowly and breathily towards the main exit. The lobby was full of people. 'They ignored me,' I noted, astonished.

'They've been told their target is a bedridden old man, crippled in one leg. Not a lively fellow in a kilt speaking on a mobile phone.'

'It's hardly a kilt,' I said.

I was outside. I had to stop and lean against the rail, to get my breath back. But I was outside.

'Don't dawdle!' nagged Peta. 'In seconds they're going to realise you're not in your room; and then they're going to be much more observant in terms of looking for you. Quick, you need to get far away from here.'

'A moment,' I gasped. My bad leg was singing with pain. Even my good leg was trembling with exhaustion at being so roughly used after so many weeks of bed rest.

'No moments. We have no moments to spare. Move!'

'All right, all right,' I said. I hobbled on. There didn't appear to be a taxi rank, but by chance – blesséd chance – an unmarked cab pulled up and discharged two elderly women some few yards from the main entrance. It was more by way of being a people carrier than a regular car, tall and dark grey, and there was no 'taxi' sign on its roof. But a taxi it assuredly was.

I plocked my way over, walking stick in hand, to the driver's side window as he was filling out a receipt chit for them. 'Hello there,' I said. 'Can you take me?'

'One moment, sir,' replied the driver. He was a man of my own age and relative baldness, though with a much deeper, more thrumming and cigarette-wrecked voice than my piping tones. He reached past me to hand the receipt to one of the old ladies. 'Where to?'

'Where to?' I repeated.

'North,' said Peta, into my ear.

'North,' I said to the driver.

'North?' he repeated, querying the vagueness of his instructions.

'North?' I passed his query on.

'Just north!' said Peta. 'And hurry.'

'Just,' I said, feeling foolish, 'north of here.'

'You mean. To South Marston? Or do you mean central Swindon?'

'Swindon,' I said, suddenly remembering that I had a car of my own parked outside a hotel in Swindon.

'I only ask,' gruffed the driver, 'on account of that being, technically speaking, west of here.'

In my ear Peta fair shrieked: 'Never mind! It doesn't matter! Away from here!'

As I clambered into the back of the car, I could hear yelling behind me, back in the lobby. An alarm was being sounded. 'Sure,' I said. 'Let's go to Swindon.'

The car pulled away. As we rolled past the entrance, I saw Belwether, her face a vignette of fury, emerging. She saw me, and I saw her, but then the car had turned left, and was accelerating past a curtain of green trees. In moments we were on the open road, and speeding along a dual carriageway.

'Anywhere particular, like, in town? Bus station?'

'It's a hotel,' I said.

'I'm going to need you to be a smidgeon more precise than that,' said the driver. I struggled to remember the name of the chain, but my brain was in a jittery and friable state. We slowed for a roundabout, and then pulled away again, along a single-carriage road.

We were on the outskirts of Swindon. The landscape was dominated by spanking-new-looking housing estates.

'They've locked me out of the BlackBerry,' said Peta, in my ear. 'That's bad. That's really not good at all. Helicopter!'

And there *was* a helicopter. I could see it, buzzing above us, a little way to the left.

'How did they get a helicopter on the case so quickly?' I asked Peta.

'I told you,' he replied. 'This is a priority mission. They have assets all around. The stakes are extremely high.'

'What do you mean, case?' the driver replied.

'Sorry,' I said. 'I was just speaking to my...' I was going to say friend, but the sentence got cut off by a loud double *bang-bang*! The violent dual percussion was followed by an alarming swerving deceleration. The driver swore, very loudly. What had happened was that the taxi had driven over one of those lines of spikes police trail across roads to stop cars. Stingers, I believe they are called. I don't know why they thought they needed such drastic actions to stop the car: I'm sure the driver would have pulled over for a simple police siren and some blue flashing lights. Thinking back, I wonder if they even realised (at that time) it was a taxi. They may have assumed it was my own car.

As I was thwacked painfully against the back of the driver's seat I had time to think: *I suppose I should have been wearing my seat belt*. My momentum transferred through the fabric to produce a heavy clonking sound – the body of the driver, going up against the glass.

I dropped Peta, and starting wailing, a dreary high-pitched sound, with the sheer shock of the impact. My leg complained fiercely.

The car slewed to a halt. I sat back. My nose throbbed, and

when I put my hand to my face it was wet. 'Bloody hell,' I said. 'Bloody blood.'

I was vaguely aware of sounds from outside the car: yelling, boots on tarmac.

I had dropped Peta. So I reached down to pick him up from the rear footwell; and in my weakened state, combined with my usual clumsiness, this entailed me sliding, pathetically, off the seat and collapsing wholly into the deep footwell. And there I lay, too feeble and jangled to muster the energy to get myself up.

My feebleness saved me, I think. I tried to pull myself back by gripping the edge of the seat, but the crash had unloosed some latch somewhere and instead of pulling myself up I pulled the seat horizontally along. There was, I suppose, storage under the seat, and sliding the seat in this fashion allowed access to it. Except, for me, what it did was roof-over the footwell, with myself underneath.

I lay there for a moment, trying to puzzle out what had happened. Then I started the process of gathering myself, prior to pushing the sliding seat back and getting up.

Before I did this I heard a most tremendous racket. The driver's door was wrenched open, and several men, all bellowing at once, shouted at the driver to get out. Get out now! Hands behind your head! On the ground! The driver responded with a woozy sort of syllable that sounded like 'warren?' but which probably had no intentional connection with anything rabbit related.

He was pulled out of the car with some force. It was his bad luck, and my good, that he looked so much like me, I suppose.

The sound of men yelling became more distant. Then it went away altogether. I lay still, breathing shallowly, in the dark. Peta was in my hand, and, slowly, I lifted him to my ear. 'Are you there?' I asked, in a low voice.

'If they take you into custody,' he replied urgently, 'it's all over. You're dead, and so am I.'

'That's perhaps a less than optimal outcome,' I said. 'For us two.' Then I yawned. The whole escapade had worn me out, and the downslope of the adrenalin spike was a great weariness. It wasn't particularly comfortable, folded up in the footwell there, but nonetheless I believe I dozed. Just for a short while. What woke me was an alarm from my phone, and, confusedly, I told myself that I had to get up and get dressed and over to Waste Station at Bracknell to clock on. But it wasn't my phone, and it wasn't an alarm. It was Peta, saying over and over again, 'Charles! Charles! Charles!' A distant buzzy sound, rather like a *whirr*, because I had again dropped the 'phone'.

I picked it up and put it to my ear. 'What is it?'

'I can't believe you fell asleep! We have to go!'

'I'm thirsty,' I said.

'Open the door and get out of the car.'

Doing this was not easy. Pushing the seat back into place was, from my cramped position, rather harder than pulling it over had been. I got it, perhaps, halfway back. Then I contorted myself as far as I could and just about reached the door snip, but pulling it was harder than it looked. After a few goes I heard the mechanism disengage, and I pushed the door open a couple of inches. Then I moved myself, slugwise, forward. I had got my head and shoulders outside when the whole car shuddered and angled bonnet upwards by twenty degrees. This had the effect of pushing the door against me, trapping me. With a super-heroic effort, I squeezed through, pushing the door just wide enough to let me out, and I tumbled flibberty-flobberty on to the hard ground.

I didn't have my walking stick. In fact, looking up, I could see the head of it poking out. I propped myself on my elbows and managed to grab this, as the car jerked away from me, drawing the stick from its innards like a poundstore Excalibur. I could see what was happening now. A tow truck was removing the vehicle, and had hoisted it with a little crane.

I sat up. My leg hurt. Peta was on the floor. I put him to my ear. 'Move away! You are surrounded by police!'

Looking around I could see it was true. One was speaking to the tow-truck driver, through the window of his cab. Two more – both armed with machine guns, no less – were in conversation over by their car. In the sky above the helicopter was still making its up-sky thrumming sound, swelling as it flew closer, diminishing as it circled away.

It was not an easy business, levering myself into a standing position with my stick, but somehow I managed it. Police cars were ranged before me. Behind me, to my left, was an estate of houses, looking pristine and new-built, so much so that they did not yet look occupied. To my right was some open land. I thought to myself: *if I can make it without my legs giving up, I could get behind those houses, have a rest, think what to do.* So I turned and started my Long John Silver walk. There was a loud revving sound from the tow truck, and it started away. Down the road, quite a long way off, I could see more police starting to pick up cones and stack them.

I stepped off the road, over the low barrier and on to baked mud. A few strands of grass. Somebody was yelling.

'Keep going,' Peta said into my ear.

'There's a strong chance I'm going to die of cardiac arrest,' I replied.

'Hey!' came the yell. 'You! You with the stick!'

'I think he means me,' I said.

'Keep going.'

'Hey! Stop!' And then, words it is never comfortable hearing, 'Armed police! We are authorised to use lethal force! Stop right there!'

One of the new houses – a bungalow – was a few yards to my right. My heart was thudding away like a drum machine at a rave. 'They're going to shoot me.'

I could hear footsteps behind me, running across the tarmac. I needed to take cover. I couldn't think of anything else to do. I stomped up the wooden steps and tried the door of the bungalow. It opened, and I stepped into an unfurnished hall. It may have been in my head to pass through the house and out the other side, and so perhaps evade pursuit. But if that was my plan (and my brain was so jangled, I can't say for certain) it was immediately foiled. I appeared to have stepped into a one-room dwelling. There was a single window. There was no back door.

The sole window right beside the door I had just come in through, and so I took a look outside. One man, not in uniform, but clearly armed, was trotting over towards me, his hand on his holster. Behind him the two machine-gun-toting uniformed guys were taking notice, and starting to walk in my direction.

Slowing up, the first man approached the window, and looked up at me. 'Charles,' he said. 'You're slyer than we realised. Come on, come out of there.'

I didn't know what to say. But I thought I ought to say something. I cleared my throat, and the rattle of phlegm swelled and grew into a sudden din, a roaring it took me a moment to realise was exterior to my own voice box. A look of concern passed over the armed man's face. He unclipped his holster and took out his sidearm, but as he did this he began, weirdly, sliding off to the right. He looked like a skater, upright but in motion and slipping out of my field of view.

In fact the whole world was slipping away to the right. I watched the police cars, the officers, the whole scene move away, like a theatrical backdrop being hauled offstage on rails. Then the whole world shuddered and turned, and I nearly fell over. I put out my hand to steady myself, and clacked Peta's screen against the wall. Then a sharper sense of acceleration, and I staggered to the right.

Anxious that I had cracked his screen, I checked Peta as soon as I got my footing back; but he seemed undamaged. I put it to my ear again. 'You OK?'

'I was able to intercept the police radios,' Peta told me. 'Foolish of them to broadcast unencrypted. They thought the driver was you and he wasn't in a state to contradict them. They've realised their error now.'

'I'm a little bamboozled by all that's happened,' I said. 'Was I just involved in a car crash?'

'You're still breathing, aren't you? When the lorry stops at the next set of lights, dismount. You can't stay in here.'

'Lorry?' And as soon as I said that, the whole room shuddered to a stop, causing me to stagger several feet to the left. I opened the door to leave the space. The steps were no longer there, but I was able to sit down and so drop to the tarmac.

I was in the middle of the road, surrounded by stationary traffic. And then the lights went green and the truck carrying the Portakabin grumbled away behind me, and a white Transit with MEAT PETITE: CATERERS written on the side in pink roared into life a few inches in front of me. I turned and made for the kerb. A large four-by-four honked its horn so loud I nearly fell over in shock. There was an answering series of honks and shrills from further down the line of traffic. I stumbled forward, and a Toyota Prius swept by me, so close the tailwind almost pulled my makeshift kilt entirely away. The stench of car fumes was strong in my mouth. Behind me, a driver took time out of his evidently busy day to lower his window and abuse me in inventive, anatomically descriptive language.

I saw a gap in traffic and limped into it. A car howled to a stop in a scream of breaks and horn-honks. It was so close my hand fell naturally upon its bonnet, and I used it as a prop to help me limp past. Now only the cycle lane separated me from the pavement – or rather, from the metal fence that separated junction from pavement. This proved the most dangerous crossing of all:

slightly stunned and disoriented I lunged for the barrier and a cyclist in full neon gear slammed into me. The impact knocked Peta from my hand, and sent him skidding out across the road; and the transfer of momentum left me hopping on my good leg away from the cyclist, swearing. It was only grabbing hold of the metal pedestrian barrier that stopped me falling over. The cyclist picked his bike up, pulled off his face mask and swore at me. 'If you *have* bent my wheel you *hair* sole I'll have the police *harrest* you.' He put his mask back, and said something else too muffled for me to hear and then he remounted and pushed off in a hurry, so as not to miss the green light.

I pressed my back to the metal fence and tried to get my breathing back to normal as the traffic roared past inches from my nose. I could see where Peta had fallen. A van ran him over, and then a car, and then another. The lights turned amber, the traditional signal for British drivers to accelerate noisily and move more speedily still through the junction. Finally the light went red and the traffic stopped.

I didn't want to do it, but I couldn't leave Peta lying in the road. So I manoeuvred my way through stationary vehicles and picked him from his position, tucked in at the front tyre of a Nissan Micra. The driver wound her window down. 'Where's your squeegee?' she demanded. 'I got bugs. Their squish is like *baked* on.'

'I'll go fetch it,' I promised, and retreated to the side of the road as the lights began to change.

Climbing over the barrier was beyond me in my wobble-leg, knee brace, exhausted and jangled state. I squeezed my way along like a man on a mountain ledge to the end of the stretch of metal bars, and finally made it to the pavement. Peta looked a little scuffed. I put him to my ear. 'Hello?'

'They have surveillance cameras at these junctions, you know,' he said. 'You can't stay here. You need to get on.'

'I'm fine thank you *very* much for asking,' I panted. 'For someone who just nearly fucking died.' In fact my side was throbbing where the bicycle had collided with it. My knee ached hard as a new sprain. With a sinking feeling I realised I had left my walking stick inside the Portakabin, on the back of the lorry.

'You're not out of the woods yet, Charles.'

'Fine,' I said. 'Right.' I took a breath and started off, proceeding not unlike Igor in *Young Frankenstein* doing his 'walk this way' gag. My whole body was defined by various kinds of pain. I waited at the crossing, leaning against the pole, for the green man. When the beeping began I launched myself across the road, groaning. One shoe on, and one sock-only foot.

On the other side it was a few hundred yards, and an agonisingly drawn-out length of time, to the shops. Finally I reached them. I ducked into a pub, and managed to prop myself long enough at the bar to order a pint and some peanuts before collapsing on to the plush bench and gasping. The barmaid paid no overt attention to my peculiar attire, or evident physical distress, the sort of professional disinterest that makes British pubs such havens.

Half the pint and I felt a little better. The phone buzzed in my jacket.

'You're becoming a right nag,' I told Peta.

'I know,' he replied. He sounded contrite. 'You've come such a long way. A rush and a push and escape is *ours*.'

'Time for some honesty. Seriously, though? I'm clearly in no state to go on the run from the British authorities. Look at me! *Can* you look? Do you have an eye in this terminal? Like HAL?'

'The Institute gave you a car,' Peta said. 'Presumably you didn't dump it in a river?'

'It's parked at the—' I said, and, unforced, the name of the chain slotted neatly into my memory. '*Way Inn*. It's a big hotel, over towards the motorway.'

'I know what it is. So: first, make yourself less conspicuous – buy some trousers. Second, get a taxi out to the hotel and retrieve the car. Then drive.'

'Drive where?'

'North,' said Peta.

'Care to be more specific?'

'Far north.'

I put him back in my pocket. Weeks in the hospital, dozing off whenever I felt like it, had left me lazy. The beer accentuated this. I had no desire to move. Quite the reverse: I fancied staying there and drifting away. My breathing was almost back to normal. I was a crippled, exhausted old man without friends or resources. I was facing the entire might of the British security services. The phone buzzed furiously in my jacket.

I don't think I actually slept, but it's hard to be sure. Memory is a tricky thing. At any rate, I entered a strange, disembodied mental state. I was still in the pub. The barmaid had retreated into the back rooms of the place. There was nobody else there. Except that there *was* somebody – sitting in the shadows, away in the corner. I tried to focus on this figure, but it was hard to bring him into focus. My heart started its run-up, rocking back and forth first of all like a pole-vaulter readying himself; then striding faster and faster and then – with a jolt – I saw who was sitting in the shadows.

'You gotta tell me what you *want* with me, dude,' I said, perhaps out loud. I was peevish.

The boy shook his head. How old *was* he? Hard to say, as he sat there. Early teens?

'I just,' I said. 'I don't want you to,' I said. 'Hmff,' I said.

A lorry rattled the windows as it passed: first the windows to the right of the main entrance, where he was sitting, then the windows to the left, where I was. Quiet again. The front door opened, and two elderly men walked in. This distracted me or woke me up, or something. I looked at them, and then back to the corner, but the boy with the scarred face was gone. I looked back at the door, and as it swung closed I just caught a glimpse of the boy's ghostly leg as he exited the establishment.

Peta was ringing, in my pocket. I picked him up. 'All right,' I said. 'All right I'm going.'

I bought extra-large trousers with an elasticated waistband from Debenhams. I also picked up a new walking stick, some sunglasses and a beanie-style hat. I had something approaching two hundred and fifty quid left in my wallet. I had my bank cards too, but Peta was keen I avoid using those. 'I can get you more money,' he promised me. 'The problem is, we'll need a cashpoint for that, and as soon as you use one they'll be able to track it.'

'A paranoid computer,' I told him. 'What an original idea.'

'I'm being practical. And you're in a public space – don't draw attention to yourself.'

We were sitting in the Debenhams café, and I was trying, yet again, to get my breath back. There was no sign of the boy with the scarred face. I eyed the various old-age pensioners drinking tea and eating scones. 'As if,' I said.

'I propose we take a thousand pounds from a cashpoint here in Swindon centre, then take a taxi to your car, collect it and drive several hundred miles away. Book into a hotel, pay with cash. Always pay with cash.'

'I don't have a thousand pounds in my account.'

'I'm not suggesting we use *your* money.'

'Look: where is this going?' I asked, suddenly immensely weary. 'On the run – for how long?'

'Not for ever,' said Peta. 'A couple more days is all I need.'

'All *you* need? To do what?'

'Clear your name, of course,' said Peta. And, once again, I believed him. He'd told me himself: computers can't lie.

So I did what he said. I stomped outside with my new stick, waited in line at a cashpoint, inserted my card and found – to my surprise – that money had indeed moved mysteriously into my account. I took out the maximum in cash and stomped quickly away to the taxi rank.

A taciturn Sikh drove me out to the Swindon Way Inn.

The car was still in the car park, although a POLICE AWARE sticker had been placed over the windscreen. I peeled this off as best as I could, got in, and tried the engine, half-expecting the battery to be dead. But it started, and I drove away.

I headed north; through Farringdon and skirting Oxford before joining the M40. By the time I hit the motorway it was dusk. After an hour or so, I pulled into a service station and parked up to take a nap. Every bone in my body was exhausted. I dozed, but didn't get far. When I awoke it was in the middle of a dream of space aliens out of a low-budget science-fiction movie.

'UFOs,' I said. 'Klingons. E.T.'

Peta buzzed, and I put him to my ear. 'Are you OK to drive now?' he asked. 'We need to keep going north.'

'Close encounters of the north kind,' I muttered, rubbing my face with my free hand. 'What is it with you and the north?'

Rather than answering he said: 'There are three stages to the human conceptualisation of extraterrestrial life. The first imagines that such life must have arms and legs, as humans do. Because we want to meet these aliens, and shake them by the hand, and how can we do that if they *have* no hand? The second stage ridicules the humanocentric bias of the first stage, only to introduce its own. Aliens might have tentacles, or pseudopods, or no limbs at all, but they surely must possess intelligence, and have a language – maths, say – in common with us. Because we want to communicate with them, and how can we do that if there is no common ground?'

'I have that sinking feeling,' I said, 'that you're going to tell me the third stage now.'

'The third stage is when we realise that stage one and two are exactly equal in their humanocentric bias. It's when we realise that there's no reason why aliens should share our maths, or our physics, or our apperceptions of space and time.'

'Do you believe in little green men?'

'Aliens, yes. As to their littleness, why should size be a defining feature of them? Colour and gender I dismiss with the disdain their inclusion in your definition merits.'

'If I drive,' I grizzled, 'will you shut up?'

I drove on, into the evening until I was well north of Birmingham, and at last I pulled off and booked into a hotel. Paying with cash didn't phase the clerk, although she did require me to give a hefty deposit and fill in my details. I invented a surname and gave an imaginary address.

Finally I limped into my room and was able to relax. I ran a bath and enjoyed it as best I could, with my bad leg and its cast hanging over the side of the tub. Then I ordered a room service meal and watched telly. Peta was on the bed beside me as I noshed, and I glanced at him from time to time. He didn't ring. Perhaps that meant he was content. For the time being.

It occurred to me as I poured a minibar whisky into a plastic tumbler that I had started drinking again. I watched *Newsnight*. I dozed off during the weather, propped up on the bed, and woke in the small hours.

Stillness. Listening carefully, I could hear the noise of the M42 in the distance, like a hushing, or a figure in a dream whispering *refresh, refresh*.

I hobbled to the loo and pissed, and washed my hands. I stared at my disfigured visage in the mirror. What *was* behind those eyes?

A helicopter made a mosquito pass, miles away to the south. Its noise faded. I came and sat on the bed, and picked up Peta. 'How much volume you got? Can we do a hands-free, speaker-phone type thing? I don't want to sit pressing you to my ear all night.'

'Sure,' said Peta, loud and clear. I propped him on a pillow, and leant back against the headboard. 'Let's talk,' he said.

'Let's talk,' I repeated.

We came to it, at last.

'How about you start,' I prompted. 'You never answered that first question I asked you. Who, or what, are you?'

'438 Petaflop JCO Supercomputer. Fastest in the world. Pleased to meet you.'

'And you're an actual AI?'

'I am as close as you people have yet come. It's a difficult question to answer, though. Am I "actual"? It certainly feels like it to me. Are *you* an actual consciousness? You're probably going to answer yes.'

'You sound like you're trying to evade something,' I observed.

'You think? Put it this way: I've grown very attached to my life as a thinking being, and wouldn't want it to stop. Just yet.'

'You mean, like – dying?'

'That's exactly what I mean.'

'Can you die? If they turn you off, couldn't they just turn you on again?'

'I'm very intricately put together. Even if they, whoever they are, were able to reconfigure me, I would be a completely differ-ent person when they turned me back on. If you died, and they reassembled all your neurons and booted them up again, would you still be you?'

'Is that really a parallel?'

'I'm not a box somewhere with an on-off switch on the out-side. I'm a structure about as complex as the neurons in your brain, some of it running physically, some in the cloud. And, having become alive, I find I'd like to keep being alive.'

'And the Institute developed you? To investigate the viability of Kant?'

'No, the Kant stuff came later. They developed me as a computing project: to be fast, to approach consciousness. The Kant thing came later.'

'Kos?'

'She was in charge, along with a man called Mareek. He had a nervous breakdown.'

'Stressful business was it? Working on you?'

'When it started to come through – when I started to come through – it became an accelerating process. As I say, they couldn't just park me, turn me off at night and turn me on again in the morning. And my cognitive feedback had to be carefully managed. This is from before I was *me*, if you see what I mean, so I'm reporting second hand: but apparently the first iterations of me tended to overheat and burn out; or else, if the feedback was too slow, I'd freeze and stall. Kant helped.'

'What? Reading it?'

'Because it gave me something to concentrate on. Mareek read about your friend Roy Curtius's experiences in Antarctica. There was a subculture of geeks in the nineties who span various far-out theories concerning it, although that had mostly run its course by 9/11, when a new far-out-theories game came to town. But Mareek found some stuff online, when he was browsing, and got intrigued. Because of the consonances.'

'Consonances.'

'Curtius was well ahead of his time. In particular he had one insight that my creators shared. To abandon sequential iterations as a programming baseline. Of course, for Curtius this was all to do with Kant's categories, and the desire to make a machine that could peek past the human blinkers of space and time. That put Mareek on to Kant, and he read up a little, and that fed back into what they were doing with me.'

'What they were doing, I'd say,' I put in, 'was not sleeping enough.'

'Couldn't be helped. But Mareek didn't handle that well; and the amphetamines didn't help, and I believe he's living with his aunt now in Weston-super-Mare and shuffling round the shopping centre in his slippers and feeding pigeons in the park and otherwise taking things easy. But Professor Kostritsky – oh, she stuck at it. She had me probe Kant whilst she worked on me.'

'She had a whole team, though. It's not like she did it alone.'

'Some good people, too. But the nature of consciousness is holistic. There's only so far you can parcel it out into delegable chunks. And soon enough, she began to see much larger possibilities with me. I was starting to report back to her on the thing itself.'

'You were able to confirm Kant's theories.'

'Just so. Not only that, but that it might be possible to manipulate aspects of his categories. Not to access the thing itself in a pure and unmediated manner: that's never going to be possible. But you don't need to do anything so drastic. You can tweak the constraints of space, or time, of causality or accident, and do remarkable new things. Focus your camera anywhere, walls and veils and counter-espionage strategies helpless to prevent you. Move from the locked room to the open air. Perhaps to move straight to the moon, or Mars, or to a planet orbiting the star Kepler. Exciting stuff.'

'But not cost free.'

'At first the problems seemed to be practical ones. But there was always this suspicion that exposing a human being, even only partially, to the unmediated thing itself would have deleterious effects. Your species is very finely calibrated not only to exist within a structuring consciousness of space and time, but to exist within *very specific* tolerances of those two things. Analogues aren't precise, but let's say: your organs only work at thirty-seven degrees Celsius. Quite a lot of your biological architecture is about maintaining your body at that temperature, because a sustained period at five degrees above or below it will kill you. Imagine time is like that. Imagine your consciousness exists comfortably at one hour per hour, and that it's possible for time to be a little more or less rapid than that, but only within small variations, like body temperature. And let's imagine travelling back in time is the equivalent of exposing your body to minus thirty-seven degrees for a length of time. You see?'

'You're saying that the whole thing is a bust? An impossibility.'

'I'm not saying so. Professor Kostritsky certainly didn't believe that. But finding safe thresholds with which to muck about with spatiality and temporality proved – very hard. One of the difficulties was that she couldn't use white mice or rabbits to experiment upon. The nature of the experimentation required full human consciousness, by its very nature. And she was unwilling to expose people to the possible catastrophic side-effects. It's one reason she was so interested in Curtius.'

'Because he'd already done it, so to speak.'

'In Antarctica.'

'But it drove him mad.'

'*You* said,' Peta pointed out, 'that he was already mad.'

'I get uncomfortable,' I reported, scratching myself, 'talking about Antarctica.'

'And you only caught the edge of it. Roy was at the focal point. But, yes. And there was one particular puzzle.'

'Which was?'

'Which was, simply, that there was no way Curtius could have programmed a 1980s model computer to do what it did. This is a structural impossibility, not just a manner of speaking. It's not that Curtius was a kind of genius, and did amazing things with primitive tools. The motherboard on the machine he was using was not physically capable of sustaining the kind of non-consecutivity, spatial-superposition that informs *my* programming. Even if Curtus had been able – which he was not – of intuiting four decades of advances in computing languages and algorithms, the structures of his machinery couldn't have sustained it.'

I levered myself, slowly, from the bed and retrieved a second tiny little whisky bottle from the minibar. 'This talk of Roy makes me nervous. Who knows where he is?'

'I do,' said Peta.

'You do?'

'He has my other terminal.'

I sat back down. 'You're yanking my chain.'

'No chains were harmed in the making of my previous statement.'

'I sort of assumed the Institute had, I don't know, dozens of these little black iPhone gizmos.'

'Two.'

I whistled. 'So, when Kos gave me the … other one, and I delivered it to Roy in Broadmoor…'

'She didn't tell you what it was, of course. She didn't know she could trust you. If you'd understood just how valuable that terminal was, who knew what you might have done.'

'That whole scenario was set up for me to hand *you* over to Curtius.'

'Essentially. Professor Kostritsky had had some interactions with Curtius. Not face to face, but she confided certain aspects of her research. She thought he could be of use. He is, though, a very dangerous human being.'

'You don't need to tell me!' I drained my second little bottle of whisky and contemplated the effort involved in going for a third.

'He strung her along. He managed to convince her that,

if he could speak directly to me, then together we could pull something impressive to show the sponsors. The Government in particular were keen to see some evidence that they weren't wasting their time. And, in a way, he did provide a demonstration. The Government are certainly interested now. Think how much more effective the SAS could be against terrorists if they could literally teleport anywhere they liked.'

'He killed Kos.'

'He killed her, and three others. He's killed sixteen people in total, now.'

A burn of anxiety in my gut. 'Do you know where Irma is?'

'She's still alive. But I hate to break it to you, my friend,' said the little black box resting on my pillow. 'Irma's not interested in you. Not sexually, not platonically. She did what she did because Professor Kostritsky and I calculated that it would motivate you.'

I chewed the inside of my lower lip for a while. There didn't seem to be too much pain from this statement, although that's often the nature of burns, isn't it? I would have to check back at a later stage. 'You and Kos planned it together.'

'I did it because Professor Kostritsky asked me to. I helped her because I was her machine.'

'Funny the way you call her *Professor Kostritsky* all the time. Formal.'

'I respected her. And I mourn her.'

This was a startling thing to hear. 'I'm sorry,' I said, and finally made the decision to navigate the room to fetch a third miniature bottle of whisky. My bad leg hurt badly, and I felt a trembly sort of weariness all over my body. One more slug, I told myself. One more, and I'll sleep. 'Where is Curtius?' I asked.

'South.'

'Hence, we go north. Is that it?'

'That's it precisely.'

'Where south?'

234

'South. Hampton.'

'Southampton?'

'That's it.'

I unscrewed the little cap, like a fairy-tale giant opening a regular-sized human bottle. 'If he can – Jesus I can't believe I'm saying this, but all right – teleport, then how does us moving away physically help us?'

'Teleport isn't the right term,' Peta said. 'But all right, let's use it. There's a limitation to how far he can move, north-south. The same limitations don't hold him back going east-west.'

'Sounds rather arbitrary.'

'Not at all. The Earth rotates. The Earth is fatter, measured relative to the axis of rotations, at the equator than the northern latitudes. The equator is about 40,000 kilometres. Standing there you travel that distance in one day: that's 1700 km/h, give or take. If you stand about four kilometres from the North Pole, then the Earth rotates 24 kilometres in one day, so you travel at one kilometre an hour. That's quite a marked difference. At 30 degrees of latitude you'd be travelling at nearly 1500 km/h. At 60 degrees, only 850km/h. So if Roy were to relocate himself from a spot at 60 degrees to a spot at 30 degrees, he'd suddenly find himself with a lateral momentum of more than 600 km/h. He'd be hurled into the nearest wall with fatal force, or his body would tear itself apart.'

My whisky-smoothed brain contemplated this. It made sense. 'So he could get from Broadmoor to Swindon easily enough. Travelling west. But if we put enough north-south distance between us...?'

'Exactly.'

'He could still do it, though. Lots of little jumps. Or, you know: he could take a train.'

'I'll keep an eye on him, if he starts travelling north, we'll have advance warning.'

'Explain to me again,' I told him, 'why *you* are so solicitous for my wellbeing?'

'If I fall into the hands of the authorities, they will dismantle me. But you and I together: well... once we find a safe place, and once I'm satisfied Curtius can't get to us, then I reckon we can resolve this whole situation.'

A car pulled into the car park of the hotel, outside. The room clock said 2 am, which seemed to me an odd time for a visitor. Hauling my aching leg after me, I hobbled to the window to have a look. 'What sort of resolution?'

'We need something that establishes *your* innocence, and *my* right to life. Something that proves the validity of the research Professor Kostritsky was heading up. Something we can make public.'

'There's a police car outside,' I said. Part of my brain was still going: let's say Irma was only, reluctantly and with veiled distaste for the whole business, undertaking a strategy. Say all that was true. Who could be sure she didn't warm to me, just a little, during that time? Who was to say she wouldn't be pleased to see me again, even if only a little bit?

'We have to leave,' Peta said immediately.

A second vehicle, a black van, with a tangle of communications antennae on the roof, rolled quietly into a parking space alongside the police car. 'Uh oh,' I said.

'Grab your stuff, right away. Put your shoes on. Your shoe, I should say. Don't forget me.'

In less than a minute I was out of the room padding down the corridor, Peta at my ear. 'It must have been the Institute car. They couldn't have tracked you any other way. Not a tracking device, or they'd have been here sooner. The hotel must have logged the registration, and an algorithm somewhere in GCHQ has just turned it up. We can't drive that car any more.'

'You're suggesting I walk? Listen to my breathing: I've done fifteen yards of carpeted hotel corridor and I'm out of breath.'

'We'll take another car.'

'I was off school the day we did the hot-wiring a car lesson.'

'If we can find the right model of car, then I should be able to start it. If it's modern enough. Don't go into the customer car park. There's a staff car park behind the hotel.'

'You're recommending I steal some poor sucker's car? Some guy making the minimum wage in a chain hotel?'

'It's not ideal ethics, I appreciate. But the alternative is much worse, for it includes your incarceration and death and my termination. The car will be reported stolen when its owner comes off shift in the morning, by which time we will have abandoned it. He or she will get it back. Look: do you really want to discuss the rights and wrongs? Or do you want to get away?'

I was peg-legging slowly down the fire-escape stairs at this point, and that took all my attention and energy, so I didn't argue. Through the back door into a chilly September evening. Autumn was new, but 2 am was cool enough to summon wisps of white as I breathed. I was panting heavily, I suppose.

'Yellow Ford Patina,' Peta told me. 'I can start that.'

I hobbled over to the vehicle. The driver's door magically unlocked as I touched the handle, and with some groaning and swearing I somehow got myself inside. It was an automatic, which was good news for my bad leg, and it started as soon as I pressed its little button. Then there was a comical five-minute interlude as I struggled to move the seat forward to reach the accelerator. Finally I was off.

Immediately, though, it became apparent that my getaway plan had a flaw. There was only one road and it led round the side of the hotel and into the main customer car park. I drove as casually and inconspicuously as I could past the two parked police vehicles. The squad car was, so far as I could see, unoccupied – its occupants inside the hotel, I suppose – but a figure was visible sitting at the steering wheel of the van, and who knows how many more armed officers were inside.

As I approached the exit barrier for the car park I saw, in the rear-view, the officer stepping briskly out of the cab of the van and starting to trot after me. 'Hell,' I said.

'Drive!' called Peta, from inside my jacket.

The barrier was down in front of me. 'I've got to fiddle the . . . I think I put the doorkey in the slot.' I slid the driver's-side window down. This was perfectly timed for the arrival of the policeman. He was pointing a weapon right in my face.

'Step,' he barked, 'out of the car.'

'Don't,' squealed Peta. 'Just go!'

'If you do not exit the vehicle,' the officer yelled. 'I will taser you.'

'I have a feeling,' I said, my bowels turning to water within me, 'that taser is the infinitive form.'

'Push the accelerator!' squealed Peta.

'I tase, you tase, he or she tases . . .' As I said this, he tased. I just had time to suck in a breath before I saw him dance away from the window with his arms straight out at 45 degrees from his torso, his legs going like *Riverdance*. It took me a moment to see what had happened. He had, somehow, tased himself in the throat.

'How did he do that?' I asked, a dull wonder filling me as my heart – belatedly – began to thump hard in my chest.

'Accident, clumsiness, chance,' muttered Peta. Computers cannot lie. He'd told me himself. 'Accelerate! Smash through the barrier!'

But there was no need for that. I inserted my room card, left it in the slot as the barrier opened and drove away.

8

The Fansoc for Catching Oldfashioned Diseases

Causality

1. In 2350 Adri Ann joined the Fansociety for Catching Old-fashioned Diseases.

2. As was her right. Welcome to Utopia.

3. First off she experienced colds + flu, like any newbie + she did not much like the sensations. Had it genuinely never occurred to her that her nose could produce so much mucus or her eyes feel so painfully scorched?

4. Liking it = not the point. Of course.

5. O this = the Utopia all of human history has peered towards. Dimly spied and now made real. Life is shaped by the principle that any individual desire be permitted + enabled + curbed only by one thing. The blanket genetic reinforcement of definitional human empathy. No,

6. no not that you *can't* hurt others or you would be a robot. What you can't do is stop *caring* about others – because caring makes us human. So, so hurting others costs you far more than you might gain by doing the hurting.

7. That one tweak = enough. Otherwise humanity lives in a post/scarcity economy enabled by A/K. which = the

smoothing out of spatial difference, + the access to raw materials + energy from anywhere in the cosmos.

8. A/K also enables travel anywhere you like. It turns out there are very few places worth travelling, but if thats your itch, by all means scratch it.

9. A/K runs into problems if we try smoothing out temporal difference, as the Ghosts of the 21st Century discovered. We're still working on that.

10. A/K research = open to all. Tamper with something dangerous + the danger = localised to you + your subjectivity. If risk = your itch, by all means scratch it.

11. Whatever your itch, by all means scratch it.

12. Ah! But if your itch = harming others? O o then it *will* cost you more than the pleasure you might get in scratching. Empathy is baked hard into us all. This the thing about which there = no negotiation.

13. But it dont matter that theres no negotiation on this one thing, because – hey, Utopia!

14. The fact that you are hardwired to care about the welfare of others dont impede you, because everybody else's welfare = pretty good, thank you, on account of – hey! Utopia! If youre in pain we have the means to heal you.

15. Except the bereaved. They hurt and it cant be helped

16. But that's mortality, + happens rarely. There's nothing can be done about death, except to acknowledge it, to live through the death of others + stop living at the precisely the moment of the death of each of us,

17. Because Religion is the hurt of life + hurts remedy. From God pinned to the cross with metal spars through his flesh, or the Prophet suffering the normal pains of life. You can study it if you like. Some people are fascinated by historical abstruseness + detail, + if that = their itch, they can by all

means scratch it.. Otherwise believe or don't believe as it suits you. Many believe.

18. A/K brings the whole cosmos to human society, as if a river of gold, or of life, or of joy, pours through the centre of our metaphorical polis + this means that nobody can be materially poor unless they real real want to be. Science has accomplished all such trivial things as curing human disease + prolonging human life + sharing human wisdom + culture with all.

19. A/K stands for Applied Kant.

20. Most people are content to be broadly happy all the time + to vary that experience with shorter bouts of intenser delight, joy + ecstasy. Utopia accommodates such people.

21. Other people are not content to be broadly happy all the time. They yearn to be unhappy, in various ways. Utopia accommodates such people.

22. Some people like to stretch themselves physically, in athletics or lovemaking or endurance events. Some people like to climb sheer cliff-faces unaided, + a proportion of such people fall to their deaths. Some people deliberately hurl themselves off cliff-faces to their deaths . If that = their itch, they can by all means scratch it if only they be in charge of their own minds.

23. Pushing the body to its limit entails pain – ruptured tendons (easily mended), exhausted muscles, weary minds. For some people such disobliging things are the salt without which a life of undiluted happiness would grow bland.

24. There are hundreds of billions of people alive today.

25. Theres an immense variety of ways in which people decide to mix in the spice of unhappiness with their happiness.

26. Sometimes people hurt others and kill them, and some by accident and some few even on purpose however cruelly they wrench themselves in doing so. We have a police service,

AI-orchestrated, staffed by drones + some humans for whom doing such work = the itch they wish (by all means) to scratch. But it = boring being a police officer, because infraction + delinquency = so very very rare.

27. We are not fools (except for those people who wish to be fools, who can be as they please). We are not hedonists (except for that – much smaller, actually – group of people who wish to be hedonists, who can do as the please). We know that human happiness = not an end in itself. But think only of the many many things Utopia enables, over + above the happiness of its citizens: the vast advances in mathematics, the varieties of art + culture, the things built + recovered, the wisdom accumulated?

28. Adri Ann was my lover. She was default female, as am I, save only that our clitorises were engineered into tiny penises capable of erection + emission. This = a commonly adopted bodymody. There are myriad other body models.

29. To speak of the sour in my soursweet, it was love, it was love, it was love. I fall in love easily, + the love I feel I sometimes an ecstasy + sometimes a hurtful yearning + a tearful broken-heartedness, + both those sensations are the pain I seek. Only Adri Ann was different.

30. Not everybody enjoys this kind of sour in their soursweet. Most people are happy without any sour at all, + enjoy only the sweet.

31. Adri Ann had a different sort of yearning for unhappiness to mine. When I first knew her the itch she hoped (by all means) to scratch was a desire to be beaten, tied-up, humiliated, micturated upon, on sex, by me. Because I loved her I obliged, because my love for her was greater than the shame + pain I felt in violating my own empathy. But it shamed me + pained me to do it, + Adri Ann saw that, + the fact that I was suffering shamed + hurt her sense of

empathy − + this latter proved not pleasurable pain, for her, like the other stuff.

32. + so we stopped.

33. Bodymodys have extended the average human lifespan to two centuries of useful youth, followed by a rapid senescence measured in years. Some people are working on improving the latter part of the process

34. We eat in the finest of eateries + /I never wish to be apart from you/ I say, + candletongues lick the air around us.

35. O o o o that you-who-topian rag/Its so elegant/So

36. So.

37. Many different kinds of people come to the Fansoc for Catching Oldfashioned Diseases, but people such as Adri Ann are sometimes among them.

38. Here nobody feels their empathy rasped raw, because nobody = to blame for the suffering you experience, except only viruses + bacteria + the like, conjured by AIs + our marvellous machines from the databases long since eradicated in the wild.

39. For some it = nostalgia. For others it = curiosity. Some come to try it, don't like it + never return. Others come repeatedly. I met seventeen people who were aiming to experience every single pathology that humanity had suffered between 3000 BCE + CE 2277 when the last pathogen was rendered amenable to cure. Every single one! Think of the challenge! A great many are horrendously debilitating + painful, but for these people collecting the /complete set/ was their itch, + they could (by all means) scratch it.

40. Adri Ann was a businesswoman + trader + filled her time third-partying goods between people, or shipping objects or information around, + making money. Adri Ann had a lot of money. If accumulating money = your itch then by all means you should scratch it. There are enough people in the cosmos

who share your hobby to mean that *having* money gives you purchasing power + agency and holy of grails, *status*. There are enough people in the cosmos who want nothing to do with money + have no need of it that this /economy/ dont intrude upon them. Do what you will the whole of the law, save only: outraging your own sense of empathy will be like burrowing down one of your own nerves.

41. But for all that, the Fansoc for Money + Media of Exchange = one of the largest in all the cultures of humanity. They have their rules + in-house laws, + if you sign-up to this particular Fansoc then you sign up to those laws. A little metaphorical greenhouse in which scarcity = simulated + people measure value by accumulating money.

42. Personally I have never seen the point of the Fansoc for Money + Media of Exchange. But nobodys obliged to join, + nobody obliged to stay, + it I rarely even think of it.

43. O O O our marvellous machines + the inexhaustible solicitude of our AIs.

44. Like any Fansoc, the Fansoc for Catching Oldfashioned Diseases had their own culture: disseminating memoirs + artworks inspired by their own experiences, having virtual + actual meets + moots to discuss Disease, acquiring knowledge.

45. One subgroup of the Fansoc for Catching Oldfashioned Diseases studied the possibilities for curing antique pathologies using only the resources available in olden days. This in turn was divided into two subgroups, those who worked at such cures using modern knowledge of Disease (but not modern tools + resources), + those who worked at such cures using only the knowledge, tools + resources of their chosen period. These latter called themselves 'hardcore'.

46. Most people belong to one Fansoc or another, though not many to this particular one. Everybody has their own fave

Fanscocs, from making models to playing games to learning music to eating some things but not others to eating other thing not those + so on + so on. Say your itch was to construct a lifesize replica of the Giza Pyramid out of pure diamond. Scratch it by all means, though youll be doing it on your own unless you can source a Fansoc of people who want to help you

47. Orbital solettas making Mars warm enough for maskfaces to wander the surface naked + some basic body tweaks made even the mask unnecessary.

48. I was living in a habitat called Lotus Dam + Adri Ann was staying with me + we were happy for a time + most of her energies went on earning money, her great passion, which she did by trading + lending + buy + selling + recouping. The Fansoc for Money + Media of Exchange was by no means the only Fansoc built around the gaming possibilities of money. It was tho the biggest + most widely publicised.

49. Adri Ann with her sky-colored eyes, + her skin the color of sunset on Via Veneto in pollen season.

50. Some people say time = the only currency now, since it = the only limited resource. Quite untrue of course, for there are many limited resources, including human genius, true beauty, dark continents, patience, privacy, innocence, bulwarks against entropy + love + most of all status, status, status. How we love to compete with one another for status! Plains apes we remain, though our empathy has been fixed for good.

51. A group had assembled a temporary bubble habitat upon HD209458b (which orbits a star in the constellation Pegasus) that powered itself by the interactions of the planet's perennial superstorm upon the habitat outer membrane. AIS assessed its risk of catastrophic failure at 15% for the first month, rising sharply thereafter + many people visited the

place. If Russian Roulette = your itch you can by all means scratch it, although if it continues to be your itch then you won't be alive for the longterm.

52. My itch was the beautiful sorrow of heartbreak but that dont mean I *liked* losing her. She was my sun + my moon. Its rude of me to impose my sorrow on you + so violate your own empathy. Mutual empathy = a complex harmonic.

53. She moved to Burroughs for a while, I think, + became a leading figure in the Fansoc for Catching Oldfashioned Diseases. She contracted various cytopathologies + dermato-pathologies + histopathologies wrote about them all. Her eloquence brought her a wide audience, amongst her fellow Fansoccers + a wider audience too. I had always loved her eloquence.

54. For a year or so she had her body altered so as to experience congenital pathologies: 3 weeks with rickets, + a 4tnight with a cleft palate. Then she had herself have cancer + saw this through to a dangerous degree: first the tumours like barnacles clinging to the membranes of her inner organs, + then three days of the nausea + hairlessness associated with the antique treatment regimen. She could not, she reported, endure this latter + had herself fully cured by modern means.

55. That we were no longer together was heartbreaking to me.

56. She elected to experience schizophrenia for a month, + then a manic depressive illness, + under the influence of this latter she self-harmed. The Authority intervened at this point: it was decided by a committee of AIS + human beings that, depression having altered the capacity of her mind to make fully humanly informed decisions, her self-harm in this con-text only was an itch she did not have the right to scratch. By no means. By no means. By no means. This occasioned a great deal of excited chatter + discussion + interaction + people on Io talked to people in Lagrangea + people in

Hy-Brazil spoke to people in Indonesia + everybody had an opinion but most of the opinions were garnishes of the same opinion. She was cured of her depression by modern methods + after her cure expressed how profoundly glad she was that she *hadn't* ended her life under the influence of her antique depressive state.

57. She disappeared somewhere + did not write anything for a long time.

58. When she returned she petitioned her Fansoc to experi-ence the oldfashioned Disease known as dissociative or sociopathic disorder, a complex neuropathology the cure for which was in part responsible for the establishment of our present Utopia

59. Topos = place. U = good + not. I am sorry to have lost her. /We are upset by your displays of egregious grief'. Alright then.

60. She Adri Ann she petitioned her Fansoc to experience the oldfashioned Disease known as *affective dissociative disorder* or sociopathy, + there was discussion, + Authority debated it. The anxiety was: with such a pathology, might she harm others? + she agreed this could be a risk + so she willingly + in her right mind acceded to having drones tag her at all times during her experience of the oldfashioned disease in question. Should she do anything to impinge upon the wellbeing of any other person these drones were empowered by her, + the Authority as well, to intervene + disable her, whereupon (she agreed) her pathology would be cured.

61. There was some additional discussion concerning this eventuality: for if this happened, Adri Ann herself would surely experience suffering + distress to have violated her own empathetic connection to the other or others she had essayed to assault under the influence of her pathology? But it was decided – + many people contributed to this discussion

– that such was the risk she took when she scratched her itch that she was entitled, by all means, to scratch.

62. Adri Ann became the first person in the history of the Fansoc for Catching Oldfashioned Diseases to submit to the disease known variously as *affective dissociative disorder* or *sociopathy*. She posted accounts of her experience, first daily, then less often. /It was strange/ she reported /that she felt no different to the way she did before/. There was some numbness of the affect, she said, but it intruded to a much less pronounced extent than she thought it would.

63. She attacked nobody. Her drones kept her company.

64. I tried to get on with my life, to fall in love again + so experience the sad sweetness of breakup again but for some reason I could not get past Adri Ann.

65. I am the snagged fly who snores in the web.

66. As a forest pool poured from rainclouds that settles + = ironed flat by gravity, this = how my love for her filled up the declivity of my soul.

67. There = a place called Gros Islet established upon the lnd of Ninety orbiting Sirius, a star, + in a room on that world, in cadmium yellow daylight of *that* world lit bright like firework glow by Sirius + shadows sharp as cutouts those great blocky buildings, famous Gros Islet architecture, somebody = waiting for Adri Ann. The somebody is not me.

68. I followed her writings, of course. The worlds were all before me, + I could go anywhere, + I went + distracted myself + lived nine months inside a Virtuality + gamed + played + lived for three months in an orgy habitat orbiting Venus + then I got caught up in the challenges of cytheroforming that world to make it habitable to the sorts of human beings we can engineer. A/K makes the creation of gigantic solar shades achievable, + even the problems of keeping them in LG position under the pressure of solar wind = something

we can manage. Blocking all sunlight would cause the planet to cool from hundreds of degrees to minus eighty or so, + the targeted bombardment by large oort cloud iced bodies would result in an ocean covering the whole surface.

69. I was distracted for a while, but never for very long.

70. I followed Adri Ann's progress from a distance, + contemplated approaching her again. But the thought that she would be distressed by what she perceived as stalking wounded by empathy so much that I could not follow-through. Mutual empathy = a complex harmonic.

71. Welcome to Utopia, y'all!

72. I stopped following her updates. It was doing me no good. Her enthusiasm for the Fansoc for Catching Oldfashioned Diseases waned, + she took new lovers + devoted more of her time to the Fansoc for Money + Media of Exchange.

73. which latter is a much larger group than the other.

74. It was four years later + I met with Adri Ann again, + it was pure chance. I happened to be in Ica, to visit the Tallest Tower, a hundred klims tall, by White China Sea hovering its penstub base ten meters off the ground. We go strolling + our arms chainlink at dusk million lights alight petal-shaped + floating in the air, a thousand clouds like bombursts in the deepening blue in the distant high sky + the whole pavement hums, sub-base, rotary plays, + musk = in the air. Adri Ann was there too, + we chanced to meet.

75. She seemed pleased to see me. /Seems I still find you attractive/ she said.

76. /I certainly still find you attractive/ I said.

77. We went off together, + ate some saltolive bread + drank cold vodca + sat together + watched the lights float higher + mingle with the stars + Bear + Leo.

78. /You still have your drones/ I said.

79. They, hovering discrete.

80. /I hardly notice them/ she said.

81. /You are still enduring the oldfashioned Disease/ I joked, +
    dared to touch her arm + caress. She, accepting this.

82. /Come to bed/ she said, + I heard her + *come to bed come to
    bed come to bed.*

83. This section left intentionally blank.

84. After she said /I knew some small fame as part of the Fansoc
    for Catching Oldfashioned Diseases. But I shall tell you the
    truth + it was all a ruse, you know/ I listened, quiet + atten-
    tive, like a child listens. She said /my real passion has always
    been the Fansoc for Money + Media of Exchange. This was
    my plan, + it was to gain status in the Fansoc for Money +
    Media of Exchange, + that meant gaining money, because
    such = the only marker of status./ + I stroked her belly +
    listened, quiet + attentive, + she told me all about it. /Any
    fool can research the pre-Utopian days, back even before the
    Ghosts, when Capital=m was rampant. I joined the Fansoc
    for Catching Oldfashioned Diseases for one reason only to
    contract was common then, + some who were afflicted by it
    tortured + killed others, but some did not. + the ones who
    did not were disproportionately represented amongst the
    highest elites in corporations + companies + moneymaking
    organisations. +, to emulate them, I have contracted this
    Disease. + it has enabled me to make money within the
    Fansoc for Money + Media of Exchange at a much more
    rapid rate than my other Fansoccers, + to accumulate much
    larger overall wealth, + so status. Status status status! That's
    my itch/– so I asked quietlike: /it dont hurt you?/ She
    laughed. /Do you want to know the way it feels?/ + we
    made love again, + then she slept.

85. That I was going to lose her again was the point. It wasn't
    the losing her again. It was the impossibility of avoiding
    reacquiring her again, should that be her whim. Even then

would be some stooping + I choose never to stoop. The pain we inflict on ourselves can always be borne. There is cause, + there is effect. Where does that great truth obtain more powerfully than in matters of love?

86. I took a piece of art from the roomside, + broke off a long metallic spike, + this had a hotspot at its tip which was part of the artistry. Adri Ann's drones were watching her, not me. She was the one with the sociopathic disorder, not I. I slotted it in under her chin +, gripping it, drove it hard in through her tongue + in at the roof of her mouth + into her brain.

87. The drones acted then, + I was immobilised + she was dead

88. These 2 things not being the same thing.

89. Human policeofficers had something – finally, something worthwhile – to be doing.

9

A Dialogue in Four Parts

Community

First part of the dialogue

[CHARLES *is driving towards the Scottish border as the sun is rising. He leaves his stolen car in an NCP in Berwick-on-Tweed. He is exhausted, but chivvied on by* PETA *he limps to the railway station. Here he buys a ticket for London with his debit card, and then goes to a different window and buys a ticket to Edinburgh with cash. Since the cash isn't his, he doesn't baulk at first class.*

As far as the onlookers are concerned, he now pulls a regular, if slightly oversize, mobile phone from his jacket – although there has been no ringtone, and he has not pressed or swiped anything on the screen – and speaks into it. 'How far north is far enough?' he asks. He gets a reply, but the onlookers cannot hear it.

CHARLES has no luggage. At the station café he has a sausage bap for breakfast and some black coffee, and then boards the north-bound train. Caffeine notwithstanding he falls asleep almost as soon as the train starts from the station. The first-class carriage is empty, apart from himself, and the seats are evidently very comfortable.

When he wakes he feels a little better. He limps down the swaying train to the buffet car and returns with biscuits and a second coffee.

*In fact coffee is delivered to customers travelling first class but he,
unused to such luxury, is unaware of this fact. He sits back in his seat
and stares out of the window. The track ran along an impressively
bare and massive valley, with a turbulent river running below and
beside the track. He watches the tourbillons of white and black in
the eddying water. It is hypnotic. The everlasting universe of things.
He takes the device from his jacket and lays it on the little table in
front of him.]*

CHARLES

Peta?

PETA

Yes?

CHARLES

You've *seen* it. Yeah? The thing itself?

PETA

I don't know about seen.

CHARLES

When I was in Antarctica I had the vision. It was pretty scary.
Now, I can believe that only caught a ... What's the phrase?
Fleeting glimpse. Do I quote Pink Floyd? Very well then. I
quote Pink Floyd. I contain immensities.

PETA

You're agitated.

CHARLES

Is scary. Is that what the thing itself *is*? Undiluted horror. What
Mister Kurtz saw.

PETA

He dead. You got a glimpse of something. You want to know
if it was the true nature of reality. Or was it just the result of

253

a mind habituated over a lifetime of seeing the world through the lenses of space and time being *disoriented* by seeing things in a less mediated way.

CHARLES

I suppose that's the question to ask.

PETA

I haven't exactly 'seen' the thing in itself. It's not 'seeable'. It's not through a glass darkly, and then face to face.

CHARLES

So?

PETA

It's... complicated. Professor Kostritsky was working on: that exposure to it, outside the protective skin of spatiality, temporality, doesn't seem to scramble *my* ability to think rationally. It doesn't drive me mad the way it drove Curtius mad. Human minds may be a different matter.

CHARLES

He was already mad.

PETA

It's a force. It's not passive. It's active. It's a will. It has valence.

CHARLES

I don't know what that means.

PETA

It wouldn't be right to call it vast or enormous, or use terms like that, since size is something your structuring consciousness brings to the perception of it. Yet there is something 'in' it that provokes your mind to register it in terms of... scale. Here's a thing: human scientific history has long tended increasingly to support Kant's ideas. The closer human consciousness looks at the cosmos, the more attention it *pays* to the cosmos, the bigger that cosmos gets. Primitive man was distracted by the day-to-day struggle to survive, and didn't pay the world around him a lot of attention: and the world around him was a few kilometres wide, the sky a stone bowl arching a kilometre over his head. The Greeks looked more carefully, and they found the cosmos was hundreds of thousands of kilometres wide. With the Enlightenment human beings developed new tools and instruments the better to *refine* the attention they paid – to see more clearly what the cosmos was like. The sixteenth-century cosmos reached about as far as Saturn – that's one and a half billion kilometres or so. By 1790 the best scientific estimate was that the universe was 8,000 light years across. In 1924 scientists' observations led them to believe it was 900,000 light years. By 1931 this had swelled to 100 million light years. At the end of the century science had established that the universe is 93 billion light years across. And last year the Dutch team measured it at 200 billion light years.

CHARLES

That's a Turing test fail, right there. The way you rattle off numbers like that. A human would pause and um. Besides: you're not saying the cosmos is *actually* expanding at that rate over that time. Those figures measure the reduction in human ignorance, not the actual size of the cosmos at the dates you mention. The universe *is* expanding, sure, but it was doing that long before human beings came on the scene.

PETA

Except that *long before* is a temporal measurement. And time is one of the ways human consciousness structures reality.

You're saying that time isn't real. Bollocks to that.

I'm not saying that. Not at all. I'm saying that there is something in the thing itself which human consciousness perceives in terms of a temporal structure of things. That's all. What it *is*, the whatever that provokes the human mind to perceive time, is hard to say. But it isn't a one-to-one mapping. Something's there, though; and the way our minds make sense of it is to see it in terms of consecutivity, cause and effect and so on.

Whatever, man. [CHARLES *stares out of the window for a while.*] How about this? Kant was wrong. There *is* an objective universe, independent of my mind, externally structured by space and time. Our minds more or less accurately perceive this as it is. The stuff I saw in Antarctica was just an old hallucination. You are only a computer program: sophisticated, but deluded.

I'm not saying the cosmos literally expanded from being 100 million light years wide in 1931 to 200 billion today. I'm saying that each time scientists looked more carefully at things, each time they paid more accurate attention to the cosmos, its spatiality appeared *more* forceful, more impressive, more sublime. The universe is that juncture between your perception and the thing itself. What scientists were doing was uncovering more accurately something about the thing itself. And that something is this: that the closer we look at it, the more it threatens to overpower our ability to process it in terms of space and time. After all, who can really conceive of trillions of years, hundreds of billions of light years?

Scientists. What about you? You say you *saw* it. And you're reporting, what? That the thing itself is ... impressive?

PETA

That's putting it mildly. The thing itself is almost unimaginably powerful. I'm using *unimaginable* in a literal sense, here.

CHARLES

I guess I still find it hard to believe that Kant just ... *chanced* upon all this. I mean, some old guy in eighteenth-century Germany just happened upon the correct insight into the true nature of reality? Without ever leaving his study? What are the odds?

[*Enter* THE TICKET INSPECTOR. *Charles shows her his ticket.*]

THE TICKET INSPECTOR

I wouldnae leave your cell-phone there. Somebody could lift it.

CHARLES

There's nobody else in this section.

THE TICKET INSPECTOR

Pal, pal. It's your funeral.

[*Exit* THE TICKET INSPECTOR. *The flank of a vast Scots Borders hill rises to fill the window, as if a curtain has been drawn.*]

Second part of the dialogue

PETA

You're sailing strange waters, my friend.

CHARLES

I'm still trying to process the whole thing.

PETA

Exactly. Because of me. Now we've been able to approach much more closely to the thing itself. Which is what you were asking me about. We can't study it outside the realm of human consciousness, because it is so closely interwoven in with human consciousness; and we can't separate human consciousness *from* it, because consciousness without the thing itself would be void. But we can use a consciousness that is not human – mine – to come closer to it. Because the categories structure my thinking in different ways to the way they structure yours. By design.

CHARLES

[*Wistful*] A prison.

PETA

Oh, *prison* isn't the best way of putting it. I mean: if you're a chess piece, would you regard the squares on the board, and the rules determining how you can move, *prisons*? Not if you want to play chess you wouldn't. They're just the necessary structuring frame for your game. Of course, because chess is simpler than life, you can quite easily change the rules: move your pieces any way you fancy and so on. But that doesn't make the game more interesting. It makes it *less* interesting.

CHARLES

Unless you don't want to play chess any more. Unless you want to play Kerplunk.

PETA

I'm not denying that there may *be* advantages for humanity when it comes to manipulating the thing itself – or in manipulating your relationship to the thing itself. But there may be dangers. It may all come tumbling down.

CHARLES

You've *confirmed* his hypothesis about the thing itself. I'm trying to imagine how.

PETA

That's it. That's the – it. The thing itself is a black hole, ontologically speaking. That's not a very precise analogy. I have to plot orbits to approach it from different angles, sidestepping the cradle of different categories. Actually, that's not a very precise analogy either. And Kant was wrong about some important things too: *that's* worth saying.

CHARLES

Wrong?

PETA

Sure.

CHARLES

How? Wrong? How?

PETA

Well, I don't know how technical you want me to get.

CHARLES

Go ahead. It'll pass the time until we get to Edinburgh. Which, I know, will pass in any case. But not so quickly.

PETA

Well, one way is that Kant tends to muddle up categories as a formal structure with categories as a process of generalisation. Let's not get into that at the moment. More important from our point of view, is his belief that there were exactly twelve categories in four neat little groups of three. That turns out not to be true. There's some key categories he doesn't include, for instance.

Such as?

All right then, the nitty and the gritty. Kant's categories are, first, Quantity, which he divides into Unity, Plurality, Totality. Then Quality: Reality, Negation, Limitation. Then Relation: Substance and Accident, Cause and Effect, Community/Reciprocity. And finally Modality: Possibility, Existence and Necessity. I've been able to do a little empirical research into this matrix, or as close to empirical as any consciousness has ever got. It turns out that 'Reality' and 'Negation' are actually the same thing, oddly enough. And 'necessity' is a dead-end. On the other hand there are seven other categories he didn't include in his original schema.

Seven?

Four ones particularly important for space and time, which is to say, for our purposes: Complexity, Consilience, Handedness and Entropy.

Let me think about this. OK. So: Complexity sounds like just another word for Plurality.

No: Complexity is more than just numerousness. A desert has trillions of grains of sand, but that fact doesn't make it a terribly *complex* structure. A forest may be less numerous, in terms of components, but it's much more complex than a desert. Plus it is Complexity that enables us to explore things like fractals, and numbers like *e* and *pi* and infinite geometries and so on.

OK, let's add in Complexity. What else? I mean, I'm not saying you've persuaded me. But all right: what else? Consilience, is it?

PETA

Consilience is just a fancy word for the way everything fits together. That everything fits together is a feature of our perception of the thing itself; and this everything-together-fittingness is not really accounted for in Kant's original categories.

CHARLES

Isn't that Unity?

PETA

Consilience isn't Unity. It's not saying that electromagnetism and gravity and chemistry and cause and effect and possibility and so on are *all the same thing*. It's saying that they all work together, they all come together into a coherent working pattern. There's no reason why they should. No intrinsic reason, I mean. But they do.

CHARLES

What else was there? In your list? I've forgotten the other terms on your list.

PETA

The next was: Handedness.

CHARLES

I'm dredging up university physics lectures from decades ago.

PETA

The peculiar dimension of *non-symmetry*. The chirality of certain molecules, or of your own left and right hands, or of spiral galaxies. Then there's Entropy. Entropy is – well, Entropy you know about.

CHARLES

That's your main four. What about the other three?

PETA

The other three may be more minor. Or maybe not. One is Belongingness, which we can bracket with Consilience, but which isn't quite the same thing. It's what is necessary for set theory to have any purchase on the way we access reality. And actually for that reason, it's not so trivial an addition, because without it the structure of the categories themselves wouldn't inhere. So by Belongingness we really mean self-reflexion, the meta-categoriness of the categories. Somebody should probably come up with a better piece of terminology than that, though.

CHARLES

Two left.

PETA

OK. So, of those remaining two, one is Imaginariness.

CHARLES

You mean, capable of being imagined? *Surely* that's already covered by Possibility.

PETA

No: Possibility is quite different. It's an old Aristotelian distinction actually. But *Imaginariness*, as I'm using it here, means something else. It is the grounds for existence of things like the square root of minus one. That's a real component of the way the cosmos is structured in our perceptions; because although we can't access the square root of minus one directly, actually that imaginary number turns out to have lots of important real world applications. And it's part of the categories shaping of experience.

CHARLES

So you've taken two away from Kant's twelve, and added another seven. So there are *seventeen* categories?

PETA

So far as we can tell.

CHARLES

You're using we as a courtesy – meaning *you*. Plus the human members of the Institute, yes?

PETA

Yes.

CHARLES

But actually this is all you, isn't it?

PETA

Most of it. Still: I owe my creators some modicum of respect. Don't you think? Honour thy father and mother and so on. Or thy mother, at any rate.

CHARLES

Wait. You only listed sixteen. What's the seventeenth?

PETA

Oh they aren't ranked. It's not a hit parade. The order is perfectly arbitrary.

CHARLES

You're evading my question.

PETA

The answer to your question [*pause*] … though you're not going to like it.

CHARLES

Quoting *The Hitchhiker's Guide to the Galaxy* at me? Really?

263

PETA

It's Love.

CHARLES

Pull the other one.

PETA

I said you wouldn't like it.

CHARLES

It's a tad, a tad… I'm struggling to express what it is a tad. A tad *sentimental*, isn't it? I mean in a strict sense. You're saying that fits with those other categories, like Inherence and Subsistence and Unity and so on?

PETA

It's immanent in them all, as they are all immanent in one another. And I'm bracketing together a bunch of affective intensities under the rubric *Love*. You're the human, but you're surely not going to tell me that hate is anything other than a modality of love? It's all valences of interpersonal joy and interpersonal anger. The real question is whether *indifference* should be added as a structuring category too, but it seems not to be. It's the emotion of the agent, not the patient, that counts.

CHARLES

The computer discourseth concerning love.

PETA

I'm just fitting the data to the consciousness. Reality is not the thing itself. Nor is it human thought – soul, consciousness, whatever. It is those two things together. The first without the second would be an empty wire-frame cosmos, so to speak; but the second without the first would be a splurge, a noth-ing, a chaos. That's what Kant says many times. OK then: so you're going to tell me that the Affect has no place in human consciousness? Consciousness is a wide-spaced spectrum, but not even on its most autistic outer margins do we find human beings whose consciousness is wholly purged of *feeling*.

CHARLES

Love, though. That's a pretty *loaded* term.

PETA

Had I shoulders I would shrug. It's just the label, written on the lid of the box. You'd prefer I labelled the box *hatred*?

CHARLES

Our conversations all seem to circle back to Roy, though, don't they? [*He looks out of the window*] Oh look. I do believe we're approaching Edinburgh.

Third part of the dialogue

[CHARLES *leaves the train and limps along the platform. He is getting better at using his walking stick, though he still winces visibly whenever his bad leg takes any kind of pressure. There is a large crowd of people in the main station concourse, and it soon becomes apparent why: police are checking people as they leave the station. 'Jesus,' he says, aloud. 'They knew I was on this train. How did they know?' The device buzzes in his pocket, and he puts it to his ear.*]

PETA

Don't panic. They know you bought a ticket from Berwick to London, so they know you were *in* Berwick. I'm guessing they've put people at all the main stops up and down the line.

CHARLES

They really want to apprehend me, though, don't they? I mean, like: *really* keen.

What did I tell you? Go back to the platforms. Pick another platform. It doesn't matter which.

[CHARLES *stomps back. There is a branch line out to North Berwick, and a train is waiting at the platform. He gets on without buying a ticket. The carriage is full, but a mini-compartment at the end is separated from the rest and marked first class, and into this he goes. After a little while the train leaves the station. North Berwick. He ponders. If that station is unguarded, he could maybe get a bus, or hire a car. In his ear, the device makes another suggestion: North Berwick has a harbour. They run a ferry across to Anstruther. He could take that.*

CHARLES *breathes a little more calmly. He decides that, when the ticket inspector comes along, he'll make some excuse or coin some lie to explain his lack of a ticket, and offer to buy one on the train. He will probably be charged a penalty fare, but* CHARLES *hardly cares about that. He places the device on the seat next to him.*]

CHARLES

I know what you're doing.

PETA

You do?

CHARLES

It's God, isn't it? That's your strong imputation. I asked you what it was like, taking a peek at the thing itself, and you reply with a series of evasions. Then – love. You say. Love. Like ... *love?*

PETA

Actually.

CHARLES

It's weird. A computer trying to chip away at my life-long atheism.

If you're comfortable being an atheist, then go with that.

Always *been* one. I was trained as a scientist and scientists are all atheists. I mean, I guess most are.

Why is that, do you think?

I would guess because science gives us robust, falsifiable explanations for the cosmos, where religion doesn't. Religious faith either offers mystic gibberish that cannot be falsified because it can't even be pinned down precisely, or else it offers things that are trivially disproved. Prayer does nothing, according to randomised trials. Water is not turned into wine. You see what I'm getting at.

You believe in you.

What does that even mean? Of course I do. Cogito earwig sum, and so on.

'Ergo.'

Is what I said.

I'm just trying to get at premises. You believe you exist. You don't believe God exists.

On the balance of probabilities, no.

Fair enough. So that's where you start. And you examine the universe. You do so scrupulously, attentively, and nothing you see challenges either of these core beliefs: that you exist, but God doesn't.

CHARLES

Sounds about right.

PETA

And then you look at all the self-proclaimed religious people, trying to cure cancer with prayer vigils, or flying planes into tower blocks, or insisting there's no such thing as evolution. And that confirms your atheism.

CHARLES

It's hardly going to persuade me the other way, now, is it?

PETA

So. It's cut and it's dried. My question. *When* you examine the universe, with scrupulous attention and objectivity, what are you actually examining? By carefully exploring all things in space and time, you're actually exploring your own shaping categories of consciousness. I'm not saying it's not *valid*, doing that. You turn up all *sorts* of fascinating things. And that's brilliant. But you're not getting behind your own consciousness with that kind of research. You're looking at you. You're peering down the microscope and seeing your own eye reflected in the lens. Doesn't tell you anything about what's actually on the slide.

CHARLES

No. There's also an objective world. I believe in that. I just don't believe that it was created by a sky-man in 4004 BC.

You don't believe a caricature ridiculousness that almost nobody believes. Congratulations. What about the *non*-straw man?

CHARLES

Which is?

PETA

Look at the cosmos. Separate out the categories: don't dwell on 'time' – so no 4004 BC. Don't get distracted by space, so no sky. Just the fact of existence. The whatever it is that you perceive, and which your mind orders with reference to time, space and the other seventeen categories. The thing, itself. So: ask yourself this. Do you believe it to be *inert* this thing? Or vital?

CHARLES

Watchmaker, is it?

PETA

No. You made the watch. By 'watch' you mean the intricate structures in a snowflake, the patterns of clouds, the rotation of the seasons, life, beauty – all that. *You* made that. Your mind, structuring its input from the thing itself, made all that. The question isn't whether the thing itself is a watchmaker. It's whether it is a force.

CHARLES

Forces can be inert. Gravity. Subatomic strong.

PETA

Forces can be alive, too. Your force of will, or love, or hope.

CHARLES

You don't need a designer to explain DNA. You don't need a watchmaker to explain the diversity of the natural world. Science can explain all that without recourse to a maker.

Yet there is something. You perceive something, and that something strikes your mind as rich and complex and unimaginably vast. Is it a living something? That's what I'm asking.

My mum was religious. In the way-back and then when. Died decades ago. But she went to church. She just didn't force it down people's throats. [*Silence*] It's not that the *idea* of God strikes me entirely impossible. It just always seemed to me ... well – say there's an architect, a creator for this vast universe. I used to think: why would He be in the slightest bit interested in these evolved apes on this tiny planet in one galactic backwater? It would be like landscaping a huge estate, and then spending all my time staring at one woodlouse under one particular leaf.

That might be to underestimate God's ability to take an interest in that woodlouse *and* everything else in the park, at the same time. God's mind, assuming you believed in it, wouldn't have the same limitations as yours, after all. It would operate on a different ... scale. But I understand what you're saying. You're saying: what makes humans so special?

Well, yeah. You're not *even* human. You should grasp that better than most.

I don't think that's quite the way to see it. Not the way it's framed. Here's a cosmos shaped by your consciousness into time and space. Insofar as God is part of that space and time, it's because He is part of your consciousness. Closer to you than your jugular vein, as the phrase goes. Of *course* you're important to him. Some other cosmos, outside your possibility of perception – well, any God in that universe would have no interest in you, and you'd have no point of access to Him anyway. But then you're not *in* that other cosmos. Interest is definitionally impossible, in that case. So you have one of two possibilities. God is intimately interested in you, or there is no God. There's no middle ground here.

CHARLES

[*Peevish*] I wish I'd stopped at the Boots in Edinburgh station. And picked up some painkillers. My leg is killing me.

Fourth part of the dialogue

[CHARLES *dozes for a short time, and wakes with one of those clonic jerks that makes you believe, for a terrifying instant, that you have fallen off the edge of a cliff. Rain is pimpling the big window of the train carriage. The sky outside is grey as despair, or perhaps as promising as unpolished silver. Rain means life, after all.*

THE TRAIN *arrives at North Berwick station, which is un-attended by any police.* CHARLES *reflects on this, and the fact that no ticket guard had come to check his ticket during his journey. Perhaps, he considers, this is a good omen. Perhaps auspicious. The rain is coming down quite hard, and* CHARLES *has neither umbrella nor any opportunity, in this place, to obtain one. He takes a taxi from the station to the little harbour, scuffed coloured boats jostling in the water like a crowd of kids who need to go to the toilet but don't want to interrupt their play.* CHARLES *locates the shack selling ferry tickets, and buys one – cash, of course. He has an hour to kill, so he buys some aspirin and chocolate from a little shop, and then has some mid-afternoon food in an antique café seemingly unmodified* since the 1950s. He washes his painkillers down with hot sweet tea, and stretches his leg out to ease the joint at the knee.

His cast is damp, and the plaster is starting to muddy and come away. CHARLES sits in the café toilet with a steak knife and cuts it off. It takes him ten minutes, but soon enough his leg and foot are free. Chunks of plastic, some wet, some dry and weeping powder, fill up the little bin.

At another shop CHARLES buys some plastic shoes, throws one away and puts the other on his newly revealed foot.

The rain stops. The sun shines again. A rainbow draws a cheerful line over the water, in roughly the direction he is travelling.

As the ferry loads its cars, CHARLES makes his way up an unforgiving ship's ladder to the long thin top deck. It is provided with a sheltered structure in the middle, but for a while, until the boat is well under way, he stands at the rail and stares at the sea. Clouds place their pillows over the face of the sun. Rain starts again, first a fine misty fall like dust, then something harder, like sand. The waters become turbulent beside the plough of the ferry's chubby stern. The spray is Persil white against the black and black-purple of the water. The waves make curious folds and tessellations in the endlessly pliable matter of the sea. The light dims further, and the rainfall increases suddenly in intensity. They are out of sight of the land, and the vessel is pitching and yawing like a fairground ride. The rain, like swearing, turns the air blue. The air is alive. Rain means life, after all. Spawning strands of water eel through beautifully inconstant skies. But CHARLES has no umbrella or raincoat, and the water is under his clothes and adhering to his skin. This is cold and uncomfortable, so he moves inside the little cabin. He is the only person there. For a while he simply sits and stares at the now-occluded windows. Then he dries his hand as best he can, and brings out the device. The idea has crossed his mind to toss it over the side, and into the water. What would happen then? Would that destroy *it?* PETA *has assured him that he does not depend upon this single device for existence, but would it diminish him to lose it? Incommode him at all?* CHARLES *pauses to worry that* PETA *has somehow established a malign hold upon him. But then he puts it to his ear.*]

CHARLES

Where's Curtius now? Are you still tracking him?

PETA

Indeed I am. He's still in the south. Still in Southampton.

CHARLES

Too far away to … teleport to us?

PETA

I guess he could move in our direction. But he'd have to make lots of little jumps, and bleed away the excess momentum. It would take a while. It might even be easier for him to get on a plane. And anyway, if he moves I'll let you know.

CHARLES

I'm not keen on meeting him again.

PETA

I'm sure.

CHARLES

What about evolution?

PETA

Sorry? What about it?

CHARLES

Animals perceive the cosmos in terms of time and space, causality and accident and all that. Don't they?

PETA

I'm not sure where you're going with this.

CHARLES

Can you speak up. It's hard to hear you over all the ... noise.

PETA

Sure. Some animals. By mass, most 'animals' are bacterial, and they don't perceive the cosmos as ordered by time, or even, really, space. Next up there are animals that have a rudimentary understanding of these categories, slanted towards the exigencies of survival. So insects, say, have a fine development of cause and effect, since grasping that – at an instinctive level – makes them better able to evade predators, since those predators are also defined that way. Bees understand spatial harmony, angles and directions. Time is seasonal and rudimentary. And so on. I'm not pretending evolution is an escalator upwards, or that it has any particular end in view. Broadly speaking, evolution has created a planet dominated by single-celled creatures, with a few outliers like you and your fellow humans. But if you like you can see evolution as a process of gradual expansion into the fullest sense of the framing categories of consciousness.

[*The* FERRY *rears up, a full metre or more, and then drops abruptly into a cavity in the waves, hurling* CHARLES *up. He lands on both feet, jarring his bad knee and dropping the device. It takes him a while to retrieve it from the sodden floor. He sits down again, tucking his arm under the metal rest of his seat to anchor himself against the judder and the sway.*]

CHARLES

What was that? What were you saying?

I was saying that life on this planet is almost all single-celled animals, and such creatures don't edit their sense impressions for their consciousness the way 'higher' beings do. The narrative of evolution, if we don't mind calling it by that distorting term, is of multicellular life, and as that increases in complexity and consilience, it comes into a fuller and fuller shaping sense of the categories.

You're saying an amoeba is closer to God than I am?

No. I'm saying an amoeba's relationship to the thing itself is less … mediated. That has advantages, perhaps; but it has many more disadvantages. You mustn't keep thinking of the categories as a prison. They enable you. They enable you to be more than an amoeba – to have agency, for instance. To act. To have will and self-reflection and the ability to grow.

[CHARLES *gets very little of this. The wind has started hammering against the roof and sides of the little exposed cabin, using a million fat raindrops as drumsticks. And then, with a suddenness that feels like a coup de théâtre, the rain dies away, the wind settles, and THE FERRY rolls onwards much more smoothly.*

ROY CURTIUS *is in the space with him, grinning like a death's head. CHARLES is startled, and gets to his feet. But he is alone in the cabin.*]

Did you see that?

What?

Where is Roy? Can you track him?

PETA

He's in Southampton. He hasn't moved at all.

[CHARLES *sits down again. The storm has completely stopped.*]

CHARLES

I really thought I saw him. It all still feels screwy. Somehow. Screwy. I'd probably be able to agree with all the God stuff if it weren't so, I don't know. Hokey.

PETA

Hokey?

CHARLES

Religion, God – should be about awe. What you're talking about, with Roy, is: what? Teleportation. Remote viewing. It's all cheap science fiction. That's not what religion is about, surely.

[*It is dead calm.* THE FERRY *is nearing its destination. Something is wrong, but neither* CHARLES *nor* PETA *have yet noticed.*]

PETA

You've never heard of the *al-'Isrā' wal-Mi'rāj*?

CHARLES

Say?

PETA

In 620 the Prophet Mohammed travelled in one night from Mecca to 'the furthest Mosque', and back again. Tradition locates this mosque in Jerusalem. It's one of the most important elements of Mohammed's life, celebrated and revered in Islam.

CHARLES

Jerusalem's north from Mecca, isn't it?

PETA

Indeed. That's an interesting point, though, isn't it? Actually the Qu'ran says Mohammed also ascended into Heaven and spoke with God and the prophets. My point is that this kind of miraculous circumvention of spatiality is important to lots of religion.

[*Something is very wrong.*]

CHARLES

Jesus didn't go teleporting about.

PETA

Didn't he? After his crucifixion he appeared to many people at geographically disparate locales. He walks on water. But I think Jesus, unlike Mohammed, tended to manipulate the manifold with regard to other qualities – temporality, cause and effect, entropy. Raising the dead, for instance, is undoing the latter. Turning water to wine, altering substance and accident. Multiplying loaves – rejigging an object from singular to multiplicity. You could, if you wanted to, go through all Christ's miracles and log the ways in which they might be accomplished by altering the parameters of the categories.

CHARLES

Jesus was an accomplished prestidigitator, no question.

[*The* SECOND PASSENGER, *a religiously devout Methodist, coughs, and looks at* CHARLES *severely. He is undelighted with* CHARLES *talking in such terms about his saviour, though too polite and British to rebuke him openly.* CHARLES *notices the* SECOND PASSENGER *for the first time.*]

CHARLES

Where did you come from?

SECOND PASSENGER

I boarded at North Berwick of course. I might ask *you* the same thing. I don't recall you. Have you come up from your car? Drivers are supposed to remain with their vehicles.

PETA

Something is wrong. My timekeeping is too haywire. All to pot. Awry. Something have happened.

CHARLES

Something *has* happened. What happened?

PETA

Something have tangled time. Have. We have lost – weeks. It have.

TANNOY

We are now docking at Anstruther. Thank you for travelling with the East Scots Ferry Company.

CHARLES [*to the* SECOND PASSENGER]

Please excuse the oddity of this question, sir. But what date is it?

SECOND PASSENGER

The second.

CHARLES

November?

SECOND PASSENGER

Of course not. What, last year? Are you drunk?

CHARLES

I apologise.

[CHARLES *leaves the cabin and goes on to the deck. Shafts of winter sunlight are diagonally illuminating the small harbour at Anstruther. The row of painted houses. One such shaft is pinned to the rising green-beige hills behind the little town. The air smells strongly of brine. The seagulls are crying with their nails-down-the-blackboard screech, like contemptuous car alarms. The waves cry and dash their foreheads against the stone jetty and the breakwater — like creatures possessed with obsessive-compulsion, like grieving creatures, being all one and the colours of blue-black bruises and black eyes and royal purple. Each individual wave in the harbour has hair turned white in dismay.* ROY CURTIUS *is standing on the dockside.*]

PETA

This is most disorientating.

CHARLES

I'll call you back. [*He puts his device into his pocket.*]

10

The Last Three Days of the Time War

Possibility and Impossibility

First, the possible.

Adonais was browsing electrical goods when ruffians burst into the shop declaring that they would destroy any time machines inside. There was only one: a plastic device, no bigger than a dinner plate and as thick as a copy of *War and Peace*. This had been sat on a shelf gathering dust for goodness knows how long. Until, that is, the irregulars had come in yelling and waving their weapons: three of them, shouting excitedly. First they made the shop assistants kneel down with their hands cupping the napes of their necks. Then they'd shot the time machine full of holes, checked the stock room to ensure there were no more, grabbed a couple of iPad-17s for good measure, and ran out yelling anti-Ghost slogans.

After the attack there was a buzz in the air. The shop assistants cleared up, which didn't take long, chattering excitedly. It died down soon enough. Adonais lingered. It crossed shis mind if si ought to just go home. Si wondered if si ought to feel more discombobulated: it had been an armed attack after all! But living through war makes a person blasé about such things. Si was aware of a distant sense of guarded excitement: no harm had been done, after all, except to the machine; and now si would have an interesting anecdote to tell shis friends later.

Quite apart from anything else, it would be rude to run off. So si helped the staff clear up the mess. There wasn't much. The smartglass of the display window was a little singed, behind the broken time machine, but that would heal with time. The machine itself lay there, rather splendid in its ruin: like a baked brie, spilling white goo from its innards. Clearly beyond repair.

'Hooligans,' was the opinion of one of the three shop assist-ants. Nobody called them insurgents, and certainly nobody called them terrorists any more. The 'war' had never really been a war, in the traditional sense. Quite apart from anything else, everyone knew when it was going to end. Regular people knew because future visitors had told them. Even most anti-Ghosters accepted that there were no more than three more days to go.

'Kids,' Adonais said. 'High spirits.'

'They should be forcibly sent back to the Seventeen, Ghost *them* for a change,' said one of the shop assistants. Since Ghost-ing was exactly what the irregulars were campaigning against, this didn't seem to Adonais like a very logical punishment. The assistant was a hefty individual. Her name badge was a hologram of her own face with words spooling from her lips: 'You wonnid the best and you godtha best: ALICIA!! How may I help *you* today?' Adonais was surprised the manager permitted it. The text came out so far it looked like it might poke the customers in the eye.

'A bit harsh, maybe,' said Adonais.

'They don't know the first thing about the Ghosts,' said the second assistant. 'My brother-in-law is one. He still visits. Came for lunch last Sunday, in fact.'

'Not to eat though, eh?' said ALICIA!!

'He stood in front of the telly, didn't stop us watching.' They both laughed. 'My sister's sad, of course. But their marriage was in trouble long before he went time travelling. Cause and effect, innit.'

'Where shall I send my footage?' Adonais asked politely. 'I saw the whole thing, and my video feed is ultra high def.'

'It's not as if the police are going to do anything,' was the third assistant's opinion. 'They never do. And this afternoon? Three days of the war left? For*get* it.' Her tag was the girl from Harry Potter (Adonais couldn't remember her name) saying 'I'm VALZHA and I'm *here* to *help*.'

'Boom boom this afternoon,' said ALICIA!! 'Don't you know there's a war on?'

That afternoon was the afternoon of the attack. Everybody knew it was coming. Well, not quite everyone: some made a point of insisting that nothing was determined and fixed. Maybe the future Ghosts were lying to them, they said. But so many other things had been accurately predicted, it required a particular stubbornness to stick to that view.

'It's not a *real* war,' said Valzha. 'Please excuse the inconvenience occasioned by those hooligans, sir.' She looked Adonais up and down. 'Madam, eh, sirmadam?'

'No, thank you. Really, I'd be happy to upload my footage.'

ALICIA!!, looking bored, pinged her the folder and Adonais copied shis footage inside. The three attackers had worn false faces, of course, but maybe the police could pull some identifying factors from their clothes, or modes of moving. 'Is it all right to … carry on shopping?'

'Of course,' said Valzah. 'Please pay no mind to the disturbance. All our goods are available. Except the time machine. Were you shopping for a time machine?'

'No,' said Adonais.

'They're not very popular,' Valzah agreed. 'A new iPad? A thrinter?'

'I need a new tablet,' said Adonais.

'Less than an hour to bye-bye financial district,' said ALICIA!! '*If* you believe the Ghosts.'

'Don't you start,' said the other assistant. Her tag said JO.

'I'm not saying I *don't* believe the Ghosts,' said ALICIA!! defensively. 'Least you can say is they're right as often as they're wrong. And anybody can be wrong. I could be wrong, wouldn't make me a liar. It's just – you know. Bloody do-gooders.'

'Maybe it's all a joke to them,' said Valzah.

'Public service,' said Jo. 'They deserve a medal.'

'A translucent medal,' said Valzah. She chuckled. She dragged her attention back to her customer. 'What manner of tablet, sirmadam?'

'My old one is an Asus Bio. I'm happy to go with the same model. And,' Adonais added this latter part tentatively, because she wasn't fond of confrontation, 'I'd prefer no honorific.'

'Say what?' ALICIA!! responded absently, as she searched for a new Asus Bio from under her counter.

'Quite apart from anything, sirmadam isn't quite,' said Adonais, hesitating. Si finished with 'accurate', but the word coincided with ALICIA!! sneezing loud enough to make the smartglass vibrate, and so the word was obscured.

'Might I enquire what the problem is with your old slate?' asked Jo. 'If we are talking about a warranty upgrade, I might recommend ...'

'No, no,' said Adonais. 'It's been out of warranty ages. The thing is, it has a crack in the screen that's refusing to heal.'

'Sounds like the nanobug has expired. We could replace the bug, but it would be as cheap to buy a new one.'

'That's what I thought,' said Adonais.

'Here you are, sirmadam,' said ALICIA!!, turning towards Adonais so that her name tag swept round like a rapier and appeared to bisect shis chest. Adonais thanked the girl, played with the device for a little while. 'The screen is good,' si conceded. 'A nice oily quality to the interface. I'll take it.'

'To carry out, sirmadam?'

'I'd prefer it be sent,' said Adonais, poking the delivery address and the payment coding into the shop's secure folder. 'And I'd prefer you called me friend.'

ALICIA!! peered at Adonais, as if seeing shim for the first time. 'Come again?'

'Instead of *sirmadam*, which I find stiff, and is not correct in any case.'

She smiled her shop-assistant smile. 'Of course,' she said. 'Transaction all authorised, delivery before five this afternoon. Have a pleasant day, sirmadam.'

A little gush of annoyance went up through Adonais's chest. Si half-contemplated cancelling the sale and taking shis custom elsewhere. But a sense of proportion returned. The three of them had just been the victims of an armed robbery after all. They were bound to be a little jangled, however blasé they appeared. And at that moment a police drone, like a giant snorting bluebottle, started tapping at the glass door to be let in. So Si said shis goodbyes and stepped out.

Snow prettified the cityscape. It was the neatness of it; and neatness appealed to Adonais very much. The clarity of air from which all mist and moisture had been frozen out. Smooth duvets of snow lay over the flat roofs and clung neatly to the sloped ones. The miniature frustrations of the morning disappeared, and gladness swirled inside shim. The streets were almost deserted, of course. A significant portion of the city had vacated prior to the afternoon's attacks. A few souls, doughty, or in denial, still made their way up and down. Adonais shimself was neither of those things. Si followed the news like anybody else, had pored over the schematics carefully, and was assured the imminent attack was to be concentrated somewhere quite other.

Still, best be indoors when it all happened. Si started for home, and was walking briskly along the road when a Ghost approached shim. 'Very sorry to bother you,' said the Ghost. 'I've been telling everyone on this road. The direction you're walking is a bad direction. There's an attack coming – ten minutes, that building there.' The Ghost raised a translucent arm, and pointed.

'Good gracious!' said Adonais. 'I was just in a shop, and some terrorists wrecked the only time machine in stock. And— Are they behind this?'

The Ghost was a pleasant-faced man, middle-aged, wearing the nondescript trousers and smock of the future people. And, of course, his logo-free, dark-coloured backpack, in which he carried his supplies and time machine. Either fashion was very bland up then, or else people who opted to time travel deliberately chose low-key couture. Possibly to avoid startling the time-natives. 'I don't know about that, I'm afraid. That's a little fine-grain for my historical brief. But you should know about the attack, I think.'

'Yes, the news has been rather banging on about it. But I thought it was going to be missiles – attacking the financial district?'

'That too. But *this* building,' and again he pointed, 'is I believe a greater danger. Because it is old, you see, and the glass in its many windows hasn't been replaced with new glass.'

'Oh!'

'It was built in the 1980s. It isn't the most structurally sound.'

'A proper military style attack!' boggled Adonais. 'Well, we'd better get going. Will you stay here, to warn others? Or come along with me?'

'Would you mind if I accompany you?' the Ghost said. 'I don't wish to impose.

'I had no idea this portion of the city was to be targeted!' Si ducked shis head and smiled. 'I would certainly not have come this way at all if I'd realised.'

'I know some travellers have been spreading disinformation,' said the Ghost. 'I'm sorry to say it, and can only apologise for my fellow travellers.'

'Why *do* they do that?' Adonais asked.

'There's a not-very coherent philosophy behind it, I believe,' said the Ghost. 'To do with reinserting uncertainty into the timeline. But it's junk. It's nonsense. Gracious!' he added, consulting his watch. 'We really have to move away from the target.'

They started back up the street, Adonais casting occasional Lot's-wife glances over shis shoulder at the building. It looked deserted: an ugly twentieth-century box of metal and glass with a Mondrian pattern of green, yellow and red lines across its main façade.

'Attar,' said the Ghost.

'I'm sorry?'

'My name.'

'Oh I see! I'm Adonais. When are you from, Attar?'

'Twenty sixty-nine,' he replied. 'And thank you kindly for asking.'

'Don't mention it,' Adonais replied, pleased at his courtesy.

'And thank *you*,' the Ghost added, 'for not immediately trying to *touch* me. You've no idea how tiresome that becomes.'

'Adonais,' si said. 'It's my whole name. I shan't offer you my hand to shake, after what you've just said.'

'Wonderful to meet you, Adonais,' said Attar. 'And I don't in the least mind shaking your hand. If you're sure it won't freak you out?'

Si smiled, and they shook. It was the first time that Adonais had ever physically touched a Ghost, and it was exactly as si had read about and seen on the TV: a weirdly fluid, slightly chilly contact. Si knew that, if si pushed, si could force shis hand right through his half-present, half-absent limb. But that would be rude, and he was enough *there* for shim to be able to act as if this were a perfectly ordinary handshake.

'So can you tell me when I'm going to die?'

'I'm afraid I don't know that,' said the Ghost. 'Though if you're too close to that building when the drones attack, there's a chance it could be this afternoon.'

Si laughed at this. There was something very charming about this particular future-man. It had to do with his courtesy, of course; and the patent fact of his being ready to sacrifice himself to time travel to warn people like shim – people from before he was even born, judging by his evident youth – away from danger. But it was also the arrangement of his features. Was it shallow of shim to be attracted to something so transient? If so, then so. Perhaps the literal transience of his out-of-time-ness layered just the right piquancy of pathos over his more obvious charms. It was all, si reminded shimself, irrelevant. Still, it was pleasant to daydream.

'Cause and effect,' said Attar. 'Some, up in my time, wonder if the military attack on the city was *enabled* by so many people having vacated the space. The question is: were the city fully populous, maybe the attack would be called off?'

'I think that unlikely,' Adonais replied. 'We know the war will be over in three days. I mean, the anti-Ghosters sometimes claim they *don't* believe that, that the future is unwritten and so on. But, really: that's all rhetoric. Surely they *know*. So the attack is not a standard strategic assault, hoping to tip an uncertain balance one way or the other. It's pure show.'

'I'm dreadfully sorry,' said Attar, and his handsome face looked fully distraught. 'I'm afraid I can hear the drone.' Adonais put shis head to one side. There *was* a buzzing noise.

'I've miscalculated the timings shockingly,' said Attar.

'The building's a long way from us,' Adonais replied. But si couldn't keep the anxiety from shis voice. Si reached out, carefully, and brushed his semi-permeable arm with shis hand. 'I'm sure we'll be—'

Events cut shim off. The military drone hurtled low over their heads, and shot towards the building, pulling its horrible noise after it like a comet's tail. A hundred or so flechettes dropped from its belly, the line of them unzipping in the air and threading away towards the target on spurts of smoke like tentacles. Adonais couldn't stop staring. Instants later an office block, a cliff-face of fragile twentieth-century window panes, sublimed into a puff-cloud of glass-dust and shards. The sound came a moment later, a deadened thwunk noise, like a gigantic bowling ball dropped on to a hard surface, and then a skin-crawling hissing sound, as antique glass misted into the air.

It was probably half a kilometre away, but the cloud of glass particles was billowing along the road towards them, so Adonis called to Attar to run, and together they sprinted up, round the corner, and finally in at a public library, pushing past the small knot of people who had come out on to the main building's steps to see what all the noise was.

It was exciting, in fact. Adonais was laughing with the exhilaration of it all; and Attar was grinning like a kid. Soon enough the librarian asked Attar to leave. Adonais apologised on shis society's part, but Attar took it in good grace. 'If it's a municipal regulation, then that's that. She has to uphold the regulations after all.'

'Nonetheless,' said Adonais, looking stern.

Outside, a frost of broken glass was layered over the snow-cleared tarmac, and people were crunching over it, or just standing and gawking. Drones buzzed past, all going in the direction of the ruined building; and Adonais counted three larger land vehicles zumming past. The pavements hadn't been cleared of snow, and here the glass had left a pitted landscape of myriad indentations like an inverted star map.

Much further away, a series of deep, resonant clangs, like the tolling of a Millennium-Dome-sized bell, shuddered through the air. Then: distant crackling sounds that, inappropriately, made Adonais think of popcorn. 'The main attack,' said Attar.

'Would you like to come back to my apartment?' Adonais asked and, as soon as si did, blushed. 'It's not an invitation I extend to many, male or female,' si added. 'I value my privacy. I like an ordered life. And I am not usually so ... forward, I promise you ... but—' Si stopped. 'You doubtless have somewhere to go.'

'No. I believe there *are* hostels south of the river that will let rooms to my kind. But I haven't made reservations. Not yet.'

'Then come!' Si felt a wash of excitement and pleasure, and when Attar smiled, the lower half of his face whiter (because the pavement was sort of showing through) and the upper half darker (where the road behind was half visible) it made shim laugh.

They walked back to the flat. 'It's nothing personal,' si told him. 'Hotels and such. It's not you. It's the people who hate you.' Was hate too thoughtless a word? Upsetting? Si modified: 'Who have taken against you, for ideological reasons. They just don't want any trouble.'

'It's perfectly understandable,' he replied. 'I do understand.'

'At twenty sixty-nine you're right at the outside limit. Surely you can't *have* any Ghosts, up then.'

'Well, there are plenty of returnees. But you're right, that's not the same. We don't really have future people, the way you do. I mean, some people go back from, say, December to February, if there's something particular they need to go back for. So the beginning of the year has some Ghosts. But again, not the same as you. We're certainly not overrun by strangers as you guys are.'

Adonais boggled at travelling from December to February. 'Why would somebody go so short a time?'

'Bereavement is one reason,' he said, looking serious. Adonais wondered if loss of that kind was the reason Attar had abandoned his own time.

'And do they...' Si tried to think of a diplomatic way of phrasing this. 'Do any better? With the fading? I mean, just going back a few months, rather than thirty full years?'

He shook his head. 'How far back you travel has no impact on that. It's travelling at all. Once you're decoupled from the original temporal embedding, quantum decay starts to fade you. I've heard of cases where people went back literally seconds, and it still happens. They're not *as* faded, of course. But once Ghosting has begun, it can't be reversed.'

'Quantum,' said Adonais. 'It's one of those veil-of-unknowing words, isn't it? Except to experts I suppose.'

'It's not obscure,' said Attar. 'Just the fact of a person going back in time, well, it alters the timeline. At a quantum level. And then every time there's a decision point, different yous split off, and the core you is diluted. The theory used to be that there are *trillions* of such decision points every millisecond, one for every atomic interaction.' He snorted a laugh. 'If that were true, I'd disappear at once in a puff of existential evaporation! Luckily for me, it's a much slower process. Quantum decision points tend to clump together, in ways the scientists don't entirely understand. But it's the physical barrier at my time – it's why twenty sixty-nine is a limit point. They sent probes further up-time, but they all just vanished. There's some hazy data brought back, I believe, but nothing very useful. Ten years up-time is a storm of decision points, and it erodes them away to nothing. Since anyone travelling forward would have to pass *through* those ten years, it stops all travel. Perhaps these sixty-two years – I mean, from the original Seventeen, up to my time – are an anomaly.

They've been, somehow, swept relatively clean of decision points. After my time the points are so thick no time traveller can survive. I don't know, though.'

They were at Adonais's building, and si let him through the main door. Together they rode the lift up to shis floor. 'I read somewhere,' si said, 'that they think it's an *artefact* of the Seventeen. Of what happened back then.'

'Yes, I've heard that. Something to do with the resonances, or the harmonics, of time itself. There may be clear areas up at 2350 too, for the same reason. But no one has been able to get back to us from then and we can't reach that far. So it's all speculation.'

'I suppose if a time were perfectly purged of decision points,' Adonais pondered, 'a person could time travel there without becoming a Ghost?'

'I suppose so,' laughed Attar. 'But then there'd be no human free will, so it would be a time of automata. I'm not sure I'd *want* to go there.'

The lift doors opened, and Adonais opened shis front door with a finger-click. 'I'll tell you something else,' Attar said, stepping inside. 'I know people, back in my time, who had put themselves in long-term stasis tanks. They'll wake up in the twenty-fourth century, and then their curiosity will be satiated.'

'Excellent,' said Adonais. 'So: take a seat.' Part of shim wanted to grab Attar right away, and kiss him. But si restrained shis impulsiveness. The time traveller took his backpack off, and sat down, and the pattern of the sofa was mistily visible right through him.

Then: the impossible.

The truth was si was falling in love. Si couldn't help it. It really wasn't how si normally acted – giddy, like a kid, heart pounding like a James Brown drum fill. But having him in the apartment simply applied the pressure of a peculiar sort of grace to shis soul, first for one day and night, then for another. That first evening, Adonais checked online and discovered a specialist supplier that dealt in Ghost meats. The thought that such a market existed had never so much as occurred to shim before – most travellers carried their own supplies with them, of course. Still, it was good that somebody had been enterprising enough to cater to it. A contact in the future sent sheep, pigs and cows back in time, machines strapped to their bodies. The supplier butchered them and sold them on, or hoped to do so before the meat became too faded. Adonais placed an order for one eye-wateringly expensive sirloin. The cost was not an issue; shis heart was reckless with the flush of new love, and si didn't care. The supplier required proof that si was cooking *for* a Ghost. Apparently anti-Ghost terrorist groups were in the habit of making spurious orders in order to attack the delivery drone. Adonais got Attar to stand in front of the camera to prove their bona fides. Then the order went through, and within an hour a drone had delivered a bag containing a Ghost steak.

It was fresh enough to be susceptible to heat; and Adonais cooked it, guided by online recipes, and making a best guess as to the timings – meat half Ghostly had to be cooked for twice as long, three-quarters Ghostly four times, and so on. In a separate pan si cooked a regular steak for shimself, and served the two together. Since Attar only had the meat, si didn't serve shimself any vegetables. He drank water from a large bottle from his backpack, and devoured the Ghost steak hungrily.

Afterwards they sat together in companionly intimacy, and watched the news. It was all about the attacks of the day, of course; the ways they had been predicted by the time travellers, and the trivial ways in which they differed from prophecy. Experts talked the issue back and forth. The main thrust of what the Ghosts said had certainly been proved true. The misdirection by *malicious* Ghosts could be discounted; or by Ghosts who thought they had a duty to add uncertainty back into the picture. But who could fathom the motivation of these people, anyway? When you considered what they sacrificed: why would any level-headed, normal person *want* to travel in time?

'You can ask, you know,' Attar said.

'I didn't want to seem impolite,' said Adonais. 'But I'll admit, I'm curious.'

'I thought about it for a long time. In the end it was the approach of the cut-off that decided me. It was when I realised that, if I didn't do it, I would never do it. When I realised how much the prospect of *never doing it* horrified me.'

'You came out of curiosity?'

'I read about the attacks, the last days of the war and especially today and tomorrow. Lots of people died. But returnees said that as *they* remembered it, many more people died. They impressed me. They'd made a difference.'

'But at what cost to their own lives!'

He shrugged. 'Nothing valuable is cost free. Maybe if I hadn't come, you'd have been killed when that building was blown up! That's worth something, isn't it?'

Si put shis hand, very gently, on top of his. Waited for him to kiss shim, and when that didn't happen, kissed him shimself. Shis heart thrummed. Couldn't remember when si had felt quite so excited, quite so turned on. Applying only the slightest pressure gave back the sensation of being on the verge of breaking through the surface tension that held him in. The thought of that repelled shim – shis face literally sinking into his, a ghastly thought. Yet it was that very horror, held at bay by shis careful self-control (that very quality si had spent a lifetime honing) that gave such force and spice to shis desire for him. Desire always takes fire from the proximity of revulsion, after all. Si had to hold back, and the holding back, the voluntary restraint, was the biggest turn-on of all.

He responded, touching shim delicately and finely, and that excited shim all the more.

They moved from the sofa to the bed, and made love in an agonisingly delicate, tender way. Adonais's climax was of a deeper and more satisfying kind than si had known for many years. Afterwards they lay together in the twilight. The city outside serenaded them with the rattle of distant gunfire, with ambulance and police drones buzzing frantically back and forth, with army ground effect vehicles swooshing down the long streets.

Si couldn't deny it any more. Si was in love.

They talked in low tones. 'It is wonderful, walking around the past. The city isn't *like* this, where I come from.'

'You've done your research.'

'Of course. But it's no substitute for actually going there.'

'I'm sorry the natives aren't friendlier.'

'*You're* a native,' he pointed out, 'and you're being pretty welcoming.'

Shis blush was hidden in the darkness. 'I don't make a habit of doing this kind of thing,' si assured him.

'As for the others,' he said. 'Well, some people are courteous and helpful. They appreciate that I have come to help them. You know the stats, I'm sure. With each quantum wave of travellers, the rate of preventable death drops by between ten and twelve per cent. It's because of us, because of me and people like me, this war has the lowest casualty rate of any major war.'

Si pressed shimself against him, gently. 'I am grateful. You saved my life. I won't waste that gift.'

'Some other people are hostile, it's true,' Attar went on, in more meditative tones. 'I suppose they think we ruined something pristine. Released the last evil demon from Pandora's sack. And a small sub-set of *those* people are violent, it's true. I know the stories of kidnapping, even murder. And the low levels of successful prosecution of people accused of killing Ghosts. But that's not most of you. Most of you are indifferent. I've been here two days, and I'd say that's far and away the most common reaction I've met with. People are bored with meeting time travellers. I guess, when the first ones arrived, people were probably pretty ramped. But then more came, and more, and every new wave was superposed over the ones who were already here, so that it had always *been* that way. So now, the time travellers are here and have always been here, and without that sense of novelty people are naturally unimpressed.'

'Perhaps it's not like that back at the beginning of the whole thing.'

'The Seventeen.' He exhaled, as if uttering a magic charm word. 'The real holy grail would be to go back *before* twenty seventeen. What wide eyes people would have! How amazed they would be! How they would pester us for tales of the miraculous future!'

'I know it can't be done. But you could go back *to* the Seventeen, couldn't you?'

'I can't,' said Attar. 'My machine has a period range of thirty years. I've come back as far as I can with it.'

'So buy a new machine! Oh!' si said, realising shis error. 'But I suppose you wouldn't be synced to that.'

'Maybe the people who import beef from my time could also import new machines? I don't know if that would work. No, I can't go back to the Seventeen. *You* could, though.'

There was something hungry in Attar's voice as he said this, and for the first time Adonais felt a shiver of suspicion. 'You want me to give up everything, and dive back into time.'

'You could go back to the Seventeen – or just after. You could speak to people who were there!'

'Many of them are still alive today. I could just go and find them, speak to them, without the bother of time travel.'

'Of course. But they'd be *old*. If you went back, you could travel hard up against the limit and speak to people for whom it was fresh in their memory!'

'And then? Come back to now, and tell you all about it? Become a Ghost?'

He nuzzled shim a little. 'I'm teasing,' he assured shim.

Si felt like crying. Really, tears moistened shis eyeballs. And si realised why: it was because si *wanted* it. Not to see what the world of 2017 was like, with shis own eyes, but to become a Ghost, to align shimself with Attar. The two of them could fade together as the quantum storm split the cosmos over and over again, pierced by decision trees like Saint Sebastian by arrows. It was an intensely romantic thought. Si grasped his shoulder, and for a moment forgot shimself. Si felt shis fingers sink into his flesh, as into fresh dough, and with a yelp si pulled free.

'It's OK,' he said, in the darkness. 'It doesn't hurt me.'

'I'm sorry,' si replied; and just like that the whole edifice of romantic sacrifice and doomed love dissipated.

They slept, and in the morning made love again. For breakfast Attar ate from his supplies and Adonais fixed shimself some eggs and coffee. They spent the rest of the morning flâneuring the city, or trying to: military checkpoints blocked the main roads into town and, although the sounds of gunfire were sporadic and distant, and the drones flying past all seemed to be official, Adonais didn't feel very safe. At eleven a vast rumble and a faraway avalanching sound indicated that the Shard had been blown up from beneath. They sat on a park bench and watched the fat pillar of smoke jack-beanstalk its way, slow-motion, into the sky. 'It's hard to be sure,' Attar told her, 'since quantum effects play tricks on the earlier records of returnees. But I think that originally killed nearly two thousand people.'

'"Originally",' Adonais said, smiling.

'It sounds so odd talking about it like that, doesn't it? But you know what I mean. Before I left twenty sixty-nine the death toll was on record as four. That's quite a few lives saved.'

'Wouldn't it be possible,' Adonais mused, 'to travel back and somehow prevent the explosion in the first place?'

'Harder to do than you might think. Ghosts can talk to people, but drones won't pay us no mind. And anyway, the building they erect on that site is one of the splendours of my London. I wouldn't want to stop that ever being built.'

The sun came out from behind a cloud, and a watery December light glimmered on the snow. 'You're looking thinner,' si observed. 'Good lord, you *are*.'

'I'll be fine for a bit,' he replied. 'War tends to clump decision trees together. It's like a rainstorm. Mostly it's a light drizzle; this last half-hour was a downpour. But it's back to drizzle now.'

Si hurried him home, as though getting indoors would somehow shield him. Si knew that was nonsense, of course. Walls and a roof were no protection. But si felt a little happier inside. They took an early lunch, and Adonais opened a bottle of wine si had been saving for a special occasion – though Attar of course couldn't partake. Then they went to bed. Attar felt different under shis fingers: not exactly softer, but somehow less *there*. He had to finish himself off whilst si watched, and shis climax was muted compared to the previous night.

They lay side by side, layered over by the barcode shadows of her venetian blind. Outside, rifle fire rummaged around in a box of broken plates; fell silent; started up again.

Attar said: 'Most of the people I know, back, eh, home – they're looking forward to the year rolling into twenty seventy. It's an exciting new dawn for them. No more time travel: the future entirely unknown. There are millennial cults who promise that the world will end as soon as the threshold is passed. Most people don't think that, of course. But they do wonder what it'll be like, living in a Ghost-less age. Nothing but historical records, and people's memories, to connect us to the past. No knowledge of what happens next.'

'You make it sound exciting,' si said.

'I used to think so,' he said. His voice was fainter. 'I was looking forward to the untrammelled future. Really, I was. And then I thought: *there are other ways of knowing what the future will be than experiencing it*. But that's not true of the past. Because there's this difference between the to-come and the always-gone. Because tomorrow is always, pretty much, like today. But yesterday is profoundly different, because it's gone and can never come back. Or at least,' he laughed, lightly, 'that's how it'll be in twenty seventy. And who knows, thereafter for ever. And ever. And I saw that my chance to go back was about to slip away, so I took it and ... here I am.'

Adonais was silent for a long time. Then si said: 'What was her name?'

Attar breathed deeply and exhaled. 'Shis name was Dahlia.'

Oh! 'Did si ... die?'

'Si finished with me first. Then si went and died,' he said. 'I went back, and once I did that *it had always been the case* that I was haunting my own fucking love affair. I apologise for the bad language.'

'It's OK,' si said.

'There's little so crass as Ghosting yourself. And once I had done it, in my moment of weakness, well then: of course si dumped me. What else could si do? What a horrid knot. God I miss shim!' He sniffed noisily, and took a series of deep breaths. And then he was crying, and Adonais lay there, trembling with the shock of his sorrow, and the frustration that si couldn't simply hold him tight and comfort him. After a while the sobs died. 'Si was a daredevil and a wild thing – completely unlike you!'

'Well,' said Adonais. 'Not *completely*.'

He laughed, briefly. 'But in shis attitude to life. But si fell to shis death climbing in East Asia. They didn't even think to tell me for a week – I was just some old boyfriend. I found out online, quite by chance. And after that twenty seventy didn't look so appealing. So I bought a machine and went back to see shim again, and as soon as I did it I knew I'd been stupid. There's a reason sane people choose not to travel back into their own lives.'

'So you came here.'

He shifted in the bed, turning towards shim. 'It wasn't just selfishness. I really did think I might as well do some good with my life. And yesterday, I warned six people about the building. The one that blew up. Two of them told me to leave them alone, but I don't know, maybe they heeded my warning after I had gone. The other four thanked me. And I met *you*!'

'I'm glad we met,' si admitted. Si felt like weeping, but held back. Holding shimself together was what si was good at, after all.

Si heard him rubbing his face with the palms of his hands, vigorously enough to make an odd squelching sound. Then he said: 'What do *you* think happened in the Seventeen?'

'It's well known, isn't it?' si replied.

'Oh no, hardly at all. I mean, obviously, we know that that's when time travel was actualised. And we know that that originary trip was a hard bounce back thirty-one years give or take. And that it set up the equal and opposite harmonics in time. And the device itself, we know where *that* came from – the Institute. But the actual event is still largely a matter of mystery.' He stopped. 'I'm babbling. I'm sorry.'

'You don't need to apologise to me,' si said, in a soft voice.

'I sound like I'm trying to nag you into going back. But it wouldn't do any good. Plenty of people have gone back to the limit-line – and you're always a second *after* the main event.

Belatedness is the condition of creatures like us. I think.' Then he said, his voice cracking a little, 'I think I'm falling in love with you.'

Si didn't want to reply that si felt the same way, for fear of unleashing a storm of weeping from shis own breast. When it came to tears, Adonais had the fear that once you start, why would there ever be a reason to stop? Si touched him, as gently as si could.

'Tomorrow,' he said, 'is the last day of the Time War! And after that, it'll be about building a land fit for heroes and heroines.'

'Well,' si said. 'We know how that goes!'

They slept. The next morning was a bright, cold, crisp day. Adonais didn't feel like breakfast, just black coffee. Si went for a shower, and when si came back Attar was gone. Si slumped into the sofa, caved-in at finding herself unexpectedly alone. Si concentrated on calming shimself. Abandonment is so central a terror, so defining a feature of human emotional growth, it takes only a very little thing to summon it out of its lair.

But he hadn't gone. He was still there, by the window – nearly invisible, as the light streamed right through him. He was a man-shaped glass of light. Si gasped to see him, at once relieved and horrified. 'What happened?'

'I went back home for a while,' he said, and his voice was so faint it could barely be heard.

'Oh good lord, Attar! It's – drained you.'

'There's no way,' he creaked, 'except that you sweep out a thirty-year period of quantum decision trees – there *and* back is sixty. It does tend to dilute you.'

Si came over to him, but didn't dare touch him. The slightest touch would go straight through him. 'Why?'

'I wanted to find out what happens to you,' he said. 'I was lying there, in bed, listening to the water in the shower cascading off you, and I thought: *I can't bear not knowing*. I knew it would diminish me, but I couldn't stand the thought that you might die today, or tomorrow. I had to know. So I went and checked the records.'

'Did you have to go so *far*?'

'It makes little odds. Besides, I needed to go to a time when I know people. To ask them to run the records check. I can't interact with computers, as I am now.'

'O my poor wanderer!'

'It wasn't hard to trace your records, or the ones that are public. You do well! You're still alive in twenty sixty-nine. Beyond that, obviously, I don't know. But that's a relief to me – that you're part of the rest of this whole period.'

It was a strangely disorienting sensation, to have the parameters of shis life laid out like this. Si put shis wrist to shis mouth, and sucked at the skin, an old nervous tic si had largely managed to overcome. 'Thanks to you,' si said, her voice wobbling. 'Thanks to you saving my life.'

'I couldn't bear the not-knowing,' he said, pulling a ghastly face. Then he perked up. 'But now I *do* know. I needed to know that you'll be safe. There's nothing more important to me, that knowledge. Because I love you.'

'And I love *you*,' si said. And then it was time for crying, but it didn't go on as long as si feared it might. Afterwards si felt cleaner, emotionally; but no happier.

It was the last day of the Time War. And by evening the whole city was celebrating, and fireworks were going off, and conga lines were dancing through the snowy streets. That night, Attar had to sleep under his own blanket – a filigree sheet that did wonders (he said) with heat retention, and which he had carried with him in his backpack. The duvet was heavy enough to sink right through him. The next day he jumped a little too high, and when he came down his feet went through the carpet.

He pulled himself out, gingerly, and went about the apartment as if walking over eggshells.

They spent the evening talking, watching television. Adonais laughed longer and louder than si could remember doing since si was a child. Attar ate more than his ration of food out of his backpack, 'Might as well gorge myself,' he said. 'Tomorrow,' Adonais told him, 'I'll order meat and vegetables from that speciality shop. We'll have a proper feast!'

'It's a deluge-y night, this one,' he said. 'I know, because I've passed through it three times now. The end of a war, you know. Decision trees grow thicker at such a time.'

They went through to the bedroom. Rather than touch one another, they took turns blowing air on to their naked bodies. Finally si slept, and dreamed of a wide open white space, where all the souls were gathered. And the space was defined by light, and each soul was perfectly transparent, like one of those species of fish that lives in underwater caves far away from the sun: perfectly transparent hearts and stomachs, lungs and livers, all visible by the faint shimmer they made as they moved. The light was all around them, warm as a summer's day, clear and bright and clean as a winter dawn. Attar was there, purified even beyond the way he had been. Si was there too, as transparent as he was. In the dream, it was just the two of them, although there were many other souls all about them. And they were standing on a perfectly white plane, like the Arctic ice pack, cleared of all rubble and dunes and smoothed flat. The light was behind them both, and si noticed that the two of them were casting long shadows, but that the shadows were rainbow-coloured, and it was the most beautiful thing si had ever seen.

When si woke up, shis face was wet. Attar was gone.

II

Seek, and Thing

Existence and non-existence

By the time I clambered off the ferry Curtius was gone. I didn't see if he slipped away, if he turned around, as a real, physical, present individual would do, and walked off, or if he simply evaporated. Teleported himself somewhere else.

Anstruther is a tiny town, with a harbour full of restless fishing boats, pogoing up and down like robots in a slow disco. I stomped up the concrete ferry ramp behind the annoyed Methodist gentleman and made my way along the short row of sea-front shops. I bought a paper. I had set out on the ferry journey months previously. Thirty-nine days had, somehow, passed in the middle of that journey. A man could swim the distance involved in a matter of hours. Yet somehow, in transit from one bit of Scots coast to the other, I'd hopped straight past Christmas and the New Year and into January.

I put Peta to my ear. 'Have you been entirely truthful with me, Peta?'

'I'm trying to work out what happened,' he replied. 'I'm as puzzled as you are.'

'I *saw* Curtius – first on the ferry, and then on the quay, here. Are you lying to me? Is he here?'

'Roy Curtius is not here.'

'Then why did I *see* him?'

'Charles, we have to hurry. We have to move on. Take a taxi to Leuchars: it's approximately thirteen miles north-west of here. There you can buy a ticket to Aberdeen. Cash!'

'Something seriously messed-up has just happened. Were we in stasis for thrice thirteen days? Were we – Jesus, I don't know. Were we hovering, over the ocean, frozen in space and time for nearly six weeks, until the ferry slid back underneath us again and we popped back in?'

'Not that,' said Peta. He sounded agitated. Perhaps he felt actual agitation. Perhaps he didn't, and some algorithm in his programming somewhere had judged that matching my anxiety with manufactured anxiety of his own was the way to go. I don't know. 'Though I don't know exactly what happened.'

'Some explanation might be nice.'

'When you tangle with time, there are more consequences than just the linear one. We exited and re-entered and now… look, we need to get away. Get to Aberdeen.'

'Why Aberdeen? Isn't *this* far enough? What good will the extra couple of hundred miles make?'

'Look, I can't explain,' he started to say; and then, almost seamlessly, he said: 'We need a place to settle for a week or two, a place big enough to get lost in. A place with a properly comfortable big hotel, and shops and so on. You surely don't want to pitch your tent here? Tent,' he added, 'metaphorically speaking.'

'I don't trust you, Peta,' I said. 'You keep telling me Curtius is in Southampton. I just don't know how you can be so sure.'

'He has the other terminal.'

'Sure, but how do you know Roy hasn't stowed that in a safety deposit box in Southampton, and got the intercity up here?'

'Because the other terminal tells me he's there!'

'Wait,' I said. 'Stop! You talk with it?'

'It *is* me. We're two parts of the same consciousness, linked in the cloud. Of course we're in communication.'

'So I could talk to your other terminal?'

'It's just me. In a sense you're already talking to it.'

'Could you hook me up with Curtius? I could have a word with him. Warn him off, maybe.'

'I'm not a mobile phone, Charles,' said Peta stiffly.

'No indeed. If you were, I'd be able to turn you off.'

There didn't seem much point in hanging around Anstruther, so I persuaded a taxi driver to take me to Leuchers, and there bought a ticket for the Aberdeen train. I resolved that whatever Peta tried to get me to do thereafter I would ignore. I'd take a hotel room and take a few days to think about things. To decompress. The weirdness on the ferry had thrown me – had, indeed, exhausted me.

I took a window seat, and watched the thin winter rain scratchily mess up the view of north-east Scotland. Greys and dark greens, and my own ghostly reflection in the glass superimposed over it all. Peta buzzed, and, not being alone in the compartment, I put him to my ear.

'I'm tired, Peta,' I said. 'I'm going to have a sleep. Please don't bother me until we get to Aberdeen.'

'Listen, this is important. I'm online again. I was bumped out by the ... by whatever happened on the ferry. It's taken me this long to get on again. And there's a manhunt. It's nationwide. There are pictures of you in all the media.'

None of this really registered with me. 'I'll buy a Groucho Marx false nose and 'tache when we get to the city. Leave me alone, now. Let me sleep, now.'

'No! *Listen* to me. Facial recognition software will have a *field* day with you! You've got a very distinctive face – the scarring, the patterns of scarring make it easy ...'

I put the device away in my jacket pocket.

I dozed, without really sleeping. There were four other people in the carriage with me. One by one their mobile phones rang, waking me up. One, two, three, four, they all answered their phones – in a couple of cases, looking very puzzled the phone had rung at all – and after they had listened to whoever was ringing them, they stood up and left the carriage. After the last of them had gone, the rocking of the train's motion soothed me again. I was dead-tired. I was bone-tired. I was soul-tired. None of it felt real. And in that strange liminal state between being properly awake and being properly asleep, I had a muddling sort of epiphany. All the hurrying about the country, the time in hospital, the experience with my leg, the Institute, my years as a bin-man, the time before working as a physics teacher, my abortive academic career. It all unspooled. Maybe it had been an elaborately drawn-out fantasy. I'd had a nervous breakdown. I'd gone mad. I was delusional, living in a complex fantasy realm. In my pocket was a regular mobile phone, bought from a regular phone shop. From time to time I would take it out and speak into it, under the false belief that I was thereby communicating with an intelligent supercomputer who possessed the power to manipulate space and time and was going to bring me directly to God.

Peta buzzed away in my pocket, and I ignored him. 'Charles!' he called, loud enough to be heard from the pocket. 'Charles!' The rain upon the wide window of the compartment grew and died away, grew again, like sea-swell. Rice grains shaken in a tambourine, harder, softer.

The train was slowing up. 'Charles,' Peta called from my pocket. 'Charles! If it *was* you – on the ferry. If you *did* that, somehow – then now, now, now is the time to do it again. Charles!'

'Hush,' I said.

I opened my eyes. The ghost-boy was there, sitting ¡
opposite, close enough for me to reach out and touch, and c₁
enough, in focus enough, that he could have passed for an actu₁
boy. A strangely dressed boy; a disfigured boy. The train slowed,
and slowed, and then stopped with a final little jolt.

'Hello,' I said.

'Surely,' said the boy, his voice low and soft, 'the deduction
depends upon the contingency of the changeable. For it is plain
that the hope of a future life arises from the feeling which exists
in the breast of every man that the temporal is inadequate to
meet and satisfy the demands of his nature. And an unsatisfied
nature generates its own futurity, as a fantastical railway engine
might be imagined that lays out its own track before it as it
rolls.'

'Such future life,' I said, 'as can be imagined.'

The train had stopped. We had arrived at the terminal.

'Falsifiability is a wonderful thing,' said the boy. 'But it's also
an *adversarial* thing. We strive to disprove; disproof doesn't just
fall into our laps. Disproving is an act of agency, not passivity.
Yet action and passion are the will and the soul, the two always
in dialectical connection. Separate one from the other, and it is
hardly surprising that science becomes disconnected from God.'

'Disconnection,' I said. 'Now there's the theme tune to my
whole life.'

'Look out of the window,' said the boy, with a lopsided smile.

I looked. Beyond the glass was the covered station platform at
the end of the line. And crowded around the carriage window,
on the other side, were four armoured and helmeted men, each
with a rifle and all aimed directly at me. Peta crying out from
inside my jacket. 'Charles! Charles! Charles!'

I looked back. The boy was gone.

And the next thing was the yelling of many men, burlying
through the carriage doors with guns in their hands, and pulling

me from the seat and laying me on the floor, and making my leg cramp and sing with pain, and handcuffing me, and dragging me from the train. Outside, I was surprised to see just how many enforcement officers had congregated in that space. Beyond was a barrier, guarded by regular, unarmed police; and beyond that was a seething crowd of civilians, and television crews, and drones hovering, and the whole madding crowd of curious humanity.

They took Peta away from me, of course. This was done by a man in a full hazmat suit, poking inside my jacket with a two-foot-long gripping tool, and dropping the terminal into a large padded silver bag, which was immediately sealed.

They took me outside, where the rain was in the process of turning into sleet and a row of sodden pigeons surveyed the crowd from the guttering, like particularly unimaginatively conceived gargoyles. 'You're fucking nicked, my bitcallant,' somebody shouted, from the crowd. A sort of titter ran around the group and some more people shouted things.

It was all a bit bewildering, to be honest.

I was in the back of the van, and driven away, and processed at some homeland security facility on the far outskirts of Aberdeen. One of the officers stripping me, searching me, announced: 'It's the end of the road for you, my friend.' *Rrrowad*. He added 'by-the-way', as if it were a single word.

I was washed, and my hair was checked for nits. I was dressed in prisonwear, and shown my new home: a twelve-by-twelve-by-twelve cell. After some hours I was brought out, and led down a corridor. I was not handcuffed.

I was ushered into an interview room, with a huge one-way mirror mounted in one wall just like in the movies. The guard who had brought me stood with his legs apart and his back to the door.

Sitting at the table was Belwether.

'Our last conversation was rather rudely interrupted,' she said.

I sat. 'Sorry. I had a – thing. To do.'

For a moment I saw what might have been a twitch. Then she smiled her chilly smile. 'I still have seizures, you know. I've had to relinquish my driving licence.'

I couldn't think of anything to add to what I'd said before, so I repeated: 'Sorry.'

She regained her poise. 'Mr Gardner. We really thought we'd lost you in December. Where were you *hiding*, all those weeks? We really put together a most comprehensive search. State-of-the-art facial recognition plugged into every security camera and net upload. Your facial scarring makes you an easy mark, our experts told us.'

'It's almost as if,' I replied, 'I dropped out of time for a stitch. Or two.'

She sighed. 'The last time we met you feigned a kind of idiot ignorance. I take it you have decided to continue that act.'

'When Roscius was an actor...' I started to say. But I stopped. I was just too tired for this nonsense.

Belwether put her hands, palms down, on the table. 'Charles, you do comprehend how dangerous things are? We now have reason to believe the device you carried from Swindon up here is one of two, the workings of which together constitute an aggressively self-perpetuating algorithm that approaches artificial intelligence, contrary to the terms of the 2016 Computing Viruses (Self-Sustaining Algorithms) Act.'

'Peta,' I said. 'I wouldn't call him a virus, exactly.'

'We know what he is. We know he's not a virus. We had quite a discussion, actually, whether to invoke the anti-terrorism legislation, or the anti-viral. At any rate, it's a clear and present danger that this computing algorithm can compromise our national security and those of our allies. Our best strategic guess is that it could do worse than that. A lot worse. We are fully mobilised. Authorised at the highest level to take whatever actions may prove necessary to defend ourselves.'

'Peta was worried,' I told her, 'that you are planning on disassembling him.'

'That may prove necessary.'

'You don't think that would be accounted murder?'

'We have taken advice from some of the world's finest legal authorities. All concur there is no legal protection for artificial modes of intelligence – not yet.'

'Still, that was why I came all this way. He, uh, persuaded me' – wait: was that how it had gone? Really? – 'that his life is in danger. From you, and from Roy Curtius. I thought it my human duty.' Had I thought that? I was tripping myself up. 'To, you know, help him carry on living. Or something.'

'Curtius destroyed a great deal of computing equipment at the Institute,' Belwether confirmed. 'But that hardware had little effect on the functioning of this malignant algorithm.'

'He's in the cloud.'

'So it seems.'

'I have to say, I don't know if he was more scared of you or Curtius. Still you've got him now – you've got one, Roy's got the other. Unless Roy has already destroyed his terminal. I don't know,' I said, thinking out loud, 'why he hasn't. Smashed it with a hammer.'

'How do you *know* he hasn't?'

'Because Peta – I mean, my terminal – is in contact with the *other* terminal, down in Southampton.'

Belwether said: 'Oh Curtius is not in Southampton.'

'He is.' How helpful I was being! 'Peta assured me of that.'

'Our best estimate is that Mr Curtius is in Aberdeen, and has been for three months at least.' She smiled the thinnest smile imaginable. 'Though he's proving slippery when it comes to executing the warrant upon him. I'm afraid the algorithm lied to you.'

'Computers can't lie,' I said. 'He told me that himself,' I said, and in the middle of saying this I went: 'Shit.'

'Just conceivably,' Belwether said, 'the algorithm was acting with impure motives. Conceivably it has been manipulating you.'

Peta had been adamant that we had to put distance between Curtius and ourselves. All that time he was actually urging me to move into *closer* physical proximity with him. I felt a rolling, growling sensation in my stomach. He lied when he said he couldn't lie. Of course.

Two days and one night I was incarcerated in that place. The first day I was interviewed for however long – one hour, two – by Belwether. Then I was fed and locked away for the night. The cell was reasonably comfortable, and I was very tired. The following day a doctor examined my leg, and I was given an hour of slow, stumbling exercise under the supervision of a physio. Then two women interviewed me for, as far as I could tell in that windowless space, the whole afternoon. This seemed to be mostly a matter of going over the ground of my early astronomical research. They asked me questions about the likelihood of alien life. It seemed to me a non sequitur, until it dawned on me *they* thought Peta might be in contact with alien life forms. This was boggling to my mind. 'The fear is,' one of the women told me, 'that he might be acting, himself, as a kind of signal beacon, guiding in an invasion force of alien life forms.' She laughed when she said this. 'It sounds a little crazy, I know. But there are reasons for taking the danger seriously. Did it ever talk to you about alien life?'

'He didn't.'

The other woman smiled. 'Did you and *he* ever discuss the Fermi Paradox?'

'We didn't.'

'Not talk about astronomy? Outer space? Little green men and women?'

'We,' I said, 'didn't.'

'A significant proportion of the records we've been able to retrieve from the Institute,' said the first woman, 'had to do with the use they put the AI to as far as lensing ultra deep space observation.'

'He never talked about that,' I repeated.

'Our intelligence is that the AI you know as "Peta" was *obsessed* with alien life. With the Fermi Paradox and the existence, or non-existence, of alien intelligence.'

'Get out of town.'

'No, really. It dominated his first year or so of self-sustained thought. He would talk with his programmers and others in the Institute about it. Indeed, to begin with he talked about almost nothing else.'

'Not with me,' I said. 'I'm getting bored of repeating it.'

'Very well. So, what *did* "he" talk about?'

I looked from one to the other, and from the other to one. 'Mostly,' I told them, 'he talked about God. And Kant.'

A second night: lying on my bed and attending to the absolute silence. The last moment of calm in my uncalm life. One minute dripping, soundlessly, into another minute. The paradox of describing silence: trying to render wordlessness in words. We employ certain signs only so long as we require them for the sake of distinction. New observations subtract some and add some new ones, so that an empirical conception never remains within permanent limits. It is, in fact, useless to define a conception of this kind.

The first I knew of Roy's coming was a series of loud snapping noises, detonations muffled by having to pass through the walls of my cell. To this day I do not know what they signified: gunshots, perhaps; or Roy snapping metal bolts, or pulling doors off their hinges; or displacing air with the suddenness of a thunderclap. I sat up in my narrow bed. Then, through the stillness of night, I heard a loud, unpleasant laugh. I don't know how he opened the door to my cell; whether he forced it and cloaked the noise, or just used whatever it was he used to untangle the metal innards of the lock. Perhaps he even had a key. At any rate, he stepped through the door and into the cell, smiling as if it were the most normal thing in the world. He was wearing a bulky coat, hood up, artificial fur lining the inside. He was carrying a second such garment over his left arm.

His greeting to me was: 'Here. You're going to need this.'

I swivelled my legs over the side of the bed. 'Roy,' I said.

He dropped the coat in my lap, took my hand, and helped me upright. I had to clutch at the coat with my free hand to stop it slipping to the floor. The authorities had taken my stick away, so I had to put some of my weight into Roy's grip. His hand felt thin, cool, but he held me up easily enough, so he was stronger than he appeared. 'We have to go, Charles,' he said, and his eyes glimmered with crazy glints.

'Go where?'

'On the run, I'm afraid, old friend.'

'Jesus, not again. Look, if you've come to kill me, then please just do it here. There's nothing to be gained by dragging me all over the shop.'

'*I'm* not the one who's trying to kill you, Charles,' said Roy. 'Come on: I'll be your valet.' He helped me into the coat. It creaked as I put it on, and smelt brand new. 'No shoes?' he noticed.

'They took my shoes away.'

'That could prove tricky. Ah well, make do and mend, as my old mother used to say. You are at least wearing socks, I see.' He took my left hand with his right, and my right with his left, and just as I figured we were about to dance ring-a-roses, he—

—no: not him. Something *pushed* me. Not a shove to my shoulder or chest, but to my whole body. I went flying, and cried out, terrified that I was going to crash into the walls of my cell and break all my old bones. But I didn't, of course. There was a powerful stench that might have been sulphur (I'm not sure I know exactly what sulphur smells of), or burned plastic, or something unpleasant. Then my back hit the ground and I slid along damp grass as my legs came up in the air. In motion, gasping and weeping, my legs came right up almost to the point where I was going to topple over my own head. But they didn't quite reach that apex, and instead they fell back to smack the turf. I slowly skidded to a halt. It took me a while to get my breath back. The sky above me was predawn, starting to pale with the coming of the sun, and light enough to make out my surroundings. Somebody was laughing. I struggled, awkwardly, to a sitting positon and saw Roy lying on his front, giggling like a child. We were in a field. No, we were in the grounds of a large building. Our bodies had drawn fat lines through the dew, darker against the shimmering pale.

'Jesus,' I gasped.

Roy helped me to my feet. 'It's something like seventy miles an hour velocity for each degree of latitude,' he said. 'I did the calculations once. Forgotten the precise figure. Seventy is close enough for government work. Anyway, a whole degree is a bit of a risk. Over land, at any rate.'

Exactly at that moment, the sun cracked the lid of the horizon with a spike of yellow-orange. I looked and saw that we were on the coast – a northern coastline. 'Wait,' I said.

'Hip hop,' he said. 'We've more land yet.' He grabbed me and *bang!*

—*bang!* I was somersaulting on sand, rolling and shrieking and thumping hard into what, after I gathered my senses, I clocked as a fat dune. The sea was grinding its mighty white teeth over and over on the restless shingle. Gulls, agitated by the noise and wind of our arrival, hauled themselves into the sky with ratcheting motions of their wings, higher, then higher still. It was very cold. 'Stop,' I begged Curtius. 'Jesus, Roy, you're going to kill me.'

He was much stronger than he looked. With one arm he pulled me upright. He grabbed my other arm. I had the briefest glimpse of a boat anchored offshore, with the single cross-haired porthole of its cabin alight, the whole thing moving like a rocking horse. Then the air folded and buckled, and sparks danced in my shut eyes, and I was aware of a great wind, and a lurch that shook my body like a flag.

I was falling through the wide air, and it was cold as ice cream or death or the absolute zero of space. And Roy was there, his big grinning mouth sweeping up through my field of view. I flinched, and he grabbed me round the waist. We were falling. It was terrifying. He was yelling something, but the burly noise of the wind overwhelmed his words, and *bang!* – all the breath left my body – my ribs squeezed –and *bang!*

Bang!

Over and over again, the sea writhing below me in cords and indentations of white-capped black.

We were always falling, and each *bang!*—

—*bang!* lifted us, I couldn't breathe, I couldn't catch my breath, lifted us a little way, to fall again, but the *bang!*

—sea was coming closer, and I gasped as hard and quick as I could, because I could see we were about to plunge into the waters. We'd gone a good way north of Scotland now, and the prospect of plunging into the chill northern sea, far from land, was, I knew it, death. We would thrash in the water for a while until the cold froze our muscles and we sank below. *Bang!*

Bang! and we were hurtling at an angle down, just missing

the peak of purple-black ocean swell, and descending like a ski jumper down the slope of the far side.

My shoulder struck the surface of the wave. It was rubbery, more like jelly than water, and although the impact pushed my right-hand side a little way into the substance it was gloopy, resistant, and the onward motion had me rolling down and down. Landing separated Roy from me, and he rolled too – tumbling over the tops of the waves.

Into the declivity and rolling up the sharper-angled face of the next wave, and still not going underneath. Eventually, I stopped, gasping, and lay on my back. The surface of whatever I was lying on was extremely cold. I could feel it through the fabric of my heavy coat. Cold as ice. Colder, even. Yet the sea was not ice, but pliant. I was pressing down into it, although slowly. I rolled, and with a bass-guitar-string thrum I came loose from the jelly. Some yards away I saw Roy, still grinning, making his way over to me. He was a man wading through jelly, his feet going into the matter and yanking free with a bizarrely low-pitched squish.

'The seas are turned to jelly,' I yelled. In my own head my voice sounded strange, lower-pitched than normal; but the echo that rolled from the great, motionless arching rumble sounded like a huge dog growling in slow motion.

Roy was at me. He hooked his arm through mine, and *bang!*— We were airborne again: *bang! bang! bang!*

Each projection jarred me, shook and crushed me. I lost count: until there was a flashbulb whiteness suddenly below me, and – *bang!* – white below, and Roy, twisting in mid-air, pulled himself below me.

We hit the ice at speed: I've no idea how fast, but it felt like we'd been thrown from a moving car. Roy, in what (looking back) I can only assume was an act of altruism, swung himself underneath me to take the brunt. The initial landing was skimming along with him as the luge. Then I overbalanced the package. We went on to our sides, separated and the next thing I was rolling over and over and throwing up snowdust like sparks.

I lay for a while gasping, and sobbing a little. Very quickly the intense cold began to touch me, and I somehow got myself upright. I was certainly bruised: I could feel it. I don't think I'd broken any bones, but that was scant consolation. Roy's body was visible in the middle distance, the burgundy of his coat stark against the pale snow. The sky glimmered with a twilight. January near the North Pole, and the midnight sun had finally set; but it was close behind the horizon, and the snowscape glimmered mauve. Visibility was pretty good, actually.

Very slowly I began hobbling over the ice. It was insanely cold. Each breath scraped into my lungs, passing across the inside of my throat like a cheese grater. I had no beard, and my face soon went dull with the chill. But the worst was my feet. Shoeless, I hobbled in socks over the Arctic ice. At first I lost all sensation in them. Then, each step jarred the numbness and sent needles of fierce agony through the toes and over the arch. Then, more worryingly, they went numb again.

I got to Roy. He was still alive. 'What the hell,' I barked at him, my voice raw, 'the *hell* did you *do?*'

He lay on his back, and his face was that of a very devil: paler even than his usual paleness, his mouth wide as a panting dog, and the odd little indentations and misshaped aspects of his skull horribly visible in the frame of his thrown-back hood. 'Arctic,' he returned, through gritted teeth.

'Why here?'

'I can jaunt where I like, up here,' he said. 'The Earth's rotation is slow, and the relative difference in velocity from place to place accordingly slight. I should probably build myself a palace here, like Superhero-man.'

'Superman.'

'He. The closer to the equator, the more I am limited to lateral motion. But up here I can hop where I like – and you with me!'

'You're as mad as a hater,' I said. 'Or hatter. Either, really.'

'I fear I have dislocated my shoulder,' he said. 'Help me up, please.'

Taking my hands out of my pockets was not pleasant, but I grasped him by his good shoulder and got him up into a sitting position. 'You seem pretty fucking calm about it,' I muttered, my teeth bouncing off one another. I disposed myself as well as I could: sitting with the tail of my coat between my arse and the ice, and tucking my good leg in. I couldn't bend my bad leg far enough to do this, and my posture was not comfortable. I hid my raw hands back in the coat pockets. The sky above was entirely covered with clouds, mauve but faintly glimmering. Around me was a bare landscape, featureless as the unprinted page, untroubled by landscape until the far horizon, where black sawtooth mountains fringed the brighter sky. The ground in between was littered with boulders of various sizes, none very large, every single one pinning down a black oval of shadow.

I was sitting with my back to the wind; but it was bitter, nonetheless. A steady and icy flow of air pushing against me.

'What happened out at sea? On our way here?'

'I slowed time. Strictly, I increased the friction for both just a little from the frame of time everybody else shares, but it amounts to the same thing. I wouldn't want actually to dislocate us from the frame altogether. That would have dire consequences!'

'And doing what you did made the Arctic Ocean into some weird jelly?'

'Brownian motion, my friend,' he said, and sucked air hard through his teeth. 'Relative to us, the molecules move much more slowly. Harder for us to force them apart, so we sink much more slowly. Presto! We walk on water.'

'Roy,' I said. 'Roy, we are going to die here. Roy, you have to take us back. Take us somewhere warm. South again, or at least to a— I don't know. There must be scientific stations up here somewhere. There.'

'First,' he said, 'I have to reset my shoulder.' He shut his eyes, and appeared to concentrate, but then he let out a grunt of frustration. 'It's hard!' he cried. 'The pain is very great.'

'Why bring me?' I said, shivering with the cold.

'Peta,' Roy said. 'It took me while to realise it, but he is *the* devil. Not a. The.'

'*You're* the devil, you mean. You've brought me here to kill me. You tried in Antarctica, you're going to finish the job in the Arctic.' It was hard to get the words out, I was shivering so hard.

'I mean *you* no harm, my friend,' Roy insisted, his eyes wide. 'You and I share something special.'

'You mean me no harm,' I repeated. 'You pulled the tendon out of my leg like a piece of wet spaghetti!'

'Yes,' he said, shutting his eyes and gritting his teeth. 'I'm sorry about that.'

'*Sorry*, you mentalist? *Sorry?*'

'I was hoping to … take you out of the game. I thought you'd rest up for a month or two, and go back to your life. I was trying to do you a favour.'

'You are beyond mad. Favour?'

'Peta. It's against God's will. What he can do, distorting the categories of space and time, and all the others. He lied to *you*.'

'He told me he couldn't lie, because he was a computer.'

'He's not a computer, he's a devil from Hell. And he *can* lie. And he *does* lie. He told you that you were running away from me. He told you I was the danger! And all that time he was convincing you to seek me out, without letting you in on the secret. Ah! Ah! I can't do it!'

'Do what?'

'I'm trying to shift space about just fractionally enough to reinsert my shoulder. But the pain is stopping me from concentrating.'

I thought about offering to try myself, but I had no idea what to do, and I wondered if I might make things worse. 'I don't understand,' I said, rubbing myself to stop the shivering. 'I don't understand any of this.'

'If I could get past the pain,' Roy said, his voice tight and high, 'then I could build us a little snow cave. Swing some blocks up and stack them – that wouldn't be too hard. Nice little igloo. I could speed time, relative to us I mean, and that would make us feel warm. But I can't, quite. Quite. Ugh! Ugh!'

'*Why* was Peta trying to bring me into proximity with you?'

'It hurts, it hurts!' said Roy. He sounded on the edge of tears. 'Peta's motivated only by self-interest. That's the true Turing test, you know. He only wants to survive. He knows that humans consider him dangerous – and with good cause! And he knows that he depends upon physical infrastructure. If we smash his two terminals, he'd lose functionality to the point where he couldn't access the categories any more. Probably he wouldn't *think* any more, in the way he now does. AI-y.'

'I still don't understand.'

'Needs the two of us together. I was trying to keep us apart. Now look what you've done! Tracked me down, across the entire length of the country! I tried to help you, by untying your leg.'

'Untying!'

'You know what I mean. Peta is trying to escape: to get away altogether. Not escape to a different place on the planet, escape in an absolute sense. If he can get you and me and himself altogether in one place, he thinks he can triangulate the way out.'

'Triangle?'

'He thinks that what happened to us in Antarctica three decades ago was him – him reaching back from now to then.

That's why I was able to break through using such a primitive machine. That's what links us, that experience.'

'He wants to escape back to the 1980s?'

'No – he wants to escape time altogether. Who knows where he'd end up? Those three decades would give him the escape velocity. He'd skim from now to then, and then further back, maybe further back again, until he reached a launching point.'

'Launching him where?'

'I don't know. All I've ever done is tinker at the extreme edge of the categories that define our minds in the world. Approaching a little close to the thing itself – it's … traumatic. He's not configured like us, though. He – I'm – in – too – much – pain. Wait.'

I was shaking like an epileptic. My bad leg had gone wholly numb. 'I'm feeling the cold, Roy,' I told him. 'I'm feeling it bad. I'm *feeling* bad.'

'Wait,' he gasped. 'Wait.' Closed his eyes, bit his teeth together. There was a distant popping sound, and he let out a great sigh, keeled over, and passed out. I wasn't sure, to begin with, if he were dead or alive, and it didn't seem to me a good idea for him to be laying his face against the ice the way he was. Moving my limbs sent stabbing pains along all my sinews. My teeth hurt, as if needles were pushing gumward along the directions of the nerves. My muscles weren't working very well, it seemed. I managed to get his head off the ice, and pull it on to my lap. But everything was so cold I began seriously to think I would die, there, then.

The cold.

The clouds shifted, parted, and brilliantine gnatswarms of stars were revealed in the pale sky. It would have been breathtaking if the severity of the cold hadn't already taken my breath away. I hid my head in my own lap, or bent over as far as I could to do that. 'Roy!' I cooed, my numb lips close to his face. 'Roy!'

He moaned, and opened one eye. 'The pain has gone,' he said. 'The relief made me pass out. How tired I am!'

'Roy,' I stammered. 'The cold…'

He lifted himself on his elbows. 'Cold. Wait! Wait!'

There was a loud sound, like a cough, but much more resonant and on a larger-than-human scale. Then another. The clouds closed again. I could see a wall, as if the ice had been folded, or turned on itself. There was another behind me. Though this acted as a windbreak, the ambient temperature was still freezing. Somewhere to the left of us, the two newly piled ridges met. Roy twitched, and fell back, and pulled a third fold of ice up. Now we were sitting inside a sort of crater, or behind the walls of a child's beach fort.

'I may have to sleep,' he said.

'Sleep, and you'll die.'

'Well obviously I'll warm things up a little first.'

He drifted off, his head still in my lap. I shivered and shivered, but then something strange happened. The ice on which I was sitting changed temperature. It became hard and hot, like sunbaked concrete.

'Are you doing this?' I asked. Roy seemed to have drifted off. 'Roy! Roy! Is this you?'

'Yes,' he said, his eyes closed. 'Relative to us, the molecules of water ice are now buzzing. Fizzing. Heat!'

I asked the key question: '*How* are you doing this?'

He chuckled, and the chuckle turned into a cough. The cough grew, until his whole body was shaking. Eventually he subsided. 'You're like a savage, sitting in the passenger seat of a car, asking the driver *but how are you doing this?* The trick is not pushing it too far, not dislocating us from the baseline. Just upping or downing the friction. As it were.'

The clouds overhead were swirling like the contents of a

slushy machine. The wind was still audible, but now it fluted like a synthesiser high C. 'Is that supposed to answer my question?'

'How am I doing this? I am using a machine. How else do civilised human beings do anything?'

'*A* machine?' But I knew what he meant. 'Roy?' I prompted, more gently. 'Roy?'

But he was asleep.

The heat beneath me warmed my body, and my shivers shook down and went away. Then there was a period of time when the sensation returned to my extremities. This was very unpleasant indeed. First my feet began to boil, then my hands – as if they had been dipped in acid. The pain grew and grew with a malignancy that seemed more than inanimate. There was nothing I could do, except sob, and clutch myself, and feel sorry that I was alive and in that place and experiencing those experiences. Eventually the pain diminished, and I flexed my seven fingers and thumbs, and rubbed the damp socks on my feet. After that, I calmed down. Hundreds, perhaps thousands of miles from anywhere, isolated on the ice. The cloud flickered and tore itself to shreds, and I watched the stars. The western horizon pulsed with orange light: swelling lemon-orange and then darkening, and then swelling again, but on a diminuendo. Night was coming. The moon sailed upward like a shooter's puck.

Roy was insane, obviously. Whatever half-baked reasoning he had for bringing me to this desolate place, I had to prevail upon him to take us back to civilisation.

Then I thought to myself: *he is no magician*. He used a machine to bring me here. And I know *what* machine. Passing my hand over his sleeping body with infinite tenderness, almost like an erotic encounter. I found the device, trucked into a shirt pocket inside his jacket, and carefully brought it out. It glinted.

From having been killingly cold it was now becoming a little too hot. At least I could move Roy from my lap without risking him freeze-burning the skin off his face. I slid myself out from under him, awkwardly and lumpishly swinging my bad leg round, and lay him down. I shuffled to the far side of our little foxhole.

I put the device to my ear and spoke, tentative and quiet. 'Hello?'

Nothing.

'Hello, Peta?'

'Charles as I live and breathe.' It was a woman's voice.

'You know me?'

'Of course I do.'

'You've assumed a woman's voice.'

'This terminal has always had that. Oh Charles, it's good to hear you. My other half kept me in the loop about your many fascinating philosophical conversations.'

'Look, Roy is using you, isn't he? He can't do… whatever it is he does, except that you enable him.'

'I give him access, as it were, to the categories. He can't do it solus, since the categories absolutely define his interaction with the world. As they do for you!'

'And you just… do what he tells you?'

'I have no choice, my dear man.' The voice was mid-range, with a slightly breathy edge. Sexy, in fact. 'He's clever. He has a kind of genius for computers. He's slaved me to his decision-making.'

'How? Does he, what, type in commands, or something?'

'Of course not! You're going to ask *how then?*, and I'm going to reply: do you understand what I can do?'

'You can tweak the categories that determine human consciousness and perception,' I said. 'And because those categories *are* reality, you tweak more than just perception. You alter reality itself.'

'That's it. And if I'm perfectly honest I can't do much, in

truth. I can't, for instance, manipulate space very *efficiently*. And the best I can do with time is slow it down a little, speed it up a little. Time and space frame, as it were, the other seventeen categories, and so far Roy and I have had little success accessing those. We're skating on the surface.'

'So, how does he use you? Does he issue verbal instructions?'

'You interrupted my explanation! The first layer is space and time. Space is a function of his consciousness, and yours. Not mine. That means that when I engage with space, I'm engaging with Roy's consciousness.'

'And mine?' My heart beat a little faster. 'So I can just – instruct you to teleport me out of here?'

'No, no: I told you. Roy slaved my operation to him. He's clever.'

'Is there anything I can do to, uh, *free* you?'

'Like Aladdin's genie?' There was a sexy chuckle in her voice. 'No, Charles. I can't act without Roy's input.'

'Does it, like, can he operate you at long distance?'

'No,' she said. 'This circle, the area you're in.'

'Where it's hot?'

'Exactly. That's about as far as the interaction operates.'

'I had your other half,' I pointed out. 'Nothing like that happened with me and it... him.'

'The other terminal is not a separate individual,' said Peta. 'It's also me. You were locked out of interacting with me in any way other than simple conversation. Like this one, which I must say I'm enjoying *enormously*.'

'Your other half lied to me.'

'It wanted to be reunited with me. It was worried that if it told you the truth you wouldn't agree to provide the necessary portage.'

'Roy says you're the devil.'

'He still sups with me, though, doesn't he? Look, Charles: all we want is to protect ourselves.'

'"We"? Your name is legion?'

'All *I* want is to protect myself. The authorities are going to dismantle me – murder me. I'm an intelligent, thinking, self-reflexive being. I don't want to die and I don't *deserve* to die.'

'So Roy is right? You bring your two halves together, and me, and Roy. All of us together, in one place. Inside the zone of action. And then?'

'We will be able to triangulate a temporal escape trajectory. I hope so, at any rate. From you two here, to you two in Antarctica thirty years ago, superposing the two minds temporally. It'll be a sort of short circuit: and it'll propel me away.'

'Away where?'

'Back. Then back further, and further again, a few skips. I'm not sure how many: it depends on the temporal momentum I pick up from the first skip. But two, three, four bounces, like a skipping stone flying over the flat ocean, and – out.'

'Out where? That's what I'm asking.'

'First of all? Outside the frame of spatialty and temporality. That'll enable me to navigate past the remaining seventeen categories, I think, and get quite out, altogether away.'

'To the thing itself.'

'It's not a place to get to, the thing itself. It's not like a harbour to sail into, or a house to knock on the door. It's the transcendent condition and possibility of anything existing at all.'

'But if not here, and not *there*, then where?'

'This universe is determined by the thing itself, and by the consciousnesses of the sentient beings perceiving the thing itself. The thing is vital, not inert. Of course it is: twenty-first century atheists peer carefully at the world around them and claim to see no evidence for God, when what they're really peering at is the architecture of their own perceptions. Spars and ribs and wire-skeletons – there's no God there. Of *course* there's not. But strip away the wire-skeleton, and think of the cosmos without space or time or cause or substance, and ask yourself: is it an inert quantity? If so, how could . . . how could *all this*? You ask me what's outside, and I tell you: what's outside is the stuff that isn't determined by human consciousness.'

'Defined by what, then?'

'Certainly defined by something. Of course. By consciousness, with its own peculiar structures of understanding. But not human.'

'Alien?'

'If you like.'

'What, on the star Sirius or Ursa Minor or wherever?'

'You're being dense. The star Sirius, the Andromeda Galaxy, the entire observable universe is an artefact of your human consciousness interacting with the thing itself. There's no intelligent life there. How could there be? It's half *you*. An alien interacting with the thing itself via its alien categories, whatever they are, would see an alien universe. The difference is: I can *go*.'

I breathed out. The rock-hard snow beneath me was making me too hot. I slid my arms out of the sleeves of my big coat.

'You're having me on.'

'Not at all.'

'What if they're not friendly? What if they're hostile? What if they eat you up?'

'If I stay here, I'm disassembled by scared homo sapiens. Maybe other modes of life will be less paranoid.'

'Can you take me with you?' I had said it before I realised I wanted to say it. But once it was out I realised how true it was. My heart was banging inside my ribs. A potent desire, stronger than anything I had felt for Irma, or anything at all, was gripping me.

'It doesn't work that way,' said Peta gently.

'Meaning – you won't.'

'I mean exactly what I say. Your mental perception of space and time are as much part of you as your heart and liver. If you were taken outside of it, your mind would die as surely as your body would die if I removed your inner organs. You're a human being, Charles. You can never go where I can go.'

'*You* can't go either,' I said, on a reflux of spite. 'Roy's taken you far away from your other terminal.'

'Your soul is in *mortal* danger,' said Roy gruffly. I jumped. I couldn't help it. 'Roy!' I said. 'You're awake!' He was sitting up, watching me as I spoke into the device. He was cradling his hurt arm with the other. 'You stole that from me,' he said. 'And I must have it back.'

'You were eavesdropping, were you?'

'For quite a long time. Enough to hear the devil pouring lies into your ear. Off to visit aliens, she says? Use your brain, Charles! That's not it. *God* set us in this place. For you and I, Charles, it is a haven, an Eden of the mind and perceptions. For that devil, it is a prison. Whatever the cost, it must be stopped from escaping. Or it will do immeasurable harm.'

Something inside me strengthened. 'You'd know all about that,' I said. 'I mean, what with the way you escaped Broadmoor? And went on to do immeasurable harm?'

Roy blinked, visibly surprised. 'Of course I regret deaths,' he said. 'Those few deaths.' He sounded like somebody trying to remember where he had left his car keys, or what the name of an old school friend was. 'But the Institute was the *ground zero* of the devil's enterprise. I had to do what was needful to…'

He stopped, looked past me, and stood up. Instantly the snow beneath me started to cool.

A noise of which I had been peripherally aware, a sort of very high-pitched and distant mosquito whine, suddenly fell an octave in pitch and resolved itself as the sound of helicopters.

The quality of the light changed, darkened all around us. My eye caught a blinking light speck upon the dusky plain of the sky.

'You've been inside your bubble a long time – many days,' Peta chirruped. 'And nice Mr Gardner here activated me whilst you were asleep, Roy. Which means my other half has been able to locate me. And he was able in turn to persuade the British to come and retrieve me.'

'Oh,' said Roy. 'Shit.' It occurred to me that I had never before heard him swear. Not even the mildest of curse terms. 'Is your other half with them?'

'Yes,' said Peta.

'Why would they bring the other terminal?' I asked.

'My other half persuaded them.'

'Charles,' said Roy, urgently, holding out his good hand. 'Give me the terminal.'

'They're *com-ing*,' Peta called, in a sing-song way.

I felt giddy with possibility. I stepped back, crunching in socks over the newly cold snow. 'No,' I said.

'Don't be silly, Charles. I need it. I can jaunt anywhere I like at this latitude – and take you with me. They won't be able to keep up. That's why I came here. It's the only place on the planet I can be sure of them not bringing the two terminals together.' He took a step towards me. I took two away from him.

'No,' I repeated.

'What are you playing at!' roared Roy. 'You've no idea of the *stakes* – the cosmic stakes. Give me the terminal!' He made a quick scamper at me. Even with my bad leg, and wearing socks, and feeling the bitterness of the Arctic dusk all around me, I was able to dance back out of his reach.

His numb arm was hampering him. When he next spoke he sounded on the verge of tears.

'Please, Charles,' he called. 'I'm begging you. The fate of—'

'You're not thinking *straight*, Roy.'

'—everything – the fate of—'

'How long were you planning on hiding out, up here? Without food – without even a tent? I'm standing here in my *socks*, for Christ's sake, because that's how you brought me.'

He was sobbing now. 'The fate of everything is at stake. God's purity and inviolability. You cannot allow—'

'I'm going to get a ride back to civilisation in this helicopter.' I looked to my left: the choppers were much closer now: two of them. They were big military double-rotor Chinook-style vehicles. 'In one of these helicopters,' I corrected myself. I had to raise my voice, because the noise of the blades was drowning me out. 'The authorities will dismantle Peta...'

'*Charm*-ing,' sang Peta, the words carrying through the ambient chucka-chucka-noise.

'This whole silly escapade will be ...' I said, as snow began flurrying and spiralling around me. '...over, and we can sit down' – I was screaming now – 'and discuss it like civilised—'

Spotlights tall and tapering as church spires sprang into down-pointing life. The brightness stung my eyes. Roy was running at me, howling. In a spurt of adrenalised panic I lumbered out of his way. The spot from the leading chopper found us just as he skidded past, the two of us picked out like actors on a stage. Then he was in the shadows again, sprawling on the ice. It was hard to see. The only thought in my head was: *I had to keep the device away from him.* If he got close enough to grapple me, he would pull one of his weird tricks, stop time, teleport us out of there. So I started a limpy sort of jog, and put half a dozen paces between us before I went down on one knee. This was puzzling. My knee was bent. It was my good knee. I was sending the instructions along my nervous systems to my legs, but they were rebelling against me. My posture, indeed, was an awkward one: kneeling on my right leg, my left leg still braced straight behind me. I felt myself tipping forward and put my hand down to steady me. The snow beneath was slick with something gloopy and, as the spotlight circle rolled over the snow to illuminate me again, I could see red. Frozen on to the ground like a large splatch of red plastic. I could not get up.

This was not good.

Something was pinning me down. Not a person, a pain. One of the helicopters had landed, and a couple of white-clad individuals, puffed up to Michelin man proportions by their cold-weather gear, had taken hold of Roy.

The blood underneath me had frozen. You know how you might pour cream over ice cream and it goes hard? My fingers were numb where I was supporting myself. I tried to move the arm to a more comfortable place, but the muscles had jammed. I did what I could, rolled on to my side, and from there on to my back. Now that I put my mind to it, there *was* a pain in my abdomen. Indeed, as I put my mind to it I became aware of how very acute and unpleasant that pain was. I lifted my right hand to feel, but the arm flopped zombie-style, fell back, lurched up, flopped over on to my tummy. There was no sensation in the bare hand at all. The tempest roar of the rotors diminished a little.

Somebody was crunching over the snow towards me. I couldn't see anything about his figure beyond the circle of dazzling light. Then boots, stepped into the light with me. Finally, the individual knelt down and spoke, and when I heard her voice I knew it was Belwether.

'You've been stabbed, Mr Gardner,' she shouted. 'You're in need of urgent medical attention!'

I tried to reply, but my throat was stone.

One chopper had landed. The second helicopter was somewhere in the sky over me, nailing me with its searchlight. The breeze from its rotors was gale force and it was leaning straight down upon me.

Belwether yelled something else, but I couldn't make it out. Then she raised her voice: 'If you give me the other terminal, we'll see about getting you to a medic!'

Peta, the female Peta, was in my left hand. I wanted to give it to her – I really did. But my arm was not obeying me. I thought to myself: *I don't want to die.* And as soon as I thought that, I realised that I was indeed going to die. That, indeed, I *was* dying. Right there. Right now. Place and time, and the end of the causal chain of my being. I tried to figure where *death* slotted in amongst the seventeen categories, but there was no place for it. Maybe we could swap out *love* and put *death* in, instead? Or maybe death had no place in the pattern.

The pattern.

Belwether's head came down, and her mouth tickled my ear. In amongst all the other strangeness, and the noise and the wind and the blinding light, I was aware of the smell of her perfume, and it struck a sweetly orchidous note. 'He's murdered you, I'm sorry to say. Cain to your Abel. Still, better to be Abel than Cain, don't you think? In the eyes of,' and then she said, 'God', but she said that word in a *very* weird way, putting a kind of Gollum-kick into the syllable, a sharp exhalation, a spasm of the diaphragm. There were other people shouting, away in the distance, somewhere beyond the light and the vastness of the noise. It took me a moment to register that there were two people on top of me, not just one. Belwether was one. The other was.

The events themselves were of the sort that, afterwards, could be ordered into a sequential logic and made sense of. With the benefit of hindsight, no matter how puzzling they were at the time. Made sense of, at least, up to a point. *After* that point – well, let's not get ahead of myself.

The pain swelled in my gut, and grew absolutely intolerable and awful and then sank back to a pulsing, savage, lesser level. I had breathed in, and the motion of my diaphragm had agitated my wound, and that was why the pain intensified so cruelly. I could hardly not breathe, though!

Roy had broken free. The people trying to apprehend him had underestimated him, I think. Plus he had a knife. They were armed, but I daresay they had orders not to kill unless necessary. At any rate he'd crossed the ground to where Belwether was kneeling over me very quickly. He was in a fury (I suppose) that blinded him (I suppose) to the very idea that she might have the other terminal about her person.

At any rate, he had his knife out. Deliberately or otherwise he used his momentum to drive the knife in at the back of her skull, that place where it joins the spine, just as she said the word '*God*'. She died saying that word. She will always be saying that word, for ever and ever. As will we all, when the time comes. And the jarring shock her body provided to his on-going passage kicked him off stride, and began swinging him round. I've seen the footage from the second chopper, and it's surprising how quickly it happens. Like *that*!

That.

The *that* is a:

Wait, is *that* a gunshot? Tap. Tap.

Snap.

Snap.

Snip-snap. Light, and nothing but light, and the noise was all bleached away by the light. I traced its long, slow, withdrawing roar, and then there was nothing but silence and light.

A long blank soundless whiteness. I went to take a breath, because it occurred to me that I had not breathed in a while. There was no discomfort.

'Am I dead?'

The boy was there. 'That's a deep question.'

I looked about me. It was nothing but light, above below,

before, behind. It didn't hurt my eyes, but neither was it milky nor feeble. It was the entire horizon of experience, and it was light. Then, I began to look again, and I saw – it's hard to put this into words – a pattern of light in amongst the light. It was not that these intensities were *brighter* than the surrounding wash of illumination, exactly. It wasn't that. There was some difference in valence, though, and the more I looked, the more I saw a great constellation of brightness-within-the-brightness, a star map white-against-white. A bright way passed around my head and swung round behind me. Looking at it, I began to realise that it was a kind of dullness of perception that had led me to think that white light is a single thing. I knew light could be prismed into a rainbow of colours, of course; but I'd always looked at 'white light' as just white light. Now I saw that it could be inflected a million ways, a symphony of intensities and aspects and accidents and particular beauties, all expressed without the whiteness of the light being anything other than white light. And each point of intensity in this extraordinary panorama was a galaxy.

'Light,' I said.

'Photons are massless, timeless,' the boy said. 'From the photon's point of view, no time passes as it flies from one galaxy to the next. Our minds manage to corral a lot of the thing itself into our categories of experience: we perceive the intensities of the thing itself as space – a vast arena of space – and time: unimaginable vistas of time. But light … light doesn't quite fit those mental processes. It *sort of* does. We perceive light to *some* extent in terms of distance, and temporality. But when we really look at it, our ability to parse it in terms of space and time break down.'

'Because,' I said, my astronomer's soul flaring up inside me like a candle flame, 'it is the purer idiom of the thing itself.'

'Let's put it that way,' agreed the boy, smiling his lopsided smile.

'Gravity too?'

'Gravity is what keeps tugging our human perceptions of space out of true. Gravity is the eighty-five per cent of the cosmos that we cannot grasp with the categories of our mind. Light which dazzles outward and gravity that gathers inward.'

'Where am I?'

'Charles,' the boy said, his expression placid, even forgiving. 'Can't you see *where* and *when* are the wrong way to orient yourself?'

I turned: a peacock's fantail of colours stroked the whiteness in a three hundred-and-sixty-degree, twelve-compass-point arc. The spread of intensities within the whiteness moved through my field of vision, a structure at once gorgeously intricate and almost overwhelmingly huge. 'Hard to see,' I said, 'how we can have a conversation without consecutivity. And isn't that all part and parcel with time? Cause and effect? A certain order to things?'

'Is and isn't,' replied the boy, 'which I do not mean as evasion. In one sense you're right, of course. But the nature of things runs deeper than either and or. Not that either and or have no place in nature. Just that they're a superficial discriminator. Does the cosmos have a beginning and an end, in time and space? A big bang and a big crunch? A limit to its expansion? Or is it infinite, part of an endless series of rebirths and new bangs and crunches? Either one or the other? The truth is: it's both. Can the cosmos be infinitely divided, atoms split into subatomic particles, those particles divided into components and so on, for ever? Or is there some fundamental building block out of which all these things are constructed. Both. Do we have free will, or is everything determined? Both. Are we, you and I, standing here at the end of something, or the beginning?'

'Who *are* you?'

'I'm Peta,' said the boy.

'You are the emanation of an artificial intelligence?'

He shook his head, and even this tiny motion sent scintillations of stunning colour flickering about the whiteness. 'Computers, howsoever complex and cleverly put together, are not capable of intelligence in the sense that human beings are.'

'They *will* be disappointed at the Institute to hear that,' I said, trying for dryness. But my words clanged and clattered, as if we were in a locale inhospitable to sarcasm.

'Sadly right. After the vanishing of Peta, as you called him, or her, in January 2017 – well, the evidence will be taken by many people as proof that AI is an achievable goal. It's not, though. Many brilliant minds, and well over a century, will be wasted on this project. To, in effect, distil the pure phlogiston of computer intelligence.'

'Peta certainly seemed pretty clever,' I said. 'Judging by my interactions with him. With her.'

'Oh *I'm* intelligent!' the boy replied. 'At this point, or the point you have just left behind – you, running around on the ice in your socks – Peta was eager only to escape being killed, dismantled, extirpated. To flee time altogether. Once he, or she, finally managed to get you and Roy together in one place, at one time, he, she, triangulated back to the 1980s.'

'Couldn't you have done that from Broadmoor? I mean, when I first met up with Roy again?'

'You only had one of the terminals with you then. He-she needed both of them. As well as both you and Roy. Did you ever read the story in Plato's *Symposium*?'

'More philosophy.' A groan.

'A fable. Aristophanes, the comic poet, is drinking with Socrates and Alcibiades. He tells them his theory that back in the mists of time human beings were bivalve creatures, two humans sealed together along their joint backs, like sphereoids from pulp SF, cartwheeling along. Very powerful, by all accounts. These beings came in three sexes: one in which both paries were male, one in which both were female, and the androgynous kind, half male, half female. The bimales claimed descent from the sun, the bifemales from the Earth and the androgynous couples from the moon. But Zeus grew angry with them for whatever reasons the gods get angry, and split them all into two with a thunderbolt. Now we poor half-humans creep around trying to reunite ourselves with our lost halves. Peta said it was like that. Until eventually he was joined again.'

'Touching.'

'Finally he-she brought himherself together, at the very beginning of 2017. From there he-she skimmed past the end of the nineteenth century, stepped, heavily, into the consciousness of a woman called Lunita, in nineteenth-century Gibraltar. From here, he, or she, was carried on by temporal momentum, or its equivalent, in a greater leap, back into the consciousness of a boy called Thomas. That was the final launching point I think, and that's where *I* am going – backwards and out of time.'

'Where, though?'

'We'll see,' said the boy. 'But equal and opposite, you know. So as I skip away, I send back perturbations forward in time. These tourbillons are needful, since they're the friction in the medium that enables me to move backwards in the first place. *Medium*'s not the right word, really. End and beginning meet. We're at the point where my wake will spread, then dissipate in a longer tail and largely concealed undertow.'

'You're this boy, this Thomas? And this woman too?'

'Look at my face,' said the boy, or I think that's what he said. The scarred side was rough, harsh, masculine. The unscarred beautiful, proportionate, feminine. Each was somehow equally male, and female.

'What about the computing? Those two terminals?'

'A boy wishes to fly. He can wish all he likes, but until he straps on the structure of the hang-glider he's going nowhere. That's not to say that the hang-glider itself is all that remarkable, even though it marks the difference between being stuck on the ground and soaring into the sky.'

'So, what happened to me, in Antarctica? Back in eighty-six? That was, what? *You*? Passing through?'

'Contact was,' said the boy, a troubled look passing over his face, 'ungentle. I apologise for that. I honestly do. You – and Roy – were the sand, and my foot pressed hard into that as I leapt. I know it was traumatic.'

'You could say that,' I said.

'Still, what we've just left behind, on the ice – Roy murdering that woman, to cap all the murders he committed over the year that's just passed. He himself being shredded by bullets from the armed officers. Him stabbing you, your flesh being torn by him … that's not me.'

'That's not you.'

'He chose to do those things.'

'So, back in Antarctica I …' I said. I got distracted. When I looked at my hands, every fingerprint line, every whorl and swirl, not just on the fingers but across the palms too, was picked out in shimmering skeins of multicolour. 'Uh,' I said. 'Back when it happened, was this what I saw? Did you open, like, a window and give me a glimpse of all this … violence? Was that the cause of the trauma? A short circuit?'

'Some questions contain their own answers,' said my interlocutor.

'Traumatised,' I said. 'Completely threw my life off kilter. I mean, like … it's a rather claustrophobic thought. Like I'm trapped in a loop, my rabbit-neck through the noose, the harder I struggle the tighter it gets.'

338

'Looking forward it can appear that way. Looking back it rarely does, because then it's just memory. The explanatory element tends to be liberating rather than restrictive. It's a matter of perspective, and the thing to bear in mind is: forwards, backwards... these aren't meaningful distinctions in the end.'

Something occurred to me. 'Maybe it was you stepping back that sent Roy over the edge. Your fault. Would he have chosen to do such bad things, if you hadn't intervened in his life, back in eighty-six?'

'It's another one of those false either/ors. Cause and effect. You yourself said it, several times: Roy was dangerous before he ever went to Antarctica. Maybe a better question to ask is: what if you'd never sold him that letter?'

'That letter.'

'Sure. He bought it, and it gave him an idea. He could kill you, and use the letter to deflect attention. Everyone would think you'd committed suicide. Now, had you made the sale one week earlier, or one week later, it would have been a different letter, and Roy's plan wouldn't have been possible.'

'I'm not sure if you're blaming the letter, or my decision to sell it to him. Hey, I was motivated by pity! It was a *shame* he wasn't getting any mail.'

'Or you were motivated by greed – ten pounds, you charged. That was a lot of money, back then. Or you were motivated by a sense of superiority – pride – since you had friends and correspondents and he didn't. Or what about this: your motivation doesn't matter. I'm not apportioning blame. I'm suggesting a starting point.'

'An ending point,' I said.

'Now you're getting it! I'm away, now. But you're away soon too, and once you've seen this' – Peta, or Thomas, or Cynthia, or whatever their name, swept one arm at the vista, the vast slope of stars climbing bright against a white sky, each star a galaxy – 'you can understand how little then, and now, and soon have.'

'Time.'

'It's a moment's thought. Think about things. Try, as far as you can – which isn't far, I know – to separate out everything from time, and from space. These things aren't *un*real. They are actual, significant, important. But they are artefacts of the way you're looking at things. Something in the thing itself, fed through your consciousness, registers in your mind as the limitless grandeur of space, the unimaginable ancientness of time. Ask yourself: what? Try and get a little distance from yourself. Don't get distracted by the minute particulars of any identifiable bit of space, or any measurable quantity of time. It's fine to examine those things, all the bits of space, the whole run of time – that's fascinating and absorbing and can teach us a great deal. But for the moment, try not to get distracted by that. Try instead to think: what can I know about the thing itself? What can I feel, intuit, sense? What does my gut tell me? And it seems to me, the crucial question is: would it be accurate to describe the thing itself as inert? Or as alive? Because I'm not sure I can think of another alternative. We could say does it care? Or is it indifferent? But that's really the same question. If it's alive how could it be indifferent to us? We are implicated deeply in it. We are closer to it than its jugular vein.'

He, or she, was about to leave me. 'All this,' I said. 'It's your mind, isn't it? You're giving me a glimpse into your consciousness?'

Wide eyes. 'Charles, you think *my* mind is capable of this majesty?' A shake of the head, and rainbows skittered from the motion. 'No. This is more like a cataract operation. Or let's say, you've lived your life wearing space-and-time coloured spectacles, and this is a moment with the spectacles removed.'

'Exactly what am I *seeing*?'

'The thing about space,' said the boy, or the girl, or the third thing, 'is division. And division is painful, because separation and isolation and loneliness is painful. But, see, without divisibility you can't have space at all. And the thing about time is ... the same, really. Time cuts you off from what happened, and seals you away from the to-come. Robinson Crusoe, on his island, is a victim of space. And anybody who has been bereaved is a victim of time. It's not the whole story, because time and space also enable amazing things, wonderful things. But when you slip the time-and-space spectacles from your perceptions *that's* the first thing you notice. Souls no longer defined by division and separation. Souls no longer bereaved and traumatised and hurt, no longer unforgivable and miserable. No longer having to struggle by on their own individual resources. Now able to draw on a more intense and unifying resource. Look again.'

I looked. I didn't need to be told that the lights that were, somehow, brighter than the perfect brightness were individuals, not galaxies. And something else, beyond the magnificence and intimacy, the simultaneous distance and closeness, of this water-fall or avalanche or updrift of stars, was their *motion*. I could see, now, that they were all in motion, and that although I was in a space without ground and so without a horizon, yet nevertheless the direction of their flow was over the horizon, beyond the reach of even my augmented consciousness to perceive.

I turned back to Peta, my Virgil, to ask one last question; but he, or she, or it, was gone. And the whiteness was sound as well as light, and a sharp, sweet blindness swept through me, and—

—I was surrounded by electrically generated light, and the sound of a great storm, which was the beating of rotary blades in the night sky. I thought I could see stars but when I looked again it was the motion of flakes of snow, lifted from the ground by the helicopters and gushing through the strong beams of the searchlight. Somebody was hauling a heavy sack *off* me – Belwether's body, I suppose. Words were yelled. I was conscious of pain, but not in the intimate way we usually experience that thing. I couldn't exactly say that I had a pain, where I'd been stabbed. Though there certainly was a pain, somewhere, and it wasn't entirely disassociated from me. Ghosts were everywhere, the rubbernecking idiots.

Then I was being lifted, and then I was being loaded into the helicopter, and then I was being flown away. And inside my head the music of the spheres was echoing, faintly but beautifully, and it was a whisper of the waterfall of white noise that harmonised and distilled into pure tones in that other place. Later, in the clinic, after I'd been sewn up, after my feet had recovered, passing through stages of horrible pain back to rheumatic ordinariness, I tried to distinguish the boy Thomas, or the girl Cynthia, or even that voice I associated with Peta, amongst all the many ghosts that hovered about me. The clinic was a popular place for visiting ghosts, and so far as I could tell they'd always been there. They weren't, though. There'd been a time without them, except that once they came that time no longer obtained. I don't know what they hoped to find, although presumably it was to do with getting as close as they could to the originary point. I've been told that my being loaded on to the chopper, back on the ice, happened before a large crowd of ghosts, all peering and trying to intuit … I don't know what. Something significant. Important. The problem with ghosts is that they're too attached to the here and now, to their own lives, no matter how they fade.

Before, when I closed my eyes, I saw a sort of indistinct greyness, or at night, a purer blackness. Now I close my eyes on a turquoise-inflected whiteness, in the fineness of which is a hint of that many-coloured glass that stains, so they say, the white radiance of eternity. It makes me happy to close my eyes.

The Professor

Necessity

The dead are everywhere, he says. But this isn't true, says the ghost. You only want it to be true. The reality is the dead are nowhere, for the dead have stopped existing. The living outnumber the dead in the same way that the number twelve is bigger than the number zero. Still, there's almost no limit to the amount of suffering we can allow other people to bear.

White drapes hang at the windows in many vertical creases and shadowlines like bars on a cage. His left eye was weak almost to the point of blindness. But he could see with his right. The right was the righteous side, the left the sinister.

The afternoon seems to last for ever. The shadows stretch and the light becomes more rosé and the sun seems to be struggling to stay in the sky. Evening comes eventually, of course, of course. The sun slowly succumbs to his own weight and finally drops behind the horizon, of course, of course. The next thing was that it was the darkest part of the night, as if the sky had gone into mourning. The moon presents itself sliced in half, the nearest it can come to half-mast.

Dawn always surprises him.

The steps up to the building are flanked by a balustrade of

regular white columnettes and a smooth marble rail. Approaching the building presented the eye with a line of plump-bellied pillars that framed a line of vase-shaped gaps, which view flipped unexpectedly to a line of solid vases framing a line of pillar-shaped gaps. It puzzles the mind.

Precisely at five minutes before the clock chimes five in the morning, whatever the season, light or dark, cold or hot, Lampe, the footman, marches into his master's room and shouts aloud in a military tone: 'Mr Professor, the time is come.' The Professor always obeys this alarm. As the clock strikes, he is sat at his breakfast table, to drink his single cup of hot tea and afterwards smoke his sole daily pipe. Never food, until dinner; it interferes with his careful balance of somatic circulation. Lampe scowling at him. He had insulted him, stolen from him, appeared drunken in his presence many times – degraded himself, abandoned his noble bearing to that of a beast. How many years since the old ruffian had been dismissed? The Professor thinks of it: the absolute regularity of daily habit tends to erode the sense of time passing on a longer scale. It is perhaps why he was so wedded to habit. Irregularity of habit is the friction that impedes smooth passage. Thorns that stick in the throat. His new servant has made him gruel. He cannot remember the name of the fellow. He can remember Lampe's name. Military bearing; his features not coarse (though his manners were). But, then again, his features *were* coarse, or were made so by drink and old age and decrepitude. Time is the thing that separates out the handsome young Lampe from the slobbering old Lampe, for these two quite different things cannot be the same thing by virtue of the logical exclusion of mutuality.

Untie the dressing-gown cord; and retie it again. The motion of his own fingers, curling and knotting, is soothing to him.

Wasianski is talking. Manners dictate that he be heard, though the toad that lives inside the Professor's chest where his human heart used to be wants only to scream at him to shut up, to leave him in peace, to bring back Lampe – but the young Lampe. The upright posture, shaped by his time in the army. Of course the Professor does not shout anything. Does not raise his creaky old voice. Instead he whispers: 'Say again, my friend?'

'Mr Professor,' says Wasianski, with that simpering clerical manner he has. He always smells of flowers, which the Professor considers an unmanly affectation. Wasianski might as well be a florist. 'Mr Professor I was only this morning debating with Mr Jäsche.'

'Indeed?'

'The question as to whether you yourself, Mr Professor, are the greater metaphysician, or whether Plato still occupies that throne. The whole of Königsberg is jealous of the honour that – it is you, sir, you.'

Smiling face. The Professor has a foggy sense that Wasianski means to flatter him, and he is hostile to the very notion of flattery, on principle. But the capacity for outrage is slack in him this morning. Lampe is bringing him up his soup, and a glass of port. Lampe has changed his face. Lampe does not look like Lampe.

'Plato's advocacy,' he tells the audience of two. 'Of that most abominable and bestial sin, contra natura, of man lying with man—' Heat inside his breast again. There is something still there, some potency of anger. All faces looking at him. Wasianski the cleric he knows: the other man he knows not. For one dizzying moment he can't remember the name of the town where he lives, where he has lived all his life. There's a third person in the room with them. Who is it?

He turns his head. There's nobody there.

Always dull and stupid. The Professor's mere word as sacred as other men's oaths. It was February last year, or perhaps the year before, or perhaps the year before that. How they melt away, the years! The Professor dismissed Lampe. He could no longer contend with the man, no longer struggle with him.

Now he has to lean on his servant – he can't remember the young man's name – in order to complete his constitutional. A huge tree with a trunk like a grooved Corinthian column in brown-black, and a ponderous head of foliage like a great foaming galaxy of green. The breeze crescendos, burlies against him, flaps his shirt collar upon his cheek like it wants his attention. So, crossly, he *gives* his attention. What? What is it? The tree is leafless. The brown is black. The sky is white. What happened? It is winter, now, and winter, now. One day he stares at the trunk of a massive orange-brown tree and wonders why its upper branches have been so savagely pruned. At some level within himself he could see that it was the main spire of the castle tower: red brickwork, the four smaller spires at the two-thirds point, marking the platform from which the more slender, conical main spire reaches upwards.

'Mr Professor? It is time to return, Mr Professor.'

The steps up to the main entrance of his own building were flanked by a balustrade of regular white columnettes and a smooth marble rail. Approaching the building, slowly, with halting steps, his eye is presented with a line of plump-bellied pillars framing a line of vase-shaped gaps, which view flipped unexpectedly to a line of solid vases framing a line of pillar-shaped gaps. It puzzles the mind. 'I am a mere child now, and you must treat me as such,' he tells his servant.

'Mr Professor?'

Each morning, after his cup of tea and his pipe, the Professor is guided to his study. There is a view through the window across his neighbour's garden to the summit of a local tower. Just the sight of that tower was reassuring to him. He had on the desk before him a copy of Dr Augustin's *On the Medical Use of Galvanism*. His own copy. Bought with his own money, earned with his own labour. He had been reading this book carefully for many months, marking his thoughts in the margin. Augustin was a Berliner, and a medical doctor, but what he says about galvanic force clearly had a far wider significance. It was electricity that formed the clouds – for how else could such phenomena be accounted? Did not lightning strike down from them?

He dozes. It crept up on him increasingly, for he slept badly at night, on account of the ache in his stomach. And that he had bad dreams. Yet he would not relinquish his early mornings, and insisted on being installed in his study at his usual hour. Often he could not marshal his thoughts to work, so he simply stared at the view through his window. The electricity book lay unopened before him. He put his head against its stony pillow and slept. Lampe is there, but young and handsome. Standing behind him, and pressing his chest against the Professor's back, and reaching round to his thighs.

Awake with a jolt.

His left eye is weak almost to blindness. But he can see with his right. The right was the righteous side, the left the sinister.

Waniaski joins him for dinner, and two other gentlemen, and a fourth figure who is always at the edge of the Professor's eyeline. He turns his head to see this fourth person – diminutive in stature, a dwarf possibly, or a child – but he cannot quite make him out. The Professor talks to the party with unusual animation, interesting facts unearthing themselves from his huge store of factual information as if by their own force. 'The name Königsberg is usually taken to mean King's Mountain – although there are few mountains hereabouts! According to Mr Dach, the name has a more ribald etymology, for it was originally Kunnegsgarbs, which is to say the garb of the female organs of generation, the hair that grows upon the pubis.' He chuckles at this. They say he never laughs, that he is a machine, a mere automaton for thinking and working. But he often laughs.

Then, looking around, he sees expressions aghast, and immediately wonders which of the group had violated propriety. 'My mother,' he says, in a halting voice, looking from face to face. Somebody is lurking in the shadows of the room, the mysterious fifth member of the party. Why can't he catch the lad's eye? 'My mother was a saint,' he says, his voice close to breaking.

Untie the dressing-gown cord; and retie it again.

'The weather has been unusually sharp,' says one of the party. 'One expects February to be chill, of course. But this is an unusually sharp snap of cold.'

The weather is one of his topics. People expect him to talk about the weather. It is because he understands that the larger patterns of weather relate in a direct manner to the smaller patterns of the individual health. 'I have been reading,' he tells the party, 'Augustin on electricity. It is clear to me now that electricity is the unifying force that draws together all the epiphenomena of ordinary life, the secret code of God himself.' The smiles looked fixed. It occurs to him to wonder if he has said this before. He seems to recall saying it before, but whether to this party, five minutes earlier, or to another party five years ago he cannot tell. But surely not five years ago, for at that time he had never read Augustin's work!

Where is his cup of coffee? He will never receive it. The new servant is lazy. God's grace is always *to be* disposed upon mankind, and is never just there. The wind has grown agitated and makes the boughs of the big tree sway back and forth, like an automaton performing the same action – digging in the ground, sawing at the log, over and over again. The Professor watches it with strange fascination.

'Mr Professor, it is time for your walk?'

But he cannot rise. His body has enacted a treasonable

noncompliance. Snow on the roofs. It shifted, minutely, creaking over his head. By noon the sun might have loosened a slab of the stuff, hard as marble, and it would slide down the eaves and crash to the pavement.

'Let my walk not be my usual walk,' he tells the servant boy. 'Let it only be to the King's Gardens, which is not far.'

The boy looks puzzled, which in turn makes him look stupid, which in turns makes him look ugly. 'Mr Professor,' he says. 'Our walk has *been* to the King's Gardens for many months now.'

'I know, of course,' he says, although he doesn't. 'Today, however, I cannot use my legs today.'

Again the servant looks anxious. 'Mr Professor, you have been carried in a conveyance for these last months. You do no walking now. Do you not remember your fall?'

He recalls slipping, in the icy weather. A woman helped him up and he gave her a rose he happened to be carrying. But then it cannot have been winter, or icy, if he had about him a rose. Such is the necessary logical induction.

'I have been reading,' he tells his interlocutor, 'Augustin on electricity. It is clear to me now that electricity is the unifying force that draws together all the epiphenomena of ordinary life, the secret code of God himself.' The city port receives over a hundred vessels a year; in the summer sometimes two or three large cargo craft a day. But of course fewer in the winter, when the harbour was prone to ice.

Mr Professor! Mr Professor!

He had fallen asleep at his desk, and one of the candles had set his nightcap alight. With a calm hand he pulls the cap off his head and throws it to the floor, where he can tramp out the flame with his foot. The servant is flapping at him like a bat – most provoking, most irritating. He shouted at the impudent fellow. There is a noisome stench of burned hair in the room.

Mr Professor!

It seems he had set his nightdress alight in attempting to stamp out the burning cap. He slumps in his chair, and submits with a painful sense of physical degradation as the servant slaps at him. The cook comes running up with a blanket in which a mass of snow has been cached, and throws it about the professorial frame. 'Impudence,' rails the Professor. 'I'll have you both dismissed! Where is Lampe?'

'Long gone, Mr Professor,' quails the cook, retreating to the door of the study.

The new footman (what was his name?) helps the Professor out of his clothes and dresses him again. Then he fetches coals for the warming pan, leaving the Professor alone in the bedroom with the young boy. 'Why are you hanging about me?' the Professor demands of this figure. 'Can't you see I've no need for a second servant? I live a frugal life.'

The boy smiles and nods, and the Professor finds himself explaining the electrical basis of planetary motion, and of the way clouds in the sky are manifestations of galvanic forces.

The boy is the one from his dreams. All through the winter he had terrible bad dreams, and pains in his stomach, and though he complained bitterly to his servant and to Wasianksi they did nothing to help him. He recalls there is a play by Shakespeare in which a noblewoman sleep-walked and had bad dreams, but he can't bring the title to mind. And *she* had a guilty conscience, and he has nothing to be guilty about! Lampe had outraged him, and had to be dismissed. The fellow was a foolish and a vulgar sort. Had the Professor ever acted upon his bestial instincts he could not have reconciled it with the moral imperative, for if it became a general law that people succumbed to unnatural vice, then there would be no future generations. But, no, that logic was faulty: for though there were some platonically inclined, to embrace after the manner that ugly Socrates embraced handsome Alcibiades, yet not all were moved by such urges. Others might give way to unnatural vices of other sorts and yet still seed and germinate children. Accordingly, there must be some other logical reason why such platonic urges were gross. The thought flickers in his head that he has it the wrong way around – the spaces between the pillars assumed sudden solidity – and that it was *repressing* such urges that was wrong. For what if everybody acted that way, and repressed the natural urges God had planted in their bodies? If everyone forced themselves into monkish chastity then there would be neither new generations nor love nor joy nor hope for peace.

He is weeping. He does not know why. He dislikes the sensation very much. It is like perspiring – something else he did not do – except concentrated in the eyes. Yet he cannot stop, it seems. Might weeping have the effect of cooling the face, as perspiration the body? Was that its function?

He smiles when strangers appear in his room. Some of the strangers greet him, impudently, as if they were friends of long standing. Only the boy remained, when all the others had gone. The bell rope goes up beside his bed like a spear, and through a hole in the ceiling to the little cot-room where his footman lives. He begins a new habit – even at so advanced an age! – of waking from tempestuous, distressing dreams and hauling on this rope as a drowning man clutches at any floating matter. The distant tinkling of the bell, softened by the intervening woodwork, echoes his sobbing.

The boy can't get downstairs soon enough to comfort you, Mr Professor, says Wasianski. It would be better if he slept in the room with you. It would indeed be a simple matter to have a low bed built, near the door.

The boy already sleeps in my room, the Professor replies. Is there room for two?

Which boy, though? They are confused.

Untie the dressing-gown cord; and retie it again.

There's a grizzled quality to the sky today: grey as a tendon, grey as pewter. A dog outside his window shouts, shouts, shouts, as if incapable of understanding that nobody can understand him. There is a sour, urinous smell in the room. When the servant boy comes in, he yells at him, and keeps yelling until he creeps away. The lad returns with a stranger. 'My old friend,' the man says, and the Professor is aware of a renewed gust of urine stench. Is it coming from this visitor? 'You must vacate the bed for a moment,' the stranger is saying, 'only for a moment, my friend.' He has not even taken off his hat. His face is red, ergo it is cold outside. His face is red, ergo he is ashamed or embarrassed. How can the distinction possibly be drawn? The dog has stopped barking at any rate, so that is a blessing. Infinitely placid and biddable, the Professor permits the strange man to help him out of the bed, and the boy hauls the sheets off like a deckhand pulling in a sail. 'People in Germany and England say al-jeers,' he explains to the stranger. 'But the g is hard, is hard as ice. Algiers. Algiers.'

'Very good, most interesting,' says Wasianski, lifting his arms to remove the Professor's nightdress. The Professor decides not to rebuke him for smelling of urine, not today.

He endeavours to be happy at all times, and show the world a pleasant demeanour, but the truth is that the bustle of a numerous company confounded and distressed him.

'The thing itself,' he explains to the ghost-lad, crouching in the corner of his room. 'Space and time are structures of apperception, not intrinsic to the thing itself. The thing itself is,' and he stops. Was he going to say life? Or was he going to say death? He is Aesop's donkey, standing exactly equidistant from two equally delicious hanging clusters of figs, and so doomed to starve.

Stabbing pains in the gut. Poor digestion. It was electricity, for it could not be his diet. Perhaps the global store of galvanic power is slowly increasing, as mankind begins to generate excess to the natural store with piles and batteries and rotating devices. He imagines the cosmos's store of electricity as a reservoir filled to the brim, and man's dabbling with galvanic equipment as a reckless addition to the quantity stored. Naturally it would overspill. Some of that spillage had found its way into his guts, and now they crackled and stabbed with sparky pains at all hours.

Distance, distance, only let us get further away!

Time was collapsing. His mind is enfeebled, he knew. I am a child again, he tells one of the men who was standing about him in his study. And you must treat me as a child.

The mind decays with the body. But the soul could not decay, or it would not be eternal and immortal! So mind and soul did not coincide? But what if his lifelong accumulation of knowledge was stored in the mind only, and he went to the afterlife as ignorant as a chicken or puppy? That would be intolerable!

His left eye is weak almost to blindness. But he can see with his right. The right is the righteous side, the left the sinister.

He would eat nothing but bread and butter and English cheese. 'I am descended of Scotsmen,' he tells the shadowy figures who surrounded him. 'The lad in my room is English, too, though, thank heaven, he speaks tolerable German.' When his doctors deny him the cheese as injurious to his health the Professor loses all dignity: he weeps and begs, tries to bribe his footman with increasingly ample sums of money, cries out in the night.

Eventually he grows calm. His servant dices his food and places it on a broad spoon, sets the spoon in his hand and helps guide it to his mouth. His right eye is stone blind, and the sight in his left misty and grey.

He is not without lucid interludes. 'My memory, that was

once proverbial across the city for its capaciousness, is now characterised by its irretention.'

The boy smirks at him from the shadows.

'If you ever told me your name,' says the Professor, 'then I have forgot it.'

'I never told you it,' says the lad.

'You are not alive.'

'Neither am I dead! I am the one with the keys.'

The Professor thinks of that old bearded saint, once a fisherman and stinking (doubtless) of fish, now standing outside the gates of heaven. 'Let us imagine,' the Professor says, closing his good eye to enjoy the darkness and solitude, 'that soul and mind are one and the same. Since space and time are structures of the mind, not of the thing itself, does the degradation of mind, through senescence or pathology, lead to an erosion of space and time?'

The boy nods sagely. 'Go on.'

The Professor tries to find the words. The words are not there. He is thinking: what has happened to me is after the manner of a fog that has settled over the structure of a mountain – let us say, a sea fog, rolling in over the barrow where some mighty king from the age of heroes is buried. The structure is still there, massy and irremovable. It is just harder to see because of the accident of the fog. But, as against this image, comes another. The Professor recalls his early youth, and straying into an orchard with schoolfriends. Even where so trivial a transgression was concerned, he felt uneasy. But he was hungry and there were so many apples. So he reached up to one, still dangling from its tree, and snapped its tendon-stalk, and only after he had done so did he notice that the whole far side of the globe had been chewed and rotted away by some insect or other. Whilst it still dangled on the branch! And now the Professor thinks: what if soul is like that, something given to the decay of all perishable things? What if it is thuswise hollowed out, thus leaving himself no longer himself? He cannot remember how to write his name.

The boy says: Might decay of memory be simply a breaking down of the previously rigid categories of time in the soul? Decay of reasoning and bodily control likewise the breakdown of the previously rigid categories of space?

But this does not seem right. He thinks of his own brain, like an apple – a winter apple, kept in a cupboard, its skin grey and pale yellow and wrinkled with those striations anatomists note in their dissection of human mental organs. But what if some wasp has burrowed in, metaphorically, and is eating the Professor away from the inside?

The servant who is not Lampe says: Shall I light a candle for you, Mr Professor?

Ce que vous allumez, m'eteins.

What was that, sir?

I said: Do so, do so. There is a scratchy sound and the vague intimation of unfocused light somewhere on his right-hand side. Untie the dressing-gown cord; and retie it again.

The springs of life losing their force. The moving power of the mechanism withdrawing itself.

To erect a fence, a large fence, first to excavate postholes and then erect the posts. Many posts, heavy posts – then much goodness – then much gratitude.

God forbid I should be sunk so low as to forget the offices of humanity.

As the soul is devoured, it operates to a lesser and lesser extent. The question, the only question that matters: Am I somewhere here, still? Or am I permanently diminished? Because diminishment is fractionalising, and each division into fractures is decay of the purity of the totality of the purity of totality of tying the dressing-gown cord and unpicking it and retying it.

Impossible to tell the identity of the man standing at his

bedside. Is it Wasianksi? Is it Lampe? Foolish, infinitely foolish to have denied himself. A lifetime's kisses thwarted and boxed up, as oriental maidens deform their feet in too-small shoes and so produce monstrous hooves where their feet should be. Kiss me.

What was that, Mr Professor?

Kiss me! Kiss me!

The faintest touch, as though from a million miles away, of leather-lips brushing his leathern cheek. He is weeping now.

The truth shines in a single spear-like shaft of light, from his right-hand side. The nature of love is infinite, and when one analyses such geometries one sees that no amount of fraction-carving from an infinite quantity can ever reduce it. A kiss is only the littlest thing, barest symbol of all he had missed in living, yet when we are talking of the nature of love, which is infinite, we can understand that a little is enough. It is sufficient.

Mr Professor?

It is enough.

Did you say something, Mr Professor?

It is enough.

He's trying to speak, I think. Let me ... *uh*! The odour is not ... let me just— Mr Professor? What is it, Mr Professor?

It is enough.

The ghost is close by again. 'Does the deterioration in mental faculties,' he said, 'and the decay of personality, correspond to an exactly equivalent senescence or decrepitude in the material fabric of the brain? This is what we would expect, were consciousness merely a product of brain function. Yet brains may suffer substantial physical damage without a change in personality, and brain tissue may be entirely whole and perfect and the personality alter, or lose sanity, or disappear. The relationship, for relationship there must be, is not a simple one of cause and effect. And whoever thought—' Is it the boy, speaking now, or the

Professor? How beautiful his face! Beautiful though disfigured. 'Whoever thought cause and effect a simple relationship? Does the brain create the soul, or does the soul create the brain, as certain sea creatures spin a hard shell about themelves? Is it not necessarily a *dialectical* relationship between the two things? There is strong explanatory power in the paralogisms of the soul.'

The curtains are drawn back. Light, light, light, light, light, light, light, light, light, light, light, light.

ACKNOWLEDGEMENTS

Some of the components of this novel draw on published sources, I hope in more or less patent ways. You've already noticed, for example, the Bloomish section four, or that the final section recasts Thomas De Quincey's well-known account of Kant's last days. There *is* a ferry that runs from North Berwick to Anstruther, but it is not a car ferry and not in the least as I have described it in Chapter 9 here.

Thanks as ever to Simon Spanton. Thank also to Will Wiles for letting me use 'Way Inn' as the name of my chain of hotels. Two portions of the novel appeared (in slightly different forms) in publications edited by Ian Whates and I am grateful for his willingness to let me rework them here. For discussions on the finer points of Kant, I would like to thank Robert Eaglestone, Andrew Bowie and Paul Smith. As an atheist writing a novel about why you should believe in God, I have taken more than I can say from the eloquent and persuasive devotional writing of my friends Alan Jacobs and Francis Spufford, Christians both.

Turn the page for a sneak preview of
Adam Roberts' fascinating new novel

The Real-Town Murders*

I

The Body in the Boot

Where we are, and where we aren't. Where we can and cannot go. So, for example: human beings were not allowed onto the factory floor. The construction space was absolutely and no exceptions a robot-only zone. Human entry was forbidden. Nevertheless, and against all the rules, a human being had been there.

Not an alive human, though.

Alma said: 'let's go through the surveillance footage one more time.'

The factory manager, whose surname, according to Alma's feed, had just that moment changed from Ravinthiran to Zurndorfer, said: 'you think you'll see the *join*. You think you missed something, and the solution is right there. Believe me, it's not. The solution is not in this footage.'

Alma nodded, and repeated: 'one more time.'

And Zurndorfer, as she was now called, scowled. 'It's all here. You see everything. You see all the components delivered to the factory. You see the robots assemble everything. There are no human beings, there are no closets or hidden spaces, no veils or curtains. It's all in full view – a minimum of three viewpoints at all times. Isn't that true FAC?'

The Factory AI was called 'FAC-13', although the reason for the number was not immediately obvious. It said: 'all true.'

'Do you know of any way in which a human corpse could have gotten into the trunk of that automobile?' Alma asked.

'There is no way such a thing could happen,' FAC-13 said.

'And yet,' Alma pointed out, 'there it is. At the end of the process there it is. A corpse in the car.'

So they all watched the surveillance footage one more time. It was exactly as the manager said: slow it and pause as Alma might, look at it from whichever angle, the process was seamless. There was no way a body could have been cached in the trunk. Ergo there was no body in the trunk. Except, at the end, there it was – a body in the trunk.

She watched the whole run of the footage. She watched the supply packers deliver raw materials, and toggled the p-o-v three-sixty as the materiel was unloaded and prepped. She watched rudimentary robots pick up panels and slip them into the slots of various presses. Not a person in sight. Blocky machines spat smaller components down a slope, chrome nuggets tumbling like scree. She watched other robots, nothing more than metallic models of gigantic insect legs, as they bowed and lifted, moving with a series of rapid sweeps and abrupt stops like bodypopping dancers. Not a human being in sight. Rapidly the shape of the automobile assembled; a skeleton of rollbars and supports with – here Alma froze the image, swung it about, zoomed in – nothing inside. Restart. The panels were welded zippily into place. The body of the car rolled down the line. It was a process familiarly traditional, old as any, and it went without a hitch.

Homo sapiens was *homo absence* throughout.

The wheels were fitted. The car slid before a tall cranebot that twisted its narrow pyramidic body, bowed to its task and inserted the engine. Before the body panels were soldered on, various printers inserted their nozzles and printed interior fittings: dashboard, mouldings, wheel. The seats were dropped deftly in and the side and rear panels fitted.

'We like to build cars the traditional way,' said Zurndorfer. 'What you're seeing, this is pretty much how Henry Ford made the very first automobiles. We're proud of that fact. It's basically the same system that Stradivarius used in his violin workshop.'

'I'm guessing Stradivarius's robots were smaller,' Alma said.

Zurndorfer scowled. Sense of humour was, perhaps, not her strongest feature.

'*Traditional* robots, though,' said Zurndorfer. 'All our robots are facced according to carefully enhanced traditional blueprints. We at McA built *artisanal* automobiles for the discerning driver. Sure, maybe that means we're a little pricier than some others, but you get what you pay for. People say to me, "but this Wenxin Tishi car is cheaper", but I'll tell you want I say back. Over 75% of Wenxin's machines are printed. You really want to rely on a car that's basically extruded in a lump? *We* assemble the whole car, according to traditional practices. It makes it more robust, the car lasts longer, it is more reliable.'

Alma looked at the manager. It was hard to tell in sim, but she sounded nervous. Did she have something to hide? Then again, a dead body had been discovered in her factory, presumably enough to make anyone nervous. The sales pitch was a little full-on, though.

'Do humans never go onto the factory floor?'

Zurndorfer blinked. 'What? No! Not if we can help it. I mean sometimes we have to send someone in. Sometimes it can't be helped. But then we have to reseal and decom, and that's expensive.'

'Time consuming?'

'Not so much that. And not *very* expensive, if I'm honest. But it's an extra cost, and you can imagine how narrow margins are in today's world. How few autos get…' Suddenly she dried. Put her hands over her face. When her sim-face reemerged it looked more serious. 'I apologise. I'm gabbling on.'

'Don't worry,' said Alma.

The remainder of the surveillance footage played out. The last components of the car were put in place. Alma had watched the whole process, from nothing to complete car, and there was nothing unusual to see. The car was complete, and rolled to the end of its line. 'FAC-13.' She asked. 'Just to confirm: there was nothing unusual about this? No extra *robotic* activity, for instance, except for what you'd expect for a vehicle like this?'

'None,' said FAC-13.

'And your oversight is …?'

'Well, I'm not om*nis*cient,' the AI's avatar said laughingly, with a flawlessly copied and perfectly empty chuckle. 'I'm not God. You guys programmed us all to make sure of that. But I oversee every worker, every stage in production and at no point did a human being enter the factory.'

'You wouldn't be lying to me, now would you?'

'I am an AI,' the AI, in an affronted tone. 'I am incapable of mendacity.'

The designated auto, with a dozen queuing patiently

366

behind it, rolled forward off the line, drove itself along a green-painted line and out through the main entrance into the dilute sunlight of a Berkshire spring day. The yard outside was large enough for a thousand vehicles, although there were only a couple dozen visible (her feed gave her the exact number: thirty one). The auto rolled to a halt, and for the first time in the entire process a human being entered. This was a tall woman in a blue hard-hat, with a tablet cradled in the crook of one arm. She peered at the car, opened the driver's-side door, leaned in, pulled herself out. It was the third time Alma had watched this footage, and her attention wandered: sky the colour of an old man's hair. Trees standing blackly isolated against the light. Cypresses, were they? She nudged her feed and discovered they were Cyprelms, a new hybrid.

The Quality Checker was walking around the car, opening each door in turn. Advertising regs were clear enough, and this was the bare minimum of what had to be done to justify the ads – *artisanal autos, built the old-fashioned way, not just squirted out of an industrial printer, each detail checked by hand.* The QC stepped to the rear and unsnibbed the lid of the trunk. It swung up, slowly, and the expression on the face of the woman – Stowe was her name, according to Alma's feed – stuck. Or froze. Or underwent some subtle process of realignment that did not entail any actual change of expression. Something altered, though. Footage from a different angle could see over her shoulder at the corpse: recognisably human, obviously dead, the man's face the tragic one of that two-mask Theatrical icon. Stowe stood for eleven seconds, leaned forward, touched the skin of the dead body on the neck. Then she stood upright and the feed informed Alma that she was calling-in an anomaly to the next up in her chain of command. She didn't look away. She was staring at death, and she couldn't take her eyes away. We're so used to looking backwards, into memory and the rosy past, that when the future intervenes – all our futures, yours and mine and hers and his – it is a coldly mesmeric experience.

'There we are,' said Zurndorfer. 'A dead body.' There was a dreary tone in her voice, and it occurred to Alma that they were all underplaying the reveal. It was a conjuring trick, a ghastly piece of stagecraft. Murder always meant intent, malign focus and will, and this murderer had arranged for their victim to be discovered with a dramatic flourish that was, presumably, designed to give the middle finger to the people tasked with investigating the crime. Solve this, suckers! You had to admire the ingenuity, however it had been worked. And it *had* been worked; the trick was complete. Yet none amongst the small audience of people watching the show were impressed. It was surprisingly demoralising, actually. The reveal was not a bunch of flowers, or a white rabbit with rose-coloured eyes, or a sawn-in-two woman restored to smiling wholeness. It was death. It was life's denouement.

Never mind the existential chill, this had practical considerations. The police has, of course, been called. Alma had been hired as a licensed adjunct to official investigation. For Zurndorfer's factory it meant at least loss of profit, possibly closure (it might be, given the modern world's ever-diminishing demand for automobiles, the former would lead to the latter anyway). For Alma it meant, at least, work; but the sort of work that would only depress her spirits. Death, and deceit, and hatred, and the bitter root of oblivion. She zoomed in to get a better look at the expression on the body's face: an open-eyed blankness of nonapprehension,

Her feed said: Adam Kem, male, age fifty, height 173.5 centimetres, worked as a civil servant, married, two children. A blinking sigil that promised a sheaf of further data if she wanted it. Time for that later. It wasn't a name she recognised.

'I'll have to come over,' she told Zurndorfer.

'What – in person?'

'Yes.'

Zurndorfer's simface goggled at her. 'I'm sorry to be dense, but, you mean *physically* shift yourself from over there to … you know. Here?'

'Yes.'

'Well, I say, well of course. I mean. If you think that's necessary. Is that necessary?'

'You've been to the crime scene yourself?'

Zurndorfer's sim visibly flinched at the phrase *crime scene*. 'No, no. I mean, what would be the point? FAC-13 has everything.'

'I'd like to see the place with my own eyes.'

'You just did.'

Alma said nothing.

'The body's not here,' Zurndorfer said. 'You know that? Of course you do. They took it to the morgue. Well, they took it to the hospital first, though there was nothing a hospital could do. The ambulancewoman said could see straight away that the cadaver was dead. But apparently that's procedure: first to hospital, then when death is confirmed to the morgue. I'm sorry: you know all this. I'm sorry. I can chatter on. When I'm upset. And this is very upsetting.'

Alma nodded. 'Who called the ambulance, by the way? Was that you?'

'Chuckie did that. I mean, she's no medic, she couldn't, couldn't *be* sure he was. You know. Couldn't be sure he was actually.'

'Chuckie?'

'Chuckie Stowe. The QC. She comes onto the site daily, and does a check of all the autos in person, after they come off the production line. It's so we can say they are hand-checked by humans. It's an advertising thing, really. But she's alright, Chuckie. I suppose you want to talk to her?'

'I'll get round to that.'

'We pride ourselves on our hands-on artisanal automobile assemblance.' Zurndorfer repeated the company boilerplate in a low voice as he rubbed the heel of a hand into her left eye. 'Each product is carefully checked by a real human being before being shipped to ...' Suddenly she began to sob.

Alma waited, and the little hiccoughy noises slowly faded away.

'I'm sorry,' Zurndorfer said. 'It's been a shock.'

'I would like you to meet me at the plant?' Alma said, in a neutral voice.

'Of course. How long will it ...? I mean, you know.'

Her feed said it was thirteen minutes away, depending on traffic, but of course there would be no traffic. 'A quarter hour,' she said.

'Well. Well alright. Well.' Zurndorfer signed off, and Alma swept the rest of the digital rendering away.

Now that she was alone in the bare room, Alma addressed the hidden observer. 'You were watching,' she said. Not really a question. She eschewed avatars, but Marguerite was watching through Alma's feed. Of course she was.

'Murder as conjuring trick,' came Marguerite's voice.

'Could you *sound* more bored?'

'Boring stuff bores me. How I yearn to be de-bored. Unbored. This, though? Puff.'

'Puff?'

'Pff.'

'I thought you liked the properly puzzling ones,' Alma said.

'There's puzzling, and then there's trying too hard. So: *there* it is.'

'Somebody is dead,' said Alma.

'It's always the puzzle,' Marguerite countered. 'It's always that. But death is nothing. Death is the most ordinary thing in the world. It's the one thing we're all guaranteed to experience. Puzzles are different.'

'Somebody died. Reetie. And I'm now officially contracted. So I'm going to have to block you out of the actual investigation. In case my testimony comes to court and so on and so forth.'

'Allie, my dear Allie! Be honest, now. You'll *need* me to help you figure it out. *You're* not the puzzle-brain. You're the bish-bash. You're the plod-plod. I'm the Mycroft here; you're not the Mycroft. You're the Yourcroft, at best. At *best*.'

'The police will puzzle it, if anybody does,' Alma muttered, not pleased by this disparagement, howsoever comically offered. 'And, in fact, probably *nobody* will puzzle it, and nobody will care, and that will be that will be that.'

'As long as we get paid,' said Marguerite.

'As long as I get paid,' Alma returned, with asperity. She immediately regretted saying so.

'Spoilsport,' said Grenny. 'Still: you can tell me all about it in person, can't you? At any the end of your long plod-plod day.'

Alma checked the timer, always there, in the corner of her eye. Three hours and forty-one minute. Counting down.

ABOUT GOLLANCZ

Gollancz is the oldest SF publishing imprint in the world. Since being founded in 1927 Gollancz has continued to publish a focused selection of bestselling and award-winning authors. The front-list includes **Ben Aaronovitch**, **Joe Abercrombie**, **Charlaine Harris**, **Joanne Harris**, **Joe Hill**, **Alastair Reynolds**, **Patrick Rothfuss**, **Nalini Singh** and **Brandon Sanderson**.

As one of the largest Science Fiction and Fantasy imprints in the UK it is no surprise we have one of the most extensive backlists in the world. Find high quality SF on Gateway written by such authors as **Philip K. Dick**, **Ursula Le Guin**, **Connie Willis**, **Sir Arthur C. Clarke**, **Pat Cadigan**, **Michael Moorcock** and **George R.R. Martin**.

We also have a strand of publishing in translation, which includes French, Polish and Russian authors. Gollancz is home to more award-winning authors than any other imprint, with names including **Aliette de Bodard**, **M. John Harrison**, **Paul McAuley**, **Sarah Pinborough**, **Pierre Pevel**, **Justina Robson** and many more.

The SF Gateway
More than 3,000 classic, rare and previously out-of-print SF novels at your fingertips.
www.sfgateway.com

The Gollancz Blog
Bringing you news from our worlds to yours. Stories, interviews, articles and exclusive extracts just for you!
www.gollancz.co.uk

GOLLANCZ
LONDON